JUST PLAIN BLOOD

Blood Trilogy 2

Chris DeFazio

TouchPoint
Press

JUST PLAIN BLOOD (Blood Trilogy, 2) by Chris DeFazio
Published by TouchPoint Press
2075 Attala Road 1990
Kosciusko, MS 39090
www.touchpointpress.com

Editor: Tamara Trudeau
Cover Design: Colbie Myles, colbiemyles.com

First Edition

10 9 8 7 6 5 4 3 2 1

Library of Congress Cataloguing-in-Publication Data is available on file.
ISBN-10: 0692281797
ISBN-13: 978-0-69228-179-6

Printed in the United States of America.

This book is dedicated to the memory of my oddly named, but completely wonderful Black Lab, *Taco*.

During a pretty rough patch in my life, he was my only day-to-day companion for close to a year. I could've done a helluva lot worse.

He was whip-smart, endearing clumsy, charmingly willful, and like any good-natured frat-boy, he was always ready to party. One time, when he was a just pup and barely knew me, he risked his life to protect me.

He died on September 12, 2010 unexpectedly and way to young at just over four years old.

I've had a lot of fine dogs in my time, but by far, Taco was the best damn dog I ever had.

More than that, he was my friend.

OTHER BOOKS BY CHRIS DEFAZIO
A History in Blood, Blood Trilogy #1

PROLOGUE

His aunts had always told him of the folly in contacting human family, even after several generations had passed. It was 160 AD, and Titus Acilius had survived nearly two hundred years as a vampire. As any "youngster" would, he thought he'd accumulated enough knowledge to disregard their advice, advice that came from several thousand years of experience. And even when Acilius was much, much older, taking sound advice would never be one of his gifts.

The two ancient women knew his mind was made up, but nonetheless tried to dissuade him from what he planned to do. They reminded him that it would be time-consuming, fruitless, and most likely dangerous. They asked him once again to reconsider.

He politely declined.

They did not command him, even though that was their nature. They never commanded Acilius, their most apt ward in well over a thousand years.

Mary, or Cornelia as she was known at that time, sighed resignedly. "Be careful, Titus. We'll be here when you return."

"Needing to dig you out of further trouble, no doubt," Licinia added. It would be nearly two millennia before Licinia would be known as Katie.

Acilius laughed. They had gotten him out of trouble many times in his vampire life, especially when he was a fledgling and just learning the trade of blood drinking.

"Come, let me kiss you goodbye," he said. "No trouble this time, I promise."

He embraced them, and Cornelia replied, "I hope not, Titus, but trouble seems to have a way of finding you."

He laughed again and started off for Greece. In the end he wished he'd listened to them.

Lucius Acilius, his older brother and their father's namesake, had moved to Athens to pursue a career as a merchant when he was a young man and had never contacted Titus again. In truth, they had never gotten along, and the younger Acilius always found his older brother to be taciturn, sullen, and self-important. Even so, curiosity about potential human relatives proved irresistible to Acilius, as it often did for many of his kind.

Given the state of that era's record keeping, Acilius's expectations were low. But under an assumed name, he was currently a sitting Roman senator and commanded the esteem of his high office, an office he'd acquired by what could best be described as "ancient identity theft", a talent vampires of the day often used to great advantage. He would use every bit of power that his senatorship afforded him to try to locate his family.

Almost unbelievably, he found a record of a Gaius Acilius, who was a soldier in Rome's 12th Legion, the very same legion that the vampire had served in when he was a human in BC times. He took this as a favorable sign. He was not able to trace the soldier's lineage at all, but reasoned that this discovery might yet be a family member, as Acilius, although not a rarefied name, was not exactly a common one either.

The 12th Legion was a part of the Roman forces fighting the Parthians, or Persians, for control of Armenia. The vampire set off quickly to find the soldiers, and given his senatorial status, he was able to have himself attached to his old legion as an adviser and legate, or general rank.

Gaius Acilius was twenty-six and already a junior centurion. He was more slender than the vampire and slightly taller, but perhaps there might have been some family resemblance. The vampire general had him transferred from his current duties and put him in command of his personal guard.

Gaius Acilius knew very little of his own family history, so he was of no help in gaining any more insight into his heritage. But he was an intelligent and competent soldier with a good disposition. As time went on, Titus Acilius grew fond of the boy and entertained thoughts of adopting him once the war ended. His plan never had a chance to come to fruition, at least not in the way he thought it would.

In the Romans' final push on Mesopotamia, Titus Acilius's advance cavalry unit was ambushed, divided, and put into full flight.

His group of six soldiers, including the young Acilius, was pursued by over twice that number of Parthians. Although the potential safety of a small forest loomed ahead, their horses were played out, and they were sure to be overrun long before they got there.

As they galloped for the woods, the vampire ruminated over the conundrum of using his superhuman powers to defend his group, but then potentially having to kill them as witnesses to such a display. Young Acilius solved the dilemma for him.

The centurion turned his horse back into the oncoming pursuers, shouting over his shoulder, "Go on, General! I'll delay them!"

The vampire rode on with the rest to the edge of the woods. The young soldier, as chief of Titus's guard, was simply doing his duty as any good Roman would, but the vampire was aghast. His feelings for the boy, along with guilt, overwhelmed him. He could not simply leave Gaius to die. As the others plunged headlong through the trees, he turned back, hoping that Gaius could somehow stay alive the few minutes it would take to reach him.

CHAPTER 1

That damn dog of mine was chewing on my arm again, trying to pull me out of bed.

"Sarge, cut it out," I sleep-mumbled. "It's too early. Go lie down."

But Sarge, my big black lab, kept right at it, whining a bit for good measure, and that was odd, because he never whined. Sarge had a deep basso voice, and his "whines" came out sounding like low, dangerous growls—if you didn't know him, that is. If you did know him, you knew he wouldn't hurt a fly, unless that fly was trying to hurt me.

I tried to shake free, but he wouldn't let go. He merely changed his grip and essentially used my arm as a large chew stick. I got what I deserved, as I'd trained him (or maybe he'd trained me) to do this when he wanted to get my attention. He'd take me by the arm and pull me toward whatever he wanted. Usually it was food, and sometimes it was the door to let me know he needed to go out. But on other occasions, it seemed random.

He'd lead me around the house to various nonsensical destinations with a happy dog-smile playing in his eyes. I couldn't help but think Sarge was laughing at the idea of the dog leading the master. At times, it seemed we were both unclear as to who actually was the master in our relationship.

Even though the mutt was quite the pain in the ass, and I didn't want to get up, I smiled a half-asleep smile. Sarge hadn't chewed on my arm like this in...well, in years.

My smile faded as I opened my eyes. This wasn't my old house in Massachusetts. I was in Provence, and Sarge was long dead. I still dreamed of him, though, even after more than two decades. As I lay there in that state between sleep and consciousness, I ran my hand over my dream-bitten forearm, and it seemed I could actually feel those long-missed phantom tooth marks.

My more superstitious friends, vampires and humans alike, have always warned me that when Sarge tries to pull me somewhere in my dreams, I shouldn't go. They think he's trying to spirit his old master over to the other side with him, or some such baloney. I do my best to gently remind them that there is no other side, and that my dream Sarge is just a manifestation of my own subconscious. But even a tried-and-true atheist vampire such as myself has to admit that when I have these dreams of Sarge, there's always something more. He seems to be attempting to tell me something.

I lay in bed watching the fading light of the day trying to fight its way through my blackout shades. I started to really wake up, and Sarge's phantom bites completely faded and disappeared. Oddly, I nonetheless thought I heard him whine again. The whine actually sounded more like a groan, however. Then the realization of what was happening slapped me hard right in the face, and I was shocked wide-awake with all the subtlety of a sledgehammer.

I heard a weak, muffled scream and high hurdled out of bed. I sprinted to the living room, shouting, "Lisa! Stop! Don't do it!"

I turned the corner to see my ex gnawing into the neck of Marie, our hapless housemaid. Lisa noisily slurped on the founts of blood gushing from Marie's ruined carotid artery.

I screamed, "Lisa! Stop!"

She took one more long, gulping drink, and then looked up at me, appearing truly perplexed as the pulses of Marie's blood faded and then petered to a halt. The maid's head lolled back on her now-boneless neck, her dead, glazed eyes seemingly locked onto mine in bitter accusation. Their upside-down orientation was disconcerting, even dizzying for a moment.

"Whatever for?" Lisa asked and dropped the body unceremoniously. It hit the hard stone floor with a loud *thwack.* I flinched at the sound.

Lisa stood stark naked with Marie's fresh red blood running down her chin, onto her breasts, and finally dripping onto the floor. She looked like a *Playboy* centerfold gone really bad.

I was livid, but at the same time I blamed myself because, you see, I was ultimately responsible. I'd turned Lisa into a vampire against her will, knowing the results would likely be horrid, but hoping that they wouldn't be. In my defense, when I turned her, I'd thought I'd done the right thing, because it was either that or kill her.

I wanted to scream at her, lose control, as I'd done many times over the past three years. But it never did one damn bit of good. Nothing did. She just kept pushing me and pushing me. My culpability for her current state had kept me in check thus far, but I had my limits. Even taking into account my guilt over what I had done to her, I felt she was fast approaching the point of no return with me, where she would have to be put down like a wild animal. And even if I didn't have the balls to do it, there was a long line of vampires who gladly would. As I watched blood drip down her breasts, I wondered if she realized that, or if she was too far gone.

Lisa noted the direction of my gaze and took on a phony, lascivious smile. But that smile never touched her eyes; none of her smiles ever did. Her eyes were crazy. She looked down theatrically at her blood-soaked body. When she looked back up at me, her arms opened wide and her fake smile grew.

"Well, would you look at me," she said sarcastically. "But it seems you already are, aren't you, Titus? I think I could use a long, hot shower."

She never called me Julian anymore, even though that was how she knew me back when we were married, when I was still pretending to be human and she didn't know I was a vampire. She'd told me once that everything about that name was a lie. Julian Brownell was dead to her.

She paused, silently taunting me with her naked, bloody body. When I didn't take the bait, she added cheerily, "I'm going out on the patio once the sun sets. Would you mind bringing out some wine?" She glanced down at the maid and then continued, "Maybe a Bordeaux. I think a French wine would be the most proper pairing with French blood, don't you?"

She winked and sauntered from the room with a grotesque hip swivel that would make a burlesque stripper blush. I limply plopped down in the nearest chair with all of my shocked-awake adrenalin driven into a hasty retreat by Lisa's antics. I stared helplessly at Marie and the blood-spattered room.

What a fucking mess.

It was sort of ironic that since the housemaid was dead, the cleaning duty would fall to me. I doubted very much Marie would've appreciated that irony.

I mumbled to the empty room, "Well, Sarge, I guess you were trying to tell me something after all."

CHAPTER 2

Even though it was after 2:00 a.m. and he was in one of the worst neighborhoods in Cleveland, the old man strolled along, carefree as could be, whistling a little tune from his childhood. There were two of them following, but Bloody Bill Harrison already knew that. His Mossberg 500 shotgun was tucked neatly under his overcoat and at the ready. His backup team was well positioned, but if all went as planned, he doubted he'd need them.

Bill wandered to a more deserted area that happened to have an overabundance of abandoned buildings to go along with its dark streets and blind alleys. He was sure they'd make their move here, trying to trap him without an escape route, but they'd be the ones who'd be trapped. The two vampires did not disappoint. They picked up their pace and began to close in on him.

Bill continued on, feigning obliviousness. If he "noticed" them too soon, it might alert them to what was really happening here: that they were the prey and not the hunters. Bill waited for a full count of "three Mississippi" and looked over his shoulder. He tensed for a moment and moved off at a quicker pace. He didn't think he'd ever win the Academy Award for his performance, but on a moonless night from a hundred yards, it would work just fine.

He trotted down one street, then another, with the footsteps of his pursuers growing louder by the moment. He broke into a run, sprinting down a dark alley to the dead-end brick wall that he knew would be there, blocking his escape.

Bill stood staring at the wall for a moment, pretending to catch his breath. A small, mean smile formed on his lips.

The two vampires waited for a moment, and then one of them spoke. "If it isn't the famous Bloody Bill Harrison. Do you know the bounty on you is up to three mill, old man?"

The other added, "Money aside, it's going to be a real pleasure to tear you limb from limb."

Harrison's smile widened. Over the past three years, the vampires who had tracked him down always seemed to want to gloat a bit and talk smack instead of just getting to the business at hand. Although his back was turned, this loquacious pair, by both speaking, had given away their locations.

They're making this way too easy for me, he thought.

Bill spun in a blinding whir, as his shotgun flipped up to firing position. Caught off guard, the vampires froze for a moment, their eyes open wide. A moment was all Bloody Bill would need.

As he squeezed off the first round, the long tail of his overcoat, tossed airborne by his quick turn, came to rest across the barrel of his gun. His battle-tested instincts told him if he paused to clear it, he was a dead man. So he fired through it, knowing the shot would be drawn askew.

The gun roared, shattering the night's stillness. The blast caught one of the vampires in the side and knocked her to the ground. It was far from the mortal wound Bill had counted on.

Despite being tangled, Bill remained calm. He swiveled, pumping the gun with the tattered remnants of his coat, now on fire, still snarled on his Mossberg. Bloody Bill moved with his usual fluid speed, but the other vampire had recovered from his initial shock and caught the gun before it could make its full pivot, and the next shot blasted harmlessly into the alley wall.

A harsh backhand struck Bill and sent him sprawling and dazed, as the vampire moved in for the kill. But before he could, a black-clad assailant dropped ninja-like from a fire escape, landing directly on the vampire's back and driving him face-first into the ground.

The vampire was up with dazzlingly fast speed, but his attacker moved faster. A sword flashed, and the vampire's head left his shoulders in a bloody spray. The teeth chattered in final death throes as the head spun in lazy circles on the alley floor.

The shotgun-wounded vampire was back on her feet and rejoined the fray. The sword struck out again, but this time it was blocked, and the vampire countered with a blow meant to shatter the skull of her attacker. The death strike was partially deflected, but landed with enough force to knock the "ninja" down and send the deadly sword clattering across the alley.

Incredibly, this second vampire, evidently the more talkative of the two, paused once again for more vampire smack talk. "You no-good fuck! I'm gonna drain you dry!"

Bloody Bill's reply was a thunderous blast that left her looking incredulously down at the huge hole that had suddenly materialized in her chest. The vampire barely had time to register the sound of a shotgun pump before her head vaporized to pulp.

Bill ambled over to his daughter and helped her to her feet. "You okay, Molly?"

Molly had a biggish welt forming over her eye, but she seemed fine. "I'm good, Dad." She picked up her samurai sword, sheathed it, and as she did, got a good look at her father. "Jesus, Dad! You're really bleeding. Let me look at you."

In the excitement of battle, Harrison hadn't even realized he was hurt. He reached up and touched his forehead gingerly and came away with a few fingers full of blood.

Molly fretted over him. "Oh damn. You're going to need some stitches, maybe a CT scan."

Bill fished a handkerchief from his pocket and pressed it firmly against the wound. "I need no such thing. And what about you? You took one hell of a shot there. You're the one who ought to have the CT scan."

As the words left his mouth, he remembered that they weren't true anymore. They would have been a year or so ago, before Molly had become enhanced. The welt on her forehead that might have indicated brain damage before signified no such thing now. That welt, which would have expanded into a full-fledged hematoma with bruising extending all over Molly's pretty face, was already healing. It would be totally gone in less than a day. Bill was overjoyed that his daughter wasn't seriously hurt, but at the same time was uneasy about the drug-induced enhancement that had just kept her safe.

She smiled at him and shrugged.

"No, I guess you don't need that scan," Bill snorted. He pawed at the charred ruin of his coat. "But I'm definitely going to need a new topcoat."

Molly laughed. "Definitely. But maybe this time you shouldn't buy anything so long and loose."

He chuckled. "You got me there. I got more tangled up than a cross-eyed rattlesnake. I must be getting old."

Molly beamed at her father. They weren't only family, they were best friends. She loved her father fiercely. "Never you, Dad."

He smiled. "Well, maybe I've got a few more tricks left in me yet."

Their pickup car quietly eased into the alley, and Bill turned his attention to it. The driver, who also happened to be Molly's husband, rolled down the window and started to say something, but Bill cut him off.

"Just what the hell do you think you're doing, Steve?"

Although Steve Conti had married Molly Harrison two years prior and was technically part of the family, Bill hadn't quite gotten used to the idea yet. Harrison knew Conti was book-smart, but thought him lacking in the common-sense department. This was another one of his goofy mistakes, but it was the kind of mistake they couldn't afford these days. It might've gotten them all killed.

Conti replied carefully. "I'm picking you up as planned, Bill."

Harrison shook his head. "You think it was the best idea to drive this big boat down a blind alley? It's like sticking a cork in a bottle. If there were more of them, we'd be trapped."

Conti looked abashed. "Oh shit, Bill, I'm sorry. That was really dumb."

He started to put the car in reverse, but Harrison stopped him. He touched his earpiece and listened. "No, we're okay for now. Observation posts say we're good. I'll stand guard; you and Molly get the bodies in the trunk. We'll dump them in the Cuyahoga."

As Molly walked by Bill, she said under her breath, "Do you have to be so hard on him all the time?"

Bill started to answer, but she'd already whisked by. And the thing was, she was right. Bloody Bill was never the nicest when it came to Steve. His treatment of the young man was partly the natural response of an old-school father thinking no man was good enough for his daughters. He'd been the same way with Molly's two younger sisters and their husbands, all four dead now after the vampire attack on the farm three years ago. The thought sent a flash of white-hot anger through him. He took a deep breath and let it pass on through.

Aside from marrying his daughter, Bloody Bill had another reason for disliking Steve Conti. In his former life, prior to becoming a full-time vampire hunter, Conti had been a talented biochemist. In an effort to take away some of a vampire's natural advantages, he'd been the one to come up with the drug that greatly enhanced human physical powers, a drug that Bill's daughter had become addicted to.

The dead vampires were loaded into the trunk, and Conti started the drive to the river. The bleeding from Bill's head had stopped, but he didn't seem to notice. He kept dabbing at it, lost in thought. This was the fourth time this year that they'd been flushed from a city, and now they would have to move again.

Bill had fully expected to be the hunted and on the defensive for some time after the attack on his home, but not for this long. He hoped at some point soon that they'd be able to stop running and start hunting vampires in earnest again. But right now, it wasn't possible.

Even though their vampire-hunting network was broken up into small, isolated cells, his wife Helen's last act as its leader, the vampires seemed to always be able to locate Bloody Bill and his group. He supposed it was the price of being famous in blood-drinking circles. But deep down, he knew something else was afoot.

And even though it was completely irrational, Bill wanted to kill at least one of the monsters who'd been at the farm that night, as a payback for Helen and his two daughters.

The way things are going, I'm never gonna get that chance, he thought.

He was beginning to believe that they might have to leave the continent just to get some breathing room. They'd stand out being foreigners, but considering the way things were in the States, it was a risk that they might have to take.

Conti started yapping annoyingly, shattering Bill's thought process. He talked too much, yet one more reason for Bill to dislike him, not that he needed another reason. Conti never seemed comfortable with even moderately long silences, especially when Bloody Bill was involved.

"We got some prelims from the video feed from the alley," Conti blabbed out. "Bill, you were as quick as ever. Bad luck with the coat. But Molly, your reaction times were even faster than the last hunt, up at least twenty-five percent. The PEDA 17 is still working wonders."

PEDA was an acronym for "performance-enhancing drug/amphetamine." The performance-enhancing drug part was a combination of very high-test steroids, human growth hormone, and several other agents that Conti always declined to elaborate on. The amphetamine was also something of Conti's own creation; super potent and not likely to be found in your neighborhood CVS.

PEDA revved human physical response to off-the-scale levels. The seventeen, Bill thought sourly, reflected the fact that this was the seventeenth version of the drug. The previous sixteen either didn't work or killed the test animals. Bill didn't understand all the biochemistry of it, but he did understand that it worked, at least in part, by altering the subject's DNA, like the human-to-vampire sub-virus, or HVSV, did for vampires. For Bill, this was a little too close for comfort to the monsters they were hunting. He even thought that on some level, using it might be morally wrong.

In addition to altering the subject's DNA, PEDA 17 was also terribly addicting. If Molly stopped taking injections, she would go through horrible withdrawal symptoms and maybe even die.

Finally, there was no way Steve could be sure about the long-term consequences of the drug. He'd go on for hours about this test and that test, and sound as sure as any puffed-up scientist who really didn't know the answer could sound. But the fact was, they'd only been trialing the drug for a year. The proof about the long-term effects would be coming down the line sooner or later, and that proof might be in the form of a pretty shitty pudding. Bloody Bill thought that if anything happened to Molly on account of the PEDA, he'd have very little chance of controlling himself when it came to what he would do to Steve.

But even Bill had to admit that Molly and the other three from his cell who were on the drug seemed fine, and by every test, *were* fine. And the results were nothing short of spectacular. If major leaguers got their hands on PEDA 17, they'd be hitting two hundred home runs a season.

Conti went on. "I don't even know how that second vamp blocked your strike, Molly. He must have been lucky, because if you ask me—"

Bill interrupted him. "Lucky? If you didn't notice, Steve, Molly and I both ended up on our asses. I'd say we were both *lucky* to get out of that alley in one piece."

Molly said, "Now, Dad—"

Conti jumped in. "No, it's okay, Molly. Bill, I didn't mean anything by that. It's just—"

Bill's short fuse was lit and blazing. "*Just* nothing! How come I don't see you taking your super-drug? Tell me that, Steve."

Conti flushed, but his voice remained calm. "We've talked about that. It's a wise precaution in case something would go wrong. I'd be the one who'd need to come up with a fix, and I couldn't be counted on to do it if I were—"

"Yeah, yeah, if you were affected. But that crap you came up with is good enough to shoot into my daughter, right?"

Conti's flush darkened to a deep red. "She's my wife, Bill, and I love her. She volunteered for it, and it wasn't as if we had much of a choice the way things were going."

"What do you mean, the way things were going?" Bill spat back. There was murder in his tone.

Conti scoffed. "Newsflash, Bill: we don't have seven hundred agents behind us anymore. We don't have the best computer network and science labs anymore. Hell, I can't even make our garlic extract out here. And if you haven't noticed, there are only ten of us left. No. . . Jesus, check that. . . nine. Somehow I just can't get it through my head that Doris is really dead. Doing just fine? If by that you mean sticking to your archaic methods and slowly getting wiped out, yeah, then I guess we were doing fine."

On autopilot, Bill's hand reached for his .357. He leaned forward and growled, "Why, you little prick."

"Will you two stop it!" Molly screeched.

Bill sat back, glowering, and Conti seemed to refocus on the road, but his eyes kept shooting up to Bill in the rearview. The three once again drove in silence.

As much as Bill hated to admit it to himself, a lot of what Conti had said was correct. They'd been fighting a losing battle until the PEDA 17 had come along. Their situation still wasn't any great shakes, but it was definitely better.

Bill willed himself to calm down. His group was already in a difficult situation, and his ongoing spats with Conti were certainly not helping morale. As the group leader, he would have to do better, but there was something about Conti that Bill didn't trust.

"I apologize, Steve," Bill began. "I was out of line. I'm worried, that's all. I'm worried about the long-term consequences of the drug, and I'm worried about our cell. Hell, I'm worried about all the cells."

Conti and Molly were both shocked by his apology, and the surprised looks on their faces didn't do much to hide it. Bloody Bill Harrison wasn't much of an apologizer.

Steve found his voice. "I'm sorry, too, Bill. Sorry about all that horseshit that came out of me. It was harsh."

"Apology accepted," Bill said. "But you don't need to be sorry for speaking the truth."

"Just so we're clear," Steve said, "I respect you, Bill, and all that you've done for the last forty years. I'm just trying to do my part. And to date, all of my studies project the likelihood of unforeseen long-term side effects to be almost negligible."

With a bemused smile, Bill replied, "Steve, how come you science types can't ever say 'I don't know'?"

Conti paused and said, "I don't know."

Bill laughed.

Conti smiled in return. "I wish we could communicate with the others, though. You know, tell them about the PEDA 17."

"Or even just find out how they're doing," Molly added. "We've got a lot of friends out there."

Bill reflected on what the two had said. "A lot of damn fine people. But the way the vamps are on us, if we tried to get in touch with anyone, it would be a death sentence for them, and us, more than likely."

"No argument there," Steve replied. "You know we're going to have to move again, and I was thinking that this move might have to be more drastic than before."

Bill leaned forward once again, but he didn't reach for his pistol this time. "I was thinking the same thing. What did you have in mind?"

CHAPTER 3

I wanted blood, and more than that, I *needed* it. I had my cap set on hunting and planned to take a ride into one of the bigger towns like Cavaillon, or maybe even Avignon. I would have a drink and a good meal, and then I'd carefully stalk my victim, taking my time and really enjoying it. At just the right moment, I'd drain him or her dry—a good, clean kill.

I would spend the night in a nice hotel, and the next morning make the leisurely return drive along the winding back roads of the gorgeous Luberon Valley. I'd take in the sumptuous views of the picture-perfect countryside, and I'd smell the lavender, that lovely, calming aroma that permeated everything in Provence at this time of year.

I could picture myself with the top down on my rented convertible, making the slow, gentle curves while deeply inhaling the lavender-soaked breeze as it blew through my hair. I would whistle along with French tunes that would be playing on the radio.

I'd been feeling so good about the idea that I was even going to invite Lisa to come along and try, yet one more time, to set her feet on the right path. But by this point it was abundantly clear that Lisa's feet weren't going anywhere near that path. Furthermore, she'd just as soon cut them off before she let me help her set them there.

After witnessing the brutal slaughter of our housemaid, I'd lost my appetite for hunting, anyway. Granted, I was planning to do the exact same thing to some poor, unsuspecting slob who happened across my path. But that didn't change the fact that Lisa had ruined my whole damn night.

She'd clearly already taken care of *her* blood requirement for the evening, albeit we were down one maid, but I was on my third day without, and definitely in need. I'd have to call down to the town manager and have a donor sent around. What a letdown. I mean, blood was blood, and it was always great, no matter how you got it, but I'd been totally jazzed for a night out topped off by a perfect kill. I am a vampire, after all.

Now I'd have to have a donor sent to me, take a unit or so from the schlub, and send him packing all smiles, secure in the knowledge that he had served his new vampire benefactor. How wonderful for him! But for me it was like being a caged lion thrown a dead slab of sirloin when he should have been hunting for fresh meat on the Serengeti. Even worse, it was like being stoked for dinner at the Ritz and then having to call out for Domino's.

Hello, I'd like to make a delivery order. One medium Frenchman, light on the cheese, no distasteful blood-borne illnesses, and please make sure he or she has showered. Yes, showered, and recently. No, I don't want any twisty bread with that. About twenty minutes? Great!

I sighed and made the call.

I randomly grabbed a bottle of cabernet from the wine cellar, and on the way upstairs, I scanned the label.

Lisa should be pleased, I thought. *This probably will go well with French blood.*

I took a deep breath and walked onto the patio. Lisa sat at the outdoor table looking across the Luberon at what was left of the sunset. The sky was mostly dark, but there were still a few lingering wisps of oranges and pinks. At dusk, I found the valley was especially lovely. On the surrounding hillsides, the lights of Bonnieux, Lacoste, and Gourdes were beginning to twinkle on, adding even more splendor to the already angelic view.

I opened the wine while Lisa smoked a cigarette, patently ignoring me. Given her beauty, I thought she might have been the perfect *piece de resistance* to this magnificent panorama. But that would've required a massive alteration in circumstances, and unfortunately, circumstances were what they were. When it came to Lisa, looks could be very deceiving.

Granted, no longer being naked, blood-stained, and holding our dead maid as the poor thing bled out did wonders for her overall demeanor. But it didn't change the fact that just below the surface of her external appearance roiled a nearly uncontrollable rage.

I noticed Lisa's face was a bit sunburned. She'd been cavalier about the sun for her three years as a vampire and sometimes suffered greatly for it. Her puffy eyes indicated she'd been crying, although she'd never admit it, especially to me. I slid her a glass of wine.

She picked it up and said softly, "Thanks. It's really beautiful here, isn't it, Titus? And so quiet."

Despite her instability, we often could have relatively normal conversations.

"I think it's one of the most beautiful places on earth," I replied.

She took a sip and wrinkled her nose, as she always did when drinking wine these days. "I'm not sure I'm ever going to get used to these vampire taste buds when it comes to wine," she said. "*Terroir* is one thing, but I feel like I'm drinking a mouthful of liquid dirt."

"You'll get used to it," I replied. "Just ignore it and concentrate on the other flavors."

She took another grimace-laden sip. "Sommelier Acilius has spoken."

In general, a vampire's enhanced sense of taste did take some getting used to. But there was something in the blend of the various components and flavors of wine that was, for us, particularly intense. Vampires can actually taste the humidity that was in the air when the grapes were grown, the sunlight, the rain, and even the soil or the terroir. And finally, the essence of the fermented grape fairly explodes to life on our palates.

"And you can't even get a buzz off the crap," Lisa grumbled.

I laughed. "Nope, only tequila and absinthe for that, but give yourself a chance. You'll learn to appreciate wine again. I'd say within the next fifty years, tops."

She actually smiled at my little joke. We drank in silence for a while.

Although I really didn't want to, I felt I had to bring up the topic of poor Marie. As calmly as I could, I said, "You know, Lisa, it probably wasn't the best idea to kill the maid."

She smiled again, but it was predatory this time. "Oh come now, *Mr. Morals*, you're not going to lecture me again, are you? I'd like to know what your headcount is over the last two millennia."

"That's not the point, and you know it. There are certain rules—"

"Rules?" she said incredulously. "You've got to be kidding, Titus. You're a killer, and you made me into one. We kill humans to drink their blood. That's about the only rule I can see that applies. I don't judge whom you choose to feed on. Why do you get to judge me?"

"It's not about that. It's about survival, and our survival depends on being covert, not getting noticed."

She laughed shrilly. My internal Lisa warning sirens started to sing. I would need to be very careful if I didn't want this conversation to break down into a full-fledged battle.

"Perhaps my idea of not getting noticed is different from yours," Lisa shot back. "The maid was only a human, and we feed on humans, don't we, Titus?"

"But why look for trouble when it's not necessary?" I asked. "You could've fed in a thousand different ways tonight, a thousand different ways that wouldn't have gotten the entire village upset. They're already scared shitless of you. Would it hurt to show them some respect?"

She looked at me coldly. "Oh, respect, is it? You mean the way you respected my wishes to let me die and not turn me into a vampire? How was that for respect?"

"Look, Lisa, we've been through this. After everything that happened, I couldn't just let you die. I couldn't just—"

Her voice was ice-cold and dangerously calm. "No, you look, Titus. I understand why you did what you did. I really do. But don't kid yourself that it was out of love or out of some warped and ancient sense of duty. You did it out of guilt, guilt about lying to me all those years and then getting me dragged into your world and tortured and marked for death."

"It wasn't about guilt," I answered.

"Oh really? What was it about, then?"

I ruminated, but didn't have an answer. *Oh fuck, maybe it was about guilt.* "I don't have a good answer for that," I replied lamely. I reached out and touched her arm lightly. "But can't we work through this somehow? I'm just trying to help, to help you adjust to our world."

She whipped her arm away as if it was snake-bit. Her voice shot back up the shrill scale. "*You* made me what I am, a monster! I won't be lectured to by another monster like you. And if I want to kill every single motherfucker in that little piss-pot village down the hill, I'll do it!"

She turned away from me, lit another smoke, and looked across the now pitch-dark valley.

I opened my mouth to answer, but let it fall shut. What would be the use? Everywhere I'd taken her—Montreal, New Orleans, the Caribbean—it had all ended in disaster. *She* was a disaster. Why should Provence be any different? I'd have to take Lisa away from here soon, or she'd probably carry out her threat.

The little piss-pot village she referred to, Saint Michel, had quietly served my aunts for generation after generation since the mid-1400s, when they'd first arrived. When they died, they'd willed me a great deal, some of which I was aware of, and some I was not. This Provence property was definitely in the "I was not" category. I'm not quite sure how they kept a villa in Provence hidden from me for six hundred years, but they did.

When looked at one way, Saint Michel was a village of the damned, quietly serving its two vampire benefactors, Mary and Katie, whenever they stayed in the town. They'd even provided volunteer blood donors when the need arose. This horrible little course of events was kept secret from the rest of the world for hundreds of years in the manner in which only small towns could keep such deep, dark secrets.

But when looked at from another perspective, the town wasn't so damned after all. My aunts had provided for the townsfolk in terms of protection, medical care, and financial support. Generations of them wanted for nothing, and through various trust funds established by my aunts, they would live on worry-free for generations to come.

Now this wonderful haven, along with its responsibilities, was mine. Only problem was that I'd brought my psycho, murdering, vampire bitch of an ex-wife into their midst. Quickly running through how Lisa had behaved over the past three years beat my already shitty mood down to pulp. Sort of like that stuff at the bottom of a juicer after you've made fresh-squeezed orange juice. You know, that gmish of mashed orange goo, with a bunch of tooth-breaking hard seeds tossed in for good measure—the crap that you tossed down the drain, unless you were a pulp lover, that is. That was where my mood was, rock bottom and sitting in a juice strainer, waited to be shit-canned and ground to bits in the garbage disposal. Dealing with my Lisa was such a fucking joy!

Suddenly, the last place on Earth I wanted to be right then was sitting next to the bitch. I got up. "I'm going into town for some dinner."

Lisa disdainfully waved a backhand as I walked away. The

gesture conjured images of my friend Jean-Luc, but of course Lisa would never possess any of his good grace or humor.

She called after me. "Make sure that donor you called for doesn't show up when you're gone. No telling what I'd do to him tonight."

The comment sent a chill down my spine. I immediately got on the phone and canceled my "delivery".

Despite Lisa's antics, nights always seemed perfect in Provence. Even she couldn't change that. This night was no exception, but it did little to improve my disposition. After a ten-minute stroll, I reached Saint Michel.

Lisa's "piss-pot" description aside, Saint Michel was a lovely, tiny town with only about twenty very old buildings making up the bulk of it. A beautiful medieval fountain and a small, but forbidding Gothic cathedral dominated the town square. And despite its size, Saint Michel was well appointed with a *boulangerie*, a *tabac*, a market, and a very nice restaurant.

I ate my lonely-hearts dinner alfresco, but barely tasted my food through my distraction. Toward the end of the meal, I went from distracted to antsy. I thought it was probably a combination of trying to come up with a new Lisa-management plan and destination, compounded by my need for blood.

Even with my rationalization, I had graduated to outright nervousness by the time my dessert arrived. I left my *tarte tatin* untouched, tossed some cash on the table, and started back to the house at a brisk walk. When I got about halfway there, a near panic set in on me, and I became sure something was dreadfully wrong. I broke into a vampire-speed run and got back to the villa in no time.

"Lisa!" I called as I burst into the house.

The only response I got was the echo of my voice bouncing around the cold stonewalls. She was gone, plain and simple. Of course she was gone.

I'm such a dope.

CHAPTER 4

Jean-Luc Leclerc sat at his regular table, musing over a glass of champagne. It was early yet, and the Absinthe House, New Orleans' vampire-only restaurant and bar, was nearly deserted. Jean-Luc still had one last foul piece of business to attend to in the subbasement, but that thought was only flitting about the fringes of his mind.

As New Orleans' vampire mayor, he felt especially satisfied that his city had not been attacked by any of Harrison's vampire-hunting cells over the past three years. A substantial amount of the credit for this was due to his security chief and resident computer wizard, Jake Lyons. The young man was absolutely tireless in his efforts to keep the city's vampire population safe.

Jean-Luc smiled and shook his head at the thought of the underachieving goofball Jake had once been. Every vampire in the city, including Leclerc himself, had given up on him. It was a pure stroke of luck that Titus Acilius, Leclerc's old friend, had shown up when he did. Acilius, with his ever-soft heart, took a liking to the boy and somehow managed to tease Jake's innate talent out of him. Lyons' success was due in no small part to the old Roman's tutelage.

Years before, Lyons had made a monumental mistake that ended up costing Jean-Luc more than a million dollars. But that was now firmly in the past, and in Leclerc's mind, Lyons had more than made up for it. He considered himself extremely lucky to have a vampire as talented as Jake in his community.

Jean-Luc may not have been quite as forgiving as Acilius, but he came close, although the little Frenchman would be loath to admit it. Leclerc said aloud in his heavily French-accented English, "I'm going to give that boy a raise."

To his surprise, he was answered by a deep basso voice. "I hope you're talking about me."

Jean-Luc looked up from his champagne glass. "Unfortunately, no."

Rodrigo Deschamps strolled over to the table. "Too bad. I could use it."

Deschamps was a former slave that Leclerc had turned into a vampire over two hundred years prior. He was one of his most trusted aides.

Jean-Luc asked, "Is everything ready?"

Looking decidedly uncomfortable, Rodrigo hesitated for a moment. "Yes, the same as usual."

Jean-Luc smiled. "Rodrigo, I really don't understand how someone as big and strong as you would get so squeamish over a little torture."

"Frankly, I find it distasteful," Rodrigo replied. "And I'll never understand why someone as prim and proper as you would enjoy it so much."

"You're wrong, my friend. I don't enjoy it at all, but it is a necessary evil in times such as these. And you have to agree that it has borne quite a bit of fruit, no?" For an instant Jean-Luc's mind wandered back a millennium to when he himself was tortured, and expertly so. He suppressed a shudder.

Rodrigo shrugged his massive shoulders. "I suppose, but I still find it offensive."

Leclerc tittered his high-pitched laugh. "Oh, stop being such a sissy. Besides, I'm a child of the Middle Ages, and torture was all the rage back then. Doing this is somewhat nostalgic for me."

"Sometimes I don't know what to think of you, Boss," Rodrigo replied.

The two of them started the long descent to the subbasement.

In the final negotiation with Helen Harrison on the night of the attack on her farm, she'd bought the safety of Bill and Molly Harrison with a list of more than 130 names. This list represented the religious zealots in her group, all loyal to the late Reverend Gary Jarvis. The members of this splinter group thought themselves fighting a holy war against vampires. Because of this, Helen knew that when she died, her controlling influence of the group's religious wing would die right along with her.

They would hunt vampires in their holy war much more aggressively and with no consideration for the vast amount of collateral damage to the general public. To them, the accidental killing of innocents was acceptable since they saw themselves as doing the will of God.

In the end, Helen Harrison had taken care of the problem by killing Jarvis and handing over the list to the vampires. She surmised that the vampires would do their very best to eliminate everyone on that list.

This task had seemed to naturally fall to Jean-Luc. It was just the type of large-scale mission that he enjoyed and thrived on beginning nearly a thousand years ago when he was a high-ranking knight of the First Crusade, the prototype large-scale mission. And as per usual when facing a great challenge, Jean-Luc had been an unmitigated success.

Due to his perseverance, there were only seven names left on the list to hunt down. Jean-Luc thought these last survivors would likely never be found. He reasoned that they had either gone deep into hiding, never to resurface into public view again, or they'd been taken in by one of the cells, or they were already dead.

As he continued his steady march down to the subbasement, he thought, *But my dear Helen, did it ever occur to you that I would instruct my teams to merely apprehend your religious friends and only kill if necessary? Hmmm, I think not.*

All of his captives eventually were killed, but not before Jean-Luc had extracted substantial amounts of information from them. Some gave it up easily, once convinced that the Harrisons had betrayed them. Others hung on, calling on their religious fervor for strength, something Jean-Luc recalled doing quite clearly all those years ago when he was at the wrong end of the torturer's instruments.

But under the expert torment he inflicted, they always cooperated in the end. The information Jean-Luc gained in his dungeon had kept Bill Harrison, and most of the other cells, on the run for the past three years and would likely continue to do so for some time.

Jean-Luc unlocked the heavy metal dungeon door and looked across at the man he considered to likely be the very last guest of his subbasement hospitality. Andrew Simmons, late of the Harrisons' network, was chained to the far wall of the dimly lit, dingy stone room. The prisoner hung limply and appeared to be unconscious. He was horribly scarred and bruised, and clad only in a filthy, shredded pair of jeans.

The roaring flames of the small fireplace danced Jean-Luc's shadow across the room as he approached his victim. The room smelled of burned flesh, blood, and urine. It smelled of death.

Simmons had provided quite a bit of useful information under Jean-Luc's substantial powers of persuasion. And once the vampire had found out it was Simmons who designed the garlic-infused bomb that had killed three New Orleans vampires, the diminutive Frenchman became downright cruel.

He'd stretched out the suffering of the doomed Simmons for more than two weeks, while most of his "guests" barely lasted one. He did it to avenge the three young ladies Simmons had helped to kill—ladies that Jean-Luc was genuinely fond of.

But also, he continued his ghoulish treatment because he believed Simmons knew something more. He could see it in his eyes. It had to be something important—so important that Simmons would fight as desperately as he had, putting up with unimaginable pain in an attempt to take the secret to his grave. Jean-Luc would not let that happen. He brought his hands down on a table in a loud, echoing crash.

Simmons started awake and screamed.

"Mr. Simmons, how nice to see you again. Time for another chat, I think," Jean-Luc said conversationally. The tone of his voice seemed more suited to an after-dinner discussion while sipping on a fine port than as a prelude to the most horrible torment conceivable.

Simmons lowered his bloody, battered face and whispered to the floor, "I've told you everything."

Jean-Luc replied cheerily, "I believe you have. I actually do—except for that one more thing *peut-être*, hmmm?"

When Simmons didn't answer, Jean-Luc went on. "Rodrigo, you've left Mr. Simmons' pants on. How terribly demure of you."

Simmons' head snapped up, and he moaned loudly.

Rodrigo gulped. "Do you want me to remove them?"

Jean-Luc noted Rodrigo's discomfort and thought, *My friend, you really are not cut out for this sort of thing*. "No matter, I can take care of that if need be," he replied. "You may go now. And one more thing. Would you mind telling Simone that I will meet her for dinner in, say, three hours?"

Simmons moaned louder.

"I'll tell her," Rodrigo replied. He gulped again and shot

Simmons a quick, pitying glance before he hustled out the door.

The edge of the fireplace was crowded with a variety of nasty-looking metal instruments. Jean-Luc carefully selected a long, narrow, hooked knife. The tip ominously glowed red-hot.

"Please, God, no! I told everything!" Simmons began to babble over and over with increasing volume. It was his usual litany.

Jean-Luc advanced on him, sporting a rather agreeable smile. "Oh come now, Mr. Simmons. Why not put an end to this unpleasantness? Just that one more thing, and all of this will stop."

Simmons continued to babble while shaking his head back and forth. Jean-Luc hesitated, his lips pursed and his head tilted to one side in a picture-perfect repose of patience as he waited for the reply that did not come.

When it was clear that his prisoner was not going to answer, Jean-Luc sighed. "No, I didn't think so. *Quel dommage*. Now please try to hold still this time, Mr. Simmons."

Rodrigo was halfway up the stairs when the shrill shrieking began.

CHAPTER 5

I spent the next several days moping around Provence. The townsfolk of Saint Michel did little to conceal that they were relieved and overjoyed that Lisa was gone. In fact, they appeared downright giddy about it. I have to admit, I was relieved as well.

Over the past three years, Lisa and her antics had worn me down. I'd failed miserably at even minimally improving her outlook and at inducing one iota of change in her aberrant behavior. After playing back my last conversation with her in my mind for the about millionth time, I'd come to the conclusion that I hadn't turned her into a vampire out of guilt. For the most part, I think I've gotten over guilt of any kind going on around seventeen hundred years now. Lisa was, however, more correct than she knew when she thought my actions resulted from a sense of duty, warped or not.

I'm a firm believer in the theory that no matter how long we live, vampires never truly escape their original human roots. I was a Roman centurion, responsible for the men under my command and for how my decisions affected them. And like my men of two millennia ago, I saw Lisa as my responsibility. I made a command decision for her, albeit a bad one, and then hadn't succeeded in getting her through the consequences of that decision. No matter how things turned out, I'd always believe I failed her in this. And honestly, I don't like to fail.

Anyway, my rental car, which Lisa had "borrowed", was found by the authorities at the airport in Marseille. She could be anywhere in the world by now, and there was nothing at all I could do about it, so I did my best to relax and stop fretting about her. For the most part, I failed on both counts.

After a Lisa-free week had passed, the people of Saint Michel must have come to the conclusion that she wouldn't return, because on the following Friday night, they threw an alfresco banquet in the town square in honor of me, their new benefactor. The entire year-round town population of slightly over four hundred was in attendance. They sat at tables set around the square, facing a small dais where I sat with the town manager and a few other prominent citizens.

For all intents and purposes, at least initially, it felt like a wedding reception. All I needed was a woman dressed in white sitting next to me instead of Anton, the troll-like town manager, and it would've completed the picture. I began to envision the gnarly faced Anton in a long wedding gown, and I had to cover my mouth to suppress my laughter. That wouldn't have done at all.

The tone of this affair seemed very serious, and I didn't want to insult the townsfolk. Fortunately, unlike most wedding receptions, this gathering turned out to be a marvelous party and an extremely interesting one, at that.

The night was warm and splendid, and the food was excellent. Soon after dinner, a quaint little three-piece band set up and began playing traditional French tunes. There were multiple toasts to yours truly, so I hoped all had been forgiven regarding my recently murdered maid. I was somewhat embarrassed to be feted this way, by a town full of humans no less, especially considering the countless numbers of them I'd fed on and killed through the centuries.

That embarrassment was nothing compared to what I felt at the end of the party, when I was formally presented three of the town's young adults to feed on. I was totally taken aback, and I began to wonder exactly how this odd little town truly viewed me.

I tried to demur, but the town manager would have none of that, and finally, good manners demanded my accession. It was clearly a ritualistic offering to the town's new vampire patron, and I concluded it must've been a ceremonial act for Saint Michel, given its long history of affiliation with my aunts. Ceremony notwithstanding, this public love fest made me a bit uncomfortable, so I planned to take small amounts of blood from the three and call it a night. I hoped this would satisfy.

As I approached the first—a slight, dark-haired young man—a disconcerting hush fell over the crowd. I stood in front of him, and he turned his head to give me easier access to his neck. An odd, surreal sensation fell over me. Our drinking of blood was always a private affair, a deep, dark secret hidden away in the shadowy places for no humans to witness. The townsfolk already knew what I was, but for the whole lot of them to actually see it clearly, that was something entirely different.

Now I was about to show them, to demonstrate my most primal urge to a crowd of over four hundred right out in the open. I was uneasy at the prospect, but excited, even titillated, at the same time.

I paused and scanned the square. Everyone's attention, even that of the young children, was focused on me. The tension in the air gave me gooseflesh. Just as any vampire would, the townsfolk were drinking me, drinking me in with their eyes.

I smiled, turned suddenly, and bit the young man on the neck. He swooned, the crowd roared, and I flinched. Straightening up from my prey, I prepared to run or defend myself. Over two thousand years of built-in vampire reflex told me I would have to do one or the other, because that's what a vampire did when confronted by a howling human mob.

But they weren't howling. They were cheering, laughing, and even urging me on. It took a moment to adjust to this odd turn of events, but then I relaxed and even began laughing right along with them. I took the young man's hand, raised it into the air, and spun him to face the crowd. The cheering became deafening. This was what it must be like to be truly worshipped. What it felt like to be a god, or at least a rock star.

I took him again with a deep bite, and a fount of blood hit the roof of my mouth like liquid electricity. Somehow the crowd managed to get louder, as it chanted, "Drink, drink, drink!"

So I listened to them and drank and drank, gulping down mouthfuls of this young man's hot, red life, rocking back and forth to the rhythmic din of the crowd. Finally, I tore myself from him, having taken far more blood than I'd meant to. I'd allowed myself to be whipped into a blood lust by the adulation of the townsfolk. I was in their thrall, and at that moment they weren't my servants, I was theirs.

I turned to the next offering, a pretty, dark-haired woman. But hands were pulling on my shoulders. Words were spoken that I didn't understand because of the noise and my overriding urge to drink more. I was turned to face the young man who was now sitting in a chair on the dais, pale and bleeding freely from his neck. I finally understood. I was needed for another part of the ritual.

I bit into my hand and dripped my blood onto his neck. In seconds his wound healed. He was quickly toweled off and pulled to his feet, his restored neck displayed for the crowd. They once again roared their approval and shouted out, "Healed! Saved!"

Even in my distracted state, I thought this chant rang a tad hollow, at least for me. After all, I'd been the one to inflict the damage on him in the first place. But what the hell, I'm easy, so I went with it.

I turned back to my second offering: a petite young lady who looked as if she might faint. Despite all the frenzy, and because of her small size, I reminded myself to be careful about how much I took from her, or I very well might kill her. Given the inherent dangers of this ceremony, I'm sure that sort of thing had happened in the past. But even so, I didn't want to make such an uncouth misstep at my very first time being treated like a deity. The French, sticklers for manners, might not forgive such a faux pas.

Her gaze was downcast, but I gently raised it with a single finger placed under her chin. Her eyes sparkled with terror. She gently placed her hand in mine, and I just as gently presented her to the square. The crowd cheered her boisterously, and shouts of her name, Jacqueline, filtered through the clamor.

I moved to face her, and she wrapped her arms around me and exposed her neck. I bit her the gentlest bite that I have ever delivered in two thousand years. Jacqueline moaned, not in fear as I expected, but in pleasure. The crowd chanted for me to drink once again, and once again I obeyed their urgings. Her body moved deliciously against mine to the beat of the mob, and once again I was lost in the chants of the crowd, and in Jacqueline, and in her blood.

For the second time I drank more than I had planned. But once Jacqueline was seated and her wound healed, I could see that she was not truly harmed and would be fine. I was beginning to feel blood sated, but that would do little to stop me on this night, and contestant number three was, in a word, breathtaking.

Her face, beautifully soft, with high, full cheeks, was framed by a shock of wavy brown hair. Her entrancing eyes were fixed audaciously on mine. Almond-shaped and startlingly blue, they spoke volumes of something other than French in her genetic woodpile. She took a step toward me, and a small but confident smile played on her full red lips. Even though we stood in the town square, engulfed by a cheering mob, at that moment we were totally alone.

The urge to take her nearly overwhelmed me, but I paused, giving myself the chance to fully appreciate her beauty. She was of middling height, slim but somehow curvy and voluptuous all at the same time. She was demurely dressed, but even so, the way her painfully conservative clothes fit her suggested a treasure trove just beneath their surface. Finally, I could wait no longer. I had to have her.

I moved forward, my mouth opened to bite, but she moved as well. She grabbed a handful of my hair and guided my lips to hers for the most delicious of kisses. We locked together for what seemed like hours. I was lost in her, but not lost enough that I couldn't hear the clamor of the crowd convert into a single voice that let out a protracted, "Ooooooooooohhhhhhh."

After an eternity, she broke the kiss, her smile large and her eyes sparkling like the ocean on a bright summer's day. Wild and untamed, she appeared every bit the hunter and not the prey. And this lovely young huntress was stalking me, and that was all right.

"What is your name?" I asked.

"*Je m'appelle Brigitte,*" she answered.

I smiled and then bit into her lovely neck. Again, she took me by the hair and pressed my greedy mouth firmly into her bleeding wound. I drank her in. Her blood tasted exactly how she looked—hot, steamy, and wild. She didn't swoon. Quite the opposite, in fact, she leaped up into me, her arms wrapped around my shoulders, her legs firmly scissoring around my hips. I caught her with one hand around the small of her back, the other under her derriere. Both felt as exquisite as I knew they would.

I began to spin in time to the crowd's chant, which grew louder and faster. I started to feel overwhelmed, dizzy, and all the while Brigitte laughed a soft, sensual laugh, which she kept up the entire time I drank her blood. I drank more and more and spun faster and faster. The crowd reached a frenzied peak, and I did as well, drinking and drinking Brigitte in.

Then there were hands on us, pulling us apart, interrupting our reverie, our connection. We fought against being separated until some semblance of reason seeped back into me. If I kept this up, I'd drain her dry and kill her. I released Brigitte, and she was set down into a chair, pale, but still smiling. I healed her wound quickly. I had no idea exactly how much blood I'd taken from her, but I knew it was a lot.

This little ceremony of Saint Michel had gotten me totally out of control, drunk with the feelings and sensations it had brought on. I was abashed, thinking I might have overstepped my bounds, but indicating the contrary, the people of the town seemed ecstatic over my "performance". They clambered to shake my hand and clap me on the back and to thank me.

I needed to think about what had just happened. I tried to take my leave, but was ushered back to the dais, where a very old-looking but sturdy wooden chair awaited me. It had clearly been repaired many times through the years, and obviously was fashioned as a throne. It was quite small, and I couldn't help but think somewhere in one of the town's buildings sat its twin, making the perfect pair for my two late aunts.

The townspeople quietly filed by me, everyone kneeling, taking my right hand and kissing it, saying, "*Merci, mon pere.* Thank you, my father."

When the last person passed, the band struck up a light, fast-paced tune that sounded medieval in nature. I and my three "offerings" were lifted, chairs and all, and danced around the square like the bride and groom in a Jewish wedding.

I wasn't totally off base, I thought. *This is a wedding reception of sorts, after all. I'm the groom, and the entire town is the bride.*

The crowd sang along with the tune, but it was in an unusual dialect that, surprisingly, I didn't recognize and could only partially translate. The gist of what the song said seemed to be that they gave thanks to me, their father, and that they'd gladly protect me and give their blood to me for my favor. Or maybe it was about the score of last night's Red Sox game, because the more I listened to the odd dialect, the less I seemed to understand.

I decided, as I was being bounced about in my throne, that once I fully regained my wits, I'd take a serious look into the history of Saint Michel and try to figure out how my aunts started and maintained this peculiar little subculture for these many hundreds of years.

The song ended, I was set down, and the crowd began to disperse. It was just after 1:00 a.m. I found the town manager, Anton, and thanked him for the wonderful evening.

He beamed with pride, saying, "This was the best *sharing* the town has seen in decades, maybe longer. Thank you, Father."

The fact that Anton was a town elder and a bent old man made it a bit odd for him to be calling me Father.

"Anton, please call me Titus," I said.

He looked confused. "But that would be unseemly."

I laughed. "Maybe so, but I'm not that formal a person. Please do it anyway."

He flashed a partially toothed smile. "I will. . . Titus."

"And please tell the three, the three. . ."

"Sharers."

"Of course, sharers, that I personally thank them. And you, my friend, saved the best for last, no?"

He raised an eyebrow. "Of course I did. She is my daughter."

Mortified at having jammed my foot in my big mouth, and then most of the way down my throat, I was also dumbfounded by the enigma of how a troll of a man like Anton, albeit a very nice troll, could have produced an absolute beauty like Brigitte.

I started to stammer out an apology, but he stayed me with a hand, saying, "There is no need to apologize. It is an honor to both my daughter and me that she participated tonight. And even more of an honor that you took special note of her."

I mentally wiped the sweat from my brow. "Thanks for letting me off the hook so easily."

"Not at all," Anton replied. "Is there anything else I can do for you tonight, Fa—I mean, Titus?"

"No, not tonight. But I wonder if sometime you and I could discuss the particulars about what is expected of me when I'm in Saint Michel. I'd also like to hear about the history of the town, especially as to how it pertains to my aunts."

"I will tell you all I know."

"Are there any written records?" I asked.

"Oh no," he said. "Our two mothers expressly forbade that."

Wasn't that just like those two cryptic old biddies? Thinking of them brought a sad smile to my face. How I missed them.

"Goodnight, Anton," I said.

With a wave, he was off, and so was I, taking a rather pleasant late-night stroll back to my house.

When I entered my room, I was greeted by the vision of the extraordinary Brigitte adorning my bed. She smiled, and I smiled back. No words were exchanged. None were needed. I turned out the lights, adding my bedroom to the pitch-dark stillness of the beautiful Provence night.

CHAPTER 6

Lisa Brownell looked out at the ocean at the end of Fisherman's Wharf in San Francisco. It was almost sunrise, and the pier was nearly deserted. It wouldn't be long now.

Since leaving Provence, she'd landed in one destination after the other, not caring one bit about the specifics of where she stayed. Lisa did care about wreaking havoc wherever she happened to be, and that she did with great aplomb.

After a short time, though, she had discovered some difficult truths about herself and her behavior. She couldn't act quite as recklessly as she had gotten used to, since now she was alone with no one there to clean up her messes. And she came to understand that she didn't behave this way for the sake of her destructive acts themselves. As a matter of fact, Lisa often felt horrible afterward. She realized she'd behaved so destructively only to upset Titus and his friends, but mostly Titus, of course.

This insight quickly led her to the depths of depression, a place she'd never been very far from over the past three years. Lisa Brownell was not one to fool herself, especially concerning important matters. She knew she'd never adjust to what she had become, to what Titus had made her: a vampire. She was done, all in, with nothing and no one to live for.

Lisa had arrived in California a few days earlier, and she took some time for one final reassessment. But nothing had changed, and this beautiful, clear morning found her at the end of the wharf, waiting for sunrise and death. She didn't relish the idea of burning alive, but given her vampire-enhanced healing powers, it was either that or somehow managing to decapitate herself. And as much as she was afraid to burn, the idea of trying to chop off her own head was, well. . . gross.

For a moment, she traveled back in time to when she was still married to Titus, whom she thought back then was the human Julian Brownell, ER doctor and boring husband. One of his habits that she had disliked, among many, was his almost continual watching of *The Three Stooges*. Even though he'd seen all the episodes hundreds of times, every time he watched, he laughed along as if he were seeing them for the first time. Lisa hated their idiotic antics, as nearly all women did, but she couldn't totally avoid some secondhand exposure to the Stooges via Julian.

Of all the dimwitted lines she half-heard through the years, there was one that she actually thought funny. When she'd heard it, it had nearly made her laugh, although she would have been loath to admit that to Julian.

The episode was in a medieval setting, and the dopes were going to be executed and had the choice of burning at the stake or being guillotined. The fat, bald one with the high voice chose burning at the stake. When asked why, he replied, and Lisa remembered that exact reply, "I'd rather have a hot stake than a cold chop."

She didn't find the joke funny anymore. Lisa had chosen the hot stake as well.

Time inched forward to slightly after six o'clock. Lisa's skin was already starting to feel itchy and uncomfortable, but she hardly noticed. She was deep within herself, in a very private place, trying to get ready for what was to come.

The sound of distant footsteps registered through her deliberations.

She thought, *If you're the curious type, you're going to be in for one hell of a pyrotechnics show.*

The footsteps grew disturbingly louder and clearly seemed to be heading directly for her. After a minute or so, they came to a stop immediately behind her. Whoever this asshole was, he or she was encroaching on what should have been the most private experience of Lisa's life. Her concentration was broken, and as this intruder stood mutely behind her, Lisa's already frayed nerves completely unraveled.

Her breathing became irregular, and her pulse bolted into an unsteady gallop as her anger flared. Lisa turned suddenly and struck a blow that would've crushed a human skull, but the blow never landed. Her wrist was nonchalantly caught, and she found herself looking into a smiling face—a vampire's face.

Slim and young, looking to be in his early twenties at best when turned, he had strong facial features and a prominent nose. His eyes seemed to sparkle with hidden knowledge, and his crooked smile shouted smugness. Lisa didn't know him, but something about him seemed familiar all the same. He held her wrist firmly, as she glared at him, panting like a bull.

He spoke with a lyrical, teasing voice. "My, my, my, the temper on you, little Lisa. Please try to calm down. We—and by that I mean you—don't have much time." He nodded in the direction where the sun would soon make its appearance as he continued to hold her wrist in a viselike grip.

She managed to gasp out between breaths, "Please, just leave me alone."

"After all the trouble it took to find you? Not quite yet," he answered easily.

That statement somehow penetrated Lisa's suicidal muddle. "To find me? You were looking for me? I don't even know who you are."

"Oh, but I know who you are," he replied. "It's taken me nearly a year to find you, as a matter of fact."

Lisa squinted toward where the sun would be rising anytime now. Her skin felt as if it were being stung by a swarm of miniature bees. "A year? Why? Why me?"

He released her wrist, and she immediately took to rubbing it.

"What would you say if I told you that I could help you, really help you to survive?" he asked. "Not by using the Boy Scout manual that Titus and the rest of his allies live by, but by my way: a practical way where you wouldn't have to compromise who and what you are. What would you say to that?"

Lisa was dumbfounded, reeling, on the edge of suicide, and now this? She felt the first true sensations of her skin burning as she stammered out, "But how? How can you possibly know. . . know what I need?"

He took her by the shoulders. His deep blue eyes were blazing as they locked onto hers. "Because I've been just where you are, and I've done it. I've done it myself."

She stared at him, not knowing what to say or do.

He glanced toward the now-imminent sunrise. "Time's up. Given the choice between burning and me, I'd choose me. But look at it this way. If you don't like what I'm selling, you can always jump back into the microwave later. What've you got to lose?"

Lisa's skin was turning a bright pink. She had trouble generating a coherent thought, but her head nodded yes, seemingly all by itself.

He smiled. "Good. Come on. We've got to go."

He took off at a run, with Lisa close behind. The burning pain from her skin was now excruciating, but she managed to catch up to him.

He looked over at her. "I'm not sure you're going to make it. We could go faster if I carried you."

Despite the pain, Lisa took the time to shoot him an evil glare.

He laughed. "Oh, I could really get to like you. My limo is at the end of the pier. I'll see you there. . . I hope."

He took off with a burst of speed the likes of which she'd only seen demonstrated by Titus. Although moving at a superhuman speed herself, in comparison, she appeared to be trudging along.

The pain was almost unbearable now, and she could see blisters appearing on her hands and arms as she furiously ran on. The edges on the blisters started to blacken, and Lisa was about to give up and simply lie down and burn, when she saw the limo.

Her new "friend" was holding the back door of the car open and waving her on. With reserves she never suspected she had, Lisa broke into an all-out sprint and dove into the safety of the oversized automobile. The door immediately slammed shut behind her.

Lisa felt instantly better, protected from the sun by the blackout windows of the limousine. The smug bastard's eyes fairly danced with glee as he looked across at her with an amused smile. Somehow, he'd managed to get himself a cocktail in the short time it had taken Lisa to get to the car. She really had to fight the urge to slap that smile off his face.

"Hell of a thing, wasn't it?" he began. "For a minute there, I didn't think you were going to make it. Would you like a drink?"

"No thanks," she answered, not completely able to keep the anger from coloring the tone of her voice. "I didn't think I was going to make it either. Would it have killed you to move the car closer?"

He waved a dismissive hand at her, as if her suggestion was the silliest thing in the world. "And where would be the fun in that?" The limo started rolling.

Great, just what I need in my life— another asshole. "Where exactly are we going?" she asked.

"My home. It's in northern Sonoma."

"And who exactly are you?"

"Lisa, how you hurt me, we being practically family and all," he said in a ridiculously overdone remorseful tone. He placed his hand over his supposedly slighted heart, leaned forward and extended an offer of a handshake. "I'm Gaius Acilius, Titus's son, as it were. Would it be too terribly awkward if I called you Mommy?"

CHAPTER 7

Saint Michel and Brigitte's company did wonders to improve my bruised psyche, but it was mostly Brigitte's company. Wonderfully refreshing, she all but moved in with me after our first night together. Although thirty-one, she looked twenty-one and often acted like sixteen. An interesting combination of traits for sure, but it did take some getting used to. Brigitte was arrestingly beautiful, with an uncontrollable wild streak, and somehow, she managed to be just the rock of consistency I needed after three years of my self-inflicted Lisa beat-down.

Unpretentious and honest, Brigitte was direct in her opinions and advice, which she administered freely, whether I asked for them or not. But even so, she never came across as overbearing. Perhaps it was how the people of Saint Michel were put together, or maybe it was how Anton had raised her. But I thought it was mostly just the way Brigitte was: a truly lovely person.

Fortunately, Anton saw our cohabitation as an honor, so there was no fatherly trouble on that account. Shortly after the Sharing, which is what the townspeople called the ceremony I had taken part in, I met with him to chat about the history of the town and my aunts. Unfortunately, there was little to learn. All he could recount, and it wasn't much, came from a passed-down oral history.

There were some interesting fables concerning my aunts, like how in the mid-1600s just the two of them destroyed an entire neighboring hilltop town whose inhabitants were threatening to attack Saint Michel. Tall tales aside, there was hardly any information on how Saint Michel's vampire-worshipping subculture had started and why it had continued into the modern era. When I asked Anton questions about the culture of Saint Michel, he merely shrugged his shoulders and said, "It is the way things always were and always will be."

I did learn that I could call on the townsfolk at any time and from anywhere in the world for their protection and their blood. I was expected to protect them in return, dispense advice, and in general, help them in any way within my means, financial or otherwise. I was also expected to participate in the Sharing ceremony at least once every two years. Given how the first one went, I would've made it a weekly event if I could. It was extremely satisfying to have such a safe haven in my life, but at the same time, it was an awesome responsibility.

The days passed pleasantly. Brigitte and I took long walks and explored other towns in the area. Our evenings were usually spent having dinners in Saint Michel, and at night we were together. It was a carefree time for me that began to erase the strain of the past few years.

Lisa, unfortunately, was a frequent topic of ours, albeit a diminishing one as time went by. Brigitte and I were discussing her one warm, clear day while we strolled hand in hand through a vineyard that bordered my villa.

"Titus, I don't understand," Brigitte said. "Why do you still feel guilty after all this time?"

"It's not a matter of guilt, but of failed duty," I answered. "I've explained that to you."

"Call it what you will, the choice was that she either lived or died, correct?"

I nodded in agreement.

"So you chose for her to live. How can she be angry at that?"

"I think a lot of it has to do with the fact that *I* chose for her," I replied. "She never abided that kind of thing from me, or from anyone else, for that matter."

Brigitte looked at me and nodded thoughtfully. "I see. She *is* that sort of woman. Very American, I suppose. What did you ever see in her, Titus?"

I laughed and looked into Brigitte's beautiful eyes. "Right about now, I have no idea."

She smiled at the implied compliment. "Besides, you did her a great honor, making her as you are."

I shook my head. "Oh, I don't know about that. She certainly doesn't see it that way."

"How could it be seen any other way?"

"It's kind of hard to explain without knowing what it's like being one of us."

"I see," Brigitte said. "Well, what do your friends say about her?"

"I haven't talked to them about it lately, since Lisa left Saint Michel, that is," I replied. "I feel like I've burdened them enough with her."

Brigitte's eyes flew open. "What? You've moped around here, and you haven't even discussed what's happened with others of your kind? Have you no true friends?"

I laughed and took her by the hands. "I haven't exactly been moping since you've been around." I pulled her to me, and we kissed for a long time.

She pushed back from me and her eyes took on a bright, wild glint that signaled wonderful things might happen anytime now. "You're very distracting, my love," she said. "But you won't sidetrack me quite yet. I know you must have close friends, and you need to speak to them to put this to rest for good."

I was touched by her concern. "As a matter of fact, my very closest friend happens to be in Paris. I'll call him tomorrow, I promise."

I tried to pull her close to me once again. The thought of making love to her alfresco, in this beautiful vineyard, with the sun warming us, started to take on a rather urgent appeal. Hell, at that moment, it seemed like the best idea I'd had in years.

Sadly, she kept me at arm's length.

"That will not do at all," Brigitte said. "We'll go back to the house, and you'll call your friend *now*."

She caught my hand and led me through the vines back toward the villa. I felt like a small child who'd played past dinnertime and had to be hunted down and escorted home in shame by his mommy. In the past few weeks I'd learned not to argue with Brigitte when she'd worked herself up into a state such as this one. It did absolutely no good.

Once we got back to my house, I made my call, and Squid answered on the first ring. "Chrissy, how the hell are you? Funny, I was just going to call you."

In the 1700s, the Squid first knew me as Christian Beauparlant and almost immediately stuck me with the nickname Chrissy. I hated the name, but it always sounded all right coming from him, for some reason. "Yeah? Great minds and all that. So how's Paris treating you?"

"Can't complain. What's up?" he asked.

"I was wondering if I could chat with you," I began. "There's been a new problem with Lisa. Who else, right?"

Squid replied, "Sure, but give me a minute. I'll call you right back."

The call disconnected, and almost immediately, my other cell started ringing. And just as immediately, I was concerned.

Squid had called me back on a special, ultra-secure cell that Jake had developed for the group of us who had attacked the Harrison farm, and for some other high-profile vampires as well. If Squid was using it, it meant trouble. Brigitte handed me the ringing phone.

"Okay, now you've got me worried," I said. "Why are you using the bat phone?"

"It's probably nothing. You go first."

"Are you sure?" I asked. When he didn't respond, I shrugged and went on. "Okay, Lisa took off. Being in Provence did absolutely no good. Go figure. Then a few weeks ago, she killed our maid and left. I have no idea where she went. I feel like shit about it, about the whole damn thing."

"You've got to stop beating yourself up, Chrissy," Squid replied. "You've done all you could do. You've got to let her go at this point. Let her find her own way, or not. There's nothing you can do anymore."

"Yeah, I know, but even so. I made her what she is—"

"Sure you did," he interrupted, "but it was either that or kill her. So, you made her a vampire, but you didn't make her so fucking nuts. She did that all by herself. Do I have to remind you of the voodoo gang riot in Jamaica?"

"Now that wasn't totally Lisa's fault. The fucking Captain could've helped."

"Jeez, what is it with you two?" Squid asked. "If you'd thrown him a bone once in a while, maybe he would've."

"There's nothing with us and I intend to keep it that way. I just don't like the prick, and I'll never send him any business. He's a fucking cutthroat."

Squid answered, "Okay, okay, leave Jamaica out of it. What about nearly burning down the French Quarter in New Orleans? Whose fault was that?"

There was no arguing there. "Well, I can't disagree on that one."

He went on. "And what about Montreal? It took her about two seconds to break up Adrienne and me."

I paused, trying to think of a way to be as diplomatic as possible. "Not to take the other side or anything, but you probably shouldn't have slept with Lisa."

He answered, "Well, I know that—*now*."

I laughed. "Why the hell did you own up so fast, anyway? Panic move, or were you just being Squid the Fearless, as usual?"

"Neither. That bitch of yours would've ratted me out, anyway. Or worse, she would've held it over my head for years."

"Good point," I replied. "But you still should've brought me along when you told Adrienne."

"Yeah, maybe," Squid said. "It might've saved me being thrown out of a three-story window."

"Again."

He laughed. "Yeah, right—again. It felt like old times."

Adrienne had tossed Squid out of a window once during a dinner party way back in the 1760s.

"It's nice to know Adrienne hates you more than me again," I replied. "It makes me feel like all is right in the world."

"Very funny, but you know what's funnier?" Squid asked. "Adrienne still hasn't cut me out of managing business deals in Montreal. I mean, I'm doing it from Paris, so I really can't be as effective as I should be. Odd, huh?"

"That's a good sign. Is she speaking to you?" I asked.

"Oh Jesus, no! I've always got to go through one of her underlings."

"I think she wants you back," I said, only half kidding. The two of them had been good together.

"I doubt that," Squid replied. "I hear she's pretty much banging everyone in town."

"Just trying to make you jealous. She'll forgive you, you'll see. I give it three, maybe four centuries max."

"Very fucking funny. Can you do me a favor, though?" Squid asked. "Talk to her for me. She's living in Montreal again, not even one of the suburbs. She got crazy security, but they found her. . . us, before. I'm afraid she'll get herself targeted again."

"I'll talk to her, but you know how she is," I answered.

"I know, but I'd appreciate you trying anyway. So listen, about Lisa—"

I cut him off. "Let's drop it. I'm good for now."

As usual, just talking with Squid about any topic made me feel leaps and bounds better. Ever since I first met him, nearly three hundred years ago, he'd always had that effect on me.

"You sure?" he asked.

"I'm sure. I can't wait to tell you about Saint Michel. It's quite the unique setup. But first, what's with all the cloak-and-dagger? Why the bat phone?"

"Shit, I nearly forgot. I'm pretty sure I've been scoped," Squid replied.

My mouth dropped open. This kind of craziness was just like him. "What? You think hunters have scoped you, and you let me prattle on about a bunch of chickenshit? Are you a fucking idiot?"

"No need for name-calling, and calm the fuck down. I'm fine."

I took a deep breath. "All right, all right. Did you go to the locals for help?"

"No, and I'm not going to," he replied. "And don't you do it either. I don't want any of them to get spotted and hurt on account of me."

"Okay, okay. How many are there? Do you know?"

"Three, maybe four. I'm not sure," Squid answered. "But if I'm seeing that many, there's got to be more. Anyway, they're being very careful, keeping their distance for now. I've probably got some time yet before they make their move."

"Why didn't you call me earlier, you dumb fuck?"

"Hey, enough with the fucking names," Squid said. "It's just that I wasn't sure until today. I nearly bumped into one of them. Can you imagine?"

"No, I can't," I answered gravely. "It's going to take me a few days to get a team together, but I'll be there as fast as I can."

"Thanks, Chrissy. I'll keep going through my routine and pick a setup spot. You'll recognize it easy, but from here on in, it'll be better if we have no contact. You know, just in case."

"Agreed," I said. "Be on the lookout for me. I'm going to hang back at first. I don't want to tip them that they're being watched."

"Got it. But in case I'm not here when you get to Paris, thanks for everything."

I winced at his comment. "Don't talk like that. You'll be there. Just keep your head low."

He laughed. "At six-five, that's kind of tough."

"Do it anyway." I answered. "I'll see you soon." I broke the connection and looked over at Brigitte.

"We will help," she said.

CHAPTER 8

Molly Harrison awoke to another beautiful day in Positano, on the Amalfi coast in Italy. She got out of bed and walked to the living room to take in the gorgeous view down the cliffs to the sea. A light breeze played sensually over her naked body. She closed her eyes, smiled, and breathed in the fresh ocean air. She felt wonderful.

Molly, Steve, Bill, and the rest of her cell had been here nearly a month, and the view still took her breath away. Steve remained sleeping in their bed, as she usually awoke before he did. That was all right by Molly, since she always enjoyed her alone time in the morning, especially in such a picturesque village.

Bloody Bill decided that since the vampires had so doggedly pursued them these past three years, it was time to go to ground. He and Steve came up with Italy, and their nine-person cell had scattered through the area these past few weeks. They remained completely inactive in terms of hunting and only passively monitored the Internet for any information.

Bill thought they needed to get entirely off the grid for a good while, and then, hopefully, they'd be able to restart their vampire hunting, and more safely this time. No one argued the decision. It had been a difficult few years in which they'd been constantly on the defensive and on the run.

Molly moved into the kitchen to put the coffee on. *This is the first time I've felt relaxed in years,* she thought.

She and Steve had whiled away the days in this lovely place, and she began to believe that maybe there was another life for her, a normal life without all of the danger and killing. She hadn't shared this with anyone yet, not even her husband, but her father was due to visit in the afternoon. She considered that she might have to tell him then. She knew Steve would back her, and in fact, would be overjoyed with the decision. But on the other hand, she didn't want to hurt her dad and leave him alone with his horrible duty that he would never give up. She knew leaving the "family business" was in no way a guarantee of safety and that she and Steve would still be hunted targets, but it certainly would lessen the danger considerably.

Molly was pouring a cup of coffee when her hand started shaking slightly. It quickly jittered its way up the scale to an uncontrollable spasm. The cup slipped from her palsied hand and shattered on the tile floor. "Shit!" she managed to hiss out before the overpowering shakes gripped her entire body. She lowered herself to the floor just before the stomach cramps hit. She squeezed her eyes shut and fought the urge to vomit.

Momentarily, she felt Steve's arms gently encircle her, and then the sharp sting of the needle in her shoulder. Valium—it was the only thing that seemed to help these attacks. After a few minutes it was over, and she opened her eyes.

Steve stared at her intensely, concern written all over his face. "Worse than before?"

"Not really," Molly lied.

He looked as if he didn't believe her, but said, "Same as all the other times. Your pulse was rock steady at sixty. I didn't get the cuff on you, but I bet your pressure would've been normal, too. We'll have to draw blood again, run some tests."

"What's the point?" Molly asked. "You've done that half a dozen times, and they all come back normal: CT scan normal, MRI normal. No blood tests today, Steve. I'm not up for it."

He nodded. "I don't get it. It looks like withdrawal, but nothing backs that up. When I increased the dose of the PEDA, nothing. When I decreased the dose, same thing. The Valium is the only thing that works some, and that was just a lucky shot in the dark."

She smiled a little. "Well, at least we've got that. It'll be okay."

"No, it won't!" he said sharply. "It's only treating the symptoms. I have no clue what's going on."

She took his hand. "Steve, you'll figure it out. I know you will. And the other three haven't had anything like this happen. Maybe it's just a fluke with me."

"Molly, you started taking the drug six months before anyone else. It's probably going to start with all of them, and soon."

"If it does, we'll deal with it," Molly said as she got up from the floor. She poured herself her second first cup of coffee of the day.

"I really think we need to tell Bill about this."

Molly whirled, nearly sending her mug to the same fate as the first one she'd handled. "No, not yet! We've talked about this."

"But—"

"But nothing," Molly interrupted. "We'll wait, wait for someone else to come down with these damn shakes. My dad will react way better if he's thinking about the whole group and not just me. Trust me, I know him. It's the best way." Molly thought that Steve didn't understand what danger he could be in. *He thinks he knows my dad, but he's not even close.*

Molly loved her father dearly, but she didn't kid herself about what he was. Bloody Bill Harrison was a dangerous killer.

Steve relented, saying, "All right, Molly, but he's going to know sooner or later. I think sooner is better, that's all."

A faint smile touched Molly's lips, but she was afraid—afraid for Steve. "Believe me, honey, when it comes to giving my dad bad news, later is always the way to go."

CHAPTER 9

Lisa Brownell sat on one end of Gaius's ridiculously long dining room table, with him at the other end; they were yards apart. The table, like the room and just about everything else to do with Gaius Acilius, was banquet-size.

The two of them were being attended to by a virtual gaggle of tense, silent, black-tie-clad human servants. Soft classical music played in the background, counterpointing the little clinks and clanks of the silverware, dishes, and glassware constantly being switched in and out for reasons well beyond Lisa's comprehension of formal dining practice. Gaius insisted on repeating this sort of dinner spectacle as many times per week as possible. Lisa found it annoying at best.

The servants had every right to be anxious, since if one of them made the tiniest of mistakes, Gaius was as likely to laugh it off magnanimously as he was to kill the transgressor right on the spot. Lisa found the behavior brutal and somewhat boorish, but she was getting used to it and getting used to Gaius. And it wasn't as if she hadn't behaved similarly on more than one occasion.

After slaughtering a luckless servant, Gaius would simply return to his seat, and the dinner would go on as if nothing had happened, but with the addition of a bloody corpse adorning the dining room floor. The effect of such ruthlessness on the surviving staff was galvanizing. They would visibly shake and perspire through the rest of the meal, quite literally serving dinner for their lives. Although having some objection to a homicide during dinner, Lisa enjoyed the secondary result: terrifying the wits out of the human servants. It always added a little spice to what might be an otherwise tedious, overlong dinner.

She realized that being entertained by such an exhibition

indicated she was already being significantly influenced by Gaius's view of the world, a view that wasn't the most forgiving and that many would describe as barbaric. But she didn't care. He'd helped her readjust her attitude toward being a vampire, and although that readjustment might be a warped one, it had proven instrumental to her survival. For the first time in her three years of being a vampire, Lisa felt like living instead of dying.

Gaius spoke, but he was too far away for Lisa to hear.

"Gaius, even with vampire hearing, I couldn't understand a word you said. Can't I just move closer?"

He raised his voice. "I said, 'You look beautiful,' and no, you can't move closer. You know how I feel about formality."

Lisa sat back in her chair, crossed her arms, and assumed a perfect pout. It was a look that she knew affected him.

Gaius's eyes took on a lustful twinkle, and he laughed. "Beautiful, intelligent, manipulative, and a killer pout—the perfect woman. All right, by all means, please move closer."

She took a seat next to him, followed by a virtual herd of footmen nervously moving about and arranging her new place setting.

Once the flurry of activity died down, Lisa said, "Now that I have your ear, let's go out."

"But we haven't had dessert yet," Gaius replied. "And besides, I may want to kill a footman tonight."

As if on cue, a piece of silverware tinkled loudly as it struck the dining room floor. Considering the hush in the room and its high-domed ceiling acoustics, it might as well have been a bowling ball crashing to the stone tile.

Acilius looked up slowly, obviously savoring the moment. With a small, mean smile on his face, he took in the culprit, a gray-haired man quaking with fear. Gaius's eyes narrowed, predator-like, as he stared at the horrified old man. The moment played out forever, until finally, Gaius threw back his head and roared with laughter.

Lisa joined him, but demurely so.

Once he regained control of himself, Gaius said, "Oh come now, Richard, you've been with me for over thirty years. It would take quite a bit more than a dropped fork to make me kill you." Gaius burst out laughing again and waved Richard away.

Unshed tears shone in the footman's eyes, and his face jittered and spasmed. He looked insane. Finally, with what appeared to be a supreme effort, he was able to paste a sickeningly phony smile on his face and make a small bow before he beat a hasty retreat from the dining room.

Gaius shook his head. "That Richard, what a card. He always fails to appreciate that I likely will never harm him. But he's so entertaining, believing each and every day that I'm going to kill him. I don't quite understand how he hasn't had a heart attack by now."

Lisa tittered. "The way you torture the poor fucker, I'm sure it'll be any day now."

Gaius laughed again and took Lisa's hand. "I *do* enjoy your company, my dear."

"Oh, so I'm not just bait for Titus anymore?"

Gaius tilted his head and smiled, trying to take on an aw-shucks look and failing miserably. There was nothing aw-shucksish about Gaius Acilius. "Well, you *are* still that, but surprisingly, I've become quite fond of you."

Lisa smiled back. "Thank you. But don't you think this obsession of yours with Titus is a bit much?"

"Considering your actions of the past few years with regard to Titus, I might ask the same of you," Gaius responded. "But what's wrong with obsession? I embrace obsession. I consider it quite the normal behavior, and I love being obsessed with my dear old dad."

"Why do you call him that?" Lisa said. "You know it's not true."

"It is. He's my vampire daddy, as he is yours. And he's pretty damn close on my human side as well, I'd guess. More than likely, we're related. But the real reason I like to call him Dad is that it pisses him off royally. Do I need another reason?"

"No, I guess you don't," Lisa replied. "But killing him, that's against every vampire code I've heard. Won't you become a pariah among your own people?"

He sat back in his chair and rubbed his hands together. "Now that's quite a complex question. First, code? There is no code. It's just that thus far, you've only been exposed to Titus's type of goody-two-fangs vampire. That type may very well think a code of some sort exists, but I've never seen it, and I certainly never voted for it. The few vampires that I count among my, and I'm loath to use this word. . . friends, would roundly disagree with the concept of never killing another vampire. And second, as you well know, I already am a pariah, but an extremely feared one."

Lisa laughed. "I see your point."

He went on. "And just because we're of the same kind, why does that mean we all have to love each other, respect each other, and oh my, never harm each other? Why? The humans don't behave this way. The world at large doesn't behave this way. Why should we?"

Lisa nodded. "I suppose you make some sense, but how can I ask this delicately? You've been trying to kill Titus for what, fifteen hundred years?"

"More like eighteen hundred," Gaius mumbled, looking deflated. Then he brightened and added with a smile, "But it isn't as if I've been trying to kill him that entire time."

"Even so, not the greatest success story I've ever heard," Lisa replied.

Gaius stewed for a moment. "He's not exactly the easiest person to kill. As much as I despise him, and that's quite a lot, even I have to admit he's powerful, wily, and extremely lucky. He *is* an Acilius, after all. Throw in the fact that he's painfully careful and seems to be always surrounded by his goddamn groupies, and there you go. Mine is not the best track record, I agree, but my hatred for your ex has given me a good reason for getting up in the morning all these years. And you, my dear, may yet prove to be his Achilles' heel."

"He's certainly not the only reason for you to go on, is he?"

"Not the only reason, but a big one. Although as of late, I've found another reason. Waking up mornings with you is extremely agreeable." Gaius took her hand once again and smiled.

The smile looks sincere enough, but with my Gaius, you never know, Lisa thought. She returned his smile. "Since you're feeling so agreeable, what do you say we head into the village?"

"And what could we possibly do in Geyser Peak that would entice me to forgo my chocolate soufflé?" he asked incredulously.

Lisa didn't answer right away. Her mind wandered, and she thought about Saint Michel. "You know, Gaius, this setup with your little town is pretty similar to Saint Michel," she said. "You know, your aunts' town in France."

He slammed his hand down hard on the table, but she didn't flinch. She had expected it, in fact. He always responded that way at the mention of the two ancient vampires.

"I told you never to speak of those two old bitches!" he growled.

"Oh, get a grip on yourself, Gaius," she said disdainfully. "Really, this sort of reaction is beneath you."

His glare was unnervingly threatening, but she met it evenly, waiting. Finally a small smile touched the corner of his mouth, and the look in his eyes made the slightest of moves away from lunacy.

"Nobody speaks to me that way," he said.

"Except me."

"Perhaps, but you realize of course that if I lost my temper, I could kill you with a single blow before I could stop myself."

"I wouldn't care in the least," Lisa answered honestly.

Gaius's smile widened. "I believe that's true. Maybe that's why I'm so attracted to you, because you don't care."

She batted her eyes, leaned toward him, and said sweetly, "You mean it's not because of the way I fuck you?"

He laughed out loud.

"To continue my point," she said, "the two villages are very similar: small populations devoted to their vampire host and keeping their secret for years, and in Saint Michel's case, for centuries. The only difference I see is that Saint Michel is kept in line out of respect to those two old hags; Geyser Peak, out of fear of you."

Gaius shook his head. "Your thinking is too focused on the present. But at your age, what could I expect? Try to think more historically. How do you think my dear old aunts initially insinuated themselves into Saint Michel? Do you think they "respected" themselves in? Of course not. They took over that town by terrorizing the villagers to gain their obedience. It was only over the course of quite a long time that they were able to become benevolent, essentially buying off the villagers with their vast financial kindnesses."

Lisa hadn't thought about this possibility. "Makes sense. But if that's the case, why don't you move in that direction? It seems to me it would be easier."

Gaius sipped his wine and replied, "It may be easier, but I don't think it's as effective, and I'm not sure I've been here long enough to make that transition. And frankly, it's not in my nature and wouldn't be nearly as fun. Remember, terror costs me nothing. Benevolence of the kind my dear departed aunties practiced is quite pricey. I'm well off, but nothing like those two old crones."

Lisa saw a pattern now. "I hadn't thought of that, but it doesn't make much of a difference, does it? It's a model of sorts, on a small scale anyway, of vampires taking over and becoming a ruling class."

Gaius clapped his hands together, beaming. "My, you are the smart one. Of course it is. It *is* small scale and slow moving, but if we're careful, we have all the time in the world, don't we? We can afford to be patient. But there are groups among our kind that think this sort of movement should be vastly accelerated."

"Are you a part of such a group?" Lisa asked.

"I'm a part of no group, but I *have* toyed with the idea of vampire domination through the years, somewhat more so as of late," Gaius responded. "I exist for me and me alone. I'm a gatherer of information, and I use it, at the proper times of course, to advance my interests. If vampire domination advances my interests, then I'm all for it. After all, isn't that the great American way?"

Lisa was confused. "I suppose, but then why would Titus's aunts take over a village if not to start such a movement? Merely to help them over the years? Titus described them as completely benign when it came to humans."

"Benign, my ass!" Gaius fairly shouted. "Those two were about as benign as great white sharks. I'll tell you why you take over a village or anything else—because you can. You do it because the people have something you want. You do it because you want to rule. It's as simple as that. Titus knows this. He's Roman, for God's sake. He fancies telling his fairytales, trying to pretend we're not killers when that's exactly what we are."

Lisa stammered out, "You mean the aunts believed in vampires becoming a ruling class?"

"Of course they did. And their little Titus went right along with them. He always went along with them. After a time, they changed their belief, and therefore his, the little automaton. But let me tell you, the three of them have oceans of blood on their teeth. Don't for a moment believe Titus was always as sweet as he projects to be now."

"And you, Gaius, what do you believe in?" Lisa asked.

"I believe in revenge and in myself, and given time, maybe in you," he replied.

Lisa sat silently contemplating as Richard carefully delivered their soufflés. Could what Gaius just said actually be true? She thought it could, especially considering how Titus had hidden so much from her in the past. Confused, she didn't know what to say. *I really need to clear my head,* she thought. *This is almost too much to take in.*

Gaius noticed her discomfort. "I've upset you with all this. Forgive me, I didn't mean to do that."

"It's just—"

He cut her off. "No, no more of this tonight. Let's go to the village as you wished. What shall we do there?"

Lisa truly appreciated the gesture of his ending dinner early, something he was in general disinclined to do, so she wanted to conjure up something to please him. Slowly, it came to her. "We should randomly pick a house, one not known to us at all, and enter unannounced," she began. "I don't care who's there—elderly, small children—it doesn't matter. Without explanation we'll join them in whatever their activity happens to be: watching TV, playing cards, or maybe just sitting around and eating popcorn. Who cares? We'll never know what they're thinking at our intrusion, but one thing we will know: their fear will be unimaginable. After a time of being the model guests, we'll slaughter them, or we won't. We won't consciously plan ahead. We'll just let it happen."

Gaius was silent for a moment, hands folded in front of him in thoughtful repose. "When I said earlier you were the perfect woman, I spoke in haste," he said quietly, almost reverentially. "But now, I sincerely mean it. You *are* the perfect woman. Your viciousness is astounding."

Lisa smiled, relishing that she had pleased him so. "After your eighteen hundred years of terrorizing humans, I know how much you like new approaches."

Nodding, Gaius returned her smile. "Richard, please have the car brought around. And we'll be taking the soufflés with us."

Lisa laughed, and Richard, who now seemed to have composed himself, raised an eyebrow at the breach in etiquette. He moved forward to pick up the desserts, but Gaius stopped him with a question. "Richard, how long have you been with me?"

Richard answered, "Just shy of thirty-three years now, Dominus."

Lisa asked, "Dominus?"

"It's an old Roman term that means master or head of the house; domina is the feminine," Gaius explained. "I'm rather fond of it in a nostalgic sort of way. Only my oldest and most trusted employees are given the privilege of using it."

Lisa contemplated the term for a moment. "I rather like it."

Gaius turned his attention back to the footman. "Just tonight I've decided that I like you, Richard. So much so that I promise never to kill you during one of my dinners."

Relief washed across Richard's face. He bowed and said, "Thank you, Dominus."

As Richard was leaving the room to face the distasteful task of preparing the soufflés to go, Gaius added, "But it's still open season on you at any other time, my friend."

To his credit, there was only a slight hesitation in the footman's step at the comment, and then, he continued smoothly out of the room.

Lisa barely managed to hold in her laughter until Richard left. "You really are too much, Gaius."

Gaius stood and chivalrously extended his hand to her. "It was the least I could do to pay you back for that wonderful plan for tonight's entertainment. To the village?"

She stood as well and placed her hand in his. The malevolent glow in her eyes perfectly matched his. "To the village," she echoed.

CHAPTER 10

Given the circumstances, I had to take Brigitte up on her offer to help. By using some of the villagers for support, I was able to be in Paris the same day I'd spoken to Squid. Option two would have been to organize a proper team. But that would've taken three days, maybe longer, and three days might have been more time than Squid had. So to me, option two wasn't really an option at all. Before I left Saint Michel, I made a call for help and hoped nothing would happen in Paris until the cavalry arrived. Until then, I would have to make do with the villagers.

Fortunately, most inhabitants of Saint Michel were hunters and good long-range shots. Unfortunately, Brigitte was among their best marksmen, and I was forced to take her along with me. The villagers had almost no experience with handguns or proper self-defense training, but since I didn't plan to put any of them directly in harm's way, with any luck, that wouldn't matter.

I took six of them, paired them off, and put them up in hotel rooms and flats with good lines of observation around Squid's apartment. I'd be the sole street operative armed with my Glock and a Remington sawed-off stashed under my overcoat. If and when the time came for action, the villagers would provide me cover fire from above. I hoped it would be enough.

I wasn't exactly chock-full of high-tech devices that might help such a venture, so I bought a bunch of temp cell phones when I got to Paris. Mine, hooked to earphones and rather obtrusively plugged in, made me look like either an old-style Secret Service agent or one of those cell phone addicts who seem to constantly bark conversations out loud while striding self-importantly down the street.

We did multiple three-way calls and kept our lines open at all times. That would surely burn up our minutes fast, but since I used a phony credit card to pay, it really didn't matter. All things considered, it wasn't the worst form of patched-together system for constant communication, but it was far from ideal. When the third night of our nerve-wracking vigil came around, I began to believe everything might stay calm until our backup arrived.

The Paris night activity in Squid's neighborhood generally slowed down after 2:00 a.m., and it was around this time that Squid had returned to his apartment the past few nights. His route home always took him by a particularly quiet area that was poorly lit. Hopefully, the hunters would take the bait and fall for this setup spot. My team served as my eyes from above, while I sat nursing a beer in a nondescript brasserie.

Brigitte's voice came in through my earpiece. "We've got movement: at least three. They look like they're going to push him to that second street, probably that little blind alley. Line of sight is okay, but not complete."

We'd done the best we could, but there were too many unknowns, and we were spread too thin.

"Damn!" I said. "Move a team to cover it. Quick!"

"Merde!" Brigitte exclaimed. "Three more from the other direction. Hurry, Titus!"

I bolted from my chair and broke into a run. I'd already planned out how I'd get to all the trap points, and this one, thank the gods, was one of the quickest. I'd cut through the basement of a back building and then into the alley. Now if only it ended up being the right alley, and if only the villagers' cover fire was enough, and if only Squid could stay alive until I got there, then everything would work out just fine.

I let myself into the pitch-black basement by a window I'd unlocked two days before. As I rounded the last corner before the alley door, I was greeted by two heavy-caliber bullets slamming into my ribcage. I was knocked backward onto my ass, and then that horrible, excruciating pain lit up my chest like a Roman candle.

Oh, just fucking great. Super-garlic-infused ammo.

We'd run into very little of that heinous shit in the past few years, and I'd hoped we'd seen the last of it, but no such luck.

I rolled through a doorway, barely avoiding a machine-gun burst from a second shooter. The pain from the two gunshot wounds seemed almost unbearable, but I ignored it and got on the move. I eluded a second burst coming right through the wall and chewing up everything in its path, which fortunately, didn't include me.

I could hear gunfire from out in the alley. Time had run out for the Squid. I had to get out there.

I heard my assailant's machine gun click empty, and I cut back suddenly and crashed directly through the wall at the point where I thought he was. Luckily, I landed right on top of him. He was fast and evidently well trained, because he smoothly rolled me off of him while simultaneously jamming a knife deep into my gut. I tore his infrared goggled helmet from his head and ripped his throat out, using my hand as a claw. He clutched futilely at his exsanguinating neck as he gurgled himself to death.

Shooting erupted from behind me, and I was struck again in the back of my neck. I nearly fainted with the agony, but managed to spin and empty my Glock in the direction of the gunfire. The shooting stopped, but I didn't have time to relax. I raced by this second dead vampire hunter and through the back door into the alley. Things weren't a hell of a lot better out here than they'd been in the basement.

Squid was down behind some barrels, bleeding profusely. There were at least seven attackers pouring heavy fire down on my friend, while another advanced with a flamethrower, getting ready to roast him. I didn't even have time to shout before a single shot rang out, and the flamethrower-toting hunter's head burst open like an overripe watermelon. The others now turned to the open end of the alley, shooting and ducking for cover, but not before another of their number was shot dead.

Brigitte had taken my "move a team to cover it" order quite seriously. She'd rolled up to the mouth of the alley in our rental car and was hanging out the back window firing potshots at the vampire hunters. I could see her wild brown hair reflecting the dim glow from the streetlights as she kept firing away. She was absolutely breathtaking and looked like the war goddess Minerva raining death down on her enemies.

I moved to Squid and quickly opened up on the hunters with my Remington, hopefully giving them something else to think about besides Brigitte. About half of their squad turned to me, but the other half kept concentrating on the car, which took a horrible fusillade of machine-gun fire. Brigitte suddenly dropped back into the window, and all I could do was hope she hadn't been killed. Her car sped away, still under heavy fire.

Squid was a bloody mess, but evidently not hurt enough to stop him from zinging me. "Jesus, Chrissy, better late than never."

"Very funny. Come on, we're going. Through the basement."

"I won't get very far," he wheezed out. "That fucking garlic shit. I'm bleeding like a stuck pig."

"Yeah, me, too. Hurts like a bitch. No time for talk. Get moving."

Squid quickly looked me over. "You don't look too good yourself. You better go. Leave the shotgun, and I'll—"

"We don't have time for this shit," I said, cutting him off. "I'm not leaving you, and that's that. When I open up, get yourself through that door. I'll fucking carry you from there if I have to."

He laughed. "*Oui, mon commandant.*"

"Finally a little respect," I said, popping up, with my Remington roaring to life.

Squid heaved himself to his feet and staggered through the door, with me close behind. I dropped the spent shotgun and half carried, half dragged him through the basement to the window I'd used to enter and heaved him up through it. I could already hear our pursuers coming into the basement from the alley side. We were totally screwed.

"You know we're totally screwed," Squid said.

I got him to his feet, supporting him into the best run we could manage, which wasn't very good at all.

"So this is the best you could come up with?"

"Shut the fuck up," I growled, but I was smiling. He always cracked me up, no matter what the circumstances. We turned a quick corner just as they got off a shot or two on us.

"Shit, they're already close," I said. "Come on. Let's pick it up."

Squid panted with the exertion, but managed to say, "This is the last time I call you for help."

"You're probably right about that," I replied as we turned another corner with more shots chasing us.

"And don't think this makes us even for Carillon."

"Bullshit. It definitely does," I shot back.

Quick as ever, he answered, "Oh really? When I rescued you, we actually both lived. I'm just not seeing that happening tonight."

I had to agree. "Good point. You got any weapons?"

He shook his head. “Fresh out.”

“We’ll be caught any second. Let’s go at them.”

He nodded. “Next corner?”

I agreed. “Next corner.”

We turned the next corner, and waited against the wall, me first, with Squid behind me. We were both weaponless and weak from blood loss, but it wasn’t in either of our natures to keep running and get shot down like dogs in the street. We’d give them a fight. Even though it wouldn’t be a very good one, we’d bring it as best we could. It was the only chance we had, but a pretty shitty one.

Squid leaned over and kissed me on the cheek. I looked back at him. “What the fuck was that for?”

He looked genuinely hurt. “For good luck.”

“Fucking faggot.”

“You wish,” he replied.

I laughed, and then all hell broke loose, with the night erupting in deafening automatic gunfire. Squid and I dropped instinctively, but the shooting wasn’t directed at us. It was coming from the street we’d just turned off of. After what seemed a very long time, the shooting petered out to single shots and finally, some weak moaning. One more loud report put an end to that.

We waited nervously in the dark as footsteps approached the corner and stopped. I readied myself into a crouch, prepared to spring out. I looked over my shoulder, and Squid had taken on the same position, ready as well.

A voice quietly spoke. “Julian, you there?”

I didn’t quite recognize it at first. It came again, louder this time. “Julian, it’s me, Dom.”

It was Dom, Dom Salvucci, my late aunts’ ex-bodyguard and the only human I implicitly trusted. So much so I had taken him on the raid on the Harrisons’ farm. Although gainfully unemployed and retired to Italy, he was always willing to help his vampire friends. I’d called him to help me with the Squid when I’d left Saint Michel, and evidently the cavalry had finally arrived. I let out a sigh of relief.

I said, “It’s me, Dom. I’m coming out with Squid.”

“Come out slow, okay, Jules?” he answered.

I smiled. Dom was always the cautious one.

Squid and I came out from our less-than-spectacular hiding place with our hands plainly in sight. Once Dom got a good look at us, relief flooded his extra-large face. He and his crew lowered their guns. The street was littered with the bodies of our pursuers.

Squid said, "Yo, Dom, we sure are glad to see you."

"Jesus, you two are shot to pieces. I thought you were goners."

"Us too," I agreed.

Right then, that odd, flat *eee-yaa* of French police sirens pierced the night. We all looked in the direction from which they were coming.

"We better go," Dom said. "No time to get rid of the bodies. They're sure gonna have a party trying to figure this one out."

We piled into two cars, along with Dom and his team.

"Why didn't you tell me you were here?" I asked. "We could've come up with a better plan than my piece of crap."

Squid coughed up some blood. "It definitely couldn't have gotten worse," he said.

"I would have if I was, but I wasn't," Dom answered, flustering himself. He paused. "What I mean is, I got into town just now. We were driving to our hotel, and it took us right by Squid's neighborhood. I figured we'd take a quick look, you know, check out the area."

I asked, "If that's all you were doing, how'd you find us?"

"We didn't, not really," Dom answered. "That crazy French girl of yours sort of found us."

"Brigitte! Is she all right?" I asked.

"She's fine, Jules," Dom said. "Her driver got winged in the shoulder, but he's going to be okay. Anyway, they tore around this corner and sideswiped my car. I saw the bullet holes and guns, and thought, 'Isn't this interesting?' Well, it's a good thing you told us about them and that they were expecting us, too. We got to talking, and even though she wasn't a hundred percent sure about us, she made a command decision and told us where she thought you'd be. I guess she figured it was the only chance you had."

Squid said, "Good thing she did. About another two minutes, and we were dead meat."

"More like one minute," Dom replied. "Anyway, after that it was easy. All we had to do was follow the bodies and the gunshots. Grand total ten dead. Probably got the whole cell."

"I hope so," I said. "I rented an apartment in the Saint Germain district for a safe house. Head there."

“I would if I knew where *there* was,” Don answered. “Your Brigitte wouldn’t tell me the address. She’s a careful one. I like that in a girl.”

CHAPTER 11

When I entered the apartment, Brigitte latched on and covered me with kisses despite all the blood and gore splattered on me and soaking into her. It took quite a while to pry myself loose.

The villager who'd been shot in the shoulder was healed posthaste. Squid and I were still dripping so much blood due to all the garlic-infused ammo we'd been shot with that we could've healed a battalion by accident. I let some of my blood fall onto the wound, and it closed up in no time. Even with the garlic, I was okay in a few hours, but for Squid, a relative baby compared to me at only 250 years old, it would take nearly two days to heal completely.

We did a quick debrief of the events, had dinner, and crashed for the night.

The next day, I sent Brigitte, the rest of the villagers, and Dom's crew back home. Squid, Dom, and I would make sure there were no "stragglers" left from the cell, and if there were, we'd deal with them. Once I was sure everything was safe, I'd get Squid out of Paris.

Brigitte protested having to leave. She wanted to stay with me in Paris, but I'd put her and the rest of the townsfolk who came in enough danger and insisted that they all go back to the safety of Saint Michel.

The next few days were uneventful, and we found no additional vampire hunters. Either we'd wiped out the entire cell, or if there were any survivors, they'd hightailed it out of Paris.

Our horrible shootout was blamed on the usual suspects of this era: a drug deal gone wrong or a terrorist plot of some kind. I'm sure the authorities knew it wasn't either, but they never like to admit they don't know what the hell is going on. And if they actually did know the truth and had broadcast it for the general public, they would've ended up in the loony bin.

Dom and I helped Squid pack up his apartment. I set him up with new identification papers and booked him on a flight for Ireland. The afternoon before he left, the three of us sat down to a nice lunch at an outdoor cafe.

About halfway through our meal, Squid heeled himself on the head and said, "Shit, Chrissy, I almost forgot."

"Forgot what?" I asked.

"Just before you got into town, I got a line on Lisa."

The Squid's complete lack of priorities and extremely selective memory could be trying at times.

"Oh, really?" I said sarcastically. "What, you forgot how important that little issue is to me? Just kind of slipped your mind, did it?"

He took a sip of his beer. "Oh piss off. I had a few issues of my own the past few days, like trying to stay the fuck alive."

Once again, he had a point. "Yeah, okay, good point. So dish."

"You're not going to like it," he said in a very un-Squid-like, serious tone. When I didn't respond, he went on. "Got a call from Davy Stein in California. He says he knows where she is."

"Oh great," I said. "Is that dope still playing 1950s gangster?"

Stein was a career criminal who'd been turned in the 1930s and worked for the Jewish Mafia in Los Angeles through the '40s and '50s. He never lost his "roots" in terms of the way he dressed and acted and his incredibly dated, thug-style parlance. He only had about eighty years as a vampire, so I supposed someday he might grow up. But I doubted it. Truth be told, on top of being a two-bit crook, he was a total idiot as well.

"Don't be so harsh," Squid quipped. "It's one of your many unbecoming traits."

"He's not so bad," Dom chimed in. "He knew my dad back in the day."

Dom's dad had been a mid-level mafioso who'd had some dealings with Stein.

I said, "Okay, let's forget about Stein. So where is she?"

"That's just it. He wouldn't tell me," Squid replied. "He wouldn't say over the phone, only in person and to you. He said he'd meet you in Napa. He sounded scared. You don't think—"

"She's with Gaius," I interrupted. "What else could it be?"

As tough as Squid and Dom were, they both looked scared at the mention of my old protégé's name. Gaius had that effect on people.

"So what if she is?" Squid asked. "She's a big girl. She's probably just made up her mind to be with him, that's all."

"What if he's holding her, you know, against her will?" I asked lamely.

Squid shot me his patented, super-intense, disbelieving glance: the Squid-eye.

Dom added his own version of it to the mix. "You know that ain't it, Jules," he said. "Nobody's being held against their will. They're both fucking nuts. It's a match made in heaven."

He was right. But even so, I knew I'd go to California anyway. "You're probably right, but I'm going to check it out. And before either of you two say anything, I'll be extra careful with Gaius."

"Then we're going with you," Squid said. "Right, Dom?"

Dom added, "Damn right. Jules, are you forgetting the last time you went to see your boy? He nearly took your head off."

I remembered it well. "I was fine. He's got a long way to go yet to get the better of me. I had him the whole time."

Squid said, "Word around the campfire is you just got lucky that day."

That comment really pissed me off. And the fact that he was correct made it all the worse. I was about to respond when my bat phone rang. I hadn't used the stupid thing in two years, and now it was ringing off the hook.

Jean-Luc's voice piped over my cell. "Titus, my friend. How are you?"

"Fine, Jean-Luc," I replied. "You'll never guess where I am and who I'm with right now. I'm having lunch in Paris with Squid and Dom."

"Oh, I see," he responded in his very best petulant, insulted tone. "A boys' weekend in Paris, and I, your supposed dear friend, was not invited?"

"No, it's not like that at all. It was purely business, but I'll fill you in later. Why the call on the secure phone?"

"Ah, oui. I've gained some information from my last *guest*. And as luck would have it, it could involve Dom."

"We're listening," I said and put my cell on speaker.

Dom and Squid leaned in.

Jean-Luc went on. "It seems that he was the boyfriend of one of the young ladies in Bill Harrison's very own cell, and against all regulation, they have been keeping in contact. How terribly romantic, wouldn't you say?"

"I suppose," I answered.

"You're such the pragmatist, Titus," Jean-Luc answered. "Well, Harrison's group has nine members and is somewhere in Italy, but I have no specifics on the location. They are not looking for Dom, but trying to hide from us."

"Are you sure about them not looking for Dom?" I asked.

"One can never be completely sure, but at the time, my guest seemed quite sincere. His name was Andrew Simmons, by the way, and it was he who designed the garlic-infused bomb that killed Maddie, Becca, and Jen."

"Son of a bitch," Squid said. "He nearly cooked Adrienne and me, too."

Dom added, "Quite a piece of work, this Simmons."

"And that's not all," Jean-Luc replied. "It seems that he was instrumental in torturing your Lisa."

Anger instantly flared in me. That torture session she'd faced probably had a lot to do with her current instability. Now if I could only forget the little detail about me turning her into a vampire, maybe I could lay the entire blame for Lisa going batty on this Simmons character. Ah, but for those fucking details. They always had a way of biting me in the ass.

Before I could reply, Jean-Luc said, "Let me assure you that he suffered greatly for his offenses."

Torture was commonplace back in Rome, but I always found it crude and uncivilized. In this case, however, I was more than fine with it. "Good. That bastard couldn't suffer enough in my book."

"Perhaps not, but it was definitely close," Jean-Luc said. "And there was one more thing of interest that the late Mr. Simmons was persuaded to divulge. He said that the humans were now using some sort of drug to enhance them physically, in an effort to overcome our advantages in that arena."

"Do you believe him?" I asked.

In my mind's eye I could see Jean-Luc's shrug. "I'm not sure. At that stage of our discussion, he would have said anything. It would be a titillating turn of events, no?"

"I'll say," I agreed. "It would certainly give us something to think about."

Squid blurted out, "Hey, Jean-Luc, did you know Lisa is probably with Gaius in California, and Chrissy is planning to go visit him there?"

"What?" Jean-Luc said exactly at the same time that I said, "Squid, you asshole!"

I took the phone off speaker just in time to stop Jean-Luc's very loud spate of French curses from wafting into the air.

When his expletives petered out, I said, "Look Jean-Luc, Lisa and Gaius are *my* problems. I've dragged all of you guys into them enough. I'm just going to make sure everything is okay, that's all."

Jean-Luc's response was brief. "You will not go alone."

"I'll call you back in a bit, and we can discuss it."

"You will not go alone," he repeated and hung up.

I said to Squid, "You happy now?"

"Pretty much," he replied with a smile.

Dom said, "He's just trying to help, Jules."

They all were. "I know, but he's so fucking annoying about it, and this information changes things."

Dom nodded. "Yeah, I'm going back to Italy. If I can find Harrison and take him out, we'll all be a whole lot safer. I'll have the advantage if they're really not looking for me."

"And if they are?" Squid asked.

Dom shrugged his massive shoulders. "Then I won't have the advantage."

I turned to Squid. "And now for you, dopey."

"Jeez, you and that name-calling."

"Shut up for once and listen. You're going to go back to Saint Michel and keep an eye on the place for me and make sure everybody's safe."

"Oh sure, you're just trying to get rid of me," he replied. "No way."

"No, I'm not," I said. "Well, I am, but not totally."

"Oh, now I get it. Makes perfect sense," Squid answered.

"Look, if Lisa is with Gaius, she probably told him about the village," I said. "They're only human there. Gaius and Lisa could wipe them out fast and with absolutely no consequences. It would be an attention-getter for sure, but nothing any vampires would do anything about. It's exactly the kind of thing he'd do to get to me."

"He's right," Dom added. "That'd be right up that prick's alley."

I went on. "If you came with me, Squid, Gaius could take your head off before you could blink. He's that fast. There'd be nothing I could do to protect you. As I recall, last time you met him didn't go so well."

Squid paled at the memory. "Good point, Chrissy. But how do you know he won't be setting up in Saint Michel already, and I'm not going to become Squid the Headless there, instead of in California?"

"No way he'd go himself," I said. "He might send people, and if he sticks to his modus operandi, they'll be human. You and the villagers should be able to handle them. If he does have Lisa, he's going to use her to make me come to him."

Squid shook his head. "And you're just the fucking idiot to do it and walk right into a trap."

"Now who's starting with the name-calling?" I asked. "Look, I have to do this, and I'll do you a favor on my way. I'll layover in Montreal and try to talk some sense into Adrienne about keeping a lower profile."

Squid's serious demeanor brightened some. "Really? Thanks, I owe you one."

"More like a hundred." I shot back.

Dom said, "Say hello to Davy for me."

I grimaced. "If you say so."

Dom laughed.

"Squid, call me when you get settled in Saint Michel," I said.

"Okay, Mommy. And Chrissy. Be careful."

"We all need to be careful," Dom added.

CHAPTER 12

Molly silently waited with the rest of them. The only sound in the room was from her father's fingers drumming a steady beat on the kitchen counter and the occasional nervous cough. Molly gazed out of her living room window, once again taking in the picturesque Amalfi coast. Even her dad's menacing reticence couldn't completely drain the joy from such a view.

The meeting had gone as poorly as she thought it would. She panned the room, taking in the rest of the team. They all looked nervous, as if they had a serious case of the jitters. Bill Harrison's foul moods had that effect on people. Steve, as the discoverer of PEDA 17, looked more nervous than most, but oddly, Amy Polanski appeared even worse. She looked as if she might shake apart.

Molly caught her eye and mouthed, "What?"

Amy shook her head and looked away.

Finally, Bill broke the silence. "Now let me make sure I got this just right. So Steve, all four members of our cell who're using your PEDA 17 have come down with symptoms that look like withdrawal, with shakes and cramps and maybe a small seizure thrown in for good measure. But it ain't withdrawal, and in fact, you have no idea what it is. And on top of all that, you've known about it for months now, but this is the first I'm hearing of it. That about it?"

Bill's voice was quite calm, but no one in the room was fooled.

Steve mumbled, "Yeah, that's about it."

Bloody Bill slammed both hands down on the countertop with a loud slap, and everyone started at the noise. "Damn it!" he shouted. "I get what's going on here, but goddamn it, I *am* the leader of this group."

Molly tried to interrupt, saying, "Now, Dad, wait a minute—"

Bill didn't look at her but said with an icy-cold calm, "Molly, you hold your tongue."

Molly knew that tone well and obeyed.

Bill's eyes drilled into Steve, who, to his credit, didn't flinch or look away. "You will never, never hold back vital information from me again, no matter who or what it involves," Bill growled. "And that goes for all of you. Is that clear?"

The group answered with either nods or mumbled yeses.

Bill went quiet again, his hands flat on the counter, his lowered head nodding, as if he was debating with himself. Finally he straightened up. "Okay, so the Valium seems to help some. That's good. But these fits are unpredictable. What if we're in the middle of an operation, and one of the team starts shaking? Then what?"

Steve answered, "I've been trialing with preventive injections. It seems to work and gives a symptom-free period of four, maybe six hours."

"Won't the Valium make them woozy?" Bill asked. "Not very good if we're under fire."

"Well, in a normal. . . an unenhanced human, that would be true," Steve replied. "But with Molly and the rest, it hardly causes any sedation at all."

Bill grunted. "So instead of having them addicted to one drug, now they're addicted to two. That's great."

Molly chimed in, "That's not fair, Dad. We all knew the risk when we agreed to take the PEDA."

"Whether it's fair or not, it's the plain truth, isn't it, Molly?" Bill replied in a clipped tone that told Molly just how much she'd hurt her father. Aside from all his other worries, she'd excluded him and kept information from him. She felt terrible about it, but knowing his tendency toward violent reactions, especially when it came to her safety, she had thought she had no choice.

"Steve will figure it out," Molly said. "I know he will."

"I hope so, because I've come across a bit of information," Bill replied. "I'm not sure it's solid yet, but if it is, it could put us onto an operation, and a big one. We'd need everybody at a hundred percent."

"But Bill, I thought we were going to keep lying low," Amy said.

"That was the idea," Bill answered, "but this just fell into my lap, and it could be huge. What are we supposed to do, ignore it?" When nobody replied, he headed for the door. "I've gotta do some more research. I'll be in touch as soon as I know anything."

Being the team's computer expert, that sort of job should have fallen to Molly. "You want me to help, Dad?" she asked.

"No, I figure I can noodle my way around a keyboard good enough for now," Bill said curtly. "I'll call you if I need you." He slammed the door behind him.

Molly felt herself close to tears. There was another uncomfortable silence in the room until Amy said, "I could use a drink."

"I couldn't agree more," Molly said. She made her way to the liquor cabinet.

CHAPTER 13

I sat at a small restaurant in the town of Napa on a warm, idyllic evening. The view of the river was breathtaking and the food was excellent, but none of that did a damn thing to improve my sour mood. I was royally pissed. That fucker Davy Stein was already two hours late for our meeting. I ordered my third tequila.

My trip from Paris had been uneventful, and shockingly, even my stop to see Adrienne in Montreal was pleasant. She was quite happy to see me despite the fact my dearest friend, the Squid, was once again at the very top of her shit list. I thought she might be harboring ill feelings toward me as well since, after all, I'd brought Lisa up to Montreal. And Lisa had been the cause of Adrienne and Squid's problem (and the problems of most other people in the known world as far as I was concerned). I was quite relieved when, despite all that, she treated me like a long-lost brother.

Once I told her about the near miss Squid had—we'd both had—her tone changed dramatically. Her questions and body language screamed out concern for my friend. By the end of my visit, I figured she'd probably forgive him within the century, rather than the two or three I'd originally thought it would take.

Common sense and our near fiasco in Paris convinced her to decrease her visibility in Montreal, a city in which she'd recently almost met her end at the hands of some of Harrison's hunters. She agreed to set up shop in a few of the lesser-known suburbs, which hopefully would be safer for her. When I was leaving, she actually told me to say hello to Squid for her when I saw him next. That little exchange took my estimate down for her forgiving the Squid by another fifty years. Would their inevitable reunion be the result of true love? Given my perpetual confusion regarding the opposite sex, and my two millennia of failures in such matters, I really couldn't say.

I'd ordered drink number four when I spotted Davy sauntering toward my table. His exaggerated, over-confident stride boasted a success that he'd never come close to having in his small-time life. He wore his hair in a 1940s slicked-back style and had a perpetual half-grin on his thick-lipped, jowly face. His garish suit, an odd maroon color, was a true mess that shouldn't have been seen in public, or anywhere else for that matter. A toothpick jauntily dangled from the side of his mouth. Old Davy sure knew how to fit in.

He sat across from me and extended his hand. "Chrissy-boy, how the hell are you?"

I ignored his offer of a handshake, leaned toward him, and said quietly, "Davy, if you call me Chrissy-boy one more time, I'm going to rip your fucking head off."

That wiped the smile off his face. "Jeez, what's the big idea? Take it easy, for Christ's sake."

"Let's see how easy you'd take it if I left you hanging around with your dick in your hand for over two hours."

"Oh come on, Chris, you know how it is," he replied, his half smile already making a comeback. "Business. I couldn't help it."

I was going to remind him there was a new fucking invention called the telephone, but my temper had already moved this meeting in the wrong direction. I didn't want it to go any further. After all, he had information that I needed.

"Yeah, I understand," I said. "Sorry, I got a little hot. I'm worried, that's all."

His smug level shot off the charts at my apology, and in a forgiving gesture, he opened his arms magnanimously.

I wanted to tear them from his shoulders and stuff them up his ass. Instead, I managed to say, "So, what do you know about Lisa?"

For the second time in as many minutes, he lost his haughty look. But this time it wasn't shock, it was genuine fear, or more like terror. His eye twitched, and he hunched over the table and looked over both shoulders before he spoke. Given his reaction, I knew the answer before he said it.

"Gaius. She's with Gaius," he whispered. "I'm taking a big risk telling you, Chris. If he ever found out, you know what he'd do to me."

I knew, all right. Even an asshole like Stein didn't deserve to be on the receiving end of what Gaius would cook up for him if he ever found out he'd been ratted on.

"I know, and I appreciate what you're doing. Is Gaius holding her against her will?"

"Are you kidding?" Stein asked incredulously. "They go out together, a lot. The two of them get a big kick out of screwing with the people in that little town of his. Nah, she's there because she wants to be. Sorry, Chris."

"Shit," I muttered, lowering my head. This was bad. The two of them together created a perfect recipe for disaster. I'd have to try to do something about it, but I had no idea what.

I looked up to find Davy waiting patiently and sporting a rare neutral expression. Even the toothpick was gone.

"Anything else?" I asked.

He shook his head. I took a neatly rolled-up wad of cash from my jacket pocket and made to pass it across the table to him. It was ten grand, Davy's usual fee for selling important information. He backed away from the money like it was on fire.

"I don't want your money, Chris," he said. "I'm not doing you much of a favor telling you this. You're going to go up there, aren't you? And when you do, no telling what's going to happen."

He was right. I had no specific idea what to do, but the one thing I *had* to do was go to Gaius's mansion and check things out. And as careful and cautious and polite as I would be, I already knew it was still going to go way, way bad. It always did when I had any dealings with Gaius.

I took Davy's right hand in both of mine, pressed the cash firmly in it, and held it there. "I appreciate the gesture, but take it anyway."

He looked concerned—in my experience, a foreign expression for him. "Okay, okay, Chris."

"I've got to run," I said. "But stay and have dinner. It's on me."

"Thanks, but no thanks," Davy said, once again nervously looking over both shoulders. "Even being within a hundred miles of Gaius is too close for my taste. I'm gonna beat it back to San Fran."

As he stood, I said, "Oh, by the way, Dom says hello."

Stein grinned at that. "How is that oversized guinea doing? Still refusing to be turned, I bet."

"He's doing great, but you're right," I said. "He'll never be turned."

"Too bad," Davy replied. "I'll miss the big lug when he croaks. Is he back in the old country?"

"Yep, Sicily, at one of his granddad's old villas. You should call him. I know he'd love to see you."

"I might do just that. But if you don't mind, I'm going to scram. Don't want one of Gaius's boys to spot me, especially talking to you."

Davy scurried off into the night, nervously flicking glances back and forth in search of the thugs who hopefully weren't there.

CHAPTER 14

The pleasant, winding trip north through wine country was pretty much ruined by the knowledge that Gaius was waiting for me at the end of the line. I couldn't have dreaded this visit to him anymore than I did. He'd hated me for centuries and was totally forthright about the fact that his greatest joy in life would be to see me dead. Over the years he'd made several attempts to make that happen. I really shouldn't have tolerated the behavior and should have destroyed him centuries ago, but I couldn't bring myself to do it.

Some might say the reason for my leniency was guilt, and that certainly played a part, but in fact, once again, it was my soldier's sense of duty. You see, Gaius had been a centurion in my command nearly two millennia ago, and I'd failed him miserably.

The few encounters we'd had in the last century were, in a word, horrible, with Gaius's bad behavior never seeming to find rock bottom. When it came to me, the boy just got worse and worse. And now with Lisa in the equation, I knew things between us would go directly into the shitter.

I took a leisurely route driving up Napa Valley, with plans to cut over to northern Sonoma and Gaius's town of Geyser Peak. It was also the most scenic route, and that was reason enough to choose it, especially on such a gorgeous day with the lid off my rental ragtop. But the real reason I chose it was that it was the longest route, and I wanted to stall having to meet the monster I had created for as long as possible. But what the hell, if this ride was going to be my last mile, at least it would be a pretty one.

As I took in the vineyard-laden rolling hills and the small, quaint towns, my mind wandered back 1,800 years to the last time I was on good terms with Gaius. It was the very last day of his human life…

~~~
~~~

As my cavalry unit advanced into Mesopotamia, the Parthians sprung their ambush, scattering us into a headlong retreat. The horses of my small group of six were blown out and flagging and were about to be overtaken when Gaius turned back into the pursuers, buying precious time for our escape. I saw what was left of us to the relative safety of the woods and then returned to help the young man. But I was too late, only arriving in time to see Gaius impaled through his back with a long pike. The point came through his chest with a gush of blood and he went crashing to the ground. He'd managed to kill two of the enemy before he fell.

I was beside myself at having let him turn and sacrifice himself for me. But what was I to do? I was a Roman general, and he was the chief of my personal bodyguard. It was his job.

Red-hot anger welled up inside of me. Simultaneously, like a child's security blanket, my calm, cold, killing place enfolded me in its loving embrace and, as always, I cherished the feeling.

I trotted my horse into the midst of the enemy, dismounted, and stood before the Parthians with only my sword and shield. I spared Gaius a brief glance. His breathing came in feeble, shallow pants. The pool of red that he was lying in kept growing larger as his chest wound bled out.

From atop their mounts the Parthians looked down at me incredulously. They probably couldn't believe their luck, considering the rewards they'd receive for killing or capturing a Roman general. I could see that any thought of pursuing the rest of my group had vanished, and they dismounted. There were fourteen of them.

Even though I had physical advantage, it wasn't as great as it would be for me today, as I was only two hundred years old, not two thousand. This, along with the Parthians' sheer force of numbers, stacked the odds against me. And these weren't some rabble, but trained soldiers.

None of that mattered to me. I'd just watched them kill perhaps my only relative on this earth, and my friend. I'd slaughter them all, or die trying.

They circled me casually, laughing and jeering the entire time. I waited. After a minute or so, they'd had their laugh, and they stopped and took up fighting stances. The ring of their swords being unsheathed pierced the stillness. The heat of the day was overpowering, and the air was laden with dust.

It began with two feinting at me from the front, but the real attack came from behind, as I'd expected. Ignoring the feint, I whirled and cleanly decapitated one attacker, and impaled the next. The metallic smell of blood began to humidify the super-dry air.

Using the skewered Parthian as a human shield, I heaved him into a group of three and quickly reversed direction, again going straight at my attackers. Two more fell to the ground, thrashing and bleeding out. But in the exchange, I took a deep wound when a sword impaled me through my back. The Parthians hesitated for a moment, watching and expecting me to keel over, lifeless. But instead, I simply pulled the sword from my back and dangled it between two fingers for effect before disdainfully dropping it into the dust.

I turned unhurriedly and carefully took in each and every one of them, smiling the entire time. They were startled, and mystified for sure, but not panicked yet, as they were hardened warriors. I tilted my head back and bellowed out a guttural war cry. It was at that moment that fear whipped through them. Some made for their horses to flee or maybe to get their pikes. The reason didn't matter; the fact that they'd broken formation did. They were vulnerable, and I attacked.

I took four more sword wounds, one quite serious in the neck, but it didn't stop me. I killed them all. It seemed like hours, but it was actually over in minutes. Weak from the exertion and blood loss, I stood panting for a moment, covered in my own gore and that of the Parthians. I watched mesmerized as the blood dripped from me, watering the barren terrain.

Suddenly, I remembered for whom I'd been fighting. I ran to where Gaius lay covered in a pool of red, a huge pike protruding from his chest. His breath came in feeble, shallow pants.

I had seconds, maybe less. There was no time to talk, to explain, or even to think. I'd never tried to turn anyone before, but the only alternative was to watch Gaius bleed to death in this desolate arena. Acting more on instinct than anything else, I bit him in the neck and drank his blood. It was over for him quickly.

~~~

Seeing Gaius's forbidding outer-perimeter electrified fence shook me from my memories. As if by magic, the gates opened as my car approached, a signal that Gaius was expecting me. This ominous realization did little to improve my already sour mood. His huge property was hidden in the woods above Geyser Peak, far enough
~~~

away from any traveled paths to ensure his privacy. Considering all the nasty goings-on that took place in his mansion, Gaius needed his privacy.

Gaius's line of security cameras swiveled, marking my progress as I drove up the meandering, mile-long drive. I finally arrived at the main house and parked my car in front. The looming edifice oozed a thick, smothering malevolence that felt like it was directed at me and me alone. Although the house was a tastefully designed Romanesque Revival, in my mind it screamed Bates Motel. The place had Gaius's nasty persona written all over it.

A gray-haired butler silently opened the door and waited patiently while I was thoroughly searched by two of Gaius's extra-large bodyguards. I didn't try to sneak in any weapons. They would've been found, anyway. Once satisfied I was weaponless, the reticent butler began our long trek to Gaius. The home was ridiculously large, even for a mansion, and the long, slow walk felt as if it took about four days.

We finally reached his theater-sized screening room located in the basement. When film came into being, movies became one of Gaius's rare hobbies, and he quickly morphed into a movie fanatic, so much so that occasionally he allowed himself out of his self-imposed isolation from the human race to produce and direct a few short films. Mostly unheard of, and never commercial successes, they were the kinds of films you walked away from depressed and scratching your head, trying to figure out what the hell just hit you.

High-ceilinged, especially for a basement, the screening room was dark, decorated in deep woods and leathers, and lined with cases that housed Gaius's other hobby—weapons. He'd acquired quite the collection of arms through the years, dating from nearly every era known to mankind. Many were expensive reproductions, but quite a few were originals.

I could see the back of his head in the most central front-row seat as he watched the movie, *Blade Runner*, probably for the thousandth time. He could do that: watch the same movie over and over again and see something new in it each and every time. As I entered, the scene was running where the android antagonist kills the human genius who had created him. This version of Frankenstein's monster crushes his creator's head with his own two hands. As the victim groans in pain, with blood spurting from his eyes, the android's facial expression changes from joy to sorrow to disgust and finally, to relief.

A disturbing scene, to say the least, and I was sure Gaius, the director that he was, had timed it perfectly for my entrance. The message was not lost on me.

The lights came up startlingly bright, and by the time my eyes adjusted, Gaius, with disturbing speed, had already moved directly in front of me, a step closer than I would've liked. He said with false cheer, "Dad, it's been too long. How the hell are you?"

I smirked and took a step away, pretending to admire a sword that was on display, but I was really putting a bit of space between me and this deadly viper of a vampire. "I'm just fine, Gaius, but don't call me that. You know I don't like it."

He laughed. "Come now, you know you're my dad. My vampire daddy, that's you."

His eyes looked even crazier than I remembered.

I asked, "How are you?"

His smile faded, and he said icily, "You know how it is, Dad. Just the same, century in and century out, and I have you to thank for it."

That was the crux of the matter. He wished I'd let him die doing his duty that day instead of turning him into a vampire, a monster. He'd always blamed me for making that decision for him, and he always would, just like Lisa.

"It was either that or let your carcass rot in Mesopotamia, you ungrateful little prick."

His hands flew to his mouth in mock surprise. "Now that's the dad I know and love. You know, I've been following your exploits since you've become a vampire again. You've made quite the splash. But I really was hoping you'd get depressed enough to kill yourself during your *human* phase. Too bad, really."

"You can't have everything," I quipped.

His phony smile reappeared. "No, you can't. But how inspiring you've become with all those new friends in New Orleans, and then, breaking up those nasty vampire hunters. But I think your most impressive act was making up with that no-good cunt, Adrienne. You must be up for Vampire of the Year."

He'd always had his sources and was well informed, but this intimate knowledge of what I'd been doing was a cut above, even for him. The details he was aware of were disturbing, and I could tell by his look that he knew it.

"I doubt either of us will win that award."

He laughed. It was at least partially genuine. "Heard about your aunties. Can't say I'm sorry, and as a matter of fact, I'm pretty damn happy those two old hags are gone."

I took a step toward him, my anger flaring. "They did nothing but treat you well, as I did. Why can't you just let things go?"

He screamed out, "Because you turned me into a fiend, that's why! And then you and those two old hags kept me prisoner for years, trapped with the three of you, listening to your constant drivel and interminable moralizing bullshit. You were so full of yourselves, it made me sick, and it still does."

His raised voice shocked me into silence. After a moment when I didn't respond, he said in a normal tone, "I seem to have forgotten my manners. May I get you something to drink?"

"Sure, why not?" I answered.

Gaius's violent mood swings always caught me off-balance, even though I was well aware he engineered them to do just that. As he walked to the bar, I opened my mouth to respond to his accusations, but held my tongue. What would be the use? We'd had similar arguments for centuries and to no avail. Gaius might've been correct about me turning him without his consent, but his "prison" was a beautiful villa in Rome, where he lived in luxury, was treated well, and was intelligently trained in how to survive as a vampire.

It was a far better opportunity than I'd had at the beginning, but even so, he was completely incorrigible. In fact he'd been far worse than Lisa could ever have imagined being. Despite his poor behavior back then, my aunts and I tolerated his antics. He was smart enough to bide his time with us and consider his options, because the chances of living a good life as a vampire in ancient times were quite a bit more limited than they are today.

The moment he lost his sun sensitivity, though, he left, but not before soundly cursing Mary and Katie. I never quite understood that. The two old girls were nothing but nice to him despite all of his ultra-sullen moodiness.

But he had saved the best for last, and I'll always remember it like it was yesterday, despite it happening nearly two millennia ago. He'd turned to me, his blue eyes simmering with anger, and said in a low, deadly tone, "And you, Titus, I pray that all the gods curse you as well for doing this to me. But I am still a good Roman soldier, after all, and despite everything thrown against me, I will march on, I will campaign on, and I'll become the absolutely best monster that the world has ever seen. And do you know why, Titus?"

I gulped down a dry swallow and shook my head.

"To torment you, year in and year out, decade in and decade out, century in and century out, until one day I have the pleasure of ending your miserable life."

With that, he turned on his heel and stormed out of the villa. I have to admit, it wasn't the most touching of farewells, but to his credit, Gaius had pretty much lived up to his word. Except for the killing me part, that is, at least not yet anyway.

Gaius moved toward me with my drink faster than he should have, trying to get me to flinch. I didn't, but just barely. It was a little game he liked to play.

He handed me a water glass filled with tequila. "Cheers," he said and knocked back a good portion of his huge drink. I followed suit, and he added, "If you were human, that would've been loaded with poison."

I smiled. "Not your style."

We drank in silence for a moment, and he said, "Penny for your thoughts, Dad."

"I really wish you'd stop calling me that," I replied, unable to keep myself from sounding petulant. "But if you must know, I was thinking how I wished things had turned out differently between us, that's all."

"Oh boohoo, poor Titus, the dejected Renaissance vampire," Gaius said contemptuously. "How sad that you have to put up with your wayward son. Save that crap for someone who doesn't know you the way I do. You're an egotistical, self-aggrandizing, overblown prick. You weren't trying to help me that day. You were just building a monument to yourself. And how shocked, how fucking shocked you were that I didn't get down on my knees and thank you for it."

"It wasn't like that at all. I went back to help you, but I was too late. I—"

He cut me off. "Titus, I grow weary of this discussion. Not to be indelicate, but what the fuck are you doing here?"

I put down my drink. "You know why I'm here."

He smiled. "Yes, but I want you to say it."

"Fine. Where's Lisa?" I asked. "I've come to take her with me."

He threw back his head and roared with laughter.

I waited patiently until he finally got himself under control.

"You're quite the comedian, Titus," Gaius said. "In the first place, if you tried, you'd never get her out of here alive. Second, she's here of her own free will. Just like me, she's quite sick of your bullshit. All those years of lying to her—naughty, naughty—and my, what a hypocrite you've become. But none of that even matters, because the moment I knew you were coming, I sent her away. You see, I genuinely like the girl. And she's doing a lot better with me than with you and your crap. I didn't want your sorry, half-assed advice dragging her down again."

I was stunned but managed to stammer out, "Gaius, come on, give her a break. You must know how unstable she is."

"Yes, thanks to you, and as I said, she's better now. You and your kind don't know how to deal with people like her or people like me, and you never will. You never seem to understand that we don't want to live a lie and deny what we are. And it galls you and all of your minions that there are some of us who don't want to live by the rules of the great Titus Acilius."

"They're not my rules. It's how we best survive."

He smirked. "Best? What a smug bastard you are. Why do you get to tell me how I best do anything? I'm sick of this conversation. Lisa stays here as long as she wishes. Now leave while you can."

I stared at him long and hard, seeing hatred blazing in his eyes. I'm sure he saw the same in mine.

I started to leave, but he stopped me, saying, "And Dad, one more thing."

I turned back, completely on my guard, but even so, he nailed me with a nose-smashing head-butt. Blood flew, and I landed flat on my ass. He was on me in an instant, but I kneed him off, and he crashed into a wall, shattering one of his display cases and scattering weapons everywhere. He was up fast, and waded in on me.

"Slowing down a bit, Dad?" he asked nonsensically.

I ignored the comment, sidestepped, and landed a quick right to his mouth, satisfyingly sending his blood to join mine on the floor. He covered and dipped and hammered my breath away with a jarring blow to my ribs. I hooked his leg with mine, and we went rolling to the deck in a tangled mess, clawing and kicking at each other. No fancy stuff for my boy and me. We fought in the no-rules, hand-to-hand combat style that we'd learned as Roman soldiers. It was nasty and vicious— the kind of thing you did when it was a real fight, a fight to the death.

I made my way back to my feet, and when he attacked, I caught him, spun, and threw him with all my force into the wall. His impact crushed stone and shattered another case, and more of his weapon collection rained down.

He slid to the floor among the pulverized stone and glass, but a moment later he popped up with a machine gun that had evidently fallen from the case. This was a new twist. Gaius had always maintained a healthy disdain for modern weaponry. I guess when it came to yours truly, he'd managed to get over it.

Oh shit, I thought, and I broke for the bar as he gleefully shouted, "Oh come on, Dad, let's play!"

The roar of the weapon was deafening as he opened up. I dove over the bar and got hit once in the small of my back and once in the ass. The bullets hurt like hell, but at least they weren't garlic-loaded. I landed with a crash as he poured out his clip, screaming with laughter. The bar was getting chopped to pieces, but no more of his bullets found me. He might have lost his scorn for modern weapons, but he obviously hadn't practiced with them much. At that distance he should have cut me in half.

I had my nose to the ground, taking cover, when I spotted a .38 police special keeping me company on the floor. It must have fallen from the display case near the bar. I hadn't favored revolvers for years, but it was loaded and would have to do.

A moment later, Gaius's clip impotently clicked empty. I was up in an instant, putting one in his head and two more in his chest. Gaius crashed to the floor and then rolled and crawled away for cover. Before he could get away, I shot him once more in the ass for good measure.

Let's see how you like it, you little fuck.

He scurried behind some theater chairs and out of sight. I stayed in my shooting stance, ready. He stood slowly, holding only a sword, so I held my fire. He was a fast healer, maybe even faster than me now. His head wound was nearly gone, and just then, the smoking .38 slug popped out of his forehead and tinkled to the floor.

He waved a hand contemptuously at another one of his gun racks.

"You're quite better than me with these toys, but even so, I feel I must apologize. I don't know what came over me, using that popgun on you."

I put the revolver in my jacket pocket. "Apology accepted. Is your spatha genuine?"

He twirled the sword a few times, and it sang a deadly *whoosh* as it cut through the air. "No, unfortunately, it's a reproduction, but a good one. It feels about right. Not like the old days, but close."

The spatha, the sword used by the Roman legions in Gaius's time, started out as a cavalry weapon but quickly made its way through the entire army. At thirty-two inches long, it was light, two-edged, and quite deadly.

I moved to another display case and turned to Gaius. "Do you mind?"

He shook his head, and I took out the sword I'd used in the legion, a gladius. It was a bit wider, and at two feet, gave away some in length, but it would do just fine. I hefted it, and as it always did, it felt as if it were a part of me.

Gaius smiled. "Ah, perfect. Just the way it should be. Your time against mine."

"You sure you want to do this, Gaius?" I asked.

He answered cheerfully, "Sure, I'm sure. I wasn't afraid to die way back in Mesopotamia, and I'm certainly not afraid to die now. Besides, I'm feeling today's my day, Titus. You?"

I was never brimming with confidence when it came to Gaius. I replied honestly, "No, I never feel it's my day when you're involved. I just wish things had turned out differently."

"Me, too," he said as his smile faded and his eyes turned an icy blue. "You ready?"

I nodded, and we went to it.

It was brutal—quite horrible, actually. Nothing like swordfights you'd see in the movies where the hero frolics about, parrying blows while making humorous remarks. This was the real deal, life or death. And although I consider myself a virtuoso with my gladius, Gaius was every bit my equal.

In the Roman legion, we were taught to be painfully patient in formation fighting, holding ground or advancing slowly, but never breaking the formation. That could weaken the entire unit and lead to its slaughter. But the training for this sort of one-on-one, broken-field fighting was totally different. You had to take more risk and strike quickly to try to end things before you tired or made a mistake. And in the melee of a chaotic battlefield, if you didn't take down your opponent quickly, it was likely another would stab you in the back.

We'd been trained to finish this sort of thing in three or four passes, ten maximum. Gaius and I lasted nine. But it seemed like a long fucking nine as we hacked huge wounds into each other, the floor quickly turning a slick red. I ended up with the advantage, but not because I was the better man that day. In fact, he may have been, but he lost his footing in a pool of blood, and I instantly pounced on him.

I held my sword to his throat, and it bit deeply into his neck. I planted my knee firmly on his sword arm. We both panted from the exertion and blood loss, but he still had a damn phony smile pasted on his face.

His eyes danced, daring me to kill him. "What are you waiting for, Titus?" he hissed. Blood-soaked bubbles of saliva gurgled from his open neck wound as he spoke.

"You brought this on yourself. I never wanted it to come to this," I answered, hesitating to deal him the fatal blow.

I heard footsteps— a lot of them—approaching from down the hall. I looked over my shoulder and then back to Gaius. His phony smile had grown enough to almost become genuine.

"You see, Dad, no matter what happens to me, you're not leaving here alive," he said happily.

I was shocked. In all of our untoward encounters, it had always been personal, man-to-man. He'd actually killed his own employees in the past for interfering in our battles. We were Romans, for God's sake. I couldn't fucking believe this.

The rage took me, and I shouted, "You little fucking chickenshit!"

I drew my gladius back and moved to take off his head, but wouldn't you know, the fuck blocked my arm. The footsteps stopped, and I heard guns cocking. I was out of time.

I reversed the sword and feinted for another head blow. He went for it, and I plunged the sword deeply through his chest, pinning him to the floor. He screamed in pain and coughed out a huge wad of blood. I snatched up his spatha and bolted for the bar once again. It was fast becoming my favorite place in the room.

His gunmen opened up, and they were far better than Gaius was. I was hit multiple times. I half dove and was half blown over the bar by the impact of the bullets. They continued firing, and by the time they'd stopped to reload, there wasn't a hell of a lot left to my hiding place. Once again, I desperately looked around on the floor for another weapon, but there were none. I pulled the revolver from my pocket and checked the load: two bullets left. A sword and two bullets against ten guys with automatic weapons. I must've been in worse situations in the past, but none came to mind.

In the temporary silence, I heard the sound of metal scraping on stone. Gaius must have been trying to work the gladius out of the floor and his chest.

He said, "Jesus, you really jammed that sword in deep. You still alive back there, Titus?"

"Yeah, I'm still here," I answered. "I can't believe how low you've sunk. You're no Roman, and you're a disgrace to the Twelfth."

The scraping continued, and he answered absently, "Oh my, I don't know how I'll live with myself. But you know what? I'll manage. And here's a newsflash for you, asshole, Rome is gone, and the Twelfth Legion's been dust for centuries."

"You can't kill me yourself, so now you're going to have your hired goons do it for you?" I shot back. "What a pussy you've become."

I heard the sword pop out of the floor, followed by Gaius's deep exhale of relief. "Oh no, Titus. You've got it all wrong. My men will keep you pinned down, disable you even, but I will most assuredly be the one to end your miserable life. The idea of doing you one-on-one has always, shall we say, held a romantic allure for me. But you see, after all these years, the shine has kind of worn off that notion. I'm just sick of the thought of you drawing another fucking breath, and I want you dead, plain and simple. Think of it as yet another rule book that I've tossed away."

"A lot of fancy words, but all it means to me is that you're a fucking coward."

"And you're a fool for coming here!" Gaius shouted. After a moment he continued conversationally. "You know, I'm thinking of cutting that poor excuse for a heart right out of your chest and eating it before your eyes. How does that grab you?"

I could hear his quiet footsteps, and many others slowly

approaching the bar. I got into a crouch, sword in one hand, pistol in the other. It was all I could do. "Why don't you come back here and try it yourself, asshole?"

He answered cheerfully, "No, I don't think so. You know, afterward I'm going to take your head and put it on a spike outside of my house. Just like the old days, eh? When I'm having a bad day, feeling agitated, I'll go look at it. I think it will calm me. What do you think?"

The footsteps stopped. They were all ready and in position. So was I, but I didn't have a chance.

An ear-shattering explosion rocked the room, then another that was even louder. I dropped and covered my head as debris rained down everywhere. Next came a few brief machine-gun bursts, then silence, except for some low moaning.

After a moment, a rather cultured voice said, "Titus, are you there?"

I peeked up over what little was left of the bar, and to my utter astonishment, there among the rubble and bodies and body parts stood Jean-Luc, his broadsword slung on his back. The diminutive Frenchman appeared unscathed in the midst of total destruction. There was a spent rocket-propelled grenade launcher at his feet, and he was covering what was left of the room with an M4 rifle.

When I continued to silently gape at him, he said, "Not much of a greeting, Titus, all things considered, but nonetheless we really must get going. Your host has a virtual army in the house."

I was immobile, still in that numbing shock a soldier feels after being plucked from the jaws of certain death. Jean-Luc's head suddenly flicked to one side, and he fired his rifle. Gaius, who unfortunately was still alive, had somehow gotten to his feet, but Jean-Luc's salvo knocked him back down.

That shook me out of my stunned reverie. Gaius. Any remote feeling I may have had for him in the past had been washed away by the events of this day. I'd rip his head off with my bare hands.

I leaped over the bar, moving toward him, but Jean-Luc shouted, "Titus, there's no time for that. We have to go. Now!"

Gaius was on the floor, squirming in pain. For a moment I stood there staring at the bastard, wanting to kill him even if it meant my death.

I'm going to do it.

I'd kill him, and his men would kill me. We'd die together. Maybe that was the way it was meant to be.

Jean-Luc's voice penetrated my killing haze. "Titus, for God's sake, come on!"

And that's what changed my mind in the end: Jean-Luc. Not what he said, but the fact that he was there. If I'd delayed to kill Gaius, Jean-Luc would likely have died right along with me. I could never do that to a friend, and especially one who'd just risked everything to save me.

I kept the spatha, picked up a rifle from the floor, and took off after Jean-Luc, who was already halfway down the hall. Gaius's gash-hoarsened voice followed us. "This is far from over, Titus. And you'll pay, too, you little French fucker!"

After all my blood loss, even a short run like this immediately winded me, but I pushed and managed to catch up to Jean-Luc.

He said rather nonchalantly, "Gaius's manners may be somewhat lacking, but he does have lavish tastes. This house of his is absolutely extravagant. The basement alone is a veritable maze."

We rounded a corner and nearly ran into two of Gaius's guards. Jean-Luc's sword was out in a blink, skewering them before I could even react. We took off again, and I said, "I thought we agreed that I would come here alone."

"That is correct," Jean-Luc replied.

"Okay, then why are you here?"

"Don't be ridiculous. You *thought* we agreed, but I lied—obviously."

I smiled. "That long lecture, the argument. You really had me fooled. I never had you pegged for such a good actor."

"Ha! You were always jealous over this," he said as we raced along. "I had a true starring role, while you were merely an extra for those horrible Westerns."

"I liked my Westerns," I replied. "And I wouldn't be so proud of starring in a 1920s D-list silent movie that nobody saw."

He laughed. "Except you. As I recall, you always thought my performance was admirable."

I did and was about to say so, when a group of four guards opened fire in front of us. Jean-Luc accelerated into them like a human bowling ball, taking them to the floor. We fell upon them with our swords. Their splattered blood painted the walls.

Finally, we saw the light of day down a long hallway, and we exited a side door. My rental ragtop miraculously waited for us in all its top-down glory. Jean-Luc took the wheel, and we pulled away fast, tossing about fifty pounds of gravel into the air.

"By the way, how the hell did you get in here?" I asked. "Gaius has more security than the Pentagon. Wait…Jake. You didn't bring him, did you?"

He took a hard, hubcap-loosening turn and replied, "Yes. Well, no. I left him in San Francisco. But his expertise helped, allowing me to shut down the security cameras and such."

"Ah, so that's how you got in."

"*Mais non* ,"Jean-Luc replied. "If I had done that, they would have known I was here. I only turned them off just before I attacked. On your right!"

I wheeled to the right and fired a long burst at two men in the woods as we sped by. I don't think I hit either one, but I got them to scatter. "Well, how did you get in, then?"

He looked over at me and smiled. "I hid in your trunk—simple, but effective. Gaius was counting on you to be your usual foolish, chivalrous self, and to come alone with no help."

"I don't know about foolish."

"I do," Jean-Luc said. "And by the way, you should be more careful. If I could get into your trunk, anyone could."

"Duly noted. How did you get Jake to agree to stay in San Francisco?" I asked.

"Oh, that wasn't difficult. I never let on how grave the situation was going to be here, and since he'd never even heard of Gaius before, it was easy to convince him. But to make sure, I left him mooning over his little sister. Another one up ahead!"

I was shocked. I couldn't believe Jean-Luc would do such a thing. I opened up on our new assailant, splattering his brains all over a beautifully maintained rhododendron. "You let Jake contact his sister? A human who knows nothing about vampires and thinks he's dead?"

He favored me with one of his patented petulant looks. "Of course not, you silly man. I said mooning over her. Absolutely no contact, and he completely understood what might happen to her if he did communicate with her. Even though he took great pains to hide it, I always knew he made trips here just to watch her. I merely took advantage of it this time."

"Don't try to pretend you're just manipulating him," I replied. "Face it. You're getting soft. And you have the nerve to call me the sensitive Roman killer."

He laughed. "Perhaps I am growing soft. But I will never sink to your indulgent level, Titus."

We took another physics-defying turn and came upon a lone gunman who'd foolishly stationed himself in the middle of the road. Our car slammed right into him with a loud thud. Knocked high into the air, he flew over the hood, pirouetting lazily and executing two perfect backflips before he crashed to the ground. He looked like an Olympic gymnast—before the landing, that is.

As if reading my mind, Jean-Luc said, "And the French judge gives him a 9.5."

I laughed out loud as we sped toward the gate which, as I expected, was locked tight and heavily guarded. It seemed like days since I had first passed through it, when in fact it had been barely over an hour.

"Just out of curiosity, how do you intend to open that gate?" I asked.

He fished out what looked like a garage door opener.

"Jake?"

"Jake," Jean-Luc agreed.

The guards started shooting, and I returned the favor. Jean-Luc pushed the button, the gate opened, and we sailed through. I turned and continued firing and saw it closing behind us. Despite a lot of commotion, it didn't reopen.

"Jammed?" I asked.

Jean-Luc answered, "Oh yes. Our Jake is a very smart boy."

"Damn thing looks like a garage door opener to me."

"Jake says it pretty much is," Jean-Luc replied. "Now where shall we go?"

"San Francisco. Where else? And by the way, thanks for saving my ass."

Jean-Luc drove on silently, smiling his purse-lipped, prissy little smile. It was his way of saying, "You're welcome."

CHAPTER 15

When the guard finally released Lisa from her dungeon deep under Gaius's mansion, the second thing she did was bolt for the stairs. The first thing was to deliver a hard roundhouse slap to the hapless fellow, breaking his jaw and knocking him out cold. She knew her imprisonment wasn't his fault and that he was just following Gaius's orders, but she had to hit something.

The moment Titus's approach was discovered, Gaius had insisted she be locked away. He said it was for her safety and to make sure she'd do nothing to interfere. Lisa had to admit the reasoning was sound. She definitely would have interfered to help Gaius if he required it. She thought he relied too much on his human guards, and considering how powerful Titus was, she felt Gaius should have had vampire backup, even if it was just a fledgling like her. And maybe more importantly than all of that, she didn't want to "run" from Titus.

Gaius had discussed it with her at length, but of course she wouldn't be convinced, and finally time had run out. In the end, he had restrained her and carried her down to the cell himself. She fought tremendously, whipping her body back and forth like a wildcat, but to no avail. Gaius was as immovable as granite.

Her temporary accommodations were of stone and reinforced steel and could have held a vampire far more powerful than she. But that didn't stop her from crashing into the door over and over again, trying to break out.

Gaius, film buff that he was, provided her with a direct video feed to the screening room so she could watch the "festivities". When Titus entered the room, Lisa stopped trying to free herself and kept her eyes glued to the monitor.

As she watched the scene play out, she was surprised by her complete lack of feeling for Titus. More than that, she wanted him dead, and was completely sure of it. In counterpoint to the nothingness she felt for her ex, she was amazed at the depth of feeling she'd already developed for Gaius. Lisa was desolate when she thought he would die. Her heart palpitated and tears sprang to her eyes as she watched Titus holding a sword to his neck.

Right then, the video went black.

"No!" Lisa shouted as she tried unsuccessfully to get the screen working again. Two jarring explosions coming from above froze her in her tracks. She felt the vibrations from the blasts even though she was deep below ground. She screamed to be released, once again throwing herself at the door and beating her hands raw against it. It seemed like an eternity before the guard opened the door.

Finally reaching the screening room, she stopped short and let out a pent-up sigh of relief. In the middle of all the carnage stood Gaius. He directed Richard, among many others, in the cleanup of the destroyed room. His clothes were tattered and bloody, and his face and hair were covered with soot, but he appeared unharmed.

She ran toward him, and he turned just in time to take her into his arms. Lisa hugged him ferociously and covered his face with kisses. When his mouth was not occupied with hers, he managed to say, "Now, now. What's all this?"

Lisa didn't answer. She rested her head against his shoulder and took a few deep breaths, feeling her heart rate slow as she calmed down. After a time, she looked up, backed away a bit, and caught him a solid slap to the face.

Gaius held his hand to his cheek. He looked remarkably surprised. "Interesting turn of events."

Now that she was sure Gaius was safe, rage exploded from her, and the verbal barrage began. "You no-good bastard, I thought you were dead! Don't you ever lock me up like that again, or you won't have to worry about Titus. I'll fucking kill you!"

She backed him across the room, her finger in his chest as she shouted at him.

Gaius retreated with his hands up in surrender. "It was for your safety, my dear. I couldn't take the chance of you being hurt." His back struck a wall. He had no more room to run.

There were many subtle, bemused looks on the faces of his men. No one, not even his lovers, ever treated Gaius like this and lived.

Lisa began rhythmically beating on his chest. Her words matched the cadence of the solid *thuds* of the blows she rained upon him. "Hurt? You idiot! Why would I care about being hurt if you were dead? You can't ever do that to me again, ever. You have to promise. Promise." The last words came out in a hoarse whisper as Lisa began to cry.

Gaius took her into his arms again and soothed her. "I'm not quite sure what I've gotten myself into with you, but yes, I promise," he said. "You can stand with me as long as you wish to."

He waved his men out of the room. Lisa stopped crying and looked at him with a tear-streaked face.

"Better?" he asked.

She nodded.

"I want you to have a look at something." He guided Lisa over to a monitor that had obviously just been installed in what was left of the room. "Titus's little friend Jean-Luc somehow jammed my security system, but we're getting some of the feed now. Look at this."

It was a short clip of Jean-Luc using his sword to dispatch two guards. Lisa cringed, watching the blood fly, and the screen went blank again after only a few seconds.

Gaius asked, "Did you notice anything?"

Lisa was still upset and hadn't paid close attention. Gaius ran the clip one more time.

After a moment, she said, "No, not really, except Titus didn't do a damn thing. He just stood there while Jean-Luc killed them both."

Gaius agreed. "Exactly. Here, watch again."

He rolled the segment once more, and this time she watched more closely. "He was fast. Almost like you and Titus."

"Yes, that's it," Gaius replied. "Granted, Titus was hurt and had lost a lot of blood, but he still would have acted if he had the time."

Lisa shook her head. "I don't get it. Why is that so important?"

"I'm not certain it is. I last ran afoul of that little French bastard a little over fifty years ago. He was powerful then, for his age, but this—this means his skills have quite literally taken off. Given time, I believe he could perhaps become the most powerful of our kind. We'll have to be very careful in dealing with him in the future, my dear, maybe even more so than my dear old dad."

Lisa responded, "I wish you'd stop calling him that."

"Sorry."

She went on. “Anyway, I spent time with Jean-Luc. He was a snooty, stuck-up French prick, but I didn’t notice anything that would make me think he was particularly talented.”

“He may be hiding it, or he might not even realize it himself,” Gaius replied. He went silent, deep in contemplation.

Lisa waited patiently. She knew Gaius was not fond of being interrupted when he was organizing his thoughts. After an appropriate time, she asked, “So what are we going to do now?”

Gaius brightened out of his reverie and favored Lisa with a winning smile. “First, I’m going to repair my screening room. Next, we need to have a meeting with an associate of mine. And then, I have no fucking idea. But one thing we will do is take action, and do you know why?”

“No,” Lisa answered.

“Because Titus won’t. You see, my dear, he’s a monumentally ponderous, slow thinker. You know, his very first commanding centurion pretty much told him that exact same thing over two thousand years ago. He’ll contemplate and ruminate, trying to figure out if what I did today was an aberrancy or not. He’ll think and think, and while he’s doing that, do you know what we’ll do?”

Lisa already knew the answer, but smiling, she asked anyway, “What, my love?”

Gaius returned her smile. “We’ll hurt him, and hurt him badly.”

CHAPTER 16

Jake seemed surprised to see Jean-Luc and me at his hotel room door that evening. But not quite as surprised as I was to see that Jake's girlfriend, Miranda, was with him. I turned to Jean-Luc and smiled. He really must have taken a shine to the boy to allow a sun-sensitive vampire like Miranda to come along on such a potentially dangerous trip. My taciturn scrutiny finally irritated him enough to drag out a remark.

"Why do you look at me so?" he asked.

"I think you may very well have become more soft and indulgent than me," I responded. "I can't believe you allowed Miranda on this little trip."

Jean-Luc directed a limp-wristed backhand at me, as if trying to wave my comment away. "Jake wished to bring his lover with him," he humphed. "I was supposed to say no to this? I *am* French after all."

The four of us shared a wonderful meal and then hunted together. We were quite the terrible group that lovely evening, like the Four Horsemen of the Apocalypse. The Tenderloin District lived up to its name, but not in the usual way. That night we feasted on human tenderloin and blood.

The next morning I could see Jean-Luc was uneasy. Just after sunrise, he was already futzing around our hotel suite, making ready to go back to New Orleans.

"What's wrong, my friend?" I said.

"Do you have to ask? Gaius, that's what's wrong. He has never been stable, but now I feel there is no telling what he might be capable of. He threatened me directly, and I want to make sure my people and my town are safe from him."

"He's always been that way when it comes to me," I replied. "He acts crazier than he is just to unnerve me, and it works every time."

Jean-Luc shook his head. "This was different, and you know it. I admit some of his encounters with you in the past, although deadly, almost had the feel of a game. This time he wanted to end it once and for all. I think he will stop at nothing to attain this goal, and he will hurt you as much as possible along the way."

What Jean-Luc was saying made sense, but I couldn't believe Gaius would escalate things further than he already had. "He wants me dead for sure, but I can't believe he'd risk involving others. That sort of thing could lead to war, and it's always been about me, and me alone. Why would he change now? And besides, what are we supposed to do, live the rest of our lives looking over our shoulders for the hunters *and* him?"

Jean-Luc shrugged. "No, never that. But it is always wise to take precautions and be ready, and that is what I intend to do. What will you do now?"

"I don't know," I said. "I need to think about this some."

"I advise you not to think too long," Jean-Luc replied. "Overthinking and overtalking are your major faults, among many others."

I laughed. "You're right about that. I think I'll stick around San Francisco for a few days. Maybe take a peek at Jake's sister myself. See what all the fuss is about."

"Now, Titus, do not do anything foolish because of your feelings for Jake. His sister has no idea about our world and thinks he is dead. Why don't you leave it at that?"

"Truthfully, I have no plan to do anything foolish," I replied. "But I'd be lying if I said I'm not swayed by the fact that this was the only person in the whole world Jake ever cared about prior to his turning. And it breaks his heart that he can't see her ever again."

"He does see her, but from a safe distance," Jean-Luc said. "*Mon Dieu,* you *are* far softer than me, my friend. But don't you have enough trouble already without adding this silly idea to it?"

"I don't have an idea, silly or otherwise. And who says I'm going to add to anything? I'm going to take a little look-see, that's all. Besides, you're right, I have enough trouble. As a matter of fact, it's all I seem to have had in the past few years. Jake's sister might prove an interesting distraction, that's all—maybe even some fun."

"Titus, you are insane."

"Now that's the first thing you've gotten right all day," I said.

"You and your friend Gaius do share one trait: you both like breaking the rules. But you do it, shall we say, much more nicely."

"I'm generally not described as nice, except when compared to Gaius. Safe journey, my friend," I said, opening my arms.

Jean-Luc and I embraced, kissing each other's cheeks in the French style.

"Be careful, Titus," he said, leaving me with Jake and Miranda sleeping in the adjoining bedroom.

Being a brand-spanking-new three-year-old vampire, Miranda would burn like a torch if she went out in the sunlight. Jake would keep her company for a good deal of the day.

This would be a good chance for me to check out his baby sis.

CHAPTER 17

Lisa waited with Gaius in the sumptuous splendor of his living room. He pretended to be reading a book, but she knew he was angrily stewing. His guest was over an hour late, and Gaius had little tolerance for tardiness. Finally, she heard the echoing approach of footsteps. Gaius's head snapped up, and he did not look happy. Richard, the footman, announced their caller and quickly left as Davy Stein swaggered into the room.

Lisa thought he looked like a cheap '50s gangster from an even cheaper '50s gangster movie.

"Gaius, my man," Stein said too loudly and then stopped to take a good, long look at Lisa. Once he had her skin sufficiently crawling from his ridiculous ogle, he added, "So this is the dame all the hoo-hah is about; nice, very nice."

Gaius remained ominously silent, and Lisa thought, *Did this idiot really just say dame and hoo-hah in the same sentence?*

As Stein turned to face Gaius, he was lifted off his feet and pinned to the wall, the back of his head ricocheting off the stone with a loud *thwack*. Lisa hadn't even seen Gaius move.

With one hand Gaius nonchalantly held him by the throat against the wall, a good two feet off the ground. Stein sputtered and choked. His face quickly transitioned from pink to red to tinges of blue, and his already buggy eyes bugged out even more. He tried to tear Gaius's hand from his neck as his feet drummed a fast, syncopated beat against the wall.

Gaius spat out, "You no-good fuck. I tell you to pass some information and make sure it gets to Titus, and what, he shows up in four motherfucking days from halfway around the world? I wasn't even close to being ready for him. And tell me, Davy, did you forget how to dial a phone?"

Stein tried to answer but could make no sound with his airway cutoff. His face had gone from blue-tinged to an alarming shade of purple by the time Gaius flung him across the room. He landed with a crash, but rolled to his feet with surprising speed. He pointed a snub-nosed.38 at Gaius.

The old Roman roared with laughter. "I do like you, Davy, always full of surprises. In a way, it'll be a shame to kill you. Now put that toy down."

"Whatdaya expect me to do, just take this shit?" Stein's voice was calm, but his gun hand had a clear case of the shakes.

Gaius replied, "I expect you to put the gun away and answer my questions before I kill you."

Stein looked nonplussed, but he shrugged and holstered his gun. He straightened his suit and slicked back his already slicked-back hair. "I don't get the rough stuff, Gaius. I really don't. I did what you said. I passed the info along. You didn't give me no time limit. It's not my fault he got here so fast."

"Now that you put it like that, I see your point," Gaius replied calmly, but then shouted, "Fucking telephone, Davy! Telephone! You met him here in the Valley, not twenty miles away. Hello, you think maybe you could've called me and let me know?"

Stein took a step back at Gaius's tone, but kept a defiant stance. He raised his voice in response. "Are you fucking serious? Titus barely tolerates me, and I know he doesn't trust me one damn bit. How could I be sure he didn't have guys watching me? Have my phones tapped? If he figured I crossed him, I'd be just as dead as if I crossed you. Which I didn't, by the fucking way."

"Lower your voice," Gaius said. He silently pondered what Stein had said.

"He's got a point, Gaius," Lisa added.

Gaius looked as if he wanted to get angry with someone—anyone—but couldn't. A prisoner whose death sentence had been commuted at one minute before midnight might have looked a bit more relieved than Stein, but it would've been close.

"Thank you, pretty lady," Stein said, his eyes once again lingering on her a bit too long.

Lisa laughed. She found Stein amusing and almost couldn't believe he was for real. Pretty lady, the over-the-top gawking—it was too much.

Gaius evidently was not amused. "Davy, you're still shacked up with that starlet you turned all those years ago, correct?"

Stein answered, "Sure, you know I am."

"She keeping you busy enough these days, is she?"

Stein smiled idiotically and actually winked. "Almost too busy, if you know what I mean."

Gaius replied, "Then keep your goddamn eyes off my woman, or I'll rip them out of your head. Oh, you'll grow them back, but it hurts like a bitch. You get me?"

Stein's head bobbed up and down, and Lisa smiled. She liked that Gaius had referred to her as his woman.

Gaius took a deep breath. "Davy, you really do bring out the worst in me sometimes. But lucky for you, I see your point about Titus. Now can we get down to business?"

"Sure thing, Boss."

"Would you mind getting us some drinks before we begin?" Gaius asked.

When Stein headed to the bar, Gaius turned to Lisa, raised his eyebrows and silently mouthed, "Pretty lady?"

She had to cover her mouth to stop herself from laughing.

Stein returned with three healthy pours of absinthe, and Gaius began, "Your message said you had some significant information for me."

Stein gulped down his drink and nodded. "I got a solid line on Dom Salvucci. He's in Italy."

Gaius rolled his eyes. "Duh, Davy. Where else would that big guinea be? That isn't exactly earth-shattering news, now is it?"

"Yeah, but you were looking in the wrong places, places your aunts—sorry, Mary and Katie—would've owned. But now I know for sure he's in one of his grandfather's old places in Sicily. Can't be more than two or three villas to scope out."

Gaius beamed at Stein. "I'm so glad I didn't kill you a moment ago. You really have outdone yourself. You're going to get your usual fee, plus a hefty bonus for this one, my friend."

Stein smiled back. "Gee thanks, Boss."

Gaius put an arm around Stein's meaty shoulder and slowly began to walk him to the door. "Now here's what I want you to do. First, pinpoint exactly where he is. Next, get on the hunter blogs we're into and get the information to one of the Harrison cells—no, even better,

Harrison's cell itself."

Stein stopped; the color drained from his face. "You want me to set up Dom? Put out a hit on Dom and use those fucking hunters? After all the vampires they killed?"

Gaius turned to face Stein, his eyes frosty. "That's exactly what I want you to do."

"But Gaius, I know Dom ain't a vampire, but he's got history. He's clearly a friend to us."

Gaius replied, "He's no friend to me. And why exactly did you think I set you to finding him?"

Stein mumbled, "I really didn't think that much about it, you know?"

"That's good, Davy. Thinking isn't exactly your strong suit."

Stein appeared unsettled. "But won't this cause a lot of trouble?"

Gaius smiled. "Oh, I'm counting on it. And by the way, Davy, who do think put the hunters onto your oversized friend, the Squid?"

Stein's already pale face somehow got a notch or two paler. His mouth fell open, and he stammered out, "You put hunters onto one of us? But why, Gaius, why would you do that? It's one thing doing the killing yourself, or having your boys do it, but using hunters to kill vampires? Why?"

"Because your Squid is a good friend of Titus, and that makes him a horrible enemy of mine," Gaius answered. "I kill my enemies, Davy, and in any way that pleases me. And frankly, I find playing with these hunters quite amusing. I kept this from you because I knew you'd be troubled by it. And I know you consider this Squid of yours a friend. But the time has come for you to make a decision."

Lisa was shocked, but did nothing to show it. This was the first time she'd heard about Gaius's use of vampire hunters. She knew he wasn't speaking only to Stein, but to her as well. She thought the Squid a big oaf, but didn't particularly want to see him dead. She pondered for a moment and quickly realized that no matter what Gaius said or did from here on, she'd already made her decision. Her lot was cast with him.

He looked away from Stein to her, and their eyes met. She could feel the intensity in his gaze, and was it possible—worry—from Gaius? Worry that she wouldn't side with him. She let the moment play out, keeping a serious, maybe even a shocked, look on her face. She thought it fun to give him a taste of his own sarcastic medicine.

Finally, she smiled and blew him a kiss, and instantly saw the relief in his eyes.

Wearing a rather pleasant smile, Gaius faced Stein and placed both hands on his shoulders.

Lisa wasn't fooled by the look. It was pleasant enough for sure, but right below the surface lay a predator's smile, a killer's smile.

"You've been a loyal employee, Davy," Gaius said. "I daresay, maybe even a friend, and you know how much I loathe the use of that term. But I need to know if you are with me on this."

Stein loosened his already loose necktie. His bulbous Adam's apple bobbed up and down like a fishing lure. His muddy brown eyes nervously darted about the room, finally coming to rest on Gaius's stony baby blues. He said quietly, "I don't really have much of a choice, do I?"

Gaius replied, "There's always a choice, Davy."

"You know, Gaius, this sort of thing could start a war."

"Quite likely, but I couldn't care less."

Stein gulped. "I'm with you, Boss. In for a penny, in for a pound."

Gaius smiled; it nearly looked real. He clapped Stein on the arms, causing him to wince in pain. "Excellent, Davy, really excellent. I knew I could count on you." He walked Stein to the door and said, "Now stay on Salvucci. I want that taken care of quickly, you get me? And why don't you and your girl come over for dinner tonight. Eight o'clock. Deal?"

Stein looked like a loyal hound dog just thrown a bone. "Really? Dinner here?"

Gaius said magnanimously, "Of course here. As I recall, your better half loves to dress up. Shall we make it black tie?"

"Oh, she'd really like that. Thanks, Boss. I'll get that job done ASAP. See you tonight," Stein fawned and scurried away.

After he cleared the room, Lisa began clapping in a slow rhythm. "Bravura performance, my dear."

Gaius turned to give her a theatrical bow.

She added, "Do you realize that when you speak to him, you take on a bit of that gangster lingo?"

He said defensively, "I most assuredly do not."

"Oh really? You get me? Deal?"

Gaius looked dismayed. "Oh my, I never noticed."

"Doesn't matter. It's quite cute, actually. By the way, I found it completely disarming that you were unsure of where I would fall when it comes to your little war plans. You're quite endearing when you're not so cocksure of yourself."

He smiled at that. "You always have a choice as well, right along with Davy."

She laughed. "One hell of a choice. Agree with me or die. And by the way, do you think it's wise trusting that dolt with so much?"

"Davy has a particular talent for collecting stray pieces of information, and despite how he seems, he's miraculously efficient. Besides, do you really think he's the only vampire in my camp on this issue?"

"No, I suppose not," Lisa said. "So now what?"

He approached where she sat on a huge armless leather chair and smiled down at her. "First, I'd like you to get naked. The chair is brand new, and I'd really like to christen it in style. Then pack your bags. Right after our black-tie affair with the Steins, we're off."

"Off where?" she asked, smiling sensually with just the touch of poutiness that she knew he loved.

"To where the action is, my love," Gaius replied cryptically.

"I really liked it tonight when you called me your woman. I could get used to that."

He leaned over her and put his face close to hers. "I want you to."

He moved to kiss her but she stopped him saying, "What if I decided to leave you? Would you kill me?"

He thought for a moment and answered truthfully. "I very well might."

She caught him by the back of the head and pulled him into a deep, long kiss.

CHAPTER 18

I'm not sure, but maybe I did intend to only observe her a bit. You know, take in Jake's human sister. But all intentions aside, that's not the way it worked out. You see, I have a very odd mind, and often what I believe to be a spontaneous action really isn't. I've come to think that some of my ideas, probably my worst, start somewhere way down deep in my brainstem and manage to slowly percolate their way up into my consciousness and give me the false feeling of spontaneity. When in reality, they've been planned and hatched in a hidden, warped corner of my subconscious far away from the prying eye of reason and good judgment.

Well, that's what I think, anyway. I know it's likely bullshit, but the theory has a certain romantic charm to it and makes me feel immeasurably better, especially after I've suffered the consequences of my fucked-up decisions.

After spending the early part of the morning stalking Jake's sister, catching a glimpse of her as she picked up the morning paper, and then peeking in at her through a window or two, I grew terminally bored. I'd read a good deal of her writing and thought I had an idea what she might be like, but my idiotic "Peeping Tom" routine certainly didn't add anything to my construct. So I decided on a direct approach, and then I'd wing it after that, which is pretty much right in line with the usual planning of my grander schemes.

I approached her well-maintained Spanish bungalow and rang the bell. She answered the door quickly, catching me off guard.

When I stood there mute, she asked, "Can I help you?"

She was petite, with strawberry-blond hair and bright blue eyes. She still had a smattering of childhood freckles randomly tossed across her cheeks and her nearly nonexistent nose. Her outfit of comfortably upscale sweats and a tank top, although I'm sure all the rage among the teen set, seemed a tad young for a woman in her early thirties. But what the hell, it was Sunday morning, after all.

None of that had gotten me tongue-tied; I'm generally not the tongue-tied type. Given the complete difference in appearance between her and Jake, I'd always presumed her dad must've been the milkman. But seeing her this close, in person, I was struck by the familial resemblance between Elise and her brother, Jake. For the life of me I couldn't tell you exactly what that resemblance was, but somehow it was as plain as the tiny nose on her face.

She smirked and raised a questioning eyebrow.

I stuttered out, "Ms. Little, Elise Little. I'm so sorry for my lapse, but seeing you in person....I'm such a big fan. I must've read everything you've written."

She stopped me with an outstretched hand. Elise Little was a freelance writer and investigative reporter. I really had read nearly everything she'd written, and most of it was quite good.

"I don't do autographs, mister..."

"Beauparlant," I replied.

"Uh-huh, Beauparlant," she said disbelievingly. She dug out a cigarette and struck it up.

It was hard to believe she'd sniffed out one of my more well-worn aliases on the very first pass. She blew out a puff of smoke and went on. "Look, Mr. Beauparlant, I appreciate you being a fan and all, but if you don't mind." She began to close the door.

I put my hand out and stopped it. "But I have a business proposition for you."

I really didn't know why that sentence came out of my mouth, as I had absolutely no idea what I was doing and should have cut and run. I'd seen her up close, even exchanged a word or two. What more could I want? Well, I sure as hell didn't know, but apparently my brainstem did.

She replied calmly, "You look like an intelligent man, Mr. Beauparlant, so you know this is no way to do business. You don't hunt me down at my house. You look me up and call my office. Now please remove your hand from my door, or I'll have to call the police."

I did as she asked, but before she closed the door, I blurted out, "What if I told you it was about your brother?"

That blurt stopped Elise dead in her tracks. Her bright blue, little-kid eyes, which somehow looked old and world-weary at the same time, intently searched my face. "What do you know about my brother?" she asked.

"Quite a bit, actually. But if you prefer, I'll leave and call your office next week."

She smirked again, took a deep drag of her cigarette, and blew it directly into my face. "You're quite a card, aren't you, Mr. Beauparlant?"

"A wild card, Ms. Little. May I come in?"

She shrugged and waved me into her house. It may seem odd that she'd let me in so easily, but I had brought up the secret password: Jake. Also, she was one of those journalists who constantly threw herself into danger. Her latest story came out of Colombia, where she had cavorted with several unsavory drug lords. Just reading it gave me the willies. Little Elise Little wouldn't scare easy.

We sat across from each other in her living room. It was warm and tastefully decorated in an Asian motif, very stylish, especially for someone as young as she.

She waited patiently for a bit, and then said, "All right, Mr. Beauparlant—"

"Please, call me Christian."

"Why not? You gave me a bullshit last name. I'd be disappointed if the first name wasn't total crap, too."

I laughed. "Fair enough. How does Titus grab you?"

"Weirdly, but I'll go with it," she said. She took another long drag.

I still could've done a quick exit, and no harm, no foul. But the truth was I was having fun, something I'd been decidedly short on since I'd turned Lisa, and frankly, I like my fun. And there was Jake to think of; he'd have his sister back if I could pull this off.

But trying to unite human family with a presumed-dead vampire family member nearly always ended in disaster. So I paused for a moment and brought to bear virtually every shred of analytical reasoning I possessed. With a near-Herculean effort, I quickly and completely immersed myself in a deep trance of deductive logic.

Despite all of my intense mental labor, the only conclusion I could come up with was, *What the fuck?*

"What do you think about Jake's suicide?" I asked.

She nearly hid the small quiver in her lip at the mention of her long-lost brother by lighting up another Winston. "It made no sense whatsoever."

Given her profession and the investigative skills that had to have come along with it, I was quite sure she'd looked into Jake's demise long and hard when she had come of age.

I asked, "How so?"

"Jake wasn't big on friends," she replied. "But as far as I can tell, he had no overt signs of depression and no seminal event prior to the suicide."

"Doesn't prove anything," I shot back. "Young males have a high success rate when they pull the plug, and they often hide their depression quite well."

"I know the stats, but he bought a plane ticket to come home only a week before. How does that make sense?" She blew another waft of smoke toward me.

I couldn't stomach any more of her smoke screen, so I pulled out my mini-Cubans and asked, "Do you mind?"

She shook her head and went on. "And what about the police report? He gets mugged and thrown in the Mississippi, and then a few days later he drowns himself in the same river. A little suspicious, don't you think? I wish I could find that mugger—"

"No good. He's dead," I said. The mugger, a vampire who'd attacked and accidentally turned Jake, had been taken out by a Harrison cell two years ago.

She stopped in mid puff. "How do you know?"

I took a drag of my Cuban; it was heavenly. "Never mind that. Go on."

She considered me for a moment and then shrugged. "Give me one of those things, will you?"

This kid was a virtual smokestack. I handed over a cigar, and she struck it up.

"Not bad," she said.

"I like them. What else?"

"A lot. Let's start with the note he left. Total bullshit. It was his handwriting, but bland, no content. Almost like it was scripted, or forced."

"Oh come on. Suicide notes aren't literary masterpieces. I thought you might really have something, but you're just grasping at straws."

She shot back. "The body was never found."

"Mississippi's a big river," I said.

Elise was clearly getting agitated and raised her voice. "The roommate said someone went through Jake's stuff after he was dead, before my parents went down to pick it up."

"The police, most likely."

Her voice got louder. "*No*, not the police, Titus, or whatever the fuck your name is. I checked it. They'd gone through his room way before this happened."

I leaned forward. "It *is* Titus, and that doesn't prove a damn thing, and you know it. You were ten when he died, so when did you get around to questioning the roommate? What, ten or fifteen years after the fact? None of this crap holds water. Is that all you've got?"

Her fist crashed down on the coffee table, and she shouted, "He wouldn't do it! He wouldn't do that to me! He loved me, and I loved him more than anything." She broke down, sobbing.

I waited, feeling like shit. I didn't figure her for the crying type, but my judgment regarding women, as per usual, sucked.

She quieted quickly and stared at me with a tear-streaked face. "Why are you doing this to me?" she asked softly. "If you've got some information about how Jake really died, please give it to me. It would at least give me some closure."

"Why do you think I'm doing this to you, *Esise*?"

Her face drained of all color. "How do you know that name? You can't know that."

Esise was a secret pet name Jake had for his sister. Only the two of them knew it, besides me, that is. "Doesn't matter. What if I called you Little Red? Is that why you chose Little for your last name when you changed it, by the way? Or how about if I told you how much Jake loved going on the playground swings with you? Or how he was so proud when he taught you to throw a baseball, when he could barely throw one himself. Or maybe I should sing that song from the school play he helped you to learn. What would you believe then? What—"

She put her hands over her ears and screamed, "Stop!"

The tears started again, and I waited until they dried up some. "What if I told you Jake is a friend of mine, a dear friend of mine, and that something inconceivable happened to him all those years ago, something that made him have to stay away from you. And that I'm just trying to put you two back together."

She wiped her eyes and viciously spat out, "Then I'd say you're full of shit or a fucking loony!"

"Both of your assertions would be correct most of the time, but not in this case."

Her hardened expression softened a bit, and then a small, mean-looking smile formed on her lips. She leaned back in her chair and lit up another Winston. "I'm so fucking stupid. Okay, I see. One of those assholes I exposed in one of my articles hired you to do this, to fuck me up. I get it; it's short of killing me, but pretty fucking nasty. Okay, Titus, or whatever your name is, you can go back to your boss and tell him you really earned your money. Bravo, you piece of shit."

I hadn't really expected this line of reasoning. But since I hadn't planned any of this, it was fair to say I couldn't have expected anything. "Or your brother could be alive."

"Or..." she said and then paused. Her eyes looked through me and traveled far away, deep in thought.

"Or?"

"Wait right there. I have to show you something," she replied and quickly left the room.

I was thinking that I'd made some progress, but she proved me quite wrong when she returned holding a .357 Magnum pointed directly at me. Not the result I was looking for, but definitely a turn of events that I could work with.

"Or you killed my brother, you no-good fuck!" Elise said.

I shrugged. "Logical, but not the explanation."

"If I was a hundred percent sure that you did it, I'd shoot you myself and save the taxpayers some money. But you're going to sit right there until the cops come, and then you can explain it all to them."

She took out her phone, never breaking eye contact with me.

"Elise," I said. "That won't do at all."

"If you even twitch," she replied calmly. "I'm going to shoot you."

"I know you would," I answered. "Any woman who'd run around rubbing elbows with crazy Colombians just to get a story certainly wouldn't be afraid of little old me. But I simply can't have the police involved."

She was about to respond when I flashed across the room. I snatched her gun and phone away and sat myself back down before she could blink.

Elise looked at her hands as if somehow they'd conspired against her. She stammered out, "How, how, did you do that?"

"Doesn't matter. You'll understand soon enough." I replied. "The gun is a marvelous idea, though. I have a Glock with me, but didn't even consider using it until you pulled your .357 out. I presume you have a basement in this house. Wouldn't want the neighbors to hear anything."

Her expression was grave and her complexion now ashen, but she didn't flinch, even though she had to be figuring I was taking her into her own basement to execute her. She was a brave one, all right.

"Yeah, I do," she replied.

"Marvelous. Do lead on."

As she walked ahead of me down the stairs, she said, "Before you kill me, I need to know. Why Jake? Why did you have to kill him? He never hurt anyone in his whole life."

"Well, that certainly has changed," I said. "But to answer you, I didn't kill him. He's quite well, and very close by, as a matter of fact."

The basement was ill lit and grimy, but had walls thick enough to muffle the gunshots.

"You're going to keep this bullshit up and send me to my grave without knowing about my brother," Elise said. "Well, fuck you, you psycho bastard!"

I walked toward her, held out the .357, and then thinking about it, took it back. It was way too loud. I took out my Glock 26 and holstered the .357. I held out the Glock to Elise, and then another thought struck me, and I pulled the Glock back as well.

"Do you always tease people with guns like this before you kill them?" she asked.

"No, not at all, but I like this shirt and jacket. I don't want them ruined."

"Oh sure, I see," Elise said eye-rolling me. "They look expensive. Who'd want them ruined?"

She waited patiently as I removed my shirt and jacket, folded them neatly, and draped them over a chair.

"You're in pretty good shape for an old guy," Elise quipped.

I walked back over to her. "You don't know the half of it. Okay, here are the rules. I'm going to give you my Glock. It's ready to go:

one in the chamber, ten in the clip. I really hope you don't have to use them all before you're convinced. I'm going to walk away from you, and if you don't shoot me, I will most assuredly shoot you with your own .357. You do believe me, don't you, Elise?"

Her gaze was dead steady as she looked directly into my eyes. "You're totally fucking nuts, so no worries there. I believe you, all right."

I smiled. "Really excellent." I handed her the Glock.

She took a moment to check the load in the chamber and then the clip. I didn't even have the chance to turn before she took one step back, brought the gun up, and put one in my chest.

Now that's a smart girl, I thought.

I staggered from the close-range impact, and she quickly added three more shots, dead center, knocking me farther back. I steadied myself and calmly faced her. She looked unsettled, but coolly adjusted her stance, aimed, and clicked off four more rapid, well-placed shots to my torso. I was happy she hadn't shot me in the head. I wasn't in the mood for that kind of a headache.

"You've got three more bullets," I said evenly. "But would you mind too much if we stopped here?"

Elise remained in her shooting stance, the gun smoking in her hand. Her eyes were wide, her mouth open. She responded by squeezing off the final three shots, direct hits, all.

"Was that really necessary?" I asked. "They're not going to harm me, but they still hurt like a bastard."

She pulled the trigger a few more times, with a hollow clicking noise the only report left in my Glock. Her gun hand floated slowly down to her waist, and she sighed. "Jesus Christ."

"Considering your penchant for investigation, you ought to come closer. You're going to want to see this."

She hesitated, but only for a second, and then she trance-walked over to me and stared at my bullet-ruined chest.

The bleeding had already stopped, and the wounds were healing rapidly.

"This can't be," she mumbled.

Her statement didn't have much conviction. She reached up to touch one of the bullet holes, but stopped short and looked up at me for my approval. I nodded, and she went ahead, reverently, like a doubting Thomas examining the wounds of Christ. By now, the healing was flying along, and my body would be back to normal in seconds. But for her, I'd saved the best for last.

At such close range, most of her shots had gone through and through, but three of them were still inside me. I could feel them being pushed to the surface by the internal wave of healing tissue, like surfers catching a really big one at Waikiki. They poked out of my chest.

Elise jumped back and let out a strangled, "Oh!"

The slugs fell to the floor with a clink, clank, and clunk. I gestured over my shoulder. "The rest are in the wall. Nice shooting, by the way."

"Thanks," she replied, looking way shocked, but somehow still maintaining a semblance of composure. Considering her job, she'd already seen a lot of crazy shit in her life, but nothing anywhere close to this, I'd wager.

"Would you mind if I used your bathroom to clean up?" I asked.

"I need a drink," she replied.

When I'd tidied up and dressed, I found her back in the living room, smoking of course, and halfway through a water glass full of bourbon.

I poured myself a bourbon as well, and said, "So?"

She looked up. Her eyes were glassy, shocked flesh rimming them. "So you want to tell me what the fuck is going on?"

"You sure you're ready?"

"Not now, not ever. But go ahead anyway. No wait, let me guess—a government experiment gone wrong? Aliens?"

"No, but close. The explanation is vampires," I replied. "I'm a vampire, and so is your brother, Jake."

Her glass fell from her hand and shattered on the floor, spilling bourbon everywhere. I got her a new glass from the kitchen and refilled it. After a while, conversation started slowly, tentatively, but then the reporter in her took over and the interview began, with Elise firing concise question after question at me. I answered them all.

Toward the end she said, "So when you're a vampire, you're still the same person you were, not evil or anything like that. But you're physically enhanced, don't age, and you have to have human blood to survive."

"As good a summary as I've heard. Yes, that's about it. About being the same person, that's true, but when you live as long as I have, you sort of forget what it feels like to be human. Maybe you become more callous, more *vampire,* if you will, and less human. I don't know. It's hard to explain."

"And my brother?"

I smiled. "He's about the most *human* vampire I know."

She smiled back. "And he'll look just the same? The same as when…well, as when he died?"

I nodded, "Like a twenty-year-old college kid, but by your counting, he'd be forty-two."

"And how old are you?"

"A little over two thousand years."

She took a belt of bourbon and let out a long, dry whistle. "I can't believe I'm buying this crap."

"Crap or not, you need to decide," I replied. "Even though you shot more holes in me than a Swiss cheese, there's only one thing that'll really convince you, and that's Jake. If this were *The Matrix*, it'd be time to decide between the red pill and the blue pill. And even if you picked the red pill, you'd still never forget my visit."

Elise replied, "Couldn't you just zap me with your vampire telepathy and make me forget? And it's the blue pill, by the way. The blue pill puts everything back the way it was."

"Telepathy really doesn't work that way, and I tried *zapping* you a few times. You're resistant. You sure about the pills?"

"Yeah, I'm sure," she said. "And who are you trying to kid about it being time to decide? The minute you walked up to my door, you'd already decided for me, didn't you?"

I thought about that. Although I hadn't decided for her consciously, I guess my faithful old brainstem had. "Yeah, I guess I did. Sorry. Blue pill all the way."

"Red pill. You really should watch that movie again."

Gods, she was infuriating. "Enough with the fucking pills. And for the record, I think you're wrong about that. So what's it going to be?"

The little redheaded smokestack lit up another cigarette. "First, I want to know why you're doing this."

That was an easy one; no brainstem needed there. "A lot of reasons, really. One is that I like breaking the rules every now and again. It makes me happy, and it helps keep me going, I think. You know what I mean?"

She nodded.

"And quite frankly," I added, "a lot of bad shit has happened to me these past few years. It feels kind of good to do something that I hope will be positive. But the main reason is that Jake decided for me a long time ago. You see, he's a very close friend, and he misses you terribly. So I really had no choice in the matter."

"What if what you told me drives me crazy or something?" she asked.

I waved a disbelieving hand at her. "Nah, you're not the type. But if you do go ahead with this, you need to keep one thing straight. This is about getting your brother back, not an invitation into our world."

"What do you mean?"

"Bringing a human family member in is frowned upon by other vampires and usually ends badly," I answered. "I'll get away with it because of my standing in the community, but remember, there are only two kinds of humans in our world: vampire hunters and VAs. I don't want you to become either one."

"I get vampire hunter, but what's a VA?" she asked.

"Vampire associate."

"Stupid name. And what exactly does a VA do?"

She was spot on about the name. "Humans that hang in our world and work for us. They provide a lot of services, and most of them want to be turned."

She was surprised. "Wait. People actually want to be turned into vampires?"

"Oh sure. You'd be flabbergasted how long the waiting list is right now. The last time I checked, it was over—"

She cut me off. "Hold on. Did Jake volunteer to be a vampire?"

"No, he was attacked and left for dead," I said. "But your brother is a survivor. His turning was a total accident."

She breathed a sigh of relief. "Well, at least there's that."

"Your thinking is very human, prejudicial, and exactly ass-backward," I replied. "Being chosen to be turned is quite an honor. You wouldn't believe the amount of screening and vetting and paperwork that needs to be done. It's totally nuts. When you're an accidental turning, you're looked down upon, like an abortion that lived, or at the very least, a second-class citizen. You have to work your way into the good graces of our society, and believe me, your brother has come an awfully long way."

"And I suppose you were one of the chosen ones?" she asked.

"Nope, dead meat that lived," I shot back. "Too stupid to die, I guess. But again, if you do this, just be happy to have your brother back. You can't be an investigative journalist in our world."

Even though I'm sure she knew the answer already, Elise asked, "Why not?"

"Because you'll end up dead. Remember when I told you there were two kinds of humans in our world? Well, there's a third kind—food. At our most basic level, even on our good days, we're natural killers, and very good ones. Being nosy is a sure way to end up dead."

She thought for a moment. "And even now, if I say no, you'll just walk away and I'll never see Jake or you again?"

"No, not really," I answered. "Remember, you invited me into your home, and now I can return whenever I wish to. You are *mine*, Elise."

She nearly fumbled a newly lit cigarette. "You mean that part of the legend is true? Oh shit, really?"

I stared at her grimly, trying—and probably failing miserably—to conjure up my very best Dracula impression. The moment played out, and finally I laughed. "No, it's a bunch of crap. I'm just fucking with you. I wanted to get you back for that red pill-blue pill shit."

"Very funny, asshole."

"No need for name-calling," I replied. "And the mouth on you, young lady. No matter though, time to decide."

She didn't hesitate. "I want my brother."

CHAPTER 19

The beautiful late-fall afternoon in Provence featured a cloudless bright blue sky and a warming, golden sunshine. But the beginnings of the mistral wind kept a little bite in the air as it blew across the beautiful, rolling landscape. The narrow, twisting hillside roads were all but deserted.

The two sleek, dark sedans peeking over the last small hillock before the final ascent to Saint Michel seemed completely incongruous with the bucolic scenery. Their windshields were blacked out, and the sun glinted savagely off the polished chrome, somehow making the cars look more like killer sharks than automobiles. Even more incongruous was the barricade set up at the base of this scenic declivity, blocking the road. The cars rolled to a stop, and several black-clad, heavily armed men got out of the lead vehicle.

A giant of a man stepped from behind a tree. He wore a peacoat that fit him like an undersized T-shirt, and he carried an extremely large shotgun. "That's far enough, boys," he said.

They stopped their advance and leveled their weapons at him, but the giant calmly went on. "This town is closed to all traffic. Why don't you just get back in your car and turn around?"

They didn't respond, but a voice did, an incorporeal voice coming from a speaker in one of the cars. The voice said, "Squid, is that you?"

The Squid squinted in concentration. He knew the voice, even though the speaker had mechanically distorted it. It only took a moment for him to lock in and recognize it. "Lisa. Lisa Brownell," the Squid said.

"Yes, darling, how have you been? And how is that girlfriend—excuse me, ex-girlfriend—of yours doing?"

Just as nasty as ever. "Doesn't matter," he replied. "What're you doing here, Lisa?"

"Oh, I think you know what I'm doing here. I'm just surprised you were ready for me so soon."

"With a bitch like you," Squid said, "it always pays to be ready."

She laughed. "I can't argue with that. But I'll tell you what. I only want the town. I'm not particularly interested in you right now, and neither is Gaius. Why don't you just walk away? You'll live, and perhaps we'll get to do this another day."

"Where is your *master* these days?" Squid asked.

"Oh, he's around, but no need to worry. He's not too close. He couldn't be bothered by such a pissant operation. He gave it to me because he knew how much I'd enjoy killing everyone in Saint Michel."

Squid smiled and shook his head. He lit up a Camel and took a puff. "I'll make you a counteroffer. Why don't we fuck one more time, you know, for old times' sake? Then you and your boys take off, and we'll call it even."

The speaker spewed out laughter. "Wouldn't be worth it, Squid. You simply weren't that good."

He smiled. "Now I know you're lying. Hey, Lisa, you're in a little over your head here, aren't you? Suppose I come over there and drag your skinny ass out into the sun and watch you roast? How'd that be?"

From the safety of her car, she said, "Try it. You'd never get close."

Squid finished his cigarette and carefully stamped it out. "Well, I guess we have nothing more to talk about."

His shotgun roared to life, blowing one of Lisa's henchmen back over the hood of his car. His second shot opened up the windshield, and the head of the driver, letting bright sunlight into the vehicle. But Lisa wasn't in it.

Shit! Wrong one, Squid thought.

He ducked back behind the tree as Lisa's cronies opened up on him with automatic weapons. The second car disgorged half a dozen men, and they added to the barrage.

Suddenly, a fusillade of gunfire burst from the woods on both sides of the road. Several of Lisa's men were killed, and the rest scurried back into the cars, which reversed their way back up the hill and out of range.

Anton, Brigitte, and two-dozen other townsfolk peeked out at the retreating cars from the cover of the trees. Anton approached the Squid and said, "That was easier than I expected. They did not have much fight in them, did they, Father Squid?"

Squid cringed. "Anton, you really have to stop calling me Father. Squid will do just fine." He turned to Brigitte and asked, "Will you check the barricade? Make sure the explosives weren't damaged, *d'accord*?"

As Brigitte did as he asked, Squid said to Anton, "They'll be back. We need to be ready. They'll probably wait until night on account of Lisa."

"I don't think they are waiting," Anton said.

Squid's head snapped around, and he looked back up the road. One black sedan nosed over the hill, then another, and then another after that. Squid stopped counting at six. It was as if the original two cars had mated and had a large litter of identical limos.

"Hold your places!" Anton barked out to his Saint Michel troops. He turned to his daughter. "Brigitte, get the rest of the town and Squid to safety. No matter what, no harm must come to him. You know what to do. We will delay them as long as we can."

Tears welled up in Brigitte's eyes. "But, Father—"

He cut her off. "There is no time for buts. If I am to die, it will be an honor defending one of the chosen ones. Now go!"

Brigitte leaped into his arms, her tears flowing. She hugged him fiercely as the sedans closed in.

With an effort, he pried himself free of his daughter and kissed both her cheeks. "From the moment I saw you, Brigitte, I loved you more than life," he said. "Now please, *go!*"

Brigitte turned away, sobbing, and took Squid by the hand.

But the Squid did not move. "Now wait a minute, Anton," he said. "Am I supposed to run away and leave you to die?"

The first of the enemy had gotten out of their cars, and the gunfire had started, but the old man said calmly, "If you stay, you will die along with our entire village. The very history of Saint Michel will be disgraced. Go now and protect my daughter, please."

The gunfire intensified. Though it wasn't in the Squid's makeup to run from a fight, even he had to admit to himself the futility of staying. The people of Saint Michel seemed to possess a deep-seated, almost genetic urge to protect their vampire benefactors. He knew the hunting-rifle-armed townsfolk had no chance against these machine-gun-toting mercenaries.

"All right, you win," Squid said. "I'll do my best by Brigitte and the rest of the town. And Anton, I'll make these bastards pay."

The old man smiled grimly at that, nodded once, and turned to the fight. Squid reluctantly allowed himself to be led away by Brigitte, with the gunfire getting louder by the second. He had no idea how they were going to make it up the hill without getting gunned down, let alone how he was going to protect Brigitte and the rest of the townsfolk. Lisa had brought a veritable army.

Their progress up the hill was far too slow, so Squid tossed Brigitte over his shoulder. He broke into his fastest vampire sprint, which was quite fast for a human, but in fact, quite slow for a vampire. The deafening roar of the roadblock exploding temporarily drowned out Brigitte's sobs.

What Squid had thought was his maximum running speed wasn't even close. He redoubled his efforts and climbed up through the forest, moving faster and faster.

CHAPTER 20

Dom Salvucci took in the picturesque ocean view from his seaside villa nestled high in the foothills above the harbor of Castellammare del Golfo, Sicily. That evening, he had a fine meal in the town that was famous for its history, fishing, and the Mafia.

So far he'd had no luck locating the Harrison cell. A few days before, he found what he thought was a promising lead tracing them to the Amalfi coast, but it had turned out to be a dead end. Dom reasoned that it was bad information, or they'd already cut and run.

No matter, he thought. *Tomorrow is another day.*

Dom had already made his rounds of the property, posting the guards for the graveyard shift. He returned to his living room, poured himself a glass of a very nice Sangiovese, and settled into a comfortable oversized leather chair. He listened to the crash of the waves and gazed at the stars sparkling in the crystal-clear night sky, while a recording of Pavarotti's version of *Pagliacci* played softly in the background.

The villa had originally been his grandfather's and then passed to Dom's father, and now to him. The many pleasant early-childhood memories of his visits to Castellammare del Golfo put him at ease. The townspeople, his people, also made him comfortable, welcoming him like a lost son. Through their long history of association with the Mafia, they were used to nefarious goings-on and knew how to keep secrets. They'd die before talking out of school about him, and they'd never give him up to anyone. Dom felt perfectly safe.

~~~

The operation had gone more smoothly than Bloody Bill had imagined. The electronic perimeter of the villa had been subverted without a hitch, and the guards, fewer than Bill expected, were efficiently and silently dispatched by his team. Steve had
~~~

premedicated the enhanced members of the squad with Valium, Molly included, and they'd performed perfectly, maybe even better than ever.

The grounds and the first floor of the house were secured. Bill and Molly alone would go to the second floor, where he knew their real target, and their final kill of the evening, would be. Protocol dictated they should've taken more backup for this last part of the mission, but Salvucci was the human bastard who'd helped vampires attack his farm, killing his wife and daughters. This was personal and would be for family only.

Steve and two others would hold the first floor and the rest would hold the grounds, but they were really standing guard over a graveyard. Everyone else was dead, save Salvucci. And Bill intended to correct that deficit posthaste.

"Vesti la giubba", one of Bill's favorites from *Pagliacci*, wafted down the stairs as he and Molly soundlessly ascended. As Bill climbed, he subconsciously timed his steps to the tempo of the music.

At the top of the stairs, he waved Molly to the right and motioned to his headphones, letting her know he would signal the go-ahead for the attack. He waited at the main entrance to the room, and after a few seconds, he heard Molly's whispered voice through his earphones.

"Ready," she said.

"Now," he whispered in reply.

They entered silently, and Bill immediately saw their target sitting in a chair with his back to the room. Having come through the side entrance, Molly was far closer to Salvucci. She had a two-handed grip on her killing sword, and her gaze locked onto her father's. There'd be no need for the headphones now.

Bill could see the rage in Molly's dark brown eyes. He could feel her anger and the devastating loss she still felt over her mother and her sisters. Bill felt it as well, felt the fury building in his heart, making it seem like it might explode as Molly's intense stare burned into him. As Pavarotti intoned "Ridi pagliaccio," Bill nodded.

Lifting her sword above her head, Molly glided silently toward Salvucci. She struck cobra-fast, and a large chunk of the chair flew into the air, but not Salvucci's head as she'd intended. Somehow at the last second, he must have heard or sensed her and rolled to the floor. He tangled Molly's legs with his, and she fell to the floor along with him—infuriatingly, out of Bill's line of sight.

Bill advanced, his shotgun at the ready.

Salvucci dragged Molly back to her feet, using her as his human shield. The oversized Mafioso had his meaty arm firmly around Molly's neck and a small pistol pressed against her temple.

A deadly calm descended upon Bill.

"Far enough, Harrison," Salvucci said.

Bloody Bill stopped. They were no more than eight feet apart. "You might as well let her go, Salvucci," he began. "Your men are dead, and the place is surrounded. You're not walking out of here alive no matter how this goes."

Salvucci smiled. "Maybe not, but I'll tell you what. If you don't do exactly what I say, you're going to be down another daughter. And as I recall, you don't have any left to spare."

Bill's flinty eyes grew flintier, and a small, cruel smile formed on his lips. He nodded. "You're quite a fucking comedian, ain't you, Salvucci?"

"I'm done talking," Dom replied. "Put that fucking shotgun down on the floor, or her brains are on the floor. Simple as that."

Bill began to lower his shotgun and looked to Molly. Her expression screamed that she was ready, and Salvucci didn't know what he was dealing with. He had no idea how strong and fast Molly had become with the drug. For the second time that night, Bill nodded to his daughter.

Moving lightning fast, she reached up and grabbed Salvucci's gun hand while at the same time delivering a short, powerful elbow to his gut. His breath woofed out as the gun went off, just missing Molly's head. She twisted away, meaning to give her father a clear shot. But even though she was enhanced, Salvucci was a powerful man and managed to hang on to her.

Bloody Bill didn't have much of a shot, especially with a shotgun at close range where his daughter was involved. But it was the only shot he had, and he took it. The blast inharmoniously interrupted *Pagliacci* and pulverized Dom's shoulder, spraying blood everywhere. Molly shook free, going to the floor. Miraculously, Salvucci held on to his pistol and tried to level it at Harrison. Bloody Bill's next shot stopped that, blowing a huge hole through the center of Salvucci's chest. He was propelled backward and crashed through a window, lazily tumbling end over end through the salty night air.

He splashed stone dead into the same ocean he'd swum in as a young child.

Bill held his shooting stance for a moment until it dawned on him that Molly was still down. He turned toward her, thinking the worst. "Molly?" he said.

She didn't answer, but a strange voice from his left did. "A virtuoso performance Mr. Harrison. And I don't mean Pavarotti."

Bill whirled and fired, shattering a doorway, but nothing else. He caught a glimpse of the speaker's feet diving to safety, but he didn't see much else. With that kind of speed, Bill knew he was dealing with a vampire.

He took cover behind a couch while speaking into his headset. "Steve, we need backup. There's a vampire up here."

There was no response. Bill repeated, "Steve, we need backup. Anybody? Respond."

The line remained ominously silent. From outside the room, the voice spoke again. "I'm afraid they can't respond. But I assure you none of them are harmed. You see, Mr. Harrison—Bloody Bill, if I may be so bold—I'm a true admirer. I have quite the soft spot for all the fine work you've done over the years."

Harrison wasn't cowed. He assumed his team was dead and this discussion was a trap, but a trap that really shouldn't have been needed. This vampire could have easily killed him from behind when he was dealing with Salvucci.

"Cut the bullshit," Bill replied. "What do you want?"

"To talk, that's all. Perhaps we might reach an accommodation."

"I'm listening."

"Oh, not like this. Face-to-face. I'd hate to bargain with a potential business partner while skulking about and with you crouching behind a couch."

"Come out, then," Bill said.

"Very well, but put down your shotgun. You're too damn good with it. You can keep your pistol if you wish."

"What if I say no?"

"Oh come now, Bill. I could've already killed you and your crew ten times over by now if I'd wanted to. What have you got to lose?"

Harrison was flummoxed. He couldn't argue with the logic, but before he exposed himself, he needed to check with Molly. He whispered into his headset, "Molly, are you okay? You're not hit, are you?"

When there was no answer, Bill became worried. He was about to call for her again when her whispered voice came back. "I'm okay. Not hit."

Her voice sounded odd and strained.

"You don't sound okay," Bill responded. "Can you cover me?"

"You got it, Dad," she replied, and Bill saw her pistol peek over the back of the loveseat where she had taken cover.

The vampire's voice said from outside the room, "You realize of course that I heard all that."

"Damn," Bill said, and then stood and placed his shotgun on the floor.

A hand waved a white handkerchief around the corner of the door, and the vampire stepped into view. Impeccably dressed and slim, he had dazzling blue eyes and wore a small smirk that suggested that he was the keeper of some dark, amusing secret. He affected a slight bow. "Allow me to introduce myself. I'm Gaius Acilius."

Bill's eyes widened in recognition of that surname. Over the past few years, his cell's research had dug out the fact that the vampire Julian Brownell's real name was more than likely Titus Acilius. "Acilius, huh? Came across another vampire named Titus Acilius a few years back. The meeting didn't go so well for us. He a relative of yours?"

The vampire's expression hardened. "Let me assure you he is *no* relative of mine. I would have much preferred that your meeting went extremely poorly for him."

Bloody Bill studied Gaius Acilius, unsure whether to believe what he'd said. "Okay. So here we are. What do you want?"

Acilius smiled. "First, let me thank you for killing that gargantuan guinea Salvucci. The fact that he drew breath all these years has been a perpetual thorn in my side."

Bloody Bill replied, "You're welcome. But can we just get to it, please, Mr. Acilius?"

"Certainly, and please call me Gaius. To get to it, as you say, I want to hire you and your group."

Bill chortled. "Oh, I see. You're a vampire, and you want to hire me, a vampire hunter, to what, kill other vampires I suppose?"

Acilius clapped his hands together and smiled. "That's it exactly."

"Sounds to me like you're nuts, and this is one big crock of bullshit."

"Well, I'm certainly insane, but I assure you the offer is not bullshit," Acilius said. "I'll pay you very well and provide you with excellent intelligence and support."

"To kill other vampires?" Bill asked disbelievingly.

"*Yes*, to kill other vampires. Do you really believe we're all one big, happy fleet living in peace and harmony while ravaging all you poor little humans? Grow up, Bill. We're as different and varied as you, with our likes and dislikes and motivations. I suspect you know this already. But it's so much easier to kill us when you can think of us all as one huge, mindless beast. I'm right, aren't I, Bloody Bill?"

The vampire was right. Through the years, Bill had learned some of the intricacies of the vampires' complex and varied society. It was in fact far easier to kill them when you didn't consider that they were living, feeling individuals.

"Why don't you take care of your own business?" Bill asked. "Kill the vampires you want to for yourself. You've wiped out my entire team in a blink. And after all, isn't killing what you do best?"

Acilius smiled. "It is. But couldn't I say the same for you? And as I told you, your team is unharmed. Why would I indiscriminately kill potential employees? But to answer your question, if I were to take care of my own business right now, there'd be certain repercussions, certain political consequences, which I'm not quite prepared to deal with yet. So why not hire a vampire hunter, and the very best one at that? It's always wise to add new weapons to one's arsenal when one can. And you and your group would be a fine weapon to have. Everything else aside, the idea is so perverse, it's absolutely irresistible."

Bill smiled at the comment. He still thought this vampire was full of shit, but he was definitely entertaining. "What if I say no?"

The vampire opened his arms and smirked. "Then you and your people simply walk away, and you can continue your less-than-ideal existence, hiding and scurrying about and waiting for death to finally find you. But I encourage you not to make your final decision now. My offer is no doubt confusing and complex, and you'll need to think seriously about it. I'm going to put a card down on this table. On it is an untraceable number. It will put you in contact with one of my associates, and he can get in touch with me."

Bill advanced carefully and pocketed the card. "And if I say yes?

What are my guarantees after my job for you is done?"

Acilius smiled widely. "Oh, there are no guarantees. I may very well end up killing you, or you me. But I hope it won't come to that."

Bill smiled back. He thought it was the first completely honest statement Acilius had made. "Okay, I'll think about it."

Bill heard an odd sound coming from behind the loveseat where his daughter had been taking cover. He turned toward it, immediately concerned, and said, "Molly?"

When she didn't respond, Bill moved quickly to the other side of the room and found her on her hands and knees, her head bowed low to the floor. The odd sucking noise that Bill had heard emanated from her, making him think that she had indeed been wounded.

He reached for her but stopped, cold dread filling him to his very bones as he realized the noise wasn't from a wound; it was from slurping. Molly was perched like a cat over a bowl of milk, but there was no milk there, only blood. She was lapping a pool of Salvucci's blood from the floor.

"Molly!" Bill shouted.

Molly slowly wavered up to a kneeling position, her face and shirt covered with blood. Her eyes were glazed, and she appeared grotesquely sated. Bill crouched over her, shocked, and he reached for her again. His normally rock-steady hands shook, and he couldn't bring himself to touch his own daughter.

Acilius tittered from behind him. "My, my, my. Just what do we have here?"

Bill spun suddenly and drew his .357, meaning to put a bullet in the vampire's head.

Acilius easily caught his hand. "No need for unpleasantness, Bill."

Bloody Bill's killer eyes locked firmly onto Acilius's. "Let go of my hand," he said through gritted teeth. "Don't say another fucking word, and leave."

The vampire's eyes turned icy cold, and he calmly replied, "I don't take orders from you, or anyone, Bill. It would be wise to remember that. As a sign of good faith, I'll give you a pass on your breach of etiquette and let you live. You're understandably stressed over your daughter. But let me give you a bit of advice. If I were you, I'd call me sooner rather than later. Considering the mess you've gotten your little girl into, I'm thinking she could use a little vampire help."

Acilius increased the pressure on Bill's hand, forcing him to release the gun. The vampire bent the barrel with his bare hands and tossed the useless weapon onto the couch. He raised his hand to his face, conjuring an imaginary phone with his thumb and pinky, and silently mouthed, "Call me." He strolled leisurely out of the room.

Bill turned back to Molly. Blood dribbled down her chin, and her eyes were half-lidded and unseeing.

Bill couldn't conceive how this had happened. Had she been bitten or infected in some other way? And then it dawned on him: the PEDA 17. That was the only explanation. Anger welled up in him, and he took it out on the only person available. He reared back and struck Molly a solid slap in the face. Her head lolled back, but she didn't fall.

She kept her kneeling position, and after a moment, her eyes cleared. She looked down at her meal, the partially congealed dark pool of Salvucci's blood. She reached to her mouth and touched the wet redness there. Slowly, as if dreading what she'd find, she pulled her fingers away from her lips and looked at them, fully realizing what she'd done. "Oh, Daddy!" she cried, reaching her arms up to her father.

When he didn't move to embrace her, she lowered her head and broke into huge, hitching sobs.

To his credit, Bill only hesitated for a short time and then took his daughter into his arms as she cried, soothing her as best he could. His wife's last words came charging back into his head.

Helen had said, "Go, and take care of Molly for me. You're all she's got now."

Bill's tears added to his daughter's, and he thought what a piss-poor job he'd made of that final admonition. He wondered what Helen would do if she were here, but he already knew. Many times they'd had to deal with friends and acquaintances that had been turned, and they always did it in the same way. Friends or no, they put them down like rabid dogs. It was a harsh fact of life, and it would leave Bill all alone, but it was the right thing to do. It was what Helen would want.

Bloody Bill stood on weak, quavering legs. He picked up his shotgun and readied himself as best he could.

Molly still knelt in front of that damn pool of blood with her head down.

"Molly," Bill said softly.

He had to repeat her name again, before she looked up. "Molly, honey. I can't leave you like this. It's not like I want to, but I just can't leave you like this."

His throat tightened to a stop as Molly looked at the shotgun in his hand and then up at her father's distraught face. She'd been a vampire hunter for years now. The resigned understanding in her eyes told Bill she knew what had to be done.

"I know, Daddy," Molly said. "I'm sorry. I love you, Daddy."

She didn't beg. Bill knew she would never do that. He raised the shotgun. Tears blurred his vision, and for a moment, Molly was transformed into his darling little five-year-old girl just as she'd been all those years ago—all skinny, scraped elbows and knees, topped off with an unruly mop of dark brown hair.

Bill viciously blinked the tears away, and there she was again, as she was now, kneeling and bloodstained and a monster.

But they're the same, Bill thought. *Aren't they?*

That Molly of long ago and the one kneeling before him were the same, no matter what. She was still his darling little girl, and she always would be. The gun spasmed from his hands, and he fell to his knees, sobbing. Molly went to him, comforting *him* this time.

In his mind's eye, Bill could see Helen's disapproving look and her head shaking back and forth. Even from beyond the grave, she still could command him. Not this time though. He answered that condemning look in his thoughts. *Damn it, Helen, you're dead. Molly's still alive, and I won't sacrifice her.*

After what seemed like a very long time, Bill opened his eyes and saw that the vampire had indeed been telling the truth, at least in part. The rest of his team stood in a loose circle around him and Molly.

"Molly, Bill, what happened?" Steve asked.

Bill stood quickly and cracked a nasty straight right directly into Steve's mouth, toppling him backward to the floor. Bill was on him in a flash, his boot knife appearing in his hand like magic. He pushed the huge blade to Steve's neck.

"Dad, no! "Molly screamed.

Bill turned to Molly, keeping the knife firmly against Steve's carotid artery, and spat out, "Even after all this, you defend him? You know it's that fucking drug he gave you! There's no other explanation."

Molly looked coldly down at Steve. Bill had never seen that look on Molly before. It frightened him, but he couldn't say why. Others in the room could have. In that moment Molly looked just like her dear old dad, Bloody Bill Harrison.

"I know it, and I'm not defending him," she answered. "That's over. But he's the only one who's got a chance of figuring this out. If you kill him, we're sunk."

Bill so wanted to cut Steve's throat, watch him as he slowly gurgled himself to death, his life's blood spraying all over the room. He deserved it after what he'd done to his daughter and the other members of his team, but the logic of what Molly said slowly sank in. It was undeniable. Bill reluctantly got up, sheathed his knife, and picked up his shotgun.

He took a look around the room at the members of his team, save Steve. Molly was last, and he favored her with a secret wink. She smiled, and he knew right then, for certain and from deep in his soul, that whatever she'd become didn't matter to him one damn bit. She was still his Molly, and her smile still melted his heart the way it always had.

"Let's get the fuck out of here," he said.

CHAPTER 21

Jake picked up after a few rings, and I said, "Hey, Jake. Come over to your sister's. She really wants to see you."

There was a long pause, a short response of "Okay," and an even shorter click as the line went dead. Jake could really conserve words when he had to, an attribute I wished I possessed at times.

I looked over at Elise, who sat on her living room couch, looking about as calm as a newly caged tiger.

"Done," I said. "Shouldn't be too long. The hotel's pretty close."

She smiled, but it came out strained and looked more like a grimace as she struck up about her ninetieth cigarette. At the rate she smoked, she'd probably have lung cancer before Jake got here. Shockingly, after only one puff, she took a quick look at it and stubbed it out. Elise apparently wasn't a nervous smoker, although I'd wager she'd smoke in almost every other state of mind, including sleep if she could manage it. She got up and started pacing back and forth in her living room.

After about two minutes of cigarette abstention, the air quality in the house had improved markedly, but her pacing was beginning to get on my nerves. "Jake's quite the pacer, too. Must be a family trait. Why don't you sit down, and we'll talk some."

"What for?" Elise asked.

"It'll pass the time and keep you from wearing out your shoes."

She sat back down, and of course, reached for her smokes.

"Could you give that a break for a bit?" I asked. "The smokescreen is just starting to clear in here. I was beginning to forget what you look like."

Elise eye-rolled me again. It was something she was quite good at. "Are all your jokes that bad?"

"Not all, but most," I replied.

She paused for a moment, assessing me. "Would you really have shot me in the basement if I didn't shoot you?"

"You didn't seem to need a lot of encouragement to empty that clip into me," I said. "But no, I wouldn't have shot you. I would've drained every drop of your blood, though."

She leaned away from me, her pretty blue eyes opening wider.

When she remained silent, I chortled. "Jesus, I'm kidding. Bad jokes or not, you really have no sense of humor. Like I'd kill my friend's kid sister after all this."

She glared at me, lit up, and blew a big puff of smoke right in my face. "It's amazing you've lasted two thousand years. With the kind of shit you pull, there must be a lot of people around who want to punch your ticket, dickhead."

I laughed. "My goodness, that mouth of yours. Lighten up, will you?"

"Oh, lighten up, is it?" she shot back. "You push your way into my house, put on a blood-and-gore show, tell me my dead brother's really a vampire, and I'm supposed to lighten up?"

I was about to reply when the doorbell rang. Elise stared at the door but didn't move, so I got up and answered it. Jake stood there looking paler than any vampire I've ever seen, and that's saying quite a lot.

He said in a whisper, "Is she…"

I nodded. "I'm leaving. I'll come back with Miranda after sunset. But Jake, take it slow. Okay?"

He was futilely trying to get a glimpse of Elise over my shoulder and hadn't heard a word I'd said, so I repeated, "Jake, you need to take it slow, okay? This is a huge shock for Elise."

He heard me this time. "Don't worry, Titus. I will. I'd never do anything to hurt her."

From behind me, I heard Elise gasp at the sound of her long-lost brother's voice. I couldn't even begin to imagine what she felt at that moment. I moved aside, and Jake took two steps into his sister's house and stopped. Elise stood in front of the couch. Her eyes were wide, and both hands appeared to have flown up to her mouth. She looked like a kid on Christmas morning waiting for the biggest surprise of her life. Except this wasn't a bike or a doll. This was her brother back from the dead.

Adding to that little kid image I had of her at that moment, she did one of the cutest and most touching things I'd ever seen. She put her hands over her eyes, and after a moment, took them off again. Peekaboo. Then she did it again. I guess it was her way of making sure that Jake was really real.

She started to cry, and Jake walked toward her, but she put her hand in front of her like a traffic cop, and Jake stopped. She wiped her tears and studied him intently, every bit the investigative journalist now. Her eyes squinted in concentration. I'd guess she was trying to reconcile the Jake she saw now with the Jake of her childhood memories.

She moved closer and reached out hesitantly to touch Jake's cheek. His hand moved up to cover hers, and he bowed his head as his silent tears fell to the living room carpet.

Elise took him in her arms and sobbed out, "Oh, Jake. How I've missed you."

"It's all right, Little Red," Jake answered. "I'm here now. Everything's going to be all right."

As I let myself out, I hoped so.

CHAPTER 22

Miranda and I picked up some Italian takeout on the way back to Elise's house. We found Jake and Elise chatting on the couch when we arrived, and after introductions were made, we went to the kitchen. The smell of tomato sauce soon filled the room. Now this wasn't my aunts' homemade stuff by a long stretch—which, by the way, was the best in the world—but it didn't matter much. The smell of tomato sauce in general always hit me the same way. It was absolutely intoxicating. I hadn't gotten sick of that aroma in well over two hundred years, and I hoped I never would.

As we set up for dinner, Elise kept stealing looks at Miranda. She finally asked, "You're really my brother's girlfriend?"

"Yeah," Miranda answered. "We live together. Why?"

"No offense, Jake, but she's way too hot for you."

I laughed, and Jake said, "Oh, thanks a lot, sis. Thought I was dead, haven't seen me in twenty years, and you're already busting my chops? Nice."

Miranda came to Jake's defense and said to Elise, "You only think that because you're his sister. You can't see it, but Jake's really cute."

Jake responded by kissing Miranda. It wasn't R rated, but at least PG-13 and lasted a tad too long for mixed company.

"Enough already," Elise said. "It's bad enough that I have to deal with this vampire shit, but seeing you make out with your girlfriend is way too much right now."

"Sorry," Jake replied sheepishly.

We sat down to dinner, and Elise settled into some surprisingly easygoing small talk, considering that she was dining with three vampires. Elise and Miranda were out in front for a lot of the conversation, comparing notes on Jake's pre- and post-vampire life, much to his chagrin. Their conversation danced from the odd weather in San Francisco, to the lousy red-eye flight Miranda would have to take back to New Orleans, to questions about Elise's job.

Toward the end of the meal, there was hardly any food left, even though we'd started with a ton. In terms of who scarfed down the most food the fastest, it was about a draw between Miranda and Elise. For two petite girls, they could really put it away.

Elise motioned for me to pass what was left of our chicken marsala, but it was gone. When I offered the remnants of the veal Parmesan, she declined, saying, "I don't eat veal."

"How come?" I asked. "You seem to eat a lot of everything else, and pretty damn fast, for that matter."

"You just eat slow," she replied. "Did you ever read about how they treat those calves? It's criminal."

"Oh right, the calves," I said. "You really think they treat chickens that much better? Or how about those meatball...animals?"

Instead of the wisecrack I expected at my shitty joke, Elise went silent. She looked confused and then quite serious. She looked from me to Miranda and then settled on Jake. "It's true. You're really vampires, aren't you?"

Miranda answered through a mouthful of pasta, "Afraid so."

Elise shook her head. "It's just that for a bunch of terrible monsters, you seem okay."

"You really know how to lay on the charm, Red," Jake said.

"I didn't mean it like that," Elise replied. "I mean you talk about food, have girlfriends and boyfriends—"

"Wives, even," I interjected.

"Really?" Elise asked.

Now that I'd brought that nasty topic up, I wished I hadn't. "Long story. Please, go on."

She did. "Well, you drink and smoke and make bad jokes and fret about the weather and bad plane flights."

Jake asked, "What did you expect? Black capes, long fingernails, coffins, and shit like that?"

"I expected—well, I don't know what I expected, but it definitely wasn't to feel like you were all so normal. I mean, even after shooting a bunch of holes through Titus, I still kind of feel like he's just a regular guy with a shitty sense of humor."

Jake's eyes widened. "You did what?"

"No big deal," I said. "Just some prep work for your arrival. And by the way, your sister's a way better shot than you are."

"Very funny, Titus," Jake replied.

"No joke," I said. "You couldn't break a bay window with a shotgun. Your baby sister unloaded on me under pretty extreme duress and didn't miss once."

Jake answered, "I haven't gotten around to seriously training, that's all."

"Save your time," I replied. "You suck."

Elise interrupted. "You see, there it is again, you two goofing on each other. You seem like me. Except…"

Miranda finished for her. "The blood drinking and the killing and the living forever."

Elise grew thoughtful for a moment. "I want to go with you tonight when you hunt."

That took me off guard. "Now wait just a damn minute. You've been through enough for one day, and I don't think that would be the best idea."

"No, it makes perfect sense," Jake responded. "That's the way Elise is. She likes jumping in with both feet and has to see things to believe them."

"You'll forgive me, Jake, but you haven't even seen Elise in twenty years," I said. "I don't think that makes you the expert in how she is. Not yet, anyway."

My comment got me dirty looks from both ladies, but Jake wasn't deterred in the least. "I've seen her, just not from up close. I've followed her career and read everything she's written, and for the first ten years of her life, I knew her better than anyone I've ever known."

Miranda piled on. "And you started all this, Titus. She's going to have to see sometime. Why not tonight?"

They might have been right, but it pissed me off for some reason. What had I gotten myself into here? The same thing I always did whenever I got involved with humans—trouble.

I sighed. "For the record, I think it's a bad idea. But okay, you win."

Elise quipped, "Gee thanks, Dad."

I pointed my finger at her. "Real funny. If this goes sour, you'll only have yourself to blame."

Miranda laughed. "You really did sound like a daddy that time,

Titus."

"Everyone's a fucking comedian around here. You want to add something?" I asked, looking at Jake. He raised his hands in mock surrender, and I went on. "Okay, let's go. But I hope you three know what you're doing."

We headed out, and fortunately Elise's neighborhood wasn't particularly well lit. To any passersby, the four of us would look like two nice couples out on a late-night stroll. How wrong they would be.

We saw him long before Elise did. Miranda and I slid out to the flanks to make sure Jake wasn't being watched. He was a young man, I'd say around thirty-five, and luckily, he was susceptible to Jake's telepathy. At least Elise would be spared watching the guy hopelessly fighting for his life.

We were next to a small, dark, wooded park. Jake took his victim by the arm and led him in with the three of us in tow. The only sound on this dark, still night was the rustle of leaves swaying in the wind.

Jake looked at Elise and said, "Maybe this isn't such a great idea."

She was pale and appeared as if she was about to bolt, but she held steady and managed to whisper, "You have to."

Jake hesitated for a moment, shrugged, and bit the man in the neck. The victim didn't make a sound, but Elise gasped. She watched, hands over her mouth, eyes shocked open, as her brother drained the poor bastard.

When he finished, he unceremoniously let go of the dead body. It thumped to the ground, and Elise jumped and squealed at the sound of the impact. She stared at Jake with silent tears running down her cheeks. Unable to face her gaze, Jake lowered his head. Elise walked toward her brother.

I had no idea what to expect. I shot Miranda a quick look. She appeared tense, and I could tell that she had no idea what was going to happen either. Images of Elise cussing out Jake, beating on him, and screaming at him to stay away from her danced through my mind.

In retrospect, it was stupid of me to even lean in this direction, because she took Jake into her arms and sobbed out, "Oh Jake, I'm so sorry. I'm so sorry you have to be like this."

Well now, Jake buried his head into Elise's shoulder, and didn't he join the tear fest with his baby sister? They stayed like that, hugging and crying, with the freshly killed stiff lying right at their feet. Elise might have been sorry, but I'm guessing if he'd had a vote, the dead guy would've said that he was sorrier.

I get the idea of family and all, but I was raised over two thousand years ago as a Roman soldier, so this type of emotional horseshit had a tough time washing with me. "Do you believe this?" I whispered, looking over at Miranda, and guess what? She was all teary-eyed, too.

Miranda moved over to Elise and Jake, and they all did one big fucking group hug.

Abso-fucking-lutely unbelievable.

Miranda and Jake were very lucky that Jean-Luc or the Squid didn't witness this sorry display, or they would never have heard the end of it. They'd be certain to catch a lot of crap from me as well, of course, but the main thing I felt as I looked on at the ludicrous scene was nausea.

"Guys, we really ought to get going," I said. "Come on, break it up."

After what seemed like an eternity, they reluctantly detached themselves from each other, with not a dry eye in the house.

"I'll help with the body," Jake said.

Miranda blubbered, "Me, too."

"No, I got this," I responded. "You two get Elise home. I'll be right along."

As if I needed two crybaby vampires helping me decapitate and dispose of a body with baby sis Elise watching the entire grisly event. I could only imagine the length of the hug-a-thon and the depth of the river of tears that would follow.

Jake and Miranda briefly and tearfully protested, but I shooed them away. If I had to watch them for a moment longer, I think I actually might have vomited.

When they'd left, I said to the corpse, "Alone at last. Do you believe this crap? After two thousand years, I thought I'd seen just about everything. But this baloney is a new one by me."

He, of course, didn't respond.

To be fair, since I'd been the softy that had started this entire course of events by putting Jake and Elise back together, I tried to force myself to get into this modern, emotional spirit of things. I even considered leaving well enough alone and seeing if this poor dead schlub would turn. But on deeper introspection, I didn't have it in me.

So I hacked off his head and threw it and the rest of him down the nearest sewer. I guess I'll never understand this generation—or this millennium, for that matter.

CHAPTER 23

This time the nine members of the cell met in Bill Harrison's cramped apartment on the outskirts of Positano. They were stuffed into what served as Bill's living room. The room had become even more crowded than before, since Molly had been using it as her bedroom these past few days. She'd moved in with her father right after the incident at Salvucci's. Steve had tried to engage her in conversation multiple times, but the only words she'd spoken to him in response were, "I can't talk to you right now."

The mood of the group was gloomy as they went through the preliminaries of debriefing as to how they'd been so easily captured on the night of the attack. There were really no surprises here, and no fault to be found. The vampire Acilius had expected them, and his ambush was well planned and perfectly executed. As this part of the meeting ended, everyone appeared to be on pins and needles, waiting for the real show, the explanation of what had happened to Molly.

The few times Steve had spoken up until this point, Molly had jumped down his throat. Shockingly, Bill found himself acting as peacemaker, a role he was decidedly unaccustomed to.

"Now for the fun part," Bill said with a small smile that didn't even come close to touching his hard, flinty eyes. "Steve, you want to let us in on what the hell is going on?"

"You mean with the PEDA 17?" Steve asked.

Considering the response, Bill knew that Steve was scared shitless. Given Steve's position, he would've felt exactly the same. "No, Steve, I mean with how the Denver Broncos are going to do this season. Yeah, I mean with your damn drug and why my girl has suddenly taken on a taste for blood. You want to explain that to me, and to the rest of the group?"

Steve looked ashen. "Okay. Well, for a bit of background, there are inherent problems with any performance-enhancing drugs: side effects, the length of time that they need to take effect, and how long they have an effect. In our case, the boost we needed was way beyond what's ever been tried before—that is, to be able to physically compete with vampires."

"We all know that," Molly said coldly. "Stop stalling and get on with it."

Steve gulped and went on. "The only way to get around all of the challenges was to have the enhancing agent intercalate directly into the subject's genome so it would have a lasting, maybe even permanent, effect. I tried all of the standard stuff, chemicals and tagging agents and the like, stuff that's used to direct chemotherapy against cancer cells. Dozens of trials later, I had nothing that even came close to working. There was no way around it that I could see, with one exception." Steve paused and looked around the room.

When he didn't speak, Bill prompted him. "Go on, Steve. Spit it out."

"The only thing that could work, at least in my mind, was HVSV, so I used it," Steve said.

Several of the team gasped.

For Bill, what Steve said was so unbelievable he was almost certain he hadn't heard it correctly—but he knew he had. "You mean to say that you injected Molly and Pete and Tracy and Ted with the sub-virus that turns people into vampires? Tell me you didn't do that, Steve. *Please* tell me you didn't do that."

Steve looked as if he were in a full-blown panic. "It's not like that, not exactly. An intact human immune system kills HVSV easily, a hundred percent of the time. And I attenuated it anyway, weakened it, a lot. It was antibody coated, protected. But that was only supposed to last until the drugs got into the subject's genome. When that happened, the HVSV should have been completely vulnerable to antibody attack like it usually is. Somehow it must've mutated and survived."

Bill looked shaken. "Jesus, Steve, I may not be a scientist, but you did something to protect that damn bug from the immune system? The one weakness of the thing is that our bodies wipe it out so easy. It's probably the only reason the whole human race ain't vampires already. How the hell could you do such a thing, and not even discuss it?"

"I thought I had it under control," Steve answered with a distinct quaver in his voice. "It worked perfectly in all the models and tests. My modified HVSV was killed every time after it delivered the enhancing agent to the genome."

"In the test tube," Bill said.

"And in some limited animal models, too."

"Limited animal models," Bill scoffed. "Well, I guess the human body is a wonder, isn't it? How long have you known?"

Steve lowered his head. "I suspected since the withdrawal symptoms started. But I really wasn't sure until Molly—until the attack on Salvucci."

Bill asked, "Are Molly and the others infectious? Could they turn a human?"

Molly's eyes laser-locked on Steve with a murderous glare.

"I don't know," he answered.

Bill picked up the movement from the corner of his eye as Molly charged at Steve with her sword already in hand. Bill barely managed to trip her to the floor. He tried to restrain her there, but he was losing that battle and badly. Molly fought like a wildcat. "For Christ's sake, help me hold her down!" he shouted.

Several members of the cell jumped in and grabbed her, holding onto her as she screamed, "You're dead, Steve! You're fucking dead!"

It took a long while for Molly to quiet down and stop fighting. When Bill was confident that she wouldn't kill Steve right then and there, he let her up. "Would you guys give us some time?" he said to the rest of the group. "We need to have a family discussion. Come back in twenty minutes."

Once the team filed out, Molly started in. "You cocksucker! You're lucky my Dad protected you, or your head would be rolling around on the floor right now."

"Molly, that's not fair," Steve said. "I was trying to help, and I made a mistake."

"Trying to help? A mistake? You turned me into a fucking vampire, you bastard!"

Steve tried to placate her. "Now, Molly, we don't really know that for sure. I'll have to run some tests, and—"

"That's your problem, Steve," Molly interrupted. "You never know anything for sure. And you can take your tests and ram them.

You're not laying a needle or a hand or anything else on me, you asshole."

Bill interjected, "Calm down, Molly. This ain't helping. Steve, what are your chances of figuring this out? Reversing it?"

"Out here in the field? Almost zero. Even if I were in the best-supplied research lab in the world, chances still wouldn't be great. If my HVSV has gotten into the genome like the naturally occurring one and mutated, there's nothing I know of that can remove it safely."

"But you can still make the drug easily enough, even out here, right?" Bill asked.

"Fortunately, it's easy to produce and getting easier since I've trained Ted and Tracy to help me."

"And the Valium? As far as you can tell, it's still okay for the side effects?"

Steve replied, "Yes."

Bill ruminated for a moment. "You got some of your drug with you now?"

"Yeah. In my backpack."

"Get me a vial, will you?"

Steve gave Bill a questioning look, but did as he was told.

Bloody Bill took the vial and turned to his daughter. "Molly, you remember back at Salvucci's when I said I couldn't leave you like this?"

Molly nodded.

"Well, that was wrong in a lot of ways, but I think I got it right now. What I should have said was that I can't leave you *alone* like this." Bill jammed the needle of the vial through his pants leg and into his thigh, injecting himself.

Molly gasped. "No, Daddy!"

Bill smiled. "In for a penny, in for a pound."

Molly went to her father, and they hugged long and hard. After a time, she said, "Daddy, I have to tell you. When things were going so nice here, I was thinking about getting out, leaving this life, and trying to go somewhere and be happy. I wanted to leave all the hunting and killing behind. I was going to tell you, talk to you about it, but now everything's different. I'll never leave you, Dad. I'm staying with you right to the end."

Bill's eyes filled with tears. He was so proud of Molly, but at the same time didn't want this for her. "I love you so much, honey. I sure didn't see this coming for the old Harrison clan. But I'll tell you what—we'll do our best with it. Somehow we'll come out on the other side. I know it." Bill beamed down at Molly. He turned to Steve, and his smile did a fast fade. "Well, Stevie-boy, I guess it's your turn."

A mean-looking sneer formed on Molly's lips as Steve's face blanched for about the tenth time since the meeting began. "What, what do you mean, Bill?" he asked.

Bill scoffed. "Oh come on, Steve. You know exactly what I mean. But if you want me to spell it out, okay. Take another vial of PEDA and inject yourself. And do it now. I don't got all day."

A sheen of perspiration broke out on Steve's forehead as he stammered out, "But, but, we agreed. I shouldn't inject myself in case of side effects, so I'd have the best chance to…"Steve trailed off, seeing the flaw in his logic.

Molly laughed. "Well, I guess you shot that theory in the foot, didn't you? You said you had pretty much no chance of fixing this fuck-up. Right, Steve?"

"But—"

"No buts," Bill interrupted. "You know what? I'm beginning to wonder just how much you ever cared about my little girl, Steve. After all, you exposed her to this shit without even telling her. Water under the bridge now, I suppose. But I've got to believe you and her are going to be on the outs for a fair while, or maybe for good. So if there's even the smallest chance of figuring this out, maybe she's not quite the motivating factor for you that she once was. Maybe she really never was, but I'm not going to try to judge that. But putting your ass in that sling, now that might be just the ticket to light a little more of a fire under your butt. What do you think, Steve-O?"

"I won't do it," Steve insisted.

Bill casually pulled out his brand new .357 from under his jacket and pointed it directly at Steve's head. "Oh, I think you will."

"You need me. You…"

Steve trailed off once again, and Molly once again laughed at him. "Sorry, sweetie. You just told us Ted and Tracy were helping with production, and I know for a fact that they've made batches all by themselves. So you see, babe, we need you about as much as we need a raging case of herpes. If I were you, I'd do what my dad says."

"That's about it, boy. Are you going to keep your brains in your head, or out? Doesn't matter one damn bit to me," Bill said, totally meaning it.

Steve's eyes flitted nervously from Molly to Bill and back again. "You're both crazy. You're totally fucking crazy."

Molly smiled meanly. "That's about the only right thing you've said all week."

"Yep, I've got to agree with you there, girl," Bill added. "But time's up." He cocked his pistol for emphasis.

Steve put his hand out as if to ward them off. "All right, all right. Damn you!"

He injected himself and sat down on the couch, crying. Bill holstered his gun and whispered to Molly, "You could've chosen a whole lot better, you know, not quite so much of a crybaby."

Molly shrugged, and Steve sobbed out, "I heard that."

"Sorry, Steve," Bill replied in a serious tone, but his eyes and Molly's danced with humor.

"What about the rest of the team?" she asked.

Bill answered, "I was just thinking about that. With Steve and me on board with the PEDA, that makes six. I figure we should give the last three the option of taking the drug or not. If not, I think they should split off and try to go back to a normal life or do whatever they want. No telling where this blood drinking is going to go."

Molly nodded grimly. "They might not be safe with us."

"Yep. And for what I'm thinking, they especially wouldn't be safe."

Molly replied, "You're thinking of throwing in with that vampire from the other night, aren't you?"

"Uh-huh," Bill said. "He was probably right when he said we needed some vampire help to get out of this. I figure we'll do some of his dirty work with the payback being he helps us reverse the effects of the PEDA 17."

"That'd be a total shot in the dark, Dad. Let's leave out the fact that he's a vampire, but he very likely has something to do with that fucker Brownell. That name thing is too much of a coincidence for my taste. Do you really think we can trust him?"

"No, we can't trust him at all," Bill said. "But as far as I can see, as slim as it is, it's the only chance we got."

"Are you sure? He seems so crazy, so dangerous."

"As your hubby pointed out, the both of us are fucking crazy too,"

Bill replied.

Molly smiled. "And I'm definitely dangerous."

Bloody Bill smiled back. He rubbed his thigh, which smarted from the injection. "And I think I just got a whole lot more dangerous myself."

CHAPTER 24

I meandered back to Elise's and found Miranda, Jake, and Elise moping about the house, talking in muted tones. I went to the kitchen and clinked and clanked around until I found some tequila. I poured myself a stiff one. Back in the living room, I plopped down on the couch next to Elise. They all looked miserable, and frankly, I found it quite amusing. Not that I'm the type to say I told you so, but I told them so.

"So what's up?" I asked in an overly cheery tone.

The response was a you-could-hear-a-pin-drop kind of utter silence. "Come on, Titus, what do you think?" Jake finally managed to mope out.

"I really don't know what to think," I responded.

Elise puffed out a cloud of smoke. "If you didn't notice, my brother just killed a man."

This was getting to be too much. "You mean the guy whose head I chopped off and tossed down a sewer? You mean he's actually *dead*?"

Elise glared at me. "You really are an asshole."

My hand shot out and took her by the throat. She gasped, and the cigarette tumbled from her mouth. Jake came to his sister's defense, moving quickly for him, but slowly for me. I caught him by the wrist and twisted it viciously, snapping it. He tumbled off-balance onto the coffee table, smashing it to pieces.

Miranda stood.

I looked directly at her and said in a deadly, calm tone, "Sit back down."

She did, and for the first time in a long while, Miranda looked as if she were afraid of me. It was a wise choice on her part because this little brother-sister act had really gotten under my skin.

In one hand I had Jake trying to get back on his feet as I applied increasingly nasty pressure on his already mangled wrist, while with the other hand I had Elise by her throat as she gasped for breath and tried to tear my hand away. All in all, I thought it was quite a nice family moment.

I looked down at Jake. "You don't get to attack me. I don't care what the reason. Don't do it again. Now, I'm going to let you go. Get up and go sit next to Miranda."

After a quick wrist rub and a long, evil glare, Jake sat with Miranda.

I turned to a now red-faced Little Red. "Human twerps such as yourself don't get to talk to me like that and live. The only reason you're getting a break is because you're Jake's sister. When I let you go, I'd advise you to shut your fucking yap." I released her.

She hitched in a huge, sucking breath and said, "Fuck you! And you owe me for the coffee table, asshole!" She punctuated her near Shakespearian sonnet by sticking her tongue out at me.

I couldn't help myself. I laughed. The kid had guts. "Fair enough," I said. "I'll make you a deal. I'll pay for your coffee table if you live through the night."

Jake said, "Very funny, Titus."

"It wouldn't be wise to assume I'm joking," I said, and I wasn't. "This entire woeful scene is your fault, not mine. The three of you wanted this, and now you've got it. You had your little group hug, so now it's time to deal with things as they really are."

Elise said, "It only happened a few minutes ago. How do you expect—"

I cut her off. "I'm not talking to you. I'm talking to these two. Okay, maybe Miranda, you have an excuse. You're still pretty much a baby vamp. But Jake? You've been a vampire for over twenty years now. Man up and stop being such a pussy."

"Don't talk to him like that," Elise said.

"You will not interrupt me again," I replied. "If you do, you're going to find yourself floating in a sewer tonight right along with Jake's midnight snack."

Elise winced at the allusion to the man that Jake had killed. She opened her mouth—to fire off another wisecrack, no doubt—but quickly reconsidered. She must have seen it in my face. There wasn't a bit of human left in me.

Their bullshit, boohoo antics had made me colder and colder, until I distilled myself down to 100 percent vampire. I'll give Elise credit. She probably didn't know what had happened to me, but she recognized that it was a bad thing and had the good sense to keep her mouth shut. This whole thing was going poorly, and as usual when dealing with humans—and women, for that matter—I'd probably made yet another colossal error.

I'd gone soft with Lisa, and look where that had gotten me. I wasn't going to make the same mistake twice. I wasn't going to leave a hysterical woman and two dysfunctional vampires in the face of another poor decision by me. I was going to fix things right now, and if I couldn't, I'd fix it the surefire way, the vampire way. I'd spill blood.

I stared at Elise and began to wonder what her blood would taste like. I couldn't help myself. I could see her carotid artery delectably beating away barely beneath the smooth skin of her lovely little neck.

Sounding as if he were far away, Jake said, "Hey, Titus. Come on, calm down."

I was in my deep, cold, killing place—my vampire place. The fool who had arranged this family get-together was long gone. I was no longer Titus the Roman soldier, the ER doc, the friend, the lover, or what have you. I was the monster that humans fear. Something in this little scene that had played out in Elise's house tonight had turned a switch in me. I don't know if it was conditioned, or physiological, or genetic, but it seemed to happen to me more as time went on.

In that moment I wondered if I continued to go on, continued to live for however long, say another two thousand years, would the monster be all that was left of me? No trace of humanity in me at all, only a cold, emotionless killer?

It hadn't happened to my aunts, and they were three times my age. Or maybe they were pretending, as if they were reading from some script titled "How to Act Human." That script might make a fine play, but maybe more importantly, it might help keep me from being seen as the total horror that I was becoming. Maybe it would even help me trick myself into thinking that I at least had one shred of humanity left in me.

Miranda broke the uncomfortable silence. "Look, maybe you were right. Taking her on a hunt so soon was a bad idea."

That statement shook me out of my thoughts, somewhat.

There was really no sense in worrying about how I could turn on a dime like this, and so quickly—no sense at all. But after it happened, it always upset me. Maybe that was a good sign. Maybe it meant that I could still feel something, at least for the time being.

I finally answered, "No, you were right. She had to see it sometime, and you assessed Elise correctly. She could take it. You just didn't do such a good job of assessing yourselves."

"What do you mean?" Jake asked.

"I mean you took a good decision and made it bad by overthinking it and jumping into how it made you feel and that sort of shit," I replied. "And the bottom line is you ended up being dishonest with your sister."

"What do you mean?" Elise asked.

"You were shaken up, understandably so, and said something like, 'Jake, I'm sorry you have to be like this.' Then he started crying along with you, and Miranda jumped in for good measure."

"That's not fair, Titus," Miranda said.

"No, it is fair," I said. "And for the record, you get a pass. You were only following your boyfriend's lead. He's the one who needs to account for his behavior."

"I really don't see what you're getting at," Jake said. "I cried. Big deal."

"Oh, suck it up for God's sake. You're a vampire. Start acting like one."

"You're out of line, and so fucking cold," Jake answered. "I can't believe—"

"Who were you crying for, Jake?" I interrupted. "Tell Elise. Because she thinks you were crying over the fact that you're a monster now. Is that it? Because, and correct me if I'm wrong, I thought you really loved your life lately. Or maybe you were crying for that poor headless bastard taking a sewer ride out to the harbor. Tell your sister, Jake. I think she's confused."

Jake stared angrily at me for a moment. Then he looked over at his sister. "I wasn't crying for that man, Red. And I wasn't crying about my life, because he's right. I do love it. I'm a vampire, and the killing is a part of it. You either accept it or you die. Same with me, I guess. You either accept me and I'm back, or you don't and I'll stay out of your life. I guess I cried because you did, and you had to witness…that. Titus's method of communication definitely blows, and he can be a real asshole, but in this case, he's right."

Oh great, I thought. *Now if only Miranda would call me an asshole tonight, we'll have a clean sweep.*

Elise got up and walked over and sat next to Jake. "Of course I accept you, no matter what. I'm glad you love your life. I wouldn't want it any other way. Now give me a hug."

Jake embraced his sister, and before I knew it, Miranda joined in. I felt my gorge rising once again.

Elise glanced over at me. "Come on, Titus. Join in. It'll make you feel good."

I doubted that, and I knew for a fact that a bucketful of warm vomit that reeked of barely digested Italian food spilling down the front of my shirt wouldn't feel good at all. "No thank you. I'm going to take a pass. But you three go ahead. Take your time, even."

After what seemed like centuries, they finally broke it up. I'd noticed the outside light had changed. The sun would be up soon. This would be a perfect excuse for me to get going. I liked the concept of having my "vampire family time", but only in small, controllable doses.

I stood. "It's nearly dawn. You'd better get Miranda settled here for the day. I'm going to head back to the hotel."

Miranda looked up at the window. "Shit. I wanted to take a quick shower."

"I wouldn't," I replied. "This place catches a lot of sun. You could set something up in the basement, though. It's nice and dark down there."

"Oh great, the basement," Miranda said. "Thanks a lot. Maybe we could find a coffin down there while we're at it."

I laughed.

Miranda stood and hugged me. "Bye, Titus. I hope I see you soon. But you really need to work on your people skills."

"Very funny," I said.

She and Elise headed down to the basement.

Jake eyeballed me silently for a long moment. Finally he said, "Thanks a lot for Elise. You don't know what this means to me, but sometimes Professor Titus's school of life really sucks. I know you're a hard-ass and all, but couldn't you lighten up a bit?"

His comments made me squirm internally. Truth was, when I got into that ice-cold state, it wasn't possible for me to lighten up even the tiniest bit. And another truth was that sadly, I wasn't sure if I liked being in that state or not. "Sorry. Just trying to help. I'll try to do better next time."

He laughed. "After tonight, I'm glad I only have one sister, and since I hate my brothers, there won't be a next time. But thanks again. I owe you one."

"You mean about a hundred." I quipped.

Jake smiled and extended his hand instead of moving in for some kind of touchy-feely embrace that seemed to be all the rage on this extremely odd evening. Palpable relief flooded through me, but to my utter consternation, my relief was sorely misplaced. As we shook hands, Jake pulled me in for a huge bear hug and actually lifted me off my feet.

By the time he set me down, I was totally abashed. "Was that really necessary?"

Jake laughed. "Yep. Just to see the expression on your face."

I'd nearly made it to my car when the little redheaded smokestack caught up to me. I couldn't take anymore raw emotionalism for one night, but Elise seemed to be more than a bit of a bitch, so I held out some hope. This time I wasn't disappointed.

"So I guess I'm supposed to thank you," she said moodily, once again blowing a puff of cigarette smoke directly into my face.

I shrugged and lit up a Cuban. "I didn't do it for you. I did it for Jake."

She stamped out her cigarette. "Could I have a cigar?"

I handed her one, and she lit up.

"These are quite good," she said. "Well, thanks anyway. Jake told me he couldn't even have considered this without the backing of someone as powerful as you."

"Even with me on board, it's dangerous," I responded. "You need to use your head and be very careful. I know it's pretty much in your genes, but don't get too nosy about us. It'll attract a lot of attention of the not-so-nice variety."

"I heard you the first time, so don't worry," Elise said. "With what I've seen tonight, I doubt very much I'll be doing an investigative piece on vampires anytime soon."

"Watching a victim go down like that, and your brother doing it, that must've been tough."

She looked surprised. "Funny, I really wasn't talking about that, even though it *was* pretty fucking gruesome. I was talking about you."

I probably looked surprised right back. "Me?"

"Yeah, you. In the living room you turned into something, something…" She paused, as if searching for the right words. "I don't know what, but it seemed like you weren't part of this world anymore. I thought I was afraid of you in the basement when I shot you, but it wasn't even close to how much you scared the shit out of me in the living room. I mean, not that I know you very well, but it was like you were a totally different person. No, that's not really it. It was like you weren't a person at all."

I winced at the comment.

She noticed. "Sorry. I didn't mean to—"

"It's okay. I really wasn't a person right then. When it happens, it feels like the best thing in the world, sublime, the way I'm supposed to be. But after, I always feel like shit."

"Is it just you, or is it from being a vampire?" Elise asked.

"From being an *old* vampire. It happens to my kind. It's genetic or physiological, or it may be that our emotions somehow wear out from living so long. I don't know. But as I said, I really don't like the idea of it one damn bit, well, at least what's left of my human side doesn't."

We leaned against my car, smoking in silence as the sky lightened and birds began singing their wake-up call.

"I'm sorry that happens to you," Elise said. "You seem like an okay guy for a total lunatic. My brother can't say enough good things about you, even though you broke his arm."

"I'm sorry, too. Sorry about what I did in the living room. But when I get that way, it's like someone else is in charge. And that someone is nobody's sweetheart."

She nodded. "If you strangled me, would it have bothered you?"

I thought about that for a moment. "After, for sure. But right then, I wouldn't have cared one bit."

She looked at me solemnly.

"But let's not dwell on that, because after tonight, you're family."

She looked incredulous. "Really?"

"Without doubt," I answered. "Jake is like a brother to me—maybe a son. I don't really know, but in any case, you're guilty by association. I'm stuck with you, whether I like it or not."

"And I'm stuck with you?"

I smiled. "Precisely."

She scratched her head. "This is a hell of a lot to take in for one night."

"You've got that right," I said as I flipped her my deck of Cubans and got in my car.

"What's this?"

I started the engine. "Consider it a welcome-to-my-vampire-family gift." I drove away, leaving Elise standing on the curb and looking quite dumbfounded.

~~~

Neither Elise nor Titus, with his vampire sharp eyes, noticed Davy Stein sitting in a car two blocks down and across the street. A small and very unkind smile played across his fleshy lips, making his already unappealing features look all the more unpleasant.
~~~

CHAPTER 25

It was once again a beautiful night in Saint Michel, uncharacteristically warm, with the evening breeze never quite gathering enough strength to become a wind. The town square was quiet, but for this time of year, that wasn't unusual. The few people who milled about or dined alfresco were all male, black-clad, and gun-toting, and that was decidedly unusual.

Lisa Brownell made her appearance in the square just after sunset. She strode up to the restaurant, and the two men sitting there immediately stood at attention. "Report," Lisa said.

A short, dark-haired man answered her. "They're all under lock and key, Domina, except the cook, and Phil's watching him in the kitchen."

Gaius had introduced Lisa to the term *domina,* and she had taken to it. Because of that, her men had to take to it as well. Lisa had broken the neck of the last man who'd forgotten to address her as such. "Well, Peter, do we have any new information?"

Lisa and her men had killed all the townsfolk who'd attacked them at the roadblock, and several more in the town proper. They'd captured another twenty, but that left well over three hundred still missing. It was as if they'd vanished off the face of the earth. Infuriatingly, the Squid was among the missing.

Lisa knew they were here in the town, or close by, hiding. For the past two days she'd systematically tortured and killed her captives in an attempt to discover where that hiding place was.

Amazingly, under the most severe duress, none of them had divulged a single thing. Reflecting on her experience with torture at the hands of Bloody Bill Harrison, she felt as if these quaint townspeople were almost inhuman in their ability to resist such anguish. Lisa cracked almost immediately on the Harrison farm, and in a short time had been reduced to a catatonic wreck. The thought made her shudder.

Peter answered, “Nothing, Domina. It’s unbelievable that they can withstand so much. Two more are dead. We have seven left, including the cook.”

“I want that big fucking oaf, the Squid,” Lisa replied. “We’ll kill every last one of them, and slowly, if we have to. Failing that, we’ll burn this shithole to the ground. Do you understand me, Peter?”

He lowered his gaze and mumbled, “Yes, Domina.”

Lisa smiled dangerously. She placed a finger under Peter’s chin and lifted it slowly. “I’m very disappointed in your performance with this.”

He gulped but didn’t respond.

Lisa went on. “I am, however, very pleased with your performance in my bed this morning. You may return at sunrise.”

Keeping a neutral expression and tone of voice, Peter responded, “Thank you, Domina.”

Lisa’s eyes flicked to Peter’s dining companion, whose lips had grown a small smirk. “Do you find something amusing, Walter?”

Walter immediately blanched and said in his Southern drawl, “No, ma’am, I mean, Domina.”

Lisa’s smile was perfectly evil this time. “I was thinking, tomorrow morning, why don’t you join Peter and me in my bedroom?”

Walter tried to speak, but the best he could do was produce a few inarticulate grunts.

“And if you aren’t every bit as pleasing as my dear Peter, I will rip your cock off and stuff it up your ass.”

Peter smiled widely. Lisa liked the fact that he knew when he was allowed to respond to her. It was a lesson she intended to teach Walter come sunrise.

She started for the church and said over her shoulder, “Send me one of the prisoners. I don’t care which, but not the cook. We’ll save him for last. Tell him I want the braised veal again in about one hour. That should be more than enough time.”

~~~

As she walked up the center aisle of the Cathedral of Saint Michel, the small woman’s footsteps thunderously echoed to the very heights of its cold stone spires. The flickering candlelight cast a giant
~~~

shadow before her, which contrasted starkly with her petite frame. She stopped before the altar, where Lisa Brownell awaited her.

Lisa stared silently at her latest victim, trying to unnerve her, but her gaze was returned evenly. "What is your name, my dear?" Lisa asked.

"Jacqueline, *Mere.*"

"Don't call me that!" Lisa responded sharply.

"As you wish."

Lisa approached the young woman and slowly ran a finger down her cheek. To her chagrin, Jacqueline did not flinch. "You know why you are here?" Lisa asked in a friendly tone.

"Of course, Madame Brownell. I am here to die."

Lisa smiled benevolently. "Yes, you are. But you don't seem the least bit disturbed by that, or are you?"

"I am of course disturbed. But that will not change anything, will it?"

"No, I'm afraid it won't. But if you tell me what I want to know, you will die quickly, painlessly. If not…"

Jacqueline smiled beatifically. "That I cannot do. You might as well ask me to stop breathing the air."

Lisa grabbed Jacqueline by the arm, and the young woman winced in pain. "You silly girl. I'm not going to ask you; I'm going to stop you from breathing the air. And before I do, you'll be begging for death."

Despite the viselike grip on her arm, Jacqueline smiled serenely. "Our people are bred to serve your kind, the chosen ones. I could not betray Father Squid, or even you, no matter what the cost."

Lisa released the girl and walked away for a moment. Running her fingertip lightly over the marble altar, she appeared calm, but she was infuriated. *These damn villagers have turned loyalty into a vice.*

They had all died gruesomely, but with great dignity just the same. None had given up a single shred of information. Lisa doubted that the people of Gaius's village would go to such lengths to protect him, or for that matter, any lengths at all. In fact, she was fairly certain that given any opportunity, they'd all be clambering to stab him in the back—if they were 100 percent sure they'd get away with it, that is. And with Gaius, you could never be sure. She turned back to the girl, who absently rubbed her bruised arm but still wore that damned peaceful smile.

At first, for Lisa, this had been about the townsfolk and their idyllic village and her childish need to destroy it because of some warped, petty sense of vengeance. What she needed to avenge she didn't know, but it didn't matter because Gaius, of course, had indulged her malevolent wish.

Perhaps she felt this way because Titus had taken her to Saint Michel against her will, and now she would hurt him through its utter destruction. Perhaps it was because the people all seemed so happy, and Lisa was miserable and wanted to make them pay for that transgression. But was she unhappy anymore? Lisa thought about that. She could honestly say that since she'd met Gaius, she might not call herself happy, but at least she wasn't depressed or suicidal any longer. And that was something.

Why, then why, continue this? Why not pick up and leave? Because of the Squid, that was why. She'd been surprised to find him here, and in an odd way, perhaps even somewhat happy to see him, as he was far more amusing than most vampires. She'd truly had no interest in killing him at first. But then he'd defied her and had nearly killed her with his bazooka-sized shotgun. So now she wouldn't be satisfied with anything less than his head on a spike. To accomplish that, she'd kill every last person in Saint Michel if need be. Lisa Brownell had never been a quitter. She always liked to finish whatever she set out to do.

She turned back to Jacqueline. "My guess is that you will be as reticent as the rest. But unfortunately for you, I have to make sure."

"I understand," replied the young woman. "Do what you must."

Lisa waved a hand upward toward the high-arched stone ceiling. "Do you want to say a prayer before we begin?"

Jacqueline replied serenely, "I am at peace. Know that the town forgives you. I forgive you."

"I don't need this goddamn town's forgiveness!" Lisa snapped.

"Perhaps just mine, then. Marie, the maid you killed all those weeks ago, was my sister."

As if pushed by an invisible hand, Lisa took a step back. Her legs weakened, and a shiver ran down her spine. She hadn't felt a single bit of remorse when she'd murdered the maid, and she had killed her for no good reason. She hadn't needed blood at the time. She'd only done it to upset Titus.

In a way Lisa couldn't understand, the revelation from this tiny, brave girl that she was the maid's sister and that she forgave Lisa finally brought out her guilt over that murder, a guilt that had been deeply buried up until now. Lisa had murdered this woman's sister and was forgiven by her, and she knew that forgiveness was genuine.

A single tear ran down the vampire's cheek. In the deserted church, Lisa's whisper played like a symphony. "I don't need your forgiveness."

"I think you do, Mere."

"Tell me what I want to know, and I'll let you go. You'll live. Your village will live. I just want the other vampire now."

Jacqueline responded wistfully, "Oh, to live, ma mere. I am young with many years before me. To live again, when I am so sure of death. I want that so much."

"Then please, please tell me."

Jacqueline shook her head slowly back and forth. "I cannot."

Fresh tears sprouted silently from Lisa's eyes.

The end came quickly, and without suffering for Jacqueline. It was the best that Lisa Brownell could do.

CHAPTER 26

Old Sarge was at it again. He was sitting right next to my bed in my hotel room. But it wasn't my hotel room. Well, it was, but from twenty-five years before. I wasn't in San Francisco anymore, but up in Napa Valley at the Old Calistoga Hotel. And even though I knew I was asleep and my eyes were closed, I could see Sarge just the same. Dreams are funny that way.

The Old Calistoga Hotel was where I was staying when I got the call from back East that my dog had died. I was on a trip to California and had kenneled Sarge in his usual digs, which were pretty much the Ritz Carleton for pooches.

He was perfectly fine when I'd left him, but that did nothing to stop me from getting the call at just about three in the morning California time, September 12, 1988. On the other end of the line was John, the owner of the kennel, and pretty much the dog lover of the century. The guy even looked like a floppy bald beagle.

Clearly broken up, he'd said, "I found him this morning, curled up just like he was sleeping. But he didn't wake up."

"No, John, that can't be," I'd replied, shocked and disbelieving. "I only left him three days ago. He's so strong. He's only six."

I tried to choke up over that conversation for about the millionth time, but my current dream just wasn't having it. You see, Sarge wasn't dead after all; he was alive and right next to me. I dream-watched him sitting there as he looked at me with those intelligent big brown eyes and then turned to look at the phone on the nightstand, and then back to me again.

He repeated this motion over and over and over again, but I couldn't respond. I was in one of those nightmarish paralyses, and couldn't seem to move or even speak. Finally, his eyes stopped bobbing back and forth and locked onto mine.

His head gave a little tilt, and his expression said just as clearly as if he had spoken, "Come on, Dad, think. I'm supposed to be the dumb animal, not you."

My eyes slowly shifted from Sarge to the big, old-style phone. I could almost feel that horrible call about my pet rushing through the phone line, hurtling straight at me with its dreadful news. I broke into a sweat, my heart raced, and I prayed for the phone not to ring. Dream logic being what it was, I thought if it didn't, then Sarge wouldn't die. But I knew the damn thing was going to ring. Even so, I wasn't giving up that easily. I knew exactly what I'd do. I wouldn't answer. I'd break the curse that way, and my wonderful black Lab would still be alive.

I could sense that bundle of negative energy getting closer and closer. My heart beat faster and faster and broke into uneven palpitations. I realized that no matter how much I'd fight the urge, when that fucking dinosaur of a phone rang, I'd be compelled to answer it. This nasty dream would never let me stop myself. No, God damn it! I would *not* answer that fucking phone.

I started out of sleep, bolted upright, and barely stifled the scream that had almost burst from my lips. I turned on the lights. I was soaked in sweat and panting like a bull.

I looked around the room, and it definitely was not Calistoga, which was a nice start in confirming the end of this nightmare. The phone on the nightstand was modern and complex, another good sign. I turned to where Sarge had been. If by some miracle he'd have been there, it would've been a hell of a shock, but I definitely could've worked my way through that one. That would've been just fine by me.

My breathing slowed as I sat on the side of the bed, still mesmerized by the phone and half expecting it to ring at any second. I sat staring at the damn thing, and it sat on the nightstand, as silent as could be. I should've been relieved, but it was actually maddening that it wouldn't ring.

Then it slowly began to seep in. The phone didn't ring. It didn't ring, damn it, and I'd told the Squid to call me when he was settled in Saint Michel. But he never had.

Now admittedly, the Squid wasn't the most tightly wound watch when it came to obeying instructions, especially about his own safety. Frankly, most would describe him as lax when it came to such matters, but I knew him better than that. He knew how important that town and its people were to me, and when the chips were down, the Squid never fucked up.

I picked up my cell and dialed. In my mind's eye, I could see an oversized doggy smile on my old boy. I hoped everything was okay with Squid and said out loud, "Thanks, Sarge."

Squid's batphone number rang, and finally, an automated answering message clicked on—not the Squid's personal message, mind you, but the phone company's. I was instantly filled with cold dread. That sort of thing could mean he had no signal, or worse. The last time I'd had trouble reaching him like this, he'd nearly been blown up in an attack by the Harrisons. I dialed again and got the same results.

I dialed the villa in Saint Michel. No answer. I dialed the tabac. No connection. I dialed Anton's house next, and the same thing happened.

Wait, I thought. *I'll call Brigitte's cell.*

Then it dawned on me. She didn't own a cell. None of the villagers did. *Damn it!*

I was panicked, and I decided to call Dom. He was the only person I trusted on the continent who was even remotely close to Provence. After several rings, Karl, Dom's valet, picked up, and I let out a sigh of relief. "Hi Karl, it's Dr. Brownell. Could I speak to Dom, please?"

There was a long pause. Karl finally said, "Oh, Doctor, you have not heard?"

The air grew thick, and I could hear my own heartbeat radiating up from my neck and trying to pulse its way through my suddenly clogged ears. I felt like I was slipping back into a dream again, a bad one—but that, as it turned out, was only wishful thinking.

"Heard what, Karl?"

"*Don* Salvucci is dead. He and several of his men were murdered nearly a week ago now. It is only today the police have let me back into the house. I'm doing my best to clean it and make the arrangements."

I lowered my head and whispered to myself, "Jesus Christ."

"I didn't hear you, Dr. Brownell," Karl said.

"Do they know who did it?"

"If so, they aren't saying. But here in Sicily, it could be many."

Maybe many for Karl, but in my book the suspect list was quite short: Gaius or fucking Bloody Bill Harrison.

"I've got to go, Karl. I'll be in touch." I quickly hung up.

I wanted to take some time and gather what little wits I still had about me. But it felt like the clock was already ticking, and thanks to my lollygagging about in California, I was way behind in a race that I hadn't even realized was taking place. I dialed Jean-Luc, and mercifully, he answered on the first ring. "Oh, thank God," I said.

"What is it, Titus? What is wrong?"

"Squid was supposed to call me from Saint Michel, but he never did. I just tried to get in touch with him, and there was no signal."

"Perhaps it is just a reception issue," Jean-Luc responded.

I shook my head. "No. I tried other landlines in the town. They're all dead. I hope the Squid and those people aren't."

"Do you think it is Harrison?"

"No, I don't think so," I replied. "They usually hit and run without a trace. They wouldn't bother shutting down the phones in a town. And how would they know about the village and that Squid was there? It has to be Gaius."

"Or Lisa," Jean-Luc said. "I presume you're leaving immediately. I will catch the next flight and meet you there."

"No, you should stay put," I replied. "If it is Gaius, you and New Orleans might be next on the hit parade."

"What do you want me to do?"

"Use your contacts in France. Send somebody to observe Saint Michel and scope out what's going on. But they can't get themselves seen, and I don't want them to do anything until I get there—unless they have to, that is."

"I will contact Godfrey and Archambaud. They're the only ones I'd trust for something as delicate as this."

Godfrey and Archambaud had been two Crusade knights turned vampire around the same time as Jean-Luc. They'd lived quietly in Europe for nearly a millennium and were our partners on the continent for our wine-importing business. They were both solid citizens, and Jean-Luc trusted them implicitly.

"Okay," I said. "Tell them I'll contact them when I arrive."

"Just the three of you against one of Gaius's battalions?" Jean-Luc asked. "Not the best of odds."

"I'm going to pick up some reinforcements along the way."

"That is wise. Be careful, Titus."

I hesitated for a moment, but then came out with it. "One more thing. Dom is dead."

"No, it can't be," Jean-Luc said, sounding totally stunned.

"I'm afraid so. I just got off the phone with his valet."

"Do we know who?"

"No," I answered. "Karl gave me very little to go on."

After a pause, Jean-Luc said, "I will miss him. He was a good man. We *are* at war, aren't we, Titus?"

"I'm afraid so, old friend."

"Send Jake and Miranda home as soon as you can," Jean-Luc said. "I want to make sure they are safe."

"And the sister?"

"I knew you would be imprudent when it came to her—quite foolish of you. I would say leave her. If New Orleans were indeed a target, she would be in danger if she came. I think she would be safer where she is."

"Agreed," I said. "Be very careful, Jean-Luc. I'll be in touch as soon as I can."

A few deep breaths later, I began packing.

CHAPTER 27

Amy Polanski called on Molly at Bill Harrison's apartment at about two in the afternoon. Bill was out for the day, and this was to be Amy's last stop before departing Italy. The two women had grown close over the past few years, and Molly was saddened by her leaving. Amy was the only one of the remaining three of their cell who had decided not to take the PEDA 17.

The other two had agreed to the enhancing agent, throwing in their lot with the rest. But Amy had declined, saying that she'd had enough of vampire hunting and wanted to go back home. No one faulted her for her decision.

Molly and Amy chatted over a glass of wine in Bill's small living room and reminisced about the past three years. Not surprisingly, there was very little to ponder in a positive way. When the words dried up, the two women hugged and said their final goodbyes. However, Amy didn't make to leave when she should have. She stood, silently considering Molly. She appeared extremely nervous.

Molly finally asked, "Amy, what is it?"

Amy hesitated and then replied, "I don't think I can tell you, Moll."

"You can tell me anything. You know that."

"Maybe," Amy said. "But if I do, you've got to promise not to tell your dad."

"I don't know if I can do that. I guess, as long as it doesn't have to do with him or the cell."

Amy couldn't have looked more serious. "That's just it. It does."

Molly took her by the hands, and they both sat back down on the couch.

"You should just come out with it, Amy," Molly said. "We'll figure out what to do afterward."

Amy took a deep breath. "Do you remember Andrew Simmons?"

Molly did indeed. He'd joined the Harrisons' network about a year or so before the attack on the farm. He seemed like a nice kid and was kind of cute, but more importantly, he was on the late Reverend Jarvis's "payroll". Prior to meeting his end, the good reverend had been the self-appointed religious leader of the group and had planned to forcibly take over once Helen Harrison died.

Helen and Bloody Bill thought this religious subset, although greatly helpful at times, was too dangerous to leave intact when Helen's cancer finally took her. Helen had been the heart and soul of the group, the glue that held all the varied parts of the network together. Bill was respected and feared, but would never be described as a heart-and-soul kind of guy.

They all knew that once Helen was gone, Jarvis would make his move and use his religious zealots to hunt vampires to such extremes that the collateral damage and resulting loss of innocent life would be terrifying. Hoping to prevent this, the Harrisons generated a list of religious fanatics among their vampire hunters and handed it over to the vampires. Andrew Simmons' name was on that list.

Molly replied tentatively, "Yes, sure, I know him."

"Well, what you might not know is that for the six months before everything went to hell, we were sort of an item."

"No," Molly said. "I didn't know that."

Amy paused again. "I've been keeping in touch with him."

Molly was shocked. "You've been what?"

"I'm sorry. I really am, and I know it's against security protocols. But I love him, and keeping in touch with him is the only thing that's kept me going."

Molly shook her head. "Oh, Amy. We've been chased around for the past three years. We've lost people. And it's probably because they've been tracking us through you, and through him."

"No way, no way, Moll. If I thought that, I would've stopped right away. We were very careful. We used payphones, public computers, and the like. There's no way we were being tracked."

Molly sat back on the couch, totally deflated. "I wish I could believe that. But why are you telling me this now?"

"Because Andrew is the reason I'm leaving," Amy said. "I've lost touch with him. I know he'd never let that happen unless…unless he's dead. But I have to be sure. I owe it to him. And anyway, maybe he's just in hiding, or there's some other reason I don't know. Either way, I've got to find out. That's why I'm leaving, to go look for him. Molly, you're my friend, maybe my best friend. I wanted you to know I would've stayed. I would've taken the drug and stayed, if not for Andrew."

Although angry that Amy might have exposed the entire cell to the vampires, Molly felt terrible for her just the same. Amy was about to leave the relative safety of the group to go off and try to find a man Molly was sure was already dead. After all, his name was on that list of religious fanatics.

Not to say that the cell's current life, and now the members' reliance on the PEDA 17, was the best of situations for Amy or anyone else choosing to stay, for that matter, but at least it was something. At least they weren't alone, and they had each other.

"Amy, Andrew is dead," Molly said. "I'm one hundred percent certain."

Amy looked disbelieving. "You can't know that, Molly. You just can't."

Molly sighed. She considered what to say next and decided that too much had already happened to be anything but honest. "But I do. Andrew's name was on a list of all the religious zealots in the group, the people who followed Reverend Jarvis."

"Andrew's religious, but he wasn't involved with Jarvis," Amy shot back.

"Maybe you didn't know him as well as you thought," Molly replied. "Because he was. I did the research myself."

"Research? You? What do you mean? What's going on, Molly?"

Molly considered stopping. Amy sounded as if she could get hysterical, but she was a friend, a fellow soldier in their war against monsters that most people didn't even know existed. She'd sacrificed her life to their cause and deserved the truth.

With the exception of Jarvis's semi-brainwashed followers, everyone in the old network knew how dangerous Jarvis was. Giving up Andrew to the vampires was a hard fact, but a fact Amy needed to hear to prevent her from running off headlong into danger, or worse.

"First," Molly began, "you must know that after my mother died, Jarvis had designs on taking over the network."

"I didn't know, but I suspected," Amy replied.

"He was going to take vampire hunting out into the open and

make it a holy war without any consideration for the innocents he'd kill in the process. If my dad, my sisters and I didn't go along, he was going to kill the lot of us."

"Jesus! I knew he was crazy, but not that crazy," Amy said. "But what's that got to do with Andrew?"

"My mom and dad and I couldn't just leave the religious subgroup intact if things went wrong at the end."

"Things couldn't have gone much more wrong," Amy replied. "So what did you do?"

Molly hesitated for a moment. "We gave the list of Jarvis's group to the vampires."

Amy jumped to her feet. "You did what?"

Molly stood slowly. Amy appeared as if she could snap, and Molly didn't want to provoke her. "Amy, try to stay calm. I know this is hard for you to hear, but that group—and Andrew was among them—was going to follow Jarvis's orders to kill me and my whole family. They were going to get a lot of innocent people killed as well."

Amy scoffed. "Well, I guess we'll never know that for sure, will we? You had them all wiped out. You and that fucking family of yours."

"I'm telling you this as a friend," Molly answered in a purposely neutral tone, "to keep you from running off for no reason and getting yourself killed. We had to do it or Jarvis would've run amok. My mom and dad couldn't abide what would happen if we didn't."

Amy's voice rose hysterically. "Oh, they couldn't abide it, could they? That psycho dad of yours and that scheming bitch of a mother. And you're just as bad as they are, aren't you, Molly?"

"Amy, please—"

"Please, my ass," Amy spat out. "I'm the fuck out of here. And you know what? I might just hunt down a vampire or two and tell them all about your little cell here. Why not? Tit for tat. After all, the great Harrisons cooperated with the vampires, so why can't I? Shouldn't be too hard to pull off with what I know, should it? With Andrew dead, thanks to you, I really don't give a shit anymore."

"Amy, don't talk like that." Molly replied soothingly. Even though she should have been increasingly nervous over where this discussion was potentially heading, for some reason Molly felt herself becoming calm, detached even.

Amy's voice climbed another notch on the hysteria scale. "Or what? You'll kill me, too? That *is* what you fucking Harrisons do best, isn't it?"

"No, of course not," Molly said as her seemingly consoling hand reached out toward Amy. It was as if her arm made the movement on its own accord, and at that moment Molly wasn't the least bit sure what it was up to.

Amy stepped back, and a small pistol materialized in her hand. She pointed it directly at Molly.

"Stay where the fuck you are," Amy said. "I'm well aware what you're capable of."

Molly's calm detachment suddenly dropped into a totally emotionless frigidity. She'd previously had no experience with such a state of mind, but in the brief moment she took to consider it, she decided that she liked it very much. Molly glanced to where her sword stood in the corner of the room and calculated the distance to it, and then to Amy.

"I can't let you leave like this, Amy," Molly said evenly. "Let's just relax and talk this through."

Just as calmly, Amy replied, "No more talk. I'm going to walk out of here, and if you so much as twitch, I'm going to put one, no check that, a whole bunch directly in your forehead. With that fucking vampire juice you take, I know you've gotten fast. But not that fast."

But she was that fast, because in the next instant, Molly plunged her sword directly through Amy's heart. Amy died almost instantly and didn't even have the time to get off a single shot, let alone a whole bunch.

For Molly's part, she'd had no volitional thoughts about the movements that allowed her to so easily kill her friend. It was as if her body had put together the murderous ballet all by itself, and it was yet another novel sensation that Molly decided she'd greatly enjoyed.

She looked down at Amy's dead body, remorseless, and still feeling very much stone cold. She pulled her sword out of Amy's chest. It made a thick, wet, sucking sound, and Amy's heart blood spilled out onto her blouse and then to the floor.

Molly stared at the growing pool of red, and a shudder rippled through her. She barely managed to get herself under control by breathing deeply and willing herself to relax. When her pulse and respiration steadied, Molly bent down and drank.

~~~

Bill quickly got back to his apartment after receiving the call from Molly. He found her calmly sitting on the couch listening to classical music as a warm sea breeze blew in from the open living room window. It would have been quite the peaceful scene if not for Amy's sheet-wrapped dead body lying on the floor at Molly's feet.

A large patch of red spread discordantly from the center of the starched white bed linen that was wound around the corpse. Bill found that bloodstain somehow compelling and stared silently at it, transfixed.

"Dad, are you all right?" Molly asked.

Shaken from his disturbing contemplation, Bill turned to his daughter. Her face was blank, and her normally warm brown eyes seemed to have cooled somehow. Bill couldn't ever remember her appearing this way to him.

"More important question is, are *you* all right?" he asked.

She stood and hugged her father. "I'm okay, I guess. She forced me to do it. I had no choice."

"What happened?"

Molly told him what had transpired just before she'd killed Amy.

"Jesus Christ!" Bill said. "She was in touch with Simmons? No wonder we've been getting our asses chased all over creation."

Molly shrugged. "She didn't seem to think that was the reason. Said they'd been careful."

"I doubt they were careful enough. But what the heck were you thinking, girl? Telling her about the list was plumb dumb."

"I was trying to get her to stay," Molly replied. "I didn't want her to go off trying to find a dead man and get herself killed. I didn't want it to turn out like this, Dad."

"No, I know you didn't," Bill said. "You were trying to help her. You sure you're okay?"

"I think so. Funny thing is I'm not feeling anything at all. I guess it'll hit me later."

"Yep, I suspect so," Bill said, and they both looked down at Amy's corpse.

Once again, Bill found his eyes lingering on the deep, red bloodstain. It seemed to be gleaming on the sheet, seemed to be speaking to him, and he felt a slight tingling on his lips and tongue.
~~~

Molly asked, "What should we do now?"

Distracted, all Bill could manage was, "Hmmm?"

"Dad, what's wrong?"

Bill tore his eyes from Amy's blood. "Nothing, girl, nothing at all. First, we need to get rid of the body. We'll wait until dark, and then I think the ocean would be the safest bet. You?"

"Yes," Molly answered. "What do we tell the others?"

"Nothing. She came to visit, and she left, that's all. Not much of a lie. She really did leave, just not the way they'd be thinking."

Molly wandered to the window, deep in thought. When her back was turned, Bill couldn't help but steal glances at Amy's blood. He couldn't stop himself. The tingling he felt on his tongue had intensified and spread down into his spine. At first he thought he might be having a stroke, but he knew he was kidding himself. He knew what this was all about, but for the life of him, he couldn't reason why it would be happening so fast.

Molly turned back to him. "I think we should tell them the whole thing about Simmons, the list, and even about me killing Amy."

"Molly, are you nuts?" Bill replied. "Do you want to screw up everything? The group would never survive it."

"Hear me out," Molly said. "We've survived an awful lot already, and I think the time for keeping secrets ended when the network ended. We don't have a huge, resource-rich machine anymore. We're small, like a family, and if we don't act like one, I don't think we have a chance.

"Eventually one of them will find out something—about Amy, or Simmons, or the list, and then what? We'll look like the liars that we are. Everyone knows what Jarvis was. It was just bad luck that Amy was involved with one of his nut jobs. I say we come clean now and let the cards fall where they may. At least we'll know who we're dealing with, and so will they. Worst comes to worst, it will be just the two of us."

Bill thought for a moment. There was a certain logic to what Molly was saying. They weren't a big "corporation" anymore. They were down to an intimate group of eight. If he and Molly kept secrets from them, it would be like lying to family. In the end, he knew that kind of behavior would bring dire consequences. His eyes once again wandered over to Amy, and the tingling in his spine turned into an overwhelming harmonic humming that shot through his entire body.

He quickly turned away. "Okay, Molly. We'll go with your idea. But I hope you know what you're doing, girl. And what if they react poorly? Then what?"

Molly met Bill's flinty gaze evenly. "Then they walk away. Or…"

Her father finished for her. "Or we kill them."

"Or we kill them," Molly echoed.

Bill laughed insincerely. "Great minds and all that, but I thought we were supposed to be the good guys here."

"I think the time for that is long gone, Dad."

Bill nodded. He kept looking at his daughter, but he could feel the force of Amy's blood pulling at him, trying to make him look over at it once again. He fought the urge, but it was as if he were trying to swim upstream against a raging torrent of whitewater. He couldn't win. The humming through his body turned into a tremor that felt as if it would shake him to pieces if left unchecked. He broke out into a sweat.

"It's all right, Dad. I know," Molly said. "It's the blood, isn't it?"

He considered lying to Molly, but how could he? And what good would it do? "Yes, damn it! It's the blood. I don't get how it's happening to me so fast. It's only been a few weeks, and it took months before it happened to you."

Molly shrugged. "I don't know. Maybe it's your age. Maybe it's that Steve's always improving the drug, making it purer, more potent. That's probably it."

Bill wiped his brow. "Fantastic. Now I've got another thing to hate that little fuck for."

"Just add it to the list," Molly said.

Bill laughed, but then grew serious. "Did you, you know…with Amy?"

"Yes," Molly replied immediately.

"How do you feel about that?" Bill asked.

Molly thought a moment. "To tell you the truth, I feel great."

Bill walked over to Amy's dead body.

Molly said, "It's okay, Dad."

"Forgive me, Amy," he whispered and gingerly touched his index finger to the blood-soaked sheet. Bloody Bill looked at Molly, and she nodded. He put the tip of his finger to his lips, and his hand suddenly flew away from his mouth as if it had received an electric shock. "Jesus Christ!" he shouted.

From that tiny drop of blood, Bill felt an energy rip through his body that he hadn't felt since he'd been in his teens. At once, he was ten years younger, vital, and his already sharp intellect seemed to sharpen even more.

This is what it's like in all those movies when a druggy sniffs cocaine and looks like he's been mind goosed, he thought. Except cocaine couldn't be anywhere near as good as this. The tremor inside his body diminished almost immediately, and then came back even stronger, but more controlled somehow, more directed, and not as random as it had been. Bill knew exactly what he needed to do to keep it completely in check.

But before he could do that, once again, an image of his dead wife, Helen Harrison, popped into his mind. The specter shook her head in admonition, judging him.

Fuck you, Helen, he thought. *I'd rather be a monster than sacrifice Molly on your goddamn altar.*

And just like that, Helen was gone.

"Is taking in blood always like that?" Bill asked.

"I don't really have a lot of experience, Dad, but yes, I think so."

Bill knew what he had to do, but once again, he hesitated.

Molly said, "I'll go into the bedroom."

Bill smiled. Molly knew him, knew that he couldn't do this thing in front of her. Not yet, anyway. "Thanks. And one more thing. In case all this honesty causes a shit-storm, we're not gonna tell the group anything until both of us learn how to make Steve's wonder drug. I don't want the two of us to be left hanging out in the breeze if everything goes to hell. Okay?"

"Okay," Molly replied. "And Daddy, we ought to contact that vampire sooner rather than later. I know it's not much, but you're right, I think it's the only chance we have of getting out of this. And I don't think we have a lot of time."

Bill contemplated Molly's statement as she left the room. After a moment, he uncovered Amy. Oddly, her sightless, accusing eyes didn't affect him in the least. Even so, he mouthed another apology to her. But this time, the words simply fell from his mouth, stale. His overwhelming craving for her blood rendered them perfunctory and hollow. He knew it, and that made what he had to do all the worse, but it didn't come close to stopping him.

In the end, he couldn't bring himself to put his mouth to the wound in Amy's chest. But he did manage to do just fine with his hand, like a man lifting cool stream water to his lips on a hot summer's day. But this wasn't cool water. This was warm blood.

Afterward, just like his daughter, Bloody Bill felt great.

CHAPTER 28

Early Sunday morning, Jean-Luc Leclerc sat in his office in the subbasement of New Orleans' Absinthe House. Not surprisingly, most visitors found this particular office of his quite unappealing. It was dark and forbidding, made of cold, perspiring stone, and located next to his torture chamber. Although Jean-Luc had far more luxurious workplaces throughout the city, when he had much to consider and wished to be undisturbed, this was by far his favorite. Dom's murder, the likely attack on Saint Michel, and the threat posed by Gaius Acilius gave Jean-Luc much to consider indeed.

He shut down his computer, got up from his oversized mahogany desk, and slowly wandered the room, absently looking over its many artifacts as his exquisitely sharp mind continued to sort the problems at hand. In this room Jean-Luc kept many of his prized possessions from the era when he was human, and that was another reason he liked it so. With its stone construction and all the mementos from his past, it reminded him of his chambers in the family castle in Vivarais back when he was a boy, nearly a thousand years ago.

Jean-Luc stopped at where his broadsword hung on the wall and gently touched it admiringly. Albeit repaired and improved many times through the years, it was, in essence, the same sword he'd carried to the First Crusade. He'd used it well, and countless times since then.

The diminutive Frenchman had carried it back with him to Europe when he finally returned from the Holy Land many decades after his Crusade was over. But by then, he was no longer human. The sword, more important to him than anyone knew, had been his anchor to his human life for nearly a millennium. They'd been through a lot together, and somehow the sword always reminded Jean-Luc of who he really was deep down at his core, back before he was a vampire.

Jean-Luc had worked feverishly the past two days to make sure his city and the people he loved were as safe as possible. He thought that he'd done everything he could do, but knew it was not even close to being enough because Gaius Acilius was tremendously dangerous and completely unpredictable.

At that moment, as if conjured by his very thoughts, Gaius's voice echoed its way down the long, winding stone staircase. "Yoo-hoo. Anybody home?"

Leclerc was surprised at Acilius's appearance, but only slightly so. In a way, he'd almost been expecting it. He calmly removed his sword from the wall and said to it softly, "One more time into the breach, my friend."

"Oh, and by the way, Jean-Luc, I brought you a little gift," Acilius added.

Jean-Luc heard something clunking and thumping its way down the stairs. He stepped out of his office in time to see a severed head take its last few bounces down to the subbasement antechamber. The head spun lazily on the floor, and after what seemed an eternity to Jean-Luc, finally came to rest. It was Rodrigo.

Jean-Luc looked sadly into the face of his dead friend. The expression on it told Jean-Luc he'd died painfully. He felt his anger burning.

Gaius went on. "Just so you know, he died quite well, buying time for that bitch of yours to get away. But don't worry, we'll find her soon enough."

Jean-Luc shed silent tears for Rodrigo, and in relief that Simone was still alive. He took off his jacket and used it as a funeral shroud, reverently wrapping Rodrigo's head.

Acilius spoke again. "Now I know you must have a secret exit down there. You are a wily little bastard, after all. But not everyone was lucky enough to get away like your darling Simone. If you leave now, I'm afraid you will lose another friend. Say something, my boy."

There was a scream of pain and then, "Jean-Luc, don't do it—"

The voice was cut off by a louder scream and then silence. It was Jake's voice.

"Your boy is quite a brave one, Jean-Luc, but I regret to inform you he's down another appendage. And he really doesn't have many left to spare. So what will it be? Will you live to fight another day, or do you have the courage to face me now? It's your choice."

Acilius had inferred correctly. There was an exit in the subbasement known only to Leclerc and his most trusted friends. He keyed the hidden door from his desk, and a panel across the room cracked open, allowing stale, damp air to rush into his office.

For a moment, he contemplated the dark, serpentine corridor. It surfaced blocks away, far from the French Quarter, and would lead to his safety. He looked at the secret door, but he would never step through it, not in these circumstances. Jean-Luc knew Jake was already a dead man, and by going up to meet Acilius, so was he, but he could do nothing else. He had been and always would be, first and foremost, a Crusade knight. He could never leave his friend like this, tortured and in the hands of the enemy.

He called up the stairs, "I'll be up shortly."

"Quickly, Hugues," Gaius replied, "Because in two minutes, your young friend dies. And don't bother calling anyone for help, or they'll end up dead, too."

Jean-Luc wished Acilius had not used his actual name. That madman speaking it out loud seemed to taint its very sound. And calling for help was not on his mind; getting prepared was. Jean-Luc knew that Acilius would kill him, but that didn't mean he would make it easy. He tied his long hair into a ponytail with a leather strap and slipped a long knife into each boot. He stuffed a Steyr M1912 machine pistol into his belt at the small of his back and put an extra clip in his pocket, although he doubted very much he'd get to it.

He hefted his broadsword and made to leave his office, but found himself stopping before a large golden cross set casually on an end table. It was his family's and well over twelve hundred years old. Jean-Luc had lost any belief in God and religion when his pope had betrayed him seven hundred years ago. But even so, he felt himself truly drawn to the relic for the first time in centuries.

Jean-Luc knelt before it with his head lightly resting on the hilt of his sword. He did not pray. He would never do that again. He knelt more as a long-lost but familiar pre-battle ritual. He took deep, cleansing breaths to clear his mind and center himself.

When Jean-Luc rose, he was not filled with religious fervor as he was during the trials of the First Crusade, but nonetheless, he felt better, poised.

Once again Acilius's hate-filled voice filtered down to him.

"Time's up, you little French fuck. Are you coming, or am I going to bowl another head down the stairs?"

Acilius's words could do nothing to penetrate Jean-Luc's self-possessed state of mind. He replied, "Rest assured, Gaius, I am coming for you now."

He started up the stairs with his small, prissy smile on his lips, and by the time he reached the top, it had grown into a full-fledged grin. He hadn't felt so alive in years. He was again who he once was, Hugues de Payans, and this was yet another crusade.

Just before he entered the bar, he said to himself, "Titus, my friend, I wish you could see this. It will be glorious."

CHAPTER 29

We met in Bonnieux, an ancient town in Provence that centuries ago had been a stronghold of the Knights Templar. Considering its proximity to Saint Michel, and the fact that Godfrey and Archambaud had once been Templars, the meeting place didn't surprise me. I'd contacted Adrienne before leaving California. The speed at which she agreed to help did much to confirm that although she'd deny it, she still had strong feelings for the Squid.

She'd brought along two humans. They were both large, square-headed, tattooed, and ex-Canadian special ops. She also had a huge four-hundred-year-old vampire named Yves in her entourage. I didn't particularly like Yves. He was as mean as they came, but for this kind of operation, that would come in handy.

The humans introduced themselves to me as Doc and Cat-Juice. Now as a nickname, I could get my arms around Doc, but Cat-Juice? Even if the reticent, hulking ex-soldier deigned to explain it, which he didn't, I'd still probably never fully understand the reason for the idiotic handle. After this operation, if things went smoothly, I hoped that he and Squid could go at it for the dopiest nickname of the year award.

We settled into a cave-like back room of a nice cafe that was carved into Bonnieux's hillside. Godfrey and Archambaud were waiting at our table. They were both slight, a bit taller than Jean-Luc, and had dark complexions and full beards. As we arrived, they rose and by way of a greeting, delivered cheek kisses all around. The two humans received only stern looks, however, as the Frenchmen had been particularly distrustful of humans ever since the Templars had been betrayed and destroyed seven centuries ago.

We sat, and Godfrey began speaking. "Gaius's men have effectively captured and isolated Saint Michel. They have a roadblock in place and seem to have set up a false story about a gas leak as a cover. The ruse has been successful so far only because Saint Michel is small, with only one road in, and it is not tourist season. But even so, the deception won't last much longer."

Archambaud continued, "They number approximately thirty, are well armed, and it appears there are only three vampires among them. I believe the leader, a female and still a nightwalker only, is your ex-wife."

"I see," I replied. It wasn't much of a response, but it was the best I could manage considering that the news of Lisa's involvement with this hit me like a lead weight. I'd half expected it, of course, but even so, it still sucked eggs.

Godfrey said, "There are very few of the villagers left as captives, only the chef and a few others. They've killed the rest."

"What?" I blurted out. "There were four hundred people there. They've killed them all?"

"The Squid? What about the Squid?" Adrienne asked in a tone barely above a whisper.

"No, you misunderstand," Archambaud answered. "That is exactly the enigma. You see, we think there are less than a hundred that have died here. The other three hundred seem to have disappeared, the Squid among them. The remaining prisoners are being tortured to death, we presume, to obtain the information as to where the others have gone."

"We should move quickly—tonight, I would think," Godfrey said. "I don't want that chef to die. He makes an excellent pâté."

"What's your plan?" I asked.

Godfrey shrugged. "We wait for nightfall, go into Saint Michel, and kill them all. Afterward, hopefully we will find the missing townsfolk, and your Squid as well, Adrienne."

Adrienne stiffened. "He is not my Squid any longer, Godfrey. I do this out of loyalty."

Godfrey smiled and took her hand. "You are such the beautiful liar, Adrienne. We're so pleased to see you, and you Titus, and even you, Yves."

Yves grunted in response, a virtual soliloquy for him.

Archambaud went on, "But why, my dear, did you bring these two humans with you? You know how we feel about that. Humans are not trustworthy and are far too slow. Nothing against them personally, it's just in their nature."

Adrienne said, "I can assure you—"

"It's okay, Addie," Cat-Juice interrupted. "I can speak for myself."

Addie? Letting herself get interrupted without even a mild rebuke? It made me wonder if old Cat-Juice had other hidden talents to go along with his special ops experience and his really fucked-up nickname.

He turned to Archambaud. "Let's get one thing straight, sir. When I go to war, I'm one thousand percent loyal to the men and women I'm fighting with. By somehow coming up with the nut-sac to question that, you've not only insulted me and Doc, but by inference, you've also insulted Adrienne. And I don't take too kindly to any of that. And as for slow—"In a blur of movement, Cat-Juice drew a small pistol and leveled it at Archambaud. It was a blur by human standards, but not by vampire standards.

Archambaud nonchalantly plucked the gun from his hand and knocked him sprawling across the room. Doc stood and drew his weapon, and at Godfrey's hand, he suffered the same fate, in an instant finding himself piled on top of his friend on the floor. Although the two humans virtually flew right by him, Yves didn't even twitch. He sat with his arms crossed, looking decidedly bored.

"Enough of this," I said. "Adrienne, please control your men. And you two, I expect better from you."

Archambaud replied, "Pardon me, Titus. But I think we behaved admirably. After all, they're still alive, aren't they?"

I couldn't argue with that. The two soldiers had regained their footing, and despite being completely overmatched, still looked to be spoiling for a fight.

"You two sit back down and keep your mouths shut," Adrienne said sternly. "And don't ever draw a gun on my friends again. Is that understood?"

The two behemoths sat back down at the command of the petite woman. Doc answered for both. "Yes, ma'am."

Archambaud tittered, reminding me of Jean-Luc. "Your men are obviously quite spirited and well trained, but Monsieur Cat-Juice was quite correct. By questioning them, I insulted you, Adrienne. My apologies." He turned to the soldiers. "And my apologies to you as well. I should not have put you in the general category of your kind before I even got to know you. But nonetheless, I must warn you, if either of you do anything tonight that even hints at betrayal, I will kill you both. Understood?"

Cat-Juice glared at Archambaud with murder in his eyes.

Doc said, "Understood, sir. And your apology is accepted."

Yves rumbled from the corner, "If this soap opera is over, can we order some food? I'm fucking starving."

I flagged down the waiter, and we ordered a gigantic lunch, sending him quickly scurrying back to the kitchen.

"After nightfall, we should go to the hill overlooking the town to the northeast," Godfrey said. "From there, we decide on an approach and take positions. I presume you've brought along the various technological toys you think we may need."

"Yes, and weapons as well," Adrienne replied.

Godfrey nodded. "One more detail. Titus, what do you wish us to do about your Lisa?"

I'd started thinking about that little problem far back in the conversation. I'd tried, and failed, to come up with any viable way to protect her if at all possible. But even if I had, it wouldn't have been right to ask any of the others to risk their lives for her sake. And frankly, Lisa had now crossed a line that I didn't think she'd ever be able to get back from.

"If you can, leave her to me," I said. "But I don't want any of you taking any chances with her. She's very dangerous, so if it comes to it, kill her."

I leaned back in my chair and sipped some wine. I'd eaten in this restaurant many times in the past, and the food was excellent, but I doubted it would taste very good today.

CHAPTER 30

Jean-Luc finished his long climb up the subbasement and turned the corner to face Gaius Acilius.

The old Roman smirked. "My, my, my, don't we look quite ready for action."

Jean-Luc quickly scanned the mostly deserted Absinthe House. Gaius and six bodyguards were spread out and heavily armed. Jake lay on the floor unconscious, his face a bloody mess and his severed left arm and leg across the room and well out of his reach. The two guards standing over him were vampires.

"Surprising for you to have vampires in your retinue, Gaius," Jean-Luc said. "I don't know these two, but most with any intelligence at all stay well clear of you for fear of being deemed insane by association."

One of the vampire guards spoke in a heavy eastern European accent. "Fuck you."

Jean-Luc recognized the accent immediately. "Ah, that explains it. Romanian. Probably descendants of Dracula himself, the archetype dolt."

Gaius smiled. "You know, Hugues, I'm going to miss you. You really are quite amusing, and especially so for someone who's about to die. But my friends are not dolts as you put it—quite the opposite, actually. And if you were to live longer than the next few minutes, you'd see more and more of our kind flocking to my banner. It is our time, Hugues. Time to stop skulking in the shadows, time to come out and live in the open. Time to rule."

"You can't be serious," Jean-Luc replied. "I know you to be a student of history, Gaius. And you know such thinking has never led to anything worthwhile. This is a dalliance for a younger vampire, not one with your experience."

"As I recall, you more than dabbled with the concept back in the day. And you don't know a damn thing about my experience."

"Perhaps, but when I dabbled, I was not yet four hundred," Jean-Luc said. "At your age you should know better. Why not get over your resentment and just enjoy life? After all, Titus was only trying to help you, and he *did* save your life."

Gaius's expression grew stony. "You do have a singular sense of humor, Hugues. But I grow tired of this."

Jean-Luc opened his arms. "What is it to be? Will you have your henchmen gun me down, as you did with Titus?"

Gaius's phony smile reappeared. He pulled out a spatha from under his coat. "With a youngster like you, I don't think so. I'm going to heartily enjoy hacking you to shreds."

"I know that the great majority of what you say is completely insincere and very hard to judge," Jean-Luc replied. "But I think for the very first time, I hear fear in your voice. Why would that be? You have me by force of years, and you have your guards. Why, Gaius?"

The Roman's smile once again faltered. "Wishful thinking of a dying man. Shall we begin?"

Jean-Luc said, "Ah, oui."

In a blur, Jean-Luc plucked the knives out of his boots and smoothly hurled them across the room. Two of the human guards seemed to instantaneously grow knife hilts from their chests. They fell to the floor, dying.

Gaius laughed. "You really are full of surprises, but there are many more from where those two came. And in the end, your little knife-throwing exhibition will do you no good."

Jean-Luc shrugged and suddenly charged across the room and attacked Gaius ferociously. Although initially surprised, Gaius repelled the attack and steadily forced Jean-Luc back as their swords crashed together over and over again.

The Frenchman varied his tactics, attacking from the sides, attacking low, then high, and bringing every bit of his knowledge of swordplay to bear while willing himself to move faster and faster.

But it did no good. The eight-hundred-year difference in their age was too much. Gaius countered every attack, his small, cruel smile growing steadily.

Jean-Luc stepped back, winded and bleeding from several wounds.

Gaius, who'd only barely been scratched on his forearm, raised his hand and did not pursue. "Take a moment to catch your breath," he said magnanimously. "I'm quite enjoying this, you know. You're very good with that oversized pig-sticker of yours, but not good enough today, I fear."

"You won't get away with this," Jean-Luc fired back. "Attacking that village, killing Dom, and indiscriminately killing our own kind. Other vampires will not look kindly upon these things."

"Tut-tut, Hugues," Gaius scoffed. "I assure you, I didn't kill your precious Dom. And I didn't attack Saint Michel; Lisa did. As for killing vampires, it wasn't indiscriminate at all. Everyone knows that I've been in a blood feud with Titus for centuries, and you entered into it by brutally attacking me right in my own home. That was highly uncalled for, by the way. As for your three friends, they just happened to get in the way."

"Three?" Jean-Luc asked.

Gaius's smile widened. "Oh, didn't I mention that?"

Jake rasped out from the floor. "Miranda. He killed Miranda. The bastards dragged her out into the sunlight. Jean-Luc, they burned her. They burned her alive." Jake burst into sobs.

Jean-Luc locked eyes with Gaius. "Why would you do that? Why? She never harmed you."

Gaius's eyes became a frigid steel blue, revealing his true nature. They were killer's eyes and perfectly matched his pitiless expression. "Because I wished to, that's why. I'll give her full credit, though. She fought like a wildcat. Harder than your boy here."

"You fuck!" Jake shouted and tried to heave himself up onto the single leg he had left. One of the Romanians issued him a vicious kick to the face, knocking him back to the floor.

Jean-Luc stared at Acilius. His barbaric acts on this day were almost too much to bear; Rodrigo dead, he and Jake soon to follow suit, but now this. This was by far the worst. Gaius had burned Miranda alive. Jean-Luc felt his fury erupt and shouted, "Sacrilege!"

"Oh save that religious ridiculousness, Hugues. I thought you were long over that." Gaius readied his sword for attack.

But Jean-Luc did not attack. He wanted to, but his body would not obey. It was as if it were acting independently and against his will. He felt his fury distill down to an emotionless calm, which entered his heart and his mind and his very being. He felt a pure, powerful energy surge through his body, an energy he'd never experienced before. Jean-Luc's muscles automatically relaxed with their newfound strength, and his breathing slowed. His wounds finished healing almost instantly. He had no idea what was happening to him.

At that moment, Jean-Luc let go of life and embraced death. He'd done it many times during the First Crusade. He and his fellow knights had faced insurmountable odds time and time again, but they had prevailed. And before each apparently hopeless battle, Jean-Luc had embraced his death and freed himself to fight to his utmost. Over the centuries, he'd somehow forgotten this until now.

"You shouldn't have harmed that girl, Gaius," Jean-Luc said softly. "I'll see you dead for it."

"You'll see me dead, will you?" Gaius replied incredulously. "I've been toying with you, you arrogant little fuck. You truly *are* beginning to bore me now. And just so you know, I intend to FedEx your head to Titus. First class all the way for you, my friend."

"You'll not take my head this day, you insane cocksucker."

Gaius roared and attacked, and once again, Jean-Luc was backed across the room, fighting defensively. But this time it wasn't because he was forced to; it was because he allowed it to happen. Strength pulsed through him, and his movements took on a fluidity and speed that he'd never possessed before. His concentration was laser-like, but at the same time diffuse as he took in the entire situation before him. Gaius's attack was not easy to handle by any means, but in Jean-Luc's current state of heightened awareness, it seemed to have slowed from the blazing speed and force that it was before. It was as if Jean-Luc could almost see the Roman's movements before they came.

As he fought, Jean-Luc gauged the position of the four remaining guards in the room. Even through the loud clanging of steel on steel, his acutely ramped-up hearing told him there were at least eight more guards waiting on the other side of the bar. He could tell his act was working, as Gaius's cruel, confident smile had reappeared.

"Considering your rather boorish behavior, I've changed my mind about FedEx," Gaius said. "I'm sending your head by the US Postal Service. With their track record, I doubt very much poor Titus will ever receive it."

Jean-Luc had reached his mark. He parried Gaius's attack and forced him to step back. Suddenly he whirled and took both of the Romanian vampires' heads off in one smooth stroke.

"What?" Gaius blurted out.

"Surprise!" Jean-Luc shouted and pressed his attack against the older vampire. Gaius strained to parry the assault, but this time it was Jean-Luc who smiled as he began hacking pieces out of the Roman and systematically pushed him back across the room.

Gaius's eyes widened in fear. Between his pants of exertion, he managed to shout out to his two remaining bodyguards, "Shoot! Shoot him, you idiots!"

Jean-Luc dipped and struck Gaius a hard sidekick, sending him sliding across the floor. He turned, plucked the machine pistol from his belt, and opened fire just as the two guards did the same. They crashed to the floor dead, but not before Jean-Luc had been shot twice in the chest as well. He knew from the excruciating pain the bullets caused that they were garlic-laced.

Jean-Luc sensed more than heard Gaius's thrown sword whooshing through the air directly at him. He barely managed to duck under it. It flew by him, missing by mere millimeters, and rammed into the wall behind him.

As the hilt lazily bobbed back and forth, Gaius shouted to the other room, "What the fuck are you waiting for? Get in here and kill him!"

Half a dozen of Gaius's armed flunkies rushed in and began shooting as Gaius raced for the exit. Jean-Luc flipped over a few tables and hit the floor. It wasn't much cover, but it was the best he could do given the circumstances.

As the tables were being chewed to shreds by machine-gun fire, Jean-Luc reloaded his pistol with his spare clip. But even with his startling new powers, he knew his situation was dire.

Jean-Luc's rapidly dwindling, bullet-demolished cover took away all his options except flight or fight. He was readying himself to do the latter when he noted a new basso report adding to the ongoing gunfire cacophony, and pitched above it, a loud soprano war cry.

He'd know that voice anywhere. Glancing to his left, he saw Simone at the basement door. Firing a G36 assault rifle, she looked like a goddess of war. Jean-Luc could not love her any more than he did at that moment.

Gaius's men were falling, but Simone was now taking fire. Struck several times, she was driven back into the doorway. The sight of this prompted Jean-Luc into action. He jumped up and emptied his pistol as he charged what was left of his assailants. The final two, vampires, fell to his sword.

He raced back to Simone, who'd heaved herself to her feet. Her chest was a bloody mess.

She touched one of her wounds and winced. "Fucking garlic."

Jean-Luc took her into his arms and kissed her. "I love you so much, Simone."

"I adore you, my love," she replied. "But how did you know I would come?"

"I didn't. But when Gaius mentioned that you'd escaped, I left the backdoor of the subbasement open just in case."

Simone looked saddened. "Rodrigo. He gave his life for me."

"I know," Jean-Luc said. "And Miranda is gone as well."

She nodded and looked to where Jake lay. "I feared so. At least Jake is still alive. But how did you defeat Gaius? I heard the fight as I climbed the stairs. It doesn't seem possible."

"I don't know how, but we'll have time to discuss it later," he said as he headed to the door.

"Where are you going?" Simone asked, a worried expression adorning her lovely, blood-spattered face.

"To try to end this. Go out the escape exit and get Jake to the house in the Garden District. Call only our most trusted friends. I will meet you there."

"Be careful, my love," Simone said as Jean-Luc raced out of the Absinthe House and up to the Quarter.

He paused on the deserted, Sunday-morning street and listened. In the distance he heard the squeal of tires. He quickly calculated his route and started off at a dead run. Fortunately for Jean-Luc, a small, long-haired, bearded man with bloodstained clothes, carrying a huge sword and racing through the streets at superhuman speed wasn't the most unusual of sights ever witnessed in the French Quarter of New Orleans.

Jean-Luc caught sight of a black limo with California plates near the river, veering off Decatur onto North Peters. It had to be them, but if it wasn't, the occupants were about to get the surprise of their life. The car was slowing, with its left signal on, so it would turn north either onto Esplanade or Elysian. Tiring from his blood loss and exertion, Jean-Luc picked Esplanade, as it was the closer. With a last burst of energy, he bolted across a side street, intercepted the limo, and leaped on top of it as the car accelerated up the avenue.

Any doubts that this was the wrong car were quickly quelled by the bursts of automatic fire that came pouring through the roof. Jean-Luc drove his sword down through the roof above the driver's seat. The horrible scream and the way the car lurched and veered told him he'd hit his mark.

But then the car took off and turned unpredictably, as if trying to flick him off like a bug. Jean-Luc held fast and drove his sword in again, working it like an oversized can opener and rending a huge tear through the protesting metal. Gaius's face appeared for an instant, and then the shotgun.

Jean-Luc moved instinctively and superfast, and the blast that otherwise would have vaporized his head only caught him a glancing blow to the face and shoulder. It was enough to blow him off of the car, however.

As Gaius's car sped away, Jean-Luc roughly bounced off a tree and crashed to the ground on the green-space median that ran the length of Esplanade. He got up and dusted himself off and turned to see a small, wide-eyed boy staring at him.

"Are you all right, mister?" the child asked.

Jean-Luc, although absolutely sure he looked a wreck, replied, "I'm quite well. And how are you on this fine morning, young man?"

"*I'm* good, but you don't look so good," the boy replied.

Jean-Luc laughed. "I am sure that you are correct, but I feel excellent. In fact, better than I've ever felt in my life. Now run along. Didn't your mother ever tell you not to speak to strangers?"

The young lad did as he was told, but not before giving Jean-Luc the finger.

The vampire sighed and started off for the Garden District at a brisk walk.

CHAPTER 31

Giorgio Zanazzi piloted his tiny outboard motorboat east down the coast of Positano. He'd graduated from *scuola superiore*, or high school, with honors a few months back, having earned a diploma in linguistics. He'd always had a natural ear for languages, and Positano was a tourist area where he'd been exposed to multiple foreign tongues since he was a young child. At nineteen he was already fluent in English and French, in addition to his native Italian.

Although the cost of higher education in Italy was quite reasonable, and Giorgio was anxious to leave his small-time life in Positano, he had decided to stay for an additional year to work and earn some extra money to help with the cost of his degree. His family was of poor fishing stock, and Giorgio was the youngest of five. His father, now old and beaten down by his years of labor at sea, had worked hard to send Giorgio's four older siblings through school. At this point he was barely able to hold on to his fishing business and make ends meet. Although Giorgio felt trapped in Positano, felt as if he were destined for greater things, he thought it wouldn't be right to let his father bear the brunt of the cost of his education alone, a cost that might push his father's business over the brink.

Giorgio knew he had to leave the village, but he also knew that even after delaying a year, he wouldn't feel completely right about it. His mother had died five years ago, and when he left, his father would be alone. Giorgio loved his father very much.

That morning he'd gone to the local grocery store where he had worked since graduating. He did his usual chores of cleaning up and restocking the shelves. Signore Ferrante, his boss and also the owner, put his hands on his hips and looked around the empty store. "Giorgio, I'm afraid once the tourist season ends, so do we."

Giorgio shrugged.

"It's a wonderful day, still warm and clear," Ferrante said with a twinkle in his eye. "Why don't you drop the apron today and head to that secret cove of yours? The sea bream might still be running."

"Signore Ferrante, I couldn't," Giorgio replied. "It would leave you all alone."

Ferrante rolled his eyes. "I know I'm getting old, Giorgio, but I think even I can handle an empty shop."

Giorgio smiled. "Are you sure, sir?"

Ferrante smiled back and put a hand on the lad's shoulder. "Do you forget I worked with your father all those years? I know you'll be going off to college soon, but I also know how much you love the sea."

Ferrante was right. Giorgio did love the sea, but not enough to make it his life's work, especially after seeing how it had ground his father down. Ferrante had worked the ocean for many years as well, but about seven years ago, nearly penniless, he'd given it up. Somehow, he had managed to scratch up enough cash to buy the grocery store and had eked out a modest living ever since. Giorgio's father was far too stubborn to ever quit fishing.

The boy replied, "Thanks, Signore Ferrante. If there's anything I can do—"

Ferrante interrupted him. "Just bring me back a fish. I know you'll catch something. You're a lucky one, my boy."

With that, Giorgio left the store and soon was piloting his dinghy east, skipping along the calm Mediterranean. The wind blew back his dark black hair as he raced along. It was unseasonably warm, and he soon took his shirt off, enjoying the feel of the breeze. He had wide shoulders, and a well-muscled, but wiry chest. It was thin in that way that all teenage boys' chests are, right before impending manhood does one of its final tricks and fills them out.

He continued east, nearly to Arienzo, until he sighted the well-camouflaged entrance to the small, protected cove he'd discovered when he was a boy. As far as he knew, no one else knew it existed. Although sorely tempted many times, he'd never told any of his friends, or his siblings, or even his father about it. It was his special place and his alone, and it was well away from the prying eyes of the tourists. In all the time he had spent there, Giorgio had never seen a single other person in what he thought of as Giorgio's Cove.

He cut the speed of the engine and deftly piloted his boat into the zigzagging channel. The landward side had a narrow, rocky beach and was protected on all sides by forbidding cliffs.

In no time, he was anchored and had his line in the water. He sat back against the gunwale and looked up at the crystal-clear blue sky. The sun shone directly overhead, and if this had been summer, it would have been scorching hot. But at this time of year, it was pleasingly warm and perfect.

The only sounds in the cove were from the waves lapping at the rocky shore. The rhythmic motion of the boat lulled Giorgio, and his eyelids became heavy. Before he nodded off, he thought, *What a beautiful day.*

He started up from sleep, thinking he might have heard a noise, but more likely he'd been dreaming. He looked up at the sun, and from its position he could tell that he hadn't dozed for long—a half hour at most. Then he heard it again, a coughing, choking kind of sound from the direction of the shore.

At first he couldn't see the source of the coughing because he was blinded by the sun's reflection coming off the water. As his father had taught him many years ago, he shielded his eyes with his hands, and using his peripheral vision, looked indirectly at where he thought the source of the sound might be.

After a moment his eyes focused, and he saw a young woman struggling, bobbing up and down and gagging up what looked to be gallons of seawater. Giorgio had no doubt that she would never make it to the beach safely.

He acted quickly. Cutting his anchor line and revving the engine, he raced toward the woman and reached her as her head once again bobbed to the surface. He took her by the scruff of the neck and tried to pull her into the boat, which nearly tipped over. Shocked by her weight, Giorgio managed to hang on to her while piloting his boat directly to shore, where he beached it.

He leaped out of the boat, maintaining his grip on the young woman, and helped her along as she struggled the final few steps to the beach, retching up more seawater the entire way. She fell flat on her face among the sand and rocks, and her back heaved up and down as her harsh, water-soaked breath whistled in and out.

Giorgio turned her over and was shocked to see an ashen, white face that belonged on an old crone, not on the body of this young woman. He blinked, thinking at first that it must be some trick of the bright sun, or that seawater had splashed into his eyes, obscuring his vision. As he studied her face more intently, he decided that it was not truly old, but looked as if it were falling apart.

The crone's eyes snapped open. They were a sickly yellow and swam about for a moment before she fixed them on Giorgio. He was about to ask her if she was okay when she opened her mouth and growled at him, exposing oversized canines. It was not a sound a human could ever make. Giorgio started back and tried to scuttle away, but she had him by the shoulders and was on him in an instant.

He struggled hard, but he couldn't get away. In fact, he could hardly move at all. She had him on his back and burrowed her face into his neck. He felt a sharp, stabbing pain and warm liquid spilling down his naked chest. Giorgio screamed and fought harder, but the crone held him immobilized.

Soon the pain faded, and his vision began to fade as well, as he drifted into shock. His brain was losing oxygen, and as he was drained of his life's blood, his thoughts became confused. He began to wonder if this was some kind of dream, and then he became quite sure of it. Yes, he was still in his boat napping in the sun. He stopped fighting. What would be the point of fighting against a dream? He was far too tired to keep fighting, anyway. His eyes wandered up to the warm Mediterranean sun floating in the clear blue sky.

He thought, *What a beautiful day.*

CHAPTER 32

Gaius Acilius sat alone, brooding, in the great room of his mansion. The dimmed lights perfectly matched his somber mood. In fact, the mood of the entire household was somber. Gaius had slaughtered his butler this morning because his Eggs Benedict had been prepared a tad too runny. Richard, his long-suffering footman, had witnessed the grisly murder and promptly vomited on the dining room floor.

Aciliushad nearly killed Richard as well, but at the last moment restrained himself, deciding that when he finally did end poor Richard's miserable existence, he was going to get the maximum pleasure out of it. Acilius wasn't one to hastily give up such a potentially enjoyable act in a fit of rage.

The vampire sipped a very old and very fine absinthe, barely tasting it as he contemplated recent events. The encounter with Leclerc and the near fiasco in New Orleans had shaken him. He could have done nothing to accurately predict the Frenchman's early emergence of power, but he'd been sloppy, nonetheless. He'd given up too easily on tracking down Leclerc's woman, and he hadn't secured the basement of the Absinthe House after Jean-Luc had come up.

On top of that, as far as he knew, the computer wizard Lyons was still alive. He felt certain that these lapses would eventually rear up and bite him in the ass, if they hadn't already. If Acilius truly wanted to lead the vampires out from hiding and into the light of day to become the rulers they should be, he would have to do better.

Just when he thought he'd had everything in hand, he'd gotten careless, and now he had a new blood enemy in Jean-Luc Leclerc. It was bad enough going up against a vampire as powerful as Titus, but it would appear Leclerc was what some of the ancient vampire texts would call a Gifted One.

He'd read through one of those texts that he had in his possession, hoping to glean any worthwhile information, but all he'd found was superstitious rubbish. The book, dating back to seventh-century Greece, stated that the explanation for Jean-Luc's power was that he was imbued with the spirit of some sort of vampire god. Acilius knew that to be ridiculous and thought the likely explanation was some unknown factor in Leclerc's physiology that had allowed him to mature faster than most.

But sometimes, if read carefully, even old, superstition-laden books gave clues to reality, and Gaius had pored over this one, trying to find some hint as to how to dispose of Jean-Luc. Despite several hours of brain-racking research in ancient Greek, a language that Gaius despised, he'd come up with exactly nothing. Even though the book was priceless, he'd nearly thrown it into the fireplace out of frustration.

Adding to his discomfort, he was extremely worried about Lisa. Given what happened in New Orleans, he'd attempted to contact her to have her return to the safety of his mansion, but was unable to reach her. No matter how often he tried, he couldn't get through to her, or to any member of her team.

Right when Gaius thought his disposition couldn't get any worse, Richard escorted Davy Stein into the room. Stein wore an outlandishly styled suit that hovered somewhere between green and yellow. He had a large red carnation pinned to his lapel.

"I'm really in no mood for you, Davy," Gaius muttered. "But may I ask, what exactly is the color of that suit? Piss yellow or puke green?"

Stein glanced down at his clothes and sounded truly insulted. "What? You don't like it? I think it's cool."

Gaius couldn't help but smile at the buffoon. "Davy, if I were you, I wouldn't fire my tailor; I'd kill him."

Stein chuckled. "Now I know you're just kidding, Boss."

"Actually, I'm not. But if you don't mind, I have rather a lot on my mind right now."

"That's why I'm here," Stein replied. "After that ass-kicking you took in New Orleans, I figured you might need something to brighten up your day."

Even if he'd been in a good mood, that comment would generally have incited Gaius to violence. But somehow, coming from Stein, it made him smile. Stein was an idiot, no doubt, but he was Gaius's idiot, and a loyal one at that. Acilius had to admit that for some inexplicable reason, he liked Davy Stein.

"Most would find their heads rolling around on the floor for that remark. But you're lucky, Davy. For reasons beyond me, I actually seem to be growing fond of you."

"Oh, that's not true, Boss. You love me, and you know it. And what did I do, anyway? You wouldn't kill me for telling the truth, would you?"

Gaius sighed. "No, I suppose not. But I'd advise you to never fuck up my eggs."

Stein looked perplexed and remained silent, apparently trying to reason through the enigma of the egg comment.

Gaius looked on in amusement and finally said, "Davy?"

Stein started from his distraction. "Huh?"

"You said something about brightening up my day?"

"Oh yeah, I almost forgot," Stein said with a smile. He put two fingers in his mouth and let out a nearly ear-shattering whistle.

Gaius winced and put his hands to his ears, but too late to protect them from the shrill blast.

Two guards escorted a petite redhead into the room.

"I appreciate the gesture, Davy," Gaius remarked. "But I don't need blood right now. And besides, ginger blood gives me heartburn."

Again, Stein looked perplexed. "Really. I didn't know that about redheads."

"You are hopeless," Gaius replied. "It's a joke, you idiot."

"Oh, sure. I get it. But that's not it. The blood, I mean. This is Elise Little. She's Jake Lyons' sister, the same Jake you ran into in New Orleans. And from what I could make out, she's a friend of your good buddy Titus."

A smile appeared on Gaius's face for the first time in quite a while. He stood to greet his guest. "A friend of Titus's, and young Mr. Lyons' sister, no less. Davy, you really have outdone yourself. Remind me to give you a raise."

"I didn't know I had a salary."

"You do now," Gaius replied as he walked over to Elise.

"There is one thing, Boss," Davy said. "She's a writer, a bit famous even. Her disappearance might raise some eyebrows."

"Oh, pish posh, Davy. Don't be such a bucket of cold water after performing so admirably."

Stein breathed a sigh of relief.

Gaius extended his hand to Elise. "Allow me to introduce myself, Ms. Little. I'm Gaius Acilius. It's such a pleasure to meet you."

Elise took a long look at the vampire and then shook his hand. "I wish I could say the same. Acilius, huh? Are you related to Titus?"

Gaius's smile widened. "You could say that. Please allow me to offer you the hospitality of my home."

Elise replied, "I don't suppose there's any way for me to decline, is there?"

"Your supposition is quite correct. Davy, please find Ms. Little appropriate accommodations down below."

Stein raised an eyebrow. "Should I…"

"No, no, Davy—our very finest room for Ms. Little. She's our guest—for now."

As Elise was taken away, Gaius sat back down and took another sip of absinthe, this time savoring the complex flavor. He smiled and said to himself, "Absolutely exquisite. This could be turning into quite the lovely day."

CHAPTER 33

We met at midnight on the hill overlooking Saint Michel. Doc determined cell phone jammers were being used in the village, so our communication would be limited as well. We were all fitted with earpieces, but the best we'd be able to do would be pulses via the send button on a low bandwidth. One click for *go*, two for *stop*, and three for *watch out*. It was kind of like a Morse code for idiots. Considering all the hubbub in the village with Lisa's men flitting about, we decided to wait until the assassins' hour, 4:00 a.m., before we made our move. Waiting that long would also be a significant disadvantage for Lisa, as the sun would be coming up soon after that.

Doc and Cat-Juice had long since left, following the plan to get to high points on opposite ends of the village and lay down cover fire when we went in. Mr. Juice had the notion of getting into the cathedral tower right in the center of town. A ballsy plan, if you ask me.

The rest of us would move in pairs from different approaches. I'd be with Adrienne, Godfrey with Archambaud, and Yves would go in alone. But he was so fucking big, he counted as a pair all by himself. We'd take out as many as we could as silently as we could, and if and when we were discovered, our special ops boys would open up from on high. It was a simple and hopefully effective plan.

From our vantage point we saw one villager escorted into the cathedral. A woman soon followed him in. At that distance, I couldn't really be sure it was Lisa. But I *was* sure. I could tell by the way that she moved.

Soon after she entered the cathedral, horrible screaming began and echoed its way up the valley. After a half hour or so, the shrieking ended abruptly, and Lisa stomped her way out of the church, obviously fuming. I guess she didn't get what she wanted from the poor bastard. A few minutes later, two of Lisa's thugs carried out the body.

Godfrey broke the silence. "Your ex seems quite the sweetheart, Titus."

Adrienne responded before I could. "You should get to know her in person, Godfrey. She's a real prize."

Yves rumbled, "She pretended to be interested in me, and then nearly ripped my balls off."

Archambaud tittered and clapped his hands together. "Now *that* I would like to have seen."

"You wouldn't have liked it so much if she'd tried it on you," Yves replied.

Godfrey said, "Fortunately, neither my friend nor I have an interest in women, so we would never fall prey to her wiles. But I grant you, she seems to be one nasty bitch."

"All right already," I broke in, somewhat exasperated. "She's a nasty bitch. Can we change the subject?"

"Oh my, Titus," Archambaud replied. "You can't possibly still have feelings for her after all that has gone on between you."

"Of course I don't," I lied. "It's only that considering how everything turned out, I feel like a fool for deciding to get involved with her in the first place, let alone turning her. All your jabbering is like rubbing salt in the wound."

Godfrey answered, "Understandable. We'll discuss it no further."

I turned to Adrienne, who looked decidedly nervous. Her black eyes blazed, even in pitch darkness. "What's wrong, Adrienne?"

"Do you have to ask?"

"Squid? He's not dead. I'm sure of it."

"How can you be so sure?" she asked.

"Because if they'd already gotten him, they would've thrown such a huge party it would've looked like the Fourth of July. Then they would've hightailed it out of here. She's already got the village. It's him she's hanging around for; I know it. He must have pissed her off pretty good, I'd guess."

Adrienne smiled. "What you're saying makes some sense. And he is quite talented at pissing people off."

I returned her smile. My logic about Squid's safety wasn't half bad, but unfortunately, these days Lisa wasn't so logical. I only hoped I was right.

Yves heaved himself to his feet and picked up a veritable arsenal of weapons that had been supplied by our two human friends. "I'm going to start down. I figure to come in from the south, so it will take me awhile."

One of the weapons he had looked like a canon.

"What is that thing, a bazooka?" I asked.

"Yeah. What of it?" he replied, sounding irritated.

"Nothing," I said. "Be careful."

He smirked at me. "Right," he said sarcastically.

Yves quickly disappeared into the dark, inky night, and I turned to see Godfrey and Archambaud already kneeling and deep in prayer. These two were quite the pair: thousand-year-old vampires who were gay and still devout Catholics. I didn't think you could purposely design a more senseless combination of traits.

I cleared my throat. "Sorry to interrupt, but we probably ought to get moving."

The two old knights stood.

Godfrey said, "You look ill at ease, Titus. Is everything all right?"

"I'm fine," I answered. "It's only that sometimes praying makes me a bit uncomfortable."

"It's really that you don't approve, isn't it?" Archambaud replied.

We had an important task to accomplish, and I didn't want to get into a religious argument that I'd already had with these two countless times in the past. I wished I'd kept my expression more neutral, but what could I say? After seeing its effects for two thousand years, organized religion pissed me off, plain and simple. Despite my best intentions, my mouth took off by itself. "Okay. You're right. I don't approve. But it's none of my business how you spend your time."

"You're correct about that. But didn't you used to pray to your gods before battle when you were a Roman soldier?" Archambaud asked.

"Of course I did," I shot back. "But that was before I was made into a vampire. The gods sort of lost their luster after that. But I have to say, if I had to pick, I'd pick my gods over your God any day of the week."

"And why exactly can't we believe anymore just because we're vampires?" Godfrey asked.

These two were absolutely flustering when it came to their faith. I should've let it drop, but I never seem to be able to when it comes to such matters.

"Okay," I answered. "For the sake of argument, let's leave that out of it for the time being. What about when your pope betrayed you all those centuries ago after he found out that the Templars had a strong vampire membership? You and your brothers were still doing the work of your God, but that didn't stop the pope from destroying your order and slaughtering its members, vampires and humans alike. You two and Jean-Luc were lucky to escape."

Archambaud gave the infuriatingly short answer. "The pope was a man, not God."

"Your friend Jean-Luc certainly didn't look at it that way," I responded.

Godfrey shrugged. "Hugues will either come back to the Lord, or he will not. It's all in His plan."

"What about the church's discrimination against women, against gays, for God's sake?" I asked, heating up as per usual when on this topic.

Godfrey said, "Rules written by men, not God. You must have faith, Titus."

"Faith. Just another word for denial for people who don't know any better," I answered.

Godfrey retorted, "We believe this is God's earth. And if we are on it, in whatever shape or form we exist, we can only infer that he must approve of us and of us being here. In that we have faith."

Archambaud added, "And when we die, our faith will be rewarded. You'll see."

I shook my head. "No, actually I won't, unless you come back to haunt me, that is. And I really don't fancy being haunted by a couple of thousand-year-old, hyper-religious, gay vampires, if you don't mind. But do me a favor. Try not to die and see the Lord tonight. We're going to need you down in the village."

Godfrey smiled. "We do not die this night. God has spoken to us."

Adrienne chimed in. "I'd feel a lot better about that if you took a modern weapon or two with you and not just your swords. Those boys down there are armed to the teeth."

"These are the only weapons we've used for a millennium," Archambaud said. "We won't change that now. And besides, the angels watch over me tonight. We will approach from the east. See you in the village."

With that, they were off, quickly melting into the night.

I turned to Adrienne. "I guess that leaves the west to us."

She was slowly spinning her index finger at her temple. "What a couple of kooks."

"No question, but they fight like bastards."

I watched as Adrienne sheathed her sword and holstered two pistols. She wore a sleek black leotard and looked absolutely stunning. My eyes played over her petite frame, a frame that I knew from experience housed a ferocious killer, and a ferocious lover. The moment took me and I drew her into my arms and firmly kissed her.

She looked surprised, but pleasantly so. "What was that for?"

"For luck."

"A little long of a kiss for luck, wasn't it?"

I shrugged. "It's the moonlight, then. Moonlight always makes me horny."

She smiled and shook her head. "You're such an ass, Chris. Come on, let's go."

CHAPTER 34

Amy Polanski sat on the beach next to the dead boy. She looked over at him once again and broke into huge, hitching sobs. There was blood splashed all over him, and her, and she knew she'd killed him, but she couldn't clearly remember doing it.

It wasn't really her fault, but she felt horrible over it. After all, the boy was only trying to help her. How could he possibly know that Amy was a vampire, and a blood-starved one at that, who had just spent a grueling and nearly mind-shattering two days and nights trapped at the bottom of the sea? When he'd dragged her to the shore, she was in desperate need of blood, and when she saw him, she snapped. It was as simple as that.

Her eyes wanted to glance over at the boy again, but she stopped herself. *No answers over there. All that will do is get you crying again.*

Instead she looked out to sea and thought back…

~~~

Amy looked into Molly's eyes, but they were all wrong. Her brown eyes, eyes that Amy knew to be bright and lively, were dark and emotionless muddy pools. They were the eyes of a predator.

Amy's head fell forward, affording her a dimming view of the sword that had been plunged through her chest. Then Amy died.

~~~

She was floating, lolling back and forth aimlessly in a fluid coolness. It felt safe, calming even, and Amy was totally relaxed.

Then she thought, *Molly! The sword!*

Amy's eyes flew open, and a distorted, angled light flooded her vision. She reached for the wound in her chest and gasped, then gagged and coughed out water.

Water!

The realization sent panic bolting through her like a runaway mustang, uncontrollably pinging back and forth around the corners of her mind. She whipped her head from side to side, frantically searching for the help that wouldn't be there.

Desperate, she looked up to the surface where the sunbeams lightly danced on the waves a good fifty feet above her.

They thought I was dead. They threw me in the ocean to get rid of me.

Sheer terror galvanized her into an all-out swimming motion, but she couldn't move. She looked down, and tied to each of her legs was a cinder block. *Fucking Harrisons!* she thought.

Even though Amy was panicked and completely unnerved, she grimly held her breath through the burning in her lungs and worked feverishly to untie the ropes. After what seemed like centuries of feeling as if her lungs would burst at any second, she finally freed herself.

She prayed that she had enough strength and oxygen left as she propelled herself upward toward those shimmering, teasing surface waves and the sweet air above. She didn't make any headway, and despite all her efforts, she sank back to the bottom.

No, I'm a strong swimmer. This can't be.

Amy kept trying, but it did no good. She was suffocating, and her lungs felt as if they were going to explode. Amy knew she was lost, and in that last moment, she thought of her home back in Iowa and the good life she'd had there before she'd started in with the Harrisons.

Despite all of her effort and her determination to live, reflex overcame her willpower, and she took a long, deep breath. She felt the cold liquid rush into her lungs, completely smothering the delicate, oxygen-starved tissue. Amy felt as if she'd inhaled a wet towel, and a final death panic overwhelmed her.

Her heart raced uncontrollably, erratically threatening to beat its way right out of her chest as the seawater burned and corroded its way into her lungs. Amy screamed, but the sound was swallowed whole by the all-encompassing ocean. She closed her eyes, and with her last thought, she cursed Molly Harrison.

The moment played out for seconds, and then a minute, and then two.

Amy was still alive.

Slowly, she squinted one eye open, thinking superstitiously that if she did anything, anything at all, she might somehow upset some secret, magical force that was miraculously keeping her from drowning.

Both eyes flew open as another reflex kicked in, and she belched out the seawater she'd inhaled. Amy reflexively inhaled a brand new batch to replace it, recreating that horrible, smothering feeling in her lungs.

Amy's heart still fluttered around her chest like a sparrow. Her vision was still distorted by the sea, and she was still panicked, but less so than she had been. She realized she wasn't dying, at least not right at that moment, and she knew the reason why.

I'm a vampire, she thought. *That bitch fed on me and turned me into a vampire.*

That sort of realization, plus being stuck at the bottom of the ocean, would have terrified any normal person, but Amy was far from normal. She appeared to be a bit like a withering rose: slim and fair-skinned, and looking as if she were barely out of her teens. But looks can be deceiving, and Amy Polanski was from strong Iowa stock. At twenty-five years old, she was already a seasoned vampire hunter.

She pushed the circumstances leading to her fantastical troubles to the back of her mind and refused to dwell on them. Amy knew that if she became distracted and didn't solve her current problem of being trapped under the sea, all the rest wouldn't matter. She had a distinct talent for logical, methodical thinking, and even though she looked quite the opposite, Amy Polanski was a hard case.

Considering her line of work, she always knew that being turned into a vampire was a risk. She thought it sucked that it had happened to her, but there was nothing she could do about that now. She would have to deal with it later, and accept it or not, but again, that would have to wait.

Amy took some time to regulate her breathing and get used to the feeling of inhaling and exhaling seawater. She hadn't drowned yet, but she knew from her studies about vampires that eventually she would. She struck out in a random direction and began her slow trudge through the quicksand-like silt at the ocean's bottom.

By the end of two exhausting days of suffocating her way through breath after painful breath of corrosive saltwater, and two terrifying nights spent in the utter, inky darkness of the nighttime sea, Amy was nearly mad.

In the end it wasn't Amy's grit and determination that got her through. It wasn't even the complete stroke of luck of having Giorgio Zanazzi's boat trail pass right over her. It was her total and absolute need for vengeance. As she slogged along, ruined and zombielike, both blood- and oxygen-starved, she had visions of hacking Molly to bits with her very own sword. Amy vowed that she would live to see the day that Molly Harrison was dead.

CHAPTER 35

No matter how much he tried to reproduce the extraordinary power he'd harnessed the day he faced Gaius, Jean-Luc failed. He reasoned that it was some inherent talent he possessed that had been brought out by the extreme duress of the situation. He felt confident that given time, he would be able to call upon his newfound powers at will. The problem was, he wasn't confident at all as to just how much time he had. The only positive Jean-Luc could see was that Gaius had no way of knowing his astonishing new skills had deserted him, and that alone might afford him and his friends some measure of protection, at least for the time being.

Jean-Luc, Simone, and Jake had holed up under heavy guard in what Jean-Luc considered his safe house in the Garden District, just west of the Quarter. Jake's physical wounds had long since healed, but the healing of the mental wound from watching his woman, Miranda, burn alive before his eyes would be a long time coming, if at all. He'd shut himself into one of the bedrooms and wouldn't speak to anyone, save Simone, and he absolutely refused to hunt. Small amounts of blood were brought to him, which he drank inconsistently and indifferently.

The vampire community of New Orleans radiated a nervous energy due to Gaius's attack. Some had left, not wanting to be involved in a vampire war. But most stayed due to the calming influence of Jean-Luc's tested and proven leadership and the fact that rumors were already circulating concerning his defeat of Gaius and his newfound strengths. Not for the first time, Jean-Luc had to increase the security of New Orleans. This time, however, to his utter disgust, it was not because of vampire hunters, but because of other vampires.

He continued to brood, staring out into the night, when the

landline in his makeshift office rang. He picked it up quickly, hoping that finally it would be Titus.

A cold chill ran down his spine when Gaius's cheery voice came piping over the wire. "My dear Jean-Luc, how are you?"

Leclerc responded with the same false good cheer. "I'm just fine, Gaius. No thanks to you, I must say. Have you found replacements for all those bodyguards and the two Romanians?"

Gaius laughed. "Well, as you correctly assessed, the Romanians were no great loss, but all of those well-trained human pets? They'll be harder to come by. I should be quite annoyed with you Jean-Luc. And by the way, how does it feel to be a Gifted One?"

"I don't believe in fairytales any longer, and neither do you. What do you want, Gaius?"

"I want you, Hugues."

Jean-Luc tittered. "My, my, Gaius, didn't you learn enough of a lesson on your last visit? But feel perfectly free to try again anytime you desire."

"No, not like that," Gaius responded. "I want you to join me. Come to my flag if you will, and bring Simone and the computer genius, and anyone else you wish, for that matter. And how is your boy Jake doing, if I may ask?"

Jean-Luc said, "He is well, but I fear he bears you an insurmountable grudge for Miranda, as I do for Rodrigo."

"Unfortunate casualties in a disagreement that for all intents and purposes was started by Titus. I didn't attack him, and I didn't come to him—he came to me. And for what reason? Because I had the gall to take in his ex-wife, a woman he had no clue how to care for, and who was ready to commit suicide when I found her."

Jean-Luc couldn't deny that there was truth in what Gaius said. Titus had become fixated with the lost cause that Lisa represented, but that was his old friend's nature. Titus could never give up on anyone. Jean-Luc had warned him that going to Gaius's mansion was looking for trouble. But at the time he made that statement, Jean-Luc could never have imagined just how much. Titus's visit had cost the life of two of Jean-Luc's friends and severe injury to a third.

Jean-Luc remained silent.

Gaius continued, "And if I am starting a movement to assert vampire dominance, why do we need to go to war over it? Others have tried it in the past. Even my sainted aunts were involved in such plans, and you, and even Titus, *Christ* himself. Why do vampires need war over my decision? The ones who don't want to be involved don't have to be and can stay out of the way. If history is any lesson, I'll fail and likely end up dead."

"Then why try?" Jean-Luc asked. "If I somehow could manage to bring myself to trust you, which I could not, why on earth would I join a venture as doomed to failure as this?"

"Why try? Frankly, it's because I'm terminally bored. Eighteen hundred years and the same old, same old, so I figure what the hell. Take a shot at world domination. If nothing else, it'll shake things up a bit."

"Not a very convincing argument. And don't feign insanity with me. I am *not* Titus, and it will *not* affect me."

After a pause, Gaius said, "All right, let's deal with the trust issue, shall we? I realize we've had our *differences* in the past, and you more than likely think me the monster, but do you really believe you'd be dealing with me alone, as if I were some kind of dictator? Certainly, I've taken the lead in this, had to pick up the spear, if you will, but there are many of our kind behind me, even now. Elders, vampires that you know, and dare I say it, respect."

"I would need to know, of course, who exactly you are speaking of," Jean-Luc replied.

"Always the coy one, eh, Hugues?" Gaius laughed. "Let's leave that aside for now, although I hope in due time that's something I will share with you. Now, as to why try to do this when history teaches such movements are always doomed to failure, it's quite simple really. Because the time is right, and I *won't* fail.

"This world is a chaotic mess, and humans of this era are too stupid to see that they're running it into the ground. They have no faith, no belief, except in serving their own needs and in their wonderfully advancing technology and little else. They've forgotten that superstition has its basis in fact, and they've forgotten about us, except in some sappy TV shows and a few banal movies. They don't believe in us at all anymore, Hugues. It would be over for them before they knew it started."

Jean-Luc was confused. The fact that Gaius argued so logically and that what he'd said made sense was completely unsettling and made Jean-Luc more wary of him than he'd ever been before. He needed to stall for some time to think. "I'm not sure I can completely agree," he quipped. "I rather liked *Blade.*"

Gaius remained silent.

After a moment, Jean-Luc asked, "Why me?"

"Your new power, of course, and that you were a part of the leadership of what I would consider the last truly viable movement for vampire domination."

"A movement you refused to join, as I recall," Jean-Luc replied sourly.

"An oversight on my part," Gaius said. "But my dear Jean-Luc, you do have one more extremely important quality that I seek. You were a member of the First Crusade. That makes you, my friend, an expert in expeditions clearly doomed to failure that ended up succeeding."

Unsettled before, now Jean-Luc was shaken to his core by mention of the Crusade. *Ah,* he thought. *But to go on a mission of that magnitude again, a mission that actually meant something. To fully live again, not merely exist.* "I...I must think about this," he replied. "There is much to consider. But if by some miracle I were to agree, I would insist that neither Titus nor any of his friends were harmed. Further, vampires who did not wish to be part of this would be left alone."

"Titus, as you know, is quite the sticking point for me," Gaius answered, "But if you were to join me, I feel that I could agree to letting him alone, as long as he let me alone and stayed out of my affairs. As for other vampires and Titus's friends, humans included, simply put, I want all hostilities to end as soon as possible. I have far too much work and planning ahead of me to be involved in this squabble."

Jean-Luc almost couldn't believe how reasonable Gaius was being—almost. As tempted as he was by the concept of vampire domination, a concept that never strayed far from his heart, Jean-Luc knew Gaius had a multitude of reasons for this conversation. And each and every one of those reasons was to give Gaius a tactical advantage.

"Then I will give your proposal my full consideration," Jean-Luc said. "I will contact you in, shall we say, three days? May I assume we have a truce until that time?"

"You may indeed. And let's make it five days. Oh hell, let's call it a week. I'm feeling quite encouraged by our potential partnership."

Gaius hung up, leaving Jean-Luc with more than a little to think about.

~~~

Gaius Acilius sat in his sumptuously decorated office and smiled across at Davy Stein. He placed his cell phone down on his gigantic and meticulously tidy desk.

Stein returned his smile.

Gaius said, “So, Davy, what do you think?”

“I think there ain’t a chance in hell that Jean-Luc’s gonna join you,” Davy replied.

“So why did I call, then?”

“To shake him. To let him know you could find him no matter what, no matter where he hides. And to get him to slip up and spill some info.”

Gaius smiled at his new right-hand man. He began to wonder if Stein’s outer persona of an out-of-date lug was little more than an act. “I grow more impressed with you each and every day, Davy. You appear to be far smarter than you look, thank the gods.”

Stein continued to smile his fleshy-lipped and thoroughly unappealing smile. “With this mug, I sure hope so. And what you were doing wasn’t exactly rocket science. After all, I was in the Mafia all those years. Shaking people up was kind of our thing. You get anything out of him?”

Gaius grimaced. “Just that the little fuck-wad Lyons is still alive.”

“That’s bad,” Davy said. “Every contact I have says he’s an absolute wiz with the computer stuff. He could cause us some serious trouble.”

“No matter. We’ll deal with him when the time comes. But there was one even more valuable piece of information that I obtained. The Frenchman is actually considering joining me. I could hear it in his voice.”

Stein looked flummoxed. “No way. What about Titus?”

“Perhaps dear old dad doesn’t have as much influence on Jean-Luc as I thought, but to other issues. Any word from Lisa?”

“No, not yet. I know she was planning to block communications in Saint Michel, but—”

Gaius finished for him. “It isn’t like her not to check in. If there’s no word by morning, send in a second team.”

Stein nodded and wrote down the order in a small notebook he’d
~~~

recently gotten into the habit of carrying. With his vampire-enhanced memory, he hardly needed self-written reminders, but Gaius approved of his effort to ensure that he didn't make a mistake.

When he was done writing, Davy looked up and asked, "Anything else?"

Gaius smiled. "As a matter of fact, there is. Come with me."

~~~

A few moments later, Gaius and Davy entered Elise Little's "guest room". She'd been sitting, watching television, and stood to meet them as they entered. Since her capture, Gaius had read quite a bit of her writing and in fact had come to admire her. He knew she wouldn't scare easily and would remain composed to the very end.

Elise appeared calm. Her arms were folded over her chest as she waited for what was to come next. If there was any fear in her, Gaius couldn't detect it. In his very limited, emotionally stunted fashion, he actually regretted what had to be done. He'd already decided that he wouldn't toy with her or terrorize her, which would be his usual procedure for his captives. He'd simply get it over with as quickly as possible.

Elise steadily returned his gaze, as Stein fidgeted near the door.

When Gaius didn't speak, Elise broke the silence. "I didn't think it would be very long before you came for your visit."

Gaius smiled sadly. It was one of the few genuine smiles he had in his repertoire. "No, I suspected you realized that from the first."

Elise's bright blue eyes were unwavering and locked onto Gaius. He felt as if they were boring into him, draining his strength away. Uncomfortable, he had to stop himself from fidgeting right along with Stein.

"It doesn't matter what you do to me," Elise said. "Seeing Jake again, even for just that one time, makes it all worth it."

Gaius sighed. She was such a brave, loyal creature, and what he was about to do was a tragedy. But he was at war, and she was a valuable asset, and he would use her. In the end, it was as simple as that for him.

"Being such a fine author, you are undoubtedly aware of the old saying about paying for the sins of the father," he began. "In your particular case, however, it happens to be for the sins of the brother. Unfortunately for you, Elise, it's time to pay."
~~~

CHAPTER 36

Adrienne and I silently approached the dark village. There were at least a dozen infrared-goggle-wearing men guarding the main square and the access road, with more on patrol around Saint Michel. We guessed about the same number were sleeping, and from our observation, they'd scattered to different houses instead of all bunking up together. That was a wise precaution, since if they had slept in the same house, it would have made killing a large group of them a hell of a lot easier.

The few remaining townsfolk being held prisoner were locked in the tabac's basement, which was a veritable underground fortress. The tabac was on the west end of town, the direction Adrienne and I were coming in from, so we decided to try for there first. We had no idea where the rest of our party was, but if and when any one of them was discovered, he'd hit the go signal. Then all bets were off, and the fun would really start.

I had the point, and was quietly creeping forward as stealthily as could be and feeling pretty calm, when I glimpsed a black blur of movement from behind me. I whirled to see Adrienne intercept my attacker. She parried a saber blow, but then she was knocked to the ground. I flew at the assailant, and we tumbled together.

When we regained our feet, I had him pinned to the wall with my gladius cutting deeply into his neck. He couldn't shout if he wanted to—unless, that is, he could somehow manage to use my blade for a surrogate vocal cord.

I was shocked. I knew this vampire. He was a six-hundred-year-old from Philly named Thomas Carson. The guy was a bit of a tool, but as far as I knew, he'd always been levelheaded. It was stunning to think that someone like him could be involved in something like this.

"Tom? What the hell are you doing here?" I asked.

His mouth moved, but no words came out, only blood. I relaxed the pressure on my sword slightly. He hissed in a breath and whispered, "It's our time, Titus. It's time to treat the humans for what they are—cattle. Gaius is right, and you're a fool for not seeing it. He'll lead us to our true place. It's our time."

I couldn't believe this. The idea of vampire domination had of course existed throughout our history. How could it not? But such doings had always ended poorly for the vampires involved. With enlightenment and modern times, such attempts had become historical footnotes, more or less, or so I thought. I couldn't believe that in this era, Gaius had found vampires, and mature ones at that, to back him in all his foolishness. Or maybe Carson was correct. Maybe I was the fool.

That thought brought my blood, and my anger, quickly to a boil. I pushed in on my sword with all my might and slashed it horizontally across Carson's neck. Blood flew everywhere, and his head tumbled in the dirt.

Adrienne came up from behind. "No great loss there. Carson was a dick."

"Do you think we've been discovered?" I asked.

"I don't think so. You were pretty—"

Adrienne's answer was cut short by a high-pitched rocket-propelled grenade trail, followed by an ear-shattering explosion.

We looked at each other and said the same thing. "Yves."

I shifted my gladius to my left hand and drew my Glock. Adrienne sheathed her sword and hefted the shotgun she'd taken along.

"He could've signaled like we planned," I said. "You know, with the walkie-talkie."

She smiled. "Not his style."

"No, I suppose not," I answered just as the black sedans of Gaius's henchmen started blowing up into fiery wrecks, one after the next. "Doc and Cat-Juice?"

"Uh-huh," Adrienne replied. "That's definitely their style."

Gunfire started up, and I could see muzzle flashes coming from the cathedral tower. It seemed that Mr. Juice had, quite impressively, made it up there unnoticed after all. Not bad for a human.

"You ready?" I asked.

"Always, darling," Adrienne answered. She raced around the

corner into the melee, with me close on her heels.

We went straight at the tabac. I gunned down the human guard, and Adrienne shotgunned the vampire. He appeared to be a fledgling, poor fellow. He staggered to his feet, and Adrienne used her sword on him, pretty much cleaving the unfortunate bastard in two.

We opened the basement door and found only three hostages left. One was the young man who had "shared" with me. The others were a middle-aged woman I didn't know and an elderly gentleman.

The woman said, "Father, we knew you would come."

Adrienne raised an eyebrow. "Father?"

"Long story," I said. "We don't have time."

Adrienne pointed at the older man. "Is that the chef?"

I nodded.

"Godfrey *will* be pleased," Adrienne replied. Handing him her shotgun, she added, "We're going to lock the door again. If anyone opens it without first identifying themselves, shoot them."

"Oui, ma mere," the chef replied.

Adrienne threw me an annoyed look. "What's all this mother and father shit, Titus?"

I laughed. "I told you, later."

We hurried back to the square. The place was lit up like a Christmas tree, and with all the dead bodies and gunfire and burning wrecked cars, it looked like a scene from a cheesy old World War II movie. Except there wasn't one slice of cheese here. This was the real deal.

I saw a group of Lisa's men taking cover behind a wall and laying down heavy fire on a building where Yves had taken cover. Thinking about how they'd abused the sweet people in this village, I totally lost it and ran right at them, firing my pistol empty and then dropping it along the way. This was going to be fun.

"No, Titus," Adrienne shouted.

I heard her footsteps fall in behind me as I took several bullets on the way in. The only upside was that I ended up shielding Adrienne. One of the men hefted a flamethrower and pointed it in my direction.

Oh shit!

I put on a burst of speed I didn't think I had in me, and suddenly I was among them, hacking away. Limbs and blood flew everywhere, and Adrienne soon joined in. We hushed their screams with the silence of death. In the end, we'd killed seven men behind this little wall. By the time I got to the last one, I'd worked myself into a frenzy and kept hacking him to pieces well after he was dead.

Adrienne put an arm on my shoulder. "Titus, I think you got him."

I looked down at the bloody mess and partially came to my senses. "Sorry, I guess I did," I replied, somewhat mortified.

I was hoping the square was secure, but heavy machine-gun fire started up, coming from the right. Once again, Adrienne and I took off toward the source of the clamor. We rounded a corner to see Archambaud backed to a wall, being peppered to the ground by two machine gunners.

The shooters stopped to reload, but as they did, one of them waved up a man with a flamethrower who'd been waiting behind. They were going to cook Archambaud, and we were too far away to do anything about it. The man with the flamethrower stepped up, aimed his nozzle, and his head exploded. I turned to the cathedral tower just in time to see the muzzle flash of the second shot that must have taken the tank on his back, because in the next instant he exploded, taking the two machine gunners with him.

When we got to Archambaud, he was a bloody mess and barely able to heave himself to his feet. He smiled and glanced up at the cathedral tower. "You see, Titus. I told you the angels watch over me."

"Godfrey?" I asked.

"I don't know," he answered. "We were separated."

The gunfire was petering out, and Adrienne said, "Come on. Let's get back to the square."

When we arrived, to my great relief Godfrey was there, and so was the rest of my team, all alive and well. Yves had a burn across the right side of his face, but he was beginning to heal. Cat-Juice and Doc stood on opposite sides of the square, keeping guard and looking particularly nasty with their full body armor and camouflage face paint. Neither appeared to have a scratch on him.

Archambaud embraced Godfrey and then strutted over to Cat-Juice. The petite Frenchman pulled him down to his five-foot-and-change level and kissed him on both cheeks, smearing him with his spilled blood. Rather than wipe it off, Cat-Juice seemed to wipe it in, adding it to his face paint and making him look absolutely fucking crazy, as opposed to just plain crazy.

"It appears I am in your debt," Archambaud said. "And once again, you have my apologies."

The Juice was in full military mode, stiff and formal. "Apology accepted, sir, but no debt. I was only doing my job."

"I see," Archambaud said. "I wonder if you might indulge me then and tell me how you came by your name."

Still at attention, looking straight ahead and well over the head of Archambaud, the soldier replied, "If you were to acquire that information, I'd have to kill you, sir."

With that, the large man looked down at Archambaud and cracked the briefest of smiles. The Frenchman's tittering laughter was drowned out by the roar of a motorcycle that suddenly filled the square, echoing from stonewall to stonewall.

I turned to see Lisa speeding away on a dirt bike, heading directly toward the access road. It was odd, but I hadn't thought about her once during the entire battle. Then again, maybe it wasn't so odd.

Doc quickly dropped to the ground and fired a short burst, exploding Lisa's rear tire. She pitched over the handlebars, but executed a perfect roll, coming to her feet smoothly and at a full sprint. She bolted down the hill.

Godfrey let out a bellowing war cry and took off after her, broadsword in hand.

Lisa didn't have a chance. Even with her substantial head start, it wouldn't take long before the thousand-year-old Frenchman ran her to ground. I felt absolutely nothing for her.

A moment later, I heard a car start up, followed by the squeal of tires. A few minutes after that, Godfrey returned.

"She got away," he said. "There was a car hidden just outside of town."

"Damn it, Doc!" Cat-Juice shouted. "I said I wanted all of their cars disabled."

"Sorry, Juice. I didn't know it was there. It must've been well hidden."

"No one is to blame," Adrienne said. "She's a crafty one. She looked around the square and added, "What should we do now?"

"If I may, ma'am," Doc answered. "We should split into teams and make sure the village is secured from hostiles. We can search for the villagers while we're doing it."

A voice from across the square answered, "I'm with you on the hostiles, but no need to search for the villagers."

I turned to see the Squid, as big as life, walking down the front stairs of the cathedral, followed by a steady stream of townsfolk.

He caught my eye and shot me a crooked grin and a wink. "Jesus, Chrissy, it took you long enough."

CHAPTER 37

Elise Little spiraled down and down, accelerating out of control into the black void. She had no conception of where she was or how she'd gotten there. In fact, she barely could recollect who she was.

She spun faster and faster, defying and then breaking the laws of physics. She tried to remember the chain of events that had led her to this, but she failed. The wind whistled by her at speeds that should have ripped her limb from limb, but Elise felt perfectly fine. In fact, she felt better than she ever had.

Even though she was in the midst of this frightening freefall, Elise broke out into laughter, exhilarated as the wind howled by, ruffling her strawberry-blond hair.

I'm dreaming, she thought. *I must be dreaming.*

The instant she thought it, though, she knew it wasn't true. She may have not been in a dream world, but she wasn't exactly a part of reality, either. At that moment, she just *was.*

Elise closed her eyes and smiled, luxuriating in the sensation of flying through this dark emptiness. When she opened them, in the distance she saw an insignificant speck of color. It grew rapidly as she sped along.

Elise was shocked when the speck grew large enough for her to recognize it as Jimmy Burke, her high school sweetheart. She plunged by, looking over her shoulder, and thought, *How can this be?*

Next it was her best friend from fifth grade, then an old college roommate, her long-dead great aunt, and dozens of other people from her life, coming faster and more frequently as she careened ahead.

She saw her first editor, the man she'd nearly married when she was twenty-seven, and then, far in the distance and long before it should have been humanly possible to do so, she recognized her father. He was the overweight, alcohol bloated version, before the heart attack took him; the way he'd been when he'd begun to beat her and tried to rape her.

Daddy-dearest reached toward Elise with a lecherous grin, and she did her best to veer away from him. She broke into a sweat, her pulse racing with the effort as he lunged out for her. Elise screamed soundlessly, tightly slamming her eyes shut, and when she opened them, her father was gone.

Elise breathed a sigh of relief, but now she was alarmed. Who would she see next? It turned out to be her mother, the drug-addled matriarch of her family, who'd stood by and done nothing even though she'd known what her husband had attempted to do to Elise.

Elise didn't try to veer away this time. She tried to get closer. Her anger flared, and she wanted to grab her mother, throttle her, and strike her again and again for failing to defend her against the monster her father had become.

As much as she tried, though, Elise couldn't come near her. As she sped past, her mom serenely waved *bye-bye*, her eyes vacant and stoned, as they always were.

Finally, she saw him, Jake, and she knew he'd have the answers. He'd tell her what was happening. He'd keep her safe. Elise thought for sure she'd slow to a stop to be with her big brother, and everything would be all right. But she didn't slow down.

She began pinwheeling her arms and legs to try to stop, but it did no good. Elise sped by him just as with all the others.

As she looked back at him, he mouthed silently, "I'm so sorry, Little Red. Be careful."

Tears welled up in her eyes as Jake grew smaller and smaller and then disappeared into the darkness with the rest of them.

Elise flew faster into the abyss, spiraling forever downward. In the distance, she once again saw a tiny speck beginning to take form, this time directly in her path. Although still too distant to recognize who it was, Elise was filled with dread. She was sure this person was to be the last on her journey through the looking glass, her last stop. But this was no *Alice in Wonderland*, no child's fairytale by a long stretch.

As the figure grew, her eyes confirmed what her heart already knew. Waiting for her at the end of this inky blackness was Gaius Acilius. Acilius's oversized predator's smile grew impossibly larger and larger, and suddenly she remembered everything, all that had happened to her at his hands.

Throwing her body back, she arched her spine to the breaking point in an attempt to force herself to stop. She tried to scream, but there was no sound. Acilius threw back his head and roared silent laughter. His mouth was now filled with razor-sharp fangs, and his eyes glowed red as he opened his arms insincerely in a perverse parody of welcome.

In the last instant before the end, Elise regained her self-control. She stopped fighting. She knew it would do no good. Clearheaded, with her journalist's eye, Elise Little calmly studied the monster that awaited her, and she saw it all. She wished she'd have the opportunity to write an editorial about this, about Gaius Acilius, but she knew she never would.

Elise hurtled forward to meet her fate.

CHAPTER 38

Bill and Molly Harrison followed the elderly butler through the maze of Gaius Acilius's huge California mansion. From the outside, the building appeared forbidding to Bill, and seeing it from the inside did nothing to dissuade him from his opinion.

The guards at the front door had confiscated Bill's shotgun, but nothing else. They didn't even bother to take Molly's sword, and only searched the two of them in the most superficial manner. Bill supposed the vampire thought this to be a gesture of good faith, but even after their initial brief meeting, he thought Acilius didn't have one speck of good faith in him. That was all right by Bill; when it came to vampires, neither did he.

Directly after the guards were through with them, the butler had made his appearance and introduced himself as Richard. With a gesture, he bade them to follow. He'd said nothing after that, and now, only the echoes of their footfalls, ricocheting around the stone walls and high ceilings, broke the ominous silence. Bill had never been in a private residence even close to this large before.

As they marched on and on without reaching their destination, he thought, *Hell, with this much walking, we ought to be in the next state by now.*

His fascination with the vampire's mansion didn't take away from the fact that he was scared—for himself, and more so, for Molly. He'd been in an uncountable number of dangerous situations in his life, but at that moment, he felt as if they all might be like a stroll in the park compared to what he'd have to face here.

But what choice did he have? If they were to have any chance of reversing the effects of Steve's drug, they'd have to have the help of a vampire. And the list of vampires who would come to the aid of Bloody Bill Harrison was mighty short. In fact, the only name on it was Gaius Acilius.

As if sensing Bill's tension, Molly spoke up. "This might not have been the best idea we've ever had, Dad."

"No arguing there," Bill replied. "I'm about as jumpy as a fart in a skillet."

Molly laughed. Even though she'd heard her father use that line a million times, it always cracked her up.

Bill laughed along with her.

"You know, it might have been smarter to bring the entire crew with us," she said, "instead of leaving them holed up safe in that hotel. Force of numbers."

Bill shook his head. "Nah. Even if we brought an army, if Acilius wanted to spring a trap in this joint, none of us would walk out alive. Besides, they're anything but safe. This is his country, and I'd wager he knows exactly where they are. If something goes wrong, at least this way they'll have a fighting chance."

"Yeah, I see your point," Molly agreed. "But do you think we should have told him about the PEDA over the phone like that? Before we met in person?"

Bill shrugged. "We had to tell him sometime. I wanted to make sure we had his attention, that's all. Couldn't risk having the meeting fizzle before it got started. Then where'd we be?"

They once again walked on in silence.

"We should've sent Steve," Molly said. "You know, as a first emissary. He did invent the drug, after all. If Acilius killed him, no great loss."

Bill looked down at his daughter and smiled.

Molly smiled right back, her eyes glowing with dark humor.

"I sure wish you'd come up with that before," Bill chortled. "When it comes to your hubby, that's the best idea you've had in a long time."

Molly's reply was stopped short when Richard ushered her and Bill into the great room of Gaius Acilius.

This isn't a room, Bill thought. *It's a cathedral.*

His eyes were drawn upward to the ceilings, which were at least fifty feet high, vaulted, with high arches reminiscent of the churches of medieval times. Authentic-looking, ancient stained-glass windows lined the long sides of the rectangular room, and although he couldn't be sure, Bill thought they were backlit with artificial light, not natural. After the serpentine journey they'd taken to get here, going up and down multiple flights of stairs, he wasn't completely sure of his bearing. But if he had to bet, he'd wager they were deep inside the building, far too deep for any sunlight to reach.

The great room, like the rest of the house, was dominated by flat, cold, gray stone. Here, however, richly stained, wide wooden beams and intricate moldings had been added for accent and gave this place a touch more warmth than the other parts of the mansion that Bill had seen on his long march to get here.

Four huge matching crystal chandeliers hung the length of the room and gave off a mellow golden light. A fire that blazed in the oversized fireplace, which dominated the far end of the chamber, added a vacillating orange-toned light to the room and created dancing dark shadows in the corners and along the walls.

To the right and in front of the fireplace, sitting on what appeared to be a wooden throne on a small dais, was Gaius Acilius. With one leg casually slung over an arm of his chair, he leaned back, chin to hand. Studying a fresco of an olive grove painted on one of the walls of the great room, Acilius patently ignored the new arrivals.

Bill finished his look around the impressive room and then glanced at Molly, who nodded her readiness. Richard had discreetly moved to one side and stood patiently waiting. Bill figured the butler was well used to this sort of gawking response from first-time visitors. When Richard saw the guests were ready, he gestured them forward.

As they started their walk toward Acilius, their footsteps acted as a signal and he stood to face them, his smile growing with every step.

If we had to walk any longer, he'd end up looking like a barracuda, Bill thought.

They came to a stop at the foot of the dais, and Acilius spread his arms in welcome. "Bill and Molly Harrison, I'm so happy you could come." Acilius descended the three steps of the platform and extended his hand to Bill, who shook it without hesitation. Next, he took Molly's hand and formally bent down and kissed it.

She rolled her eyes at her father over the vampire's head.

When he rose, Acilius's eyes sparkled with a malevolent glee. "May I offer you some refreshments?"

"No thanks," Bill replied. "We'd rather get down to business."

"Really? I've opened a lovely pinot noir that I thought you might like," Acilius said, sounding disappointed. When there was no response from the Harrisons, he continued, "Very well. Richard, you're dismissed."

The butler bowed and quickly exited through a small side door that Bill hadn't noticed before. He wondered what else he hadn't noticed about the room. "Your butler must need a GPS to find his way around here," he said.

Acilius waved dismissively. "Oh, you mean Richard. He's a footman, actually. You wouldn't know of any good butlers, would you, Bill? Mine left quite suddenly, as it were, so I'm in the market."

Bill scoffed. "I'm afraid I left my list of butlers at home."

Acilius smiled dryly. "Yes, I suppose you did. Before we start, I'd like to introduce my associate Davy Stein." The vampire gestured toward an alcove.

A stocky, dark-haired man stepped out of the shadows. He wore an outlandish maroon suit, accented by an extra-wide purple floral tie. His fleshy face was adorned with a bland smile.

Bill knew he was a vampire by the way he moved.

"Meet'cha," Stein said, tipping an imaginary hat in the Harrisons' direction.

Sounding somewhat alarmed, Molly whispered, "The lighting. It's by design. It throws off your vision somehow."

Acilius laughed. "Good golly, Miss Molly, aren't you the suspicious one? You have nothing to fear. We *are* allies, after all."

"Being suspicious around vampires is good for my health," Molly shot back.

Acilius grinned. "Oh, really? Perhaps you should start being suspicious around yourself then."

Molly was about to respond, but stopped short when the meaning of what the vampire had said sunk in.

Bill jumped in before things took a turn for the worse. "Okay, okay. We're very impressed with your big room here and your camouflage lighting. But if you're all out of tricks from the shadows, can we just get to it?"

"How about one more trick?" asked a female voice from a murky corner on the opposite side of the room.

Bill turned to face it, but as much as he stared into the darkness there, he couldn't make out a person. It was like trying to see into a black hole.

High-heeled footsteps echoed from the shadows as the owner of that hidden voice approached. "I'm insulted that you didn't introduce me to our guests, Gaius, but then again, I've already had the pleasure. I'm so, so hurt that you don't recognize me, Bloody Fucking Bill."

The thing was, Bill did recognize the voice, only he couldn't place it right away.

Lisa Brownell stepped out of the shadows and came to a stop about twenty feet away from Bill and Molly. She wore a long, blood-red dress with a side slit going pretty much up to her neck. Her "fuck-me" pumps were as black as coal and shinier than diamonds. She placed her hands on her hips and spread her feet wide enough for her dress slit to show every inch of her well-turned thigh. Her ruby-red lips stretched into a calm, predatory smile, and she only had eyes for Bill.

Bill said, "Oh shit."

Lisa answered, "You're right about that, old man."

Molly drew her sword, but Bill put out his hand and said, "Stand down, Molly. Put that thing away."

"But Dad, that's the one you…held prisoner at the farm on the night of the attack," Molly replied. "I recognize her. She's one of them now."

Bill looked at Lisa. "Yep, she is. And none too happy with me, I reckon. But sheath that sword and step back. This is between Lisa and me."

Molly reluctantly did as she was told.

Bill went on. "Acilius has us here on business, important business. I don't think he's gonna let something as petty as this get in the way."

Acilius shrugged, smiled smugly, and reseated himself on his "throne". Stein kept his place, and Lisa didn't move. She was so still she might have been mistaken for a slutty mannequin in one of those high-end and very fashionable women's boutiques.

"You sure about this, Dad?" Molly asked.

Without taking his eyes off Lisa, Bill replied, "No, not really."

In fact, not taking preemptive action on an impending attack went against every fiber of his being. But if he and his daughter and the rest of his team were going to be cured of the effects of Steve's enhancing drug, effects that seemed to have them well on the way to become vampires, they'd need Acilius's help. Bill would not destroy that chance now by starting a shoot-out and killing Lisa Brownell.

Bill's flinty eyes locked onto Lisa's for what seemed an eternity. He had never been the shy, retiring type, and a grin formed on his face. "You know, Lisa, after that little workout I gave you in my torture chamber, I'm kind of surprised you let yourself get turned. Didn't I show you the error of your ways?"

Stein stifled a nervous cough with his hand, but Acilius laughed out loud.

Lisa's smile faltered, and her eyes turned murderous. She spat out, "You think you're funny, you slimy old pervert? You're going to pay for what you did to me."

Bill scoffed. "Is that all you can do is talk? Come on, bitch, let's see what you got."

Lisa's eyes went flat cold, and the corner of her mouth twitched a time or two. Bill expected her to run at him, but to her credit, she started for him with an unhurried but determined walk.

Bill's hand wanted to drop to the butt of his pistol, and it took every bit of willpower he possessed to stop it from doing so. As she made her final approach, she reached behind her back and quickly pulled something out. In the last instant, Bill recognized it for what it was—a Taser.

He didn't move to defend himself as she jammed the Taser directly into his crotch. An indescribable electric jolt of pain coursed through his testicles and up into his abdomen, and every muscle in his body spasmed. His knees unhinged, and he dropped to the floor like a stone.

"There, you dirty old fuck!" Lisa screamed. "How do you like that?" She began raining kicks down upon him.

He tried to turn away and cover up as best he could. As he did, he saw Molly racing forward, her sword drawn once again.

Stein moved in fast and tackled her, but Molly rolled with it and smoothly double kicked him across the room. He crashed head first into the wall and fell to the floor, unconscious.

Lisa intently continued to kick Bill for all she was worth, completely unaware of Molly and the danger she was in. Bill actually intended to warn her, but it was too late.

From his position on the floor he had an excellent view of Lisa's severed arm, still holding the Taser, as it tumbled through the air, spraying blood out in every direction. In Bill's injured, Tasered state, things seemed to be moving in super slow motion.

Lisa screamed and screamed.

Bill thought absently, *If she'd introduced herself by screaming, I would have recognized her right off. That's exactly how she sounded when I hooked the electrodes to her. Well, her head should be joining her arm any minute now. So much for this meeting.*

Bill looked up, expecting to see just that, but Molly's death stroke was caught in the grip of Gaius Acilius. His voice was low and deadly, completely devoid of its false gaiety. "That's quite enough of that. Give me that damn sword."

Molly continued to struggle.

"Don't make me hurt you."

Molly paused, handed over the sword, and went to her father.

Acilius quieted Lisa, reattached her arm, and set her on his seat on the dais. Next he went to Stein and got him on his feet. By the time Acilius returned to the Harrisons, Bill was already standing, although feeling decidedly shaky.

The vampire eyed him up and down. "You shouldn't be standing already. As a matter of fact, you ought to be dead after that beating. You've taken the drug as well, haven't you?"

Bill shrugged.

Acilius went on. "I already knew about your daughter, but you didn't want to tip your hand to us that you were in the same boat, hmmm, Billy-boy?"

Bill rubbed his shoulder where he'd received a particularly nasty kick, but he noted it was already feeling better. And even after Lisa's high-test electric shock therapy, his balls were a lot better as well. They no longer felt as if they were stuck in his throat, and in fact, seemed to have made their way down to somewhere in the middle of his chest and clearly en route back to where they belonged. *I can't believe I'm feeling better so soon,* he thought. *This damn drug is incredible.* He replied, "I just didn't want to screw up our meeting before it got started, that's all."

The vampire smiled. "Oh, there's that, but there's my surmise as well. You are a crafty old fucker, aren't you, Bill? I think I could get to like you."

"What about you?" Bill said. "You must have your reasons for letting this little act play out."

Acilius's eyes told Bill he was correct, but the vampire said,

"Nope. Just for kicks."

Bill scoffed. "Right, just for kicks. And what about having Lisa Brownell here with you? She's Julian's ex, as I recall. I suppose that's just another big fat coincidence, is it?"

"No, not this time. I actively sought her out to piss Titus off," Acilius said, "but as luck would have it, our relationship has bloomed. Rest assured, however, Titus and I could not be any further apart in philosophy."

Lisa chimed in. "If he'd been here today, old man, I would've ripped his balls off instead of just electrocuting them."

Bill thought they both sounded quite sincere, but he asked, "Why the same name?"

Acilius's look grew stony. "He turned me. Any more questions?"

Assessing the look in Acilius's eyes, Bill decided there weren't any more, even though there were several. He shook his head.

"Wonderful," Acilius said with a broad smile. He turned his attention to Molly. "And you, Molly, disposing of my Davy so easily. He's nearly a hundred, you know, and you flicked him off like a flea. I'm impressed."

Molly remained silent.

Acilius held out her sword. "Keep this in its sheath."

Molly took her weapon and put it away. "Then you keep your bitch under control."

For a moment it looked as if Acilius would fire back a nasty reply, but he shrugged apologetically and put on a small, almost boyish smile. Despite the fact that he was an ancient and very unstable vampire, the effect was totally disarming.

He sighed. "I'll try."

~~~

When everyone had calmed down sufficiently, Acilius moved the group to an office just off the great room. They sat around a boardroom-size table, with the Harrisons well apart from Lisa Brownell. Despite the previous declination, the alluded-to pinot noir made its appearance, and as billed, was lovely.

The Harrisons handed over the specifications of the PEDA 17. Steve had redacted the production details and had added several small mistakes into the chemistry of the drug. He was sure it wouldn't hurt the vampires' analysis of it, but would prevent them from reproducing the compound, at least initially. Unfortunately, however,
~~~

to get the help they needed, they also agreed to hand over a sample of the drug to Acilius. With that, Steve felt it was 50/50 at best as to whether the vampires would be able to reproduce it on their own.

Bill knew it was a chance they had to take, and he didn't feel the need for such secrecy about the compound. He reasoned that they had no choice and that Acilius and his group were already vampires, so what difference could the drug possibly make to them? Steve had argued that he wasn't at all sure what the drug was capable of at this point, and pushed for caution. In the end, Bill took his advice and let him alter the design specifications before they handed it over.

After about an hour and a half, the meeting was winding down.

Bill said, "About this vampire bar in Montreal, you never did explain why it's our target."

Acilius smiled. "That's right, I didn't. Suffice it to say the owner is, by association, an enemy of mine, and I want to teach her a little lesson. Since you now have the location and the plans of the building, why does it matter? You'll likely be able to kill more vampires there in one swoop than you have in your entire career. Quite an achievement, yes?"

Bill didn't believe Acilius at all. "Might not get the owner, and a lot of your kind who have nothing to do with this fight will get killed."

"I don't care in the least, and neither should you. It's a job, and after all, you're only killing vampires." Acilius smiled broadly and went on. "Oh, wait. That might matter to you now. I almost forgot."

Bill smirked, and Molly added, "One more thing. There'll be eight of us going up against maybe a hundred or more. Who knows? Five million isn't going to cut it. We want ten."

Lisa spouted, "Ten million, my ass. Don't listen to this crap, Gaius. Five was too much. Let me take care of this little girl. I've handled tougher deals selling houses in Needham."

Molly smirked. "I doubt you left your arm on the floor during any of your open houses, bitch."

Lisa's color drained, and she slowly stood. Molly remained seated, but her hand rested lightly on the hilt of her sword.

"Lisa, sit down," Gaius said sternly.

For a moment it looked as if she would attack Molly, but after several seconds and seemingly with great effort, Lisa took her seat.

Gaius shook his head. "You two will really have to learn to play nice. Regarding your proposal, I'll agree to the ten million, but I need something additional from the two of you: blood samples, and right now. I think three tubes each should suffice."

Bill was taken aback by the request, but he could think of no good reason to refuse at this point. They'd already handed over the drug, and the vampires having some of their blood to analyze might give some additional information to help in reversing the effects of the PEDA. "Okay," he said.

Stein produced blood-drawing equipment from a drawer in the table and did the honors. When he was finished, he presented the six tubes to Gaius, who immediately opened one of Bill's and one of Molly's. The Harrisons watched with fascination as the three vampires sipped and swished their blood before swallowing it. After drinking the pinot noir earlier, this display struck Bill as the oddest wine tasting he'd ever seen.

Acilius turned to Stein. "What do you think, Davy?"

Stein took another sip and actually gargled it a little.

Molly laughed and had to cover her mouth with her hand to stop herself from totally cracking up.

Stein shot her an annoyed look. He took one more swish of blood and said, "It's okay, but not great, Gaius. Not dead flat like vampire blood, but nowhere near human. Like it's been watered down, and a lot."

Acilius turned to Lisa. "You?"

She answered, "I think Davy is correct."

"Agreed," Acilius said. He turned to the Harrisons, sporting his usual false smile. "I've got some good news and some bad news, totally depending on your perspective. You're not quite vampires yet, but it shouldn't be too, too much longer."

~~~

Once the Harrisons left, Acilius turned to Stein. "When the girl attacked you, what did it feel like?"

Stein appeared thoughtful. "Nowhere near someone like you, Gaius, but powerful. I'd put her at three or four hundred years a vampire, if she was a day."

Acilius rubbed his chin, thinking. "That's just how it appeared. Davy, this drug of theirs may be quite a danger. Get it and the blood samples to our people right away."

Davy stood to leave, but hesitated. "Can I ask you something
~~~

before I go?"

Acilius nodded.

"Why send them to Montreal? News travels fast, and Adrienne is no dope. She'll know being a friend of Titus puts her at risk with you. She's gonna be ready."

Acilius smiled, thinking not for the first time that Stein was not the idiot he appeared. He might not have all the answers, but he certainly could be counted on to ask the right questions. "Harrison doesn't trust us, so he'll be prepared as well. He'll know I'm sending him into a nasty situation, but what choice does he have? It'll be a test for them to see how good they are, and who knows, Bloody Bill might get lucky and kill that nasty bitch Adrienne. Won't that just rankle dear old Dad and that big idiot friend of his? And if the Harrisons get wiped out, so be it. They may prove to be too dangerous to handle in the long run, anyway. At the very least, it'll send a strong message to any who might oppose us."

Davy glanced over at Lisa. "Why'd you let Lisa attack the old man?" he asked Gaius.

"Two reasons. It was a test of her self-restraint. I allowed her to exact revenge for the torture Harrison subjected her to, and she promised not to kill him. I'm afraid she failed miserably in this."

"I didn't fail at all," Lisa insisted, pouting. "I didn't kill him."

"Random chance," Acilius replied. "He survived only because he was enhanced, and his daughter intervened."

Lisa folded her arms across her chest, her pout dramatically increasing. "Well, at least I didn't kill him on the first pass."

Acilius reached out and took her hand. "There's that, my love."

"You said there were two reasons," Davy said. "What's the second?"

Acilius smiled widely. "The same as I told Bloody Bill—just for kicks."

CHAPTER 39

Amy washed her clothes in the ocean water and laid them out on the beach to dry. She looked up into the beautiful blue sky, and for the first time the thought struck her, *I'm not burning. The sun's not burning me.* "At least there's that," she said out loud. She smiled. "I'm really more of a day person, anyway."

Amy napped naked in the warmth of the noonday sun. When she awoke, she dressed and once again looked over at the dead boy. He was covered in dried blood. As she looked at that blood, her body told her that she would need more of it, and soon. But she would have to deal with that later. For now, Amy felt that she had to do her best by the boy.

She carried him down to the waves and gently washed the blood from him. She planned to bury him on the beach even though she had his boat, and the sea beckoned. She could never dispose of him that way, not after the ordeal she had suffered in the ocean's depths.

Amy found an oar in the boat and used it to dig a shallow grave on the beach. It went far easier than it would have if she were still human. Even though she dug through sand and rocks in the hot afternoon sun, she didn't even come close to breaking a sweat.

Amy laughed. "This vampire crap might come in handy after all. From here on in, yard work is gonna be a breeze."

The dead boy lay serenely next to the makeshift grave. All that was left to do was to drag him in and cover him up.

Amy hesitated, looking at him. He was so young and handsome, pretty almost. As she continued staring at him, spellbound, a terrible thought struck her. "Oh, no," she said out loud. "He could turn." She paced up and down the beach. She'd had a lot to deal with over the past few days and hadn't even once considered the consequences of her new feeding habits. Amy stopped and shouted to the sky, "God damn it!" She ran back to the grave and picked up the oar. She raised it up to smash the boy's head. Her eyes filled with tears. "I'm sorry. I can't let this happen. I can't take the chance."

The boy took a small breath, instantly shattering Amy's resolve.

She dropped the oar and flopped down next to him, sobbing. She looked over at the vampire she had made.

He took another small breath.

~~~

It would be soon now. The boy's breathing was more regular, his chest rising and falling with increasing depth, and his color had greatly improved. While she waited, Amy tried to logically map out what her next moves would be. Her planning was concise, logical, and to the point. After all, she was a disciple of Bloody Bill Harrison.

Thinking of him made Amy fully realize the predicament she was in. She was going to kill Molly, there was no denying that. But if that were true, she'd have to kill Bill as well, and Bloody Bill was not an easy man to kill. Well, she'd just have to cross that bridge when she came to it.

More importantly, she and her new companion were going to need blood. The PEDA-changed vampires seemed to require less of it than their more naturally occurring cohorts, but she wasn't at all sure where she fell on that spectrum. At this point, she didn't acutely need blood, at least not yet.

Amy was sure that she could get the specs for PEDA 17, since she knew all the computer codes of her former colleagues, and they thought her dead. She was reasonably sure she could make the drug. She'd helped Steve on more than one occasion. But getting her hands on specimens of HVSV and the other materials needed was another matter.

Oh well, another bridge to cross, she thought.

One thing she did know for sure was that she would not make any more vampires. She may have cracked on this first one, this boy, due to guilt and her fragile state of mind, but he would be both the first and the last. She'd been a hunter too long not to realize what a blight on the world vampires were, and now she was one. She would kill each and every "donor" from here on in.

A particularly long, deep breath from the boy got her attention, and she looked over just as his eyes blinked open. He put his hands behind his head and looked up at the sky in the perfect repose for
~~~

contemplating life after waking up from a particularly restful nap alfresco. He looked wholly relaxed until he took a quick, harsh breath. His hand flew up to his neck, searching for the wound that was no longer there.

He sat up suddenly and appeared frightened, with his eyes flitting about the beach until they rested on Amy. "*Dove si torva la vecchia strega?*" he asked.

Amy shook her head. "*Non parlo italiano. Parli inglese?*"

"Where is that old hag?" he repeated in perfect, though accented, English. He looked more closely at Amy, his eyes narrowed in concentration. Then they opened wide in shock. "It's you! You attacked me. You're that old crone." He scuttled backward away from her until his back struck the harsh cliff wall and he had nowhere else to run.

He panted in terror as Amy approached him slowly with her arms open in what she hoped was a gesture of friendliness. "I don't know what old hag you're talking about, but. . ."Amy stopped, realizing that she was the hag. She could only imagine what she'd looked like when he first saw her. From her experience as a hunter, she knew just how much new vampires could degenerate if they didn't get blood fairly soon after being turned. *Throw in a few days underwater*, she thought. *I must have looked like something straight out of a nightmare*. She laughed. "I guess that hag *was* me. But I'm better now."

"How can that be?" he asked, his eyes still wide. "You were hideous, and now, your eyes are so blue, your hair like the sun. You're beautiful."

Typical Italian. And you're not so bad yourself, kiddo, Amy thought as she admired how the boy's turning had made him even more handsome than he had been as a human. She smiled. "What's your name?"

"Giorgio. Giorgio Zanazzi."

Amy's smile widened. "Giorgio. I like that. Well, Giorgio, we have a lot to talk about. Can you get us out of here on that boat of yours?"

Giorgio looked insulted. "Of course."

"Good. First stop, Positano. After that, who knows? I have to find some. . . friends of mine, and Giorgio, I want you to come with me. Truth is, you really need to come with me. After what happened to you, I think it's your only chance."

With that kind of a lead, Amy expected a dozen questions to follow, but Giorgio was silent. He stared intently at her, his coal-black eyes drilling into hers so fixedly she felt as if her knees would buckle.

Finally, he asked, "Where would we go?"

Amy laughed a bit nervously under his scrutiny. "I don't know. Everywhere."

With that, his laser-like stare let up, and his eyes softened. His face took on an expression that Amy easily recognized. Wanderlust.

"Before we leave, if I decide to go, you will explain all to me?"

Amy replied, "I'll cover most of it on the boat ride."

Giorgio nodded. "I would insist on seeing my father before we left."

Amy weighed the pros and cons of doing this, with the scale tipping precipitously to the con side. Even so, she knew there'd likely be no stopping her new apprentice from seeing his father if he wanted to.

"Sure, what the hell." She chuckled. "I'd love to meet your dad."

"What would we be doing in all our travels?" Giorgio asked.

Amy thought of Molly and smiled a small, tight smile. "Looking for some old friends of mine. And the beauty of it is they have no idea I'll be coming. It will be such a surprise."

Giorgio looked as if he wanted to ask more about this, but he didn't. He swallowed, grimacing slightly. "I'm so thirsty."

Amy nodded. "We'll cover that on the boat ride, too."

The boy shrugged, walked over to where the oar was, and picked it up from the sand. For the first time, he noticed the shallow furrow that Amy had dug into the beach. He stared down at it for a moment and then at Amy. "You were going to bury me there! I was dead?"

Amy shrugged apologetically. "Boat ride."

Giorgio stared inquisitively at her for a moment and then started walking toward the boat.

Amy called after him. "Oh, and don't go for a swim."

Giorgio kept walking and said over his shoulder, "Let me guess. Boat ride."

Amy laughed. "There is one more thing."

This time Giorgio stopped and turned around.

Amy walked toward him, extended her hand and said, "I'm Amy

Polanski."

Giorgio took her hand and smiled. But instead of shaking it, he bent and kissed it ever so gently, never taking his dark eyes from hers. Amy felt a shiver run down her spine.

Giorgio lingered over her hand for a moment too long. "A pleasure to meet you, Signorina," the young man said.

Typical Italian, Amy thought.

CHAPTER 40

I thought I had it tough detaching myself from Brigitte, but when I glanced over at the Squid, he was having exactly the same trouble, and maybe even more so, with Adrienne. My estimate for the time it took her to forgive him just dropped to about ten seconds.

The people of the town filed out of the cathedral, thanking the members of my group and embarrassing me by fawning over me for having rescued them. Frankly, I felt I'd let them down terribly, and even more, I had put them in grave danger by bringing Lisa into their midst.

The children were led off to bed, and despite the late—or early—hour, depending on how you looked at it, the rest of the townsfolk started right in cleaning up the town square. When Brigitte released me from her bear hug, I spotted Squid and Adrienne sitting at the tabac, whispering quietly to each other. As much as I didn't want to interrupt them, I had to know just what the fuck had happened.

I was nearly within talking distance when Cat-Juice and Doc unceremoniously cut in front of me. They stood at attention and snapped off crisp salutes to the Squid.

He stood, returned the salute in kind, and said, "At ease, boys."

The soldiers relaxed a smidge from their rigid attention posture.

"Damn good to see you, Major," Cat-Juice said.

Major? I had yet another "what the fuck" moment to ask Squid about.

"Good to see you, too, Lieutenant," Squid replied. "You have any trouble?"

"Piece of cake," Doc answered. "They were amateur hour at best. Their leader got away, though. My fault."

"That's too bad," Squid said. "But I'm sure it couldn't be helped."

"Maybe," Doc said. "But I don't like leaving loose ends, sir. They have a way of coming back to bite you in the ass."

Cat-Juice added, "We can debrief later, sir, but if you don't mind, I'd like to take the rest of the group to search the village for any hostiles we might have missed."

"Good idea," Squid replied. "Carry on."

The two soldiers saluted and about-faced. They picked up Yves and Godfrey and Archambaud in their wake and began their search-and-destroy mission for any of Lisa's stragglers who might still be in Saint Michel.

I was left standing there, shaking my head. "You want to tell me what the fuck that was all about?"

Squid looked truly perplexed. "What?"

"Major, lieutenant, sir—not to mention all that saluting shit."

"Oh that. I did a turn in Canadian Special Ops about twenty years ago," Squid said. "I'm sure I told you about it."

"No, you never told me about it," I answered.

"You sure?" Squid asked. "I have a distinct memory of us discussing it."

Adrienne chimed in. "If it makes you feel any better, Titus, I didn't know about it either until about six months ago."

Given the fact that I was supposed to be Squid's best friend, and up until three years ago, Adrienne hadn't passed a word with him in over two and a half centuries, no, it really didn't make me feel any better.

"You're full of shit, Squid, and you know it," I fired back. "You never said a word to me."

Squid rolled his eyes. "Jesus, you're such a pussy. So big deal, it must've slipped my mind. Do we have to get into this now?"

I was certainly miffed, but he was right about this being a stupid time to delve into his special ops career.

"Okay, okay, let's leave that for now. But tell me, where the hell were you and all the villagers hiding?"

"Underground," Squid replied. "You and Adrienne are going to want to see this."

With that, he led Adrienne, Brigitte, and me back into the cathedral and to the front of the church. Brigitte fiddled with something on a sidewall, and the small Gothic altar slid silently to the left. I walked over and looked down to see the beginning of a very old-looking flight of stone stairs hidden under the altar. Even with my vampire vision, I couldn't see very far. After only a few feet, the staircase was swallowed up by an absolute darkness.

"Can you believe it, Chrissy?" Squid asked. "No modern machinery on the altar at all. Some kind of weighted pulley contraption from five hundred years ago, and it still works like a charm."

"Closer to six hundred," Brigitte said. She produced a flashlight. "Shall we go down?"

With Brigitte in the lead, we slowly descended the narrow, winding stone steps single file. Our descent into that blackness and the skittering, bobbing illumination coming from the flashlight was disorienting.

"How far down are we going?" I asked, and nearly jumped at the sound of my own echo-distorted voice.

"Nearly one hundred and twenty meters," Brigitte answered. "This was a cavern beneath the village discovered centuries ago. The original entrance at the base of the hill has long since been sealed. This is the only way in now."

We went down and down, with the temperature steadily dropping and the sound of our footfalls ricocheting about the narrow staircase, making the four of us sound like a small army.

Finally, I thought I could make out a tiny bit of light coming from beneath us. It was so faint, I couldn't be sure if my eyes were tricking me or not. It turned out not, because a few more minutes found us at the bottom of the steps and staring at a large, formidable-looking ancient wooden door. The small tad of light that I'd first noted from up above eked out from beneath it. The door looked as if it might have come from some old knight's medieval stronghold, and perhaps it had.

Brigitte inserted an oversized skeleton key into the lock, and the huge door swung smoothly open. Light bathed the hallway and us, and my hand reflexively shielded my eyes. I turned away from the brightness and waited for my eyes to adjust. Brigitte passed through the door, and after a moment, I followed her.

We entered a large, circular, high-domed room that must have been nearly a hundred feet across. I recognized the many arches and design of the dome to be derived from ancient Roman architecture. In fact, the room bore a striking resemblance to Agrippa's Pantheon. It was amazing to me that such a structure could be buried so far underground.

Although only torch-lit, the room was extremely well illuminated and allowed me to clearly see its most striking feature: the murals. There were several high up on the walls, and they appeared to have many of the same characters in them going from panel to panel. This sort of period art would clearly be telling a story, or stories, like some kind of medieval, oversized picture book.

I stood gazing up, admiring the pure art of the murals. Whoever the painter was clearly had talent. I didn't recognize the style, something I was more often than not able to do with paintings, given my age and status as an amateur art buff.

But many a great artist didn't make the cut of history, as Rembrandt and Michelangelo and da Vinci had. It wasn't because of any particular lack of talent, but because of the random ebb and flow of passing time and luck. This was someone I could add to the list of artists I'd simply never come across in my two millennia of living.

I felt lucky to have been able to see such great art all through my overlong life, and right then, felt particularly fortunate to be seeing this hitherto unknown work for the very first time. I found myself wondering who the artist might have been. As I contemplated this, my appreciation for the strokes and the general beauty of the work slipped to the background of my mind, and I concentrated more on each panel and the characters and story that it might be telling.

Vague recognition seeped into my consciousness, and suddenly it became crystal clear. The effect of this perception hit me like a breath-stopping body punch. I took a staggering step back, feeling like I'd been pushed. "What the fuck," I gasped.

Of all the "what the fucks" I had to deal with tonight, maybe in my entire life, this was by far the worst. I turned slowly at first, then faster and faster, taking in panel after panel. A sheen of perspiration broke out on my forehead, and I suddenly felt as if I was going to puke.

Looking down at me from nearly all the panels were the serene faces of my two late aunts, Mary and Katie. But in many of the panels, and appearing very much in favor with the two old girls, was Gaius-fucking-Acilius.

The painter had captured him perfectly. He wore his usual small, mean smirk, and his eyes sparkled with secret knowledge. I swear, as I stared at the son of a bitch, he winked at me. As I continued to study

Gaius's portrait, transfixed, I could feel his painted eyes boring into mine, saying, "How do you like these apples, Daddy-O?"

I turned to my three companions. Adrienne was as mesmerized as I had been, staring up at the murals, but Squid and Brigitte seemed to be waiting for me.

"Do you want to explain exactly what the fuck is going on here?" I asked.

Squid and Brigitte glanced at each other for a moment and then back at me.

"Shit, Chrissy," Squid said. "We thought you were going to explain it to us."

CHAPTER 41

The nondescript dark sedan hurtled through the crisp Montreal night at ridiculous rates of speed, executing turn after gut-wrenching turn as it danced and dodged in and out of traffic. A sporadic tire squeal was the only outward sign that every now and again, the automobile was being pushed to its maximum.

Bloody Bill Harrison maintained a relaxed but steady grip on the steering wheel of the Audi RS5 he piloted, occasionally tossing glances into the rearview, looking for his pursuers, who were once again falling behind. They were good, but he was better.

Bill had taken several counterterrorism driving courses through the years, and now, with the enhancements from Steve's drug, his driving skills were off the map. Bill nudged the speed of his souped-up, new-age muscle car to just over a buck ten. He was sure he'd lose them in the next few minutes.

He had sped out of the center of town under fire and hit Route10 flying. He'd just crossed Pont Champlain when he'd executed a U-turn right on the highway and recrossed the Saint Lawrence. But somehow they'd stuck with him. Bill admired them for that. He'd doubled back on 15 and was now racing through the side streets of Laval, a northern suburb of Montreal.

Stevie Ray Vaughn's burnt, bluesy voice and smooth guitar riffs blasted out "Boot Hill" from the car's speaker system. Bill loved opera and classical music, and when it came to pop, he was a strict country and western fan. Stevie Ray was about as far afield as he could stray toward the mainstream. Bill especially liked listening to him when he had serious driving to do. This was about as serious as it got.

Molly leaned over from the passenger seat and turned the music down. "You're going to lose them for sure this time, Dad."

"I reckon so," Bill agreed.

From the backseat Steve spoke up. "You're going over a hundred, for Christ's sake. Would you at least turn on the headlights?"

Bill sourly glanced back at Steve. "Stop your bellyaching, Steve. My vision's always been 20/20, and now with that PEDA of yours, it's a *helluva* lot better than that. You know I don't need the lights on."

"Yeah, I know," Steve mumbled. "I just can't seem to get used to it, though."

"How's that shoulder of yours doing, by the way?" Bill asked.

Steve looked surprised, as if he'd forgotten about the two bullets that had penetrated the shoulder crease of his vest, drilling into his upper arm. He reached up and touched his shoulder, then moved it all around. "Hardly hurts at all, and the bleeding has nearly stopped. That last batch of PEDA must've been high-test."

Bill laughed. "Molly here's the one who made it. She may be a natural chemist. If we were all druggies, I bet she could cook up one helluva crystal meth."

"Like we don't have enough troubles," Molly replied.

"Molly," Steve said, "thanks for coming back for me. If you hadn't—"

Molly cut him off coldly. "I would've done it for anyone on our team."

Bill knew that was true, but he also knew Molly still harbored some tender feelings for Steve, despite everything that had happened. However things went between the two of them, Bill vowed to himself to stay the heck out of it, at least, as much as he could.

Molly asked, "What next, Dad?"

"First, we get to the rendezvous and see how many of us are left."

"I know Pete won't be there," Steve said. "I saw him get it. It was horrible."

"Yeah," Bill replied, as he took another hairpin turn. "I saw that, too. And Darlene, she's not going to be there either."

"I'm pretty sure I saw Ted and Tracy make it out a side door," Molly said hopefully. "Maybe Jack made it out, too."

In the rearview Bill saw Steve shaking his head at that last comment, but he already knew the truth. Bill had seen Jack decapitated. "Not sure about Ted and Tracy, hon, but Jack didn't make it. I'm sorry."

Molly stifled a sob, and her eyes welled up with tears. "Oh no. He was barely twenty, just a kid."

In fact, Jack's twentieth birthday would've been next week. Given the circumstances, Bill decided to keep that information to himself. "Okay, so we go to the rendezvous and hope Tracy and Ted show up. Next, we pay a visit to Gaius Acilius."

Steve exploded in the backseat. "What! That son of a bitch set us up! They were ready for us. It was a trap."

Bill had been in many a similar circumstance and knew that they hadn't walked into a trap. "They were ready, all right, but it was no trap. If it was, we'd all be dead instead of just three of us."

"Hopefully *only* three of us," Molly added.

"Hopefully," Bill echoed and went on. "We knocked down twenty-five, maybe thirty of them. Granted, most were human, but I'd wager there were at least eight or nine vampires in the mix. That's the most we've ever put down at one time."

"But Bill—"

"But nothing, Steve. I don't trust Acilius either, but he's been as good as his word so far. He even sent four of his own security along with us as reinforcements, and they're all dead now. The ten mill is in our account, and he never said this would be easy. He was testing us, and I just hope we were good enough."

Steve was incredulous. "Testing us? Three, maybe more of us are dead and you're talking about being good enough?"

Bill raised his voice. "Damn right I am. How else are we going to get out of this fucking mess you got us into? If we don't get this bastard's help, and soon, we're gonna end up full-fledged bloodsuckers in no time. What other choice do we got?"

With that, except for Stevie Ray, the car went silent as they all stewed. Bill continued to twist and turn along, putting their pursuers farther and farther back in his rearview.

Steve's horseshit and the silence and the cluster-fuck that had resulted from their attack on the V Bar in Montreal made Bill irritated, almost jittery in fact. But Bloody Bill Harrison didn't do the jitters. It only took him a moment to figure out what was really bothering him.

It was as if he could sense the same tension coming from both Steve and Molly. It added to his own, somehow making the feeling exponentially worse, almost unbearable.

Bill looked over at Molly, who met his gaze steadily and nodded. She knew, of course. He looked at Steve in the mirror, expecting him to look away quickly, but he didn't. He looked back at Bill with the same even gaze that Bill's daughter had. Steve felt it, too. They all felt it. It was *just plain blood.*

"Somehow, I'm guessing we're all on the same wavelength here," Bill said, breaking the silence. "There's gotta be at least a couple of humans in that car following us."

"I suspect so," Molly chimed in.

"Count me in," Steve added.

Bill smiled. It wasn't a pleasant one at all. "Good. What do you say we set an ambush for these fuckers?"

CHAPTER 42

After a long and impressive tour of underground Saint Michel, Adrienne, Brigitte, Squid, and I found ourselves seated where we'd started, in this grotto's version of the Pantheon. Once again my eyes were drawn to the murals where the images of my aunts—and unfortunately, Gaius—stared down upon me.

The "town beneath the town" was, in a word, astonishing. At close to six hundred years old, it was perhaps the world's first fallout bunker. Through the centuries, and in strict secrecy, the villagers had worked on the cavern, making it habitable for the entire town in times of crisis. Brigitte informed me that the attack by Lisa and her men was far from the first time that it had to be used in this way.

The engineering of the place was marvelously simple, with five large common rooms, three kitchens, a multitude of "private" dwellings, and even a small chapel—all carved out of the stone. There were no modern power supply lines, which was somewhat inconvenient, but safe. Such lines would be traceable and could be cut off. Power was supplied by burning wood and by the occasional propane tank, with any smoke vented through the chimneys of the houses above.

Air naturally circulated through small vent pockets on the side of the hill and up through the spires of the cathedral, making the church one of the draftiest in all of Europe, I'd suspect. An underground spring supplied the water, and a turbine was ingeniously fitted to it to supply the cavern with additional electrical power when needed. There was only canned food down there, however, which, like any true Provençals, the Saint Michelers vigorously disdained except in times of crisis. All in all, it was quite the setup.

We sat in silence, and I tried to take in all that I'd seen. The only sounds in the room came from a fairly constant drip of water running down one of the stone walls and the counterpoint of Squid nervously drumming his sausage-sized fingers on a large oak table.

A disquieting thought entered my mind. I turned to Brigitte. "Exactly when did you plan to tell me about all this?" I asked, sounding irritated and harsher than I'd meant to.

She blinked, startled at the tone of my voice. "I'm sorry, Father—"

"Cut the *Father* shit and answer the question," I snapped. Her use of the term "Father" quickly jumped me up the pissed-off scale from irritated to angry.

Squid and Adrienne glanced at each other nervously. Brigitte gulped, but the fact that she still didn't answer, added to my rapidly worsening shitty mood.

I went on, the volume of my voice dangerously increasing. "I mean, after all, I've only been living here for months now, and I *am* supposed to be some kind of patron of this place, and, oh, I almost forgot, we've been sleeping together for weeks. You want to tell me why you didn't let me in on this little secret?"

I punctuated the last statement by slapping my hand down fiercely on the hard oak. The gunshot-like report echoed off the high ceiling, making Brigitte, and even Adrienne and Squid, jump. Squid cleared his throat to speak, and without taking my eyes off Brigitte, I pointed a finger in his direction. Mercifully, he remained silent.

Brigitte composed herself and said, "Because of Lisa. That is why it was decided at first that you would not be told. You were clearly a chosen one, but our mothers never brought you here to meet the village before they passed on. And you brought *her* among us, that horror. What were we supposed to do? We love you, Father, and serve you, but the village must come first. The village must go on, no matter what the sacrifice. My own father died defending it." Brigitte's eyes filled with tears and her lower lip trembled. I thought that she would surely break down crying, but she got herself under control and went on. "After a time it was clear you truly had our interests at heart, but then we had to go to Paris, and then you went to California, and now this. I would have told you, but there wasn't time."

On autopilot, my mouth opened to retort, and as usual, it was way ahead of my brains. But what could I say in argument to such logic? My anger headed for the exit, leaving me feeling like shit, as one final kick in the ass before it left. "You were correct to be wary of me," I said. "I apologize for my outburst."

"Your apology is never needed in Saint Michel, Father," Brigitte responded rigidly, leading me to wonder if I'd just permanently fucked up yet another relationship. After all, it would hardly be the first time, and at last count in the relationship department—if you excluded dogs, that is—I was officially zero for 3,647. But I couldn't worry about that now.

"Are there any other paintings, or perhaps some written records that might help us figure out some of the history between my aunts and Gaius?" I asked.

"He was known to us as *Gaetan*, Father," Brigitte replied. "And no, there are no other records of any kind, Father."

Oh great, I thought. *She's going to "Father" me to death.*

"Well, what do you make of the mural?" I asked.

Squid jumped in. "Actually, it's pretty clear."

"Oh?" I answered. "What are you, some kind of an art critic now?"

"Well, it wasn't like I had a whole lot to do down here while I waited for you to *finally* show up," he snapped back.

"Down, boys," Adrienne said. "I'm sure Brigitte told you all about them, Squid."

Squid looked abashed. "Hey, I figured out some for myself—some."

Brigitte glared at me and then perked up, smiling her thousand-watt smile for Squid. "Actually, Father Squid was quite accurate in his analysis. I hardly had to help him at all."

It's official, I thought. *Now I'm zero for 3,648.* But Brigitte wasn't really a relationship. She was only a fling, and flings didn't count, did they? Because if I had to tally up all the flings I'd totally screwed up, I'd need to use a fucking calculator. "How wonderful," I added sourly.

Adrienne reached out and patted Squid's hand. "Art? I didn't think you had it in you, babe."

At Adrienne's use of the term "babe", Squid briefly caught my eye, subtly moving one eyebrow up and down a fraction of a millimeter. Even though I was royally pissed at him, I nearly laughed out loud. The guy could crack me up in a heartbeat with one of his goofy looks. Neither Adrienne nor Brigitte seemed to have caught on.

Barely hiding a smile, I said, "Okay, wise-ass, enlighten us."

Squid pointed at a mural. "Here's the first one. No sign of Gaius, and your aunts are clearly in Saint Michel. You can tell by the cathedral. Look at the last one. Almost the same, and again, the two of them in Saint Michel, and once again no Gaius. But going clockwise, now here you see Katie—"

"Angelique," Brigitte interrupted.

I was dumbfounded. I might not have known my aunts' real names until the very end, but up until this point, I was certain I knew all of their aliases. I'd never heard of Katie using the name Angelique.

Squid went on. "I forgot. Angelique. Well, anyway, here she's welcomed in another town, maybe Lacoste, but it's hard to tell. Now here's Mary—Justine. Same deal in yet another town. No clue as to which one it might be. Then the two of them destroying a town together."

"Was that the town that was going to attack Saint Michel?" I asked Brigitte.

She shrugged, and Squid said, "Maybe. Or maybe it was because that village didn't welcome your aunts. Anyway, now we have Gaius in the picture, and again, there's town after town looking happy to have him, either alone or with one of your aunts. Then here, the three of them argue, and finally he's sent away. Once again, we're back to your aunts in Saint Michel."

The sequence of these murals was sobering and was made much worse by the fact that my aunts had been secretly involved with Gaius.

"Would you excuse us, please, Brigitte," I said. "We'll be up in a moment."

Brigitte favored me with an extremely arid look. She gave the Squid another smile, and finally bowed slightly to Adrienne.

When she'd left the room, Squid started right in. "I kind of like it down here. I mean, it's a bit gloomy and could use some curtains or maybe a bowling alley or something, but otherwise, I could see myself here for the long haul."

I sighed. "Could you be serious just for a minute?"

"Jeez," he said. "What's the big deal? So what, your aunts and Gaius took over the Luberon Valley five hundred years ago. Big deal. You told me yourself they were all for vampires being a ruling class at different times in their lives. You even helped them, and more than once, as I recall."

"Yeah, but I thought they'd stopped that shit. The last time I knew about them trying it was in the tenth century, and boy, did that ever go sideways."

"I have to agree with Squid, Chris," Adrienne said. "Why is this so different?"

"Because I thought I knew them, and they lied to me. I never had the beginning of a clue that they'd interacted with Gaius in any significant way since he left us in Rome eighteen hundred years ago. It makes me wonder what else I didn't know about them, and if I really knew them at all, for that matter. I mean, partnering up with that loon, especially knowing how I felt about him?"

Adrienne said, "Maybe they were trying to protect you, trying to bring Gaius back into the fold, and when that failed, they thought it best not to mention it."

"No offense, but that sounds like a bunch of crap," I said. "And it makes me wonder who they were really rooting for in all those fights between Gaius and me."

"Not to pile on, Chrissy," Squid said, "but how did they pull this off without you knowing it? You guys were tight. I mean, I realize that communication and travel back then wasn't what it is now, but this whole deal here took a hundred and fifty, maybe two hundred years. It's evident by changes in clothing styles in the murals."

I started to respond, but Squid didn't give me time.

"Before you say it, no, I didn't notice the clothes thing. Brigitte told me. But even so, the question stands."

Damn it! I so wanted to call him out on his supposed clothes analysis. "I was into my New World thing at the time," I replied. "First with Cartier, and then with Champlain over to Canada."

Squid shook his head. "Even so, before that you must have been in some contact."

"No, not really. I was bored to death with Europe, and the travel bug had bitten me hard. Before Canada, I was busy with Cortes in Mexico."

Squid's eyes opened wide. "You, with Cortes? Jesus, you were a part of bringing down a whole civilization, and you're bitching about Gaius and your aunts? Wait, hold on a minute. Cortes conquered Mexico with what, ten guys and a horse, right?"

"No, more like five hundred men and thirteen horses," I answered.

He rolled his eyes. "Oh, I get it now. He was able to do that because he happened to have a very powerful fifteen-hundred-year-old vampire with him."

I shrugged. "I may have helped some."

His eyes opened wider. "Wait, the Aztecs, the human sacrifices?"

I nodded. "Vampires. Primitives really. I felt like they needed to be taught a lesson."

"Holy shit!" Squid replied. "And you're pissed at me for not telling you about Canadian Special Ops? You really are an asshole."

There was really no argument with his final premise. I paused for a moment and then finally remembered the question I'd meant to ask Brigitte before I dismissed her. "Damn! I wanted to ask Brigitte who painted the murals, but I got so flustered I forgot."

Squid laughed. "I know. Your aunts, dummy."

"Jesus Christ." I spouted. "Is there anything else I don't know about those two old biddies?"

"That I can't answer," Godfrey said, poking his head into the room. "With Gaius's men eliminated, cell phone reception has resumed. I have Jean-Luc on my phone up above. The signal won't penetrate this cavern, though. He says he needs to speak to you right away. He says it's important."

"I don't know, Chrissy," Squid said. "Smart money says it ain't good news."

CHAPTER 43

Gaius Acilius sat in his office with his feet up on his desk, finishing a phone conversation. He was all smiles. "Excellent, Juan Carlos, excellent. I'll be in touch with you very soon." Acilius looked up at Lisa, who sat across from him.

"More good news?" she asked.

"Better than I expected. It seems I have misjudged the prevailing sentiment. Many of our kind are in favor of attempting to become a ruling class. Granted, most don't want to be actively involved. But on the other hand, they'll do nothing to interfere, either, as long as I don't do anything to disrupt their lifestyles. Many of those I've spoken to would even support the movement financially. It seems many of my brethren vampires are just looking for a leader and a plan."

Lisa laughed. "Well, you've got at least half of that covered. But I haven't even heard the beginning of a plan out of you. It isn't like you can take over the world by winging it."

Acilius favored Lisa with one of his most sour looks. "Very funny, my dear. I have no intention of *winging it*, as you would say. As a matter of fact, you've already been watching me execute the first part of my plan. It's called gathering support."

"You haven't talked much about the vampires who are against your grand scheme," Lisa replied. "The ones who support Titus and his group."

Acilius put his feet on the floor and leaned forward, elbows on the desk, chin in his hands, ruminating. "A substantial group, no doubt," he said. "And Jean-Luc has many friends as well. Even the boy, Jake Lyons, has quite a following due to his computer skills, but now he garners a great deal of sympathy as well. In retrospect, perhaps it was unwise to burn his girlfriend."

"Not one of your nicer moves, hon."

Acilius waved the comment away and leaned back in his chair. "No matter. There's nothing that can be done about that now. But do you know what's the most surprising thing?"

Lisa shook her head.

"It's that idiot, the Squid," Acilius replied. "He's still quite young, and such a buffoon, but you'd be shocked to know how much support he has in our community."

"No, I probably wouldn't," Lisa said. "He's a very charming buffoon, and his courage and loyalty are unquestioned."

"I suppose so. But the point that I take away from things is this: I believe *their* supporters would do very little to interfere with any plans of mine, as long as we left them and Titus and his group alone. Granted, to do that would take some deft political maneuvering and some severe restraint on my part, but all in all, it's not impossible in the least. I must say that things are going quite swimmingly."

"I have to agree, mostly anyway," Davy Stein said as he entered the office and plopped himself down in the chair next to Lisa's.

Acilius and Lisa eyeballed him, clearly in shock, and Lisa's mouth actually fell open. In stark contrast to his usual dated and clownish attire, Stein was dressed quite stylishly in light gray pants, a steel-blue shirt, and a very expensive-looking, tailored black jacket.

The ogling silence went on, with Stein looking back and forth between Lisa and Acilius. Finally, he asked, "What?"

Acilius responded, "It's just that you're dressed so well, when you usually look like such a fool."

"Oh, great," Stein spewed out. "You give me so much shit about how I dress, and when I actually listen and change, you give me shit anyway."

Acilius laughed out loud.

"Quiet, Gaius," Lisa said. "Davy's right. Leave him alone. You look great, Davy."

Stein still appeared a bit deflated, but Lisa's comment brought out a small smile. "Thanks, Lisa."

Acilius had to suppress another chuckle at Stein's antics. "My apologies. You do look quite good. It will take a little getting used to, but I highly approve."

Stein looked like the loyal dog that he was. "Thanks, Boss."

"Now if you don't mind," Acilius replied, "please bring me up to date on your activities."

"Oh, sure," Stein said, pulling his little notebook from his jacket. He flipped it open. "Los Angeles, Chicago, New York, Mexico—all pretty much in line. They'd either help some or stay out of it, but I don't get the sense any would interfere, unless you screwed around with Titus. Then I think there'd be a war."

Acilius nodded. "Pretty much the same as what I found. We can definitely work with that sort of attitude. I think things are looking excellent. Well done, Davy."

Stein suddenly looked serious as he flipped to another page of his notebook. "One more thing. The initial reports are in from our science guys. The formulas Harrison gave us are purposely a little screwed up, just like you figured. But with the sample of the drug, they're pretty sure they'll be able to reproduce it, and soon. They did what you instructed and tried to figure what the drug would do to someone who already was a vampire. They think it would increase our strengths and decrease or maybe eliminate sun sensitivity in new vampires. Hell, they even think it could decrease the amount of blood we need."

"No sun sensitivity?" Lisa murmured.

"That's right, kid," Stein answered.

Acilius had asked the scientists to hypothesize about the effects on vampires just to be thorough. He hadn't expected any significant results and was taken aback by Stein's report. "Would these effects be permanent?"

Stein shook his head. "They think temporary, only while you're on the drug. And they have no idea what the long-term effects of PEDA might be. This was only a first pass, and a rush job at that."

"Then why the long face?" Acilius asked. "That's all good news."

Stein swallowed. "The other thing is this: they ran through the blood samples and found that Bill and Molly Harrison are very infectious. Something about a mutation of the HVSV, but they lost me on the explanation. It was way over my head. Anyway, they figure that any human turned like them, by the drug, will be super-infectious, too—way more than we are. Our guys think they might be able to turn people with a completely intact immune system. Wouldn't have to kill them. Maybe even a single bite could do it."

Acilius couldn't believe what Stein had just said. The effect was galvanizing. He cleared his throat and managed to croak out, "Are they sure?"

Stein's normally pasty face had gone several degrees pastier than usual. "About the other stuff, who knows? But about the infectious part, they seemed pretty damn sure."

"My gods," Acilius whispered.

He was completely stunned, horrified. He felt as if his mind could barely work, and that his body would be quite content to remain paralyzed in his office chair for an eternity. Exerting every bit of willpower at his command, Acilius forcefully cleared the dense fog of terror that had clouded his reasoning and pushed himself into action mode. "Davy, I want you to get every man we've got into the field and find the Harrisons. We've got to bring them in, and now."

Stein replied immediately, "I've already done it, Boss."

Acilius nodded. "Good. No, wait. Call them off. If that old buzzard even senses we're coming for him, he'll go to ground, and we'll never find him."

Stein seemed flummoxed. "What do we do, then?"

Acilius sighed. "Nothing. We just have to wait. After Montreal, he'll come in. What choice does he have? We have to be patient. Redistribute the men, California only. I don't want the Harrisons intercepted, but I want to know when they're within a hundred miles of here. And I don't want them to know they're being watched. Understood?"

Stein stood. "I'm on it, Boss. Anything else?"

"Yes," Acilius replied. "Get me a copy of the scientists' reports. I want to look at them myself."

"I knew you would," Stein said. He pulled out a neatly folded stack of papers from his jacket and handed them over to Acilius.

Acilius almost worked up a smile at his apprentice's efficiency, but the situation was too grave. "Thank you, Davy," he said. "That will be all."

Stein nodded and briskly walked from the office, already dialing his cell phone.

Acilius spread the reports on his desk and began reading.

Lisa, who had been silent through the entire exchange, said, "I don't understand. What is it?"

Acilius looked up slowly from the papers on his desk. "The end of everything, my love."

CHAPTER 44

The Squid was right; it wasn't good news. Over the phone, Jean-Luc brought us up to speed on the attack in New Orleans. He also alluded to an even larger attack in Montreal but didn't have details. Adrienne quickly plumbed her contacts there and confirmed that there'd been over twenty vampires and humans killed at the V Bar in Montreal. There'd only been a half dozen killed in New Orleans, but among them was an old friend, Rodrigo, and heartbreakingly, Miranda.

If was difficult for me to deal with the fact that Miranda was dead, and from what Jean-Luc told me, impossible for Jake to deal with it. Her death at Gaius's hands only emphasized that my former protégé needed to be put down for the mad dog that he was. I should have taken care of it centuries ago, but I never could bring myself to do it.

And now look where it had gotten me. That beautiful young girl, Miranda, died horribly, burned to death, and it was all my fault. I swore an oath to myself right then that no matter how everything turned out, I would make Gaius pay for her with his life.

Adrienne immediately dispatched Doc and Cat-Juice to Montreal to get to the bottom of what went on there. Godfrey and Archambaud volunteered to stay in Saint Michel to help get the town back to a semblance of working order, and, more importantly, to stand guard.

Shockingly Yves, nobody's sweetheart on the best of days, offered to stay as well. But then I noticed how he'd steal moony-eyed glances at Brigitte. Clearly, the big lug was smitten with her. What I thought at first was a one-way street was not, as she would moony-eye him right back.

What I'd believed were true feelings Brigitte had for me must have been nothing more than a first-rate case of vampire "groupieism". On the one hand, it was distressing to realize that even after two thousand years, I still didn't have the beginning of a clue as to how the female mind functioned. But on the other hand, it was comforting to know that my streak of shitty relationships with the opposite sex was still intact and going strong. Oh well.

Squid, Adrienne, and I left for New Orleans immediately to try to come up with our next move. From the airport we went directly to the Absinthe House and met Jean-Luc there. The place was crawling with armed guards, making it look more like a military base than the very chic vampire bar that it was.

The four of us, along with Simone, took the long, dark stairway down to the subbasement and Jean-Luc's dungeon office. Simone selected a nice French cabernet for the meeting, but Squid, never being the wine connoisseur, drew himself two pitchers of draft and lugged them all the way down. We'd just finished our descent when Adrienne's cell phone rang.

"Hello. Doc, is that you?" she said. "I can barely hear you."

"The reception down here is spotty at best, my dear," Jean-Luc interrupted. "You may have to go back up."

Adrienne nodded and started her climb, while Jean-Luc sat behind his huge desk, and the Squid and I settled into some chairs. Simone opened the wine, and we sipped the exquisite cabernet. Squid drank his beer—directly out of the pitcher, I might add—as he ogled the dripping stonewalls and the various medieval artifacts in the office.

This kind of behavior from Squid would clearly save on dishwashing, but it was the sort of uncouth display that would usually set off someone as "Miss Manners" as Jean-Luc. Oddly, he didn't seem to notice. I guess over the past three years, he'd gotten used to the Squid and his eccentricities. That was a pretty short breaking-in period, considering it had taken me the better part of a century to get used to the big dope.

Jean-Luc steepled his hands in a repose of contemplation and asked, "Shall we begin?"

"Yeah, the quicker the better," Squid answered. "This place gives me the creeps. It's like being in a torture chamber."

Jean-Luc nodded toward his left. "Next door."

Squid's eyes opened wide, and he took another huge slug of beer. "No way."

Jean-Luc shrugged. "Way."

"You should be the last one to talk about choice of office space," I added, sounding a little harsher than I meant to. "That telephone booth shit hole you call an office isn't exactly the Taj Mahal."

Squid rolled his eyes. "Jeez, Chrissy, did anyone ever tell you that you had an anger problem?"

"Sure, plenty of times, but they were usually dickheads like you."

"Oh, real nice," Squid replied. "Like I said, an anger problem."

Jean-Luc cleared his throat. "If you two don't mind, we have quite a bit to discuss."

Even after 250 years, the Squid and I could still fire barbs at each other at the drop of a hat, no matter what the circumstances. Considering the gravity of the situation, I was more than a little embarrassed. And the fact that the Squid was right about my anger problem didn't help.

I shrugged and turned to the Squid. "Sorry, big guy."

Squid slugged down another huge pitcher swig and favored me with his patented over-the-top wink. "Pussy."

I laughed out loud, along with Simone.

Jean-Luc sighed. "I'm glad you two are in such a jocular mood," he said, "but this is serious business—deadly serious."

"You know we're all in with you, Frenchy," Squid replied. "It's just that Chrissy and I like keeping it light, no matter how bad things are. It's our way of dealing with it."

"I know, my friend," Jean-Luc answered, "but things are very bad. Rodrigo is dead, and so are Miranda and four other vampires, along with a half dozen of our humans."

Simone had taken a seat next to Jean-Luc. Her eyes welled with tears. "Rodrigo gave his life to buy me time to escape. If he hadn't…"

Jean-Luc patted her on the hand. "It's all right, Simone."

Her head snapped toward him. "No, it isn't. You know better than to placate me. And none of us are safe while that madman lives."

I interrupted. "And how is Jake dealing with. . . you know."

"Not well, I'm afraid," Jean-Luc replied. "The first thing he wanted to do was go and try to kill Gaius. I told him that would be suicide, but it didn't matter to him. I've had to put him on a twenty-four-hour watch. Now he hardly takes any blood at all. He's deteriorating rapidly, and if he doesn't come out of his malaise, he will be dead very soon."

I'd had no idea about this, and it shocked me. "I want to see him right after we're through here."

Jean-Luc nodded. "Very well, but now to the details. The attack in New Orleans wasn't a general terrorist-like action. It consisted of pointed assassinations or assassination attempts aimed at me and my closest associates and lieutenants. It was clearly in retribution for my interfering with his doings with you, Titus. His usual fare, I would say, brutal and for show mainly. But the conversation I had with Gaius a few days later was the interesting part."

I thought I had been shocked about Jake. Now I was dumbfounded. "Wait. What?"

Simone sounded cross. "Oh, the conversation with that psychopath doesn't matter. You skipped over the most important part. Tell them you defeated him."

"Simone, that's neither here nor there—an aberration, or a fluke, if you will," Jean-Luc replied. "The important part—"

"Tell them," Simone interrupted coolly. When her voice took on that temperature, it meant watch out, a fact that Jean-Luc was well aware of.

"Very well, my love," he replied.

Squid chuckled through a gulp of beer. "Sounds like me and Adrienne, doesn't it? When she's speaking to me, that is."

Jesus, the Squid could be annoying. The big oaf could take a runaway freight train off track with a single comment.

"Will you please shut the fuck up, Squid?" I said, exasperated.

He opened his mouth to respond, but mercifully decided on another chugalug instead.

"Jean-Luc, please, tell us," I said.

The small Frenchman appeared somewhat abashed. "I had to meet him in single combat with our swords, right up in the bar. I really had no choice. At first it went as you'd suspect, with him toying with me. But then, when I learned how he had killed Miranda by burning her to death, something happened. I felt a sort of pure energy surge into me, calming me, making me feel powerful. When we began again, it was as if Gaius was eight hundred years my junior and not the reverse. I would have killed him, and easily so, if his guards hadn't interfered."

"Whoa," Squid said. "You could've taken out Gaius? How the hell could you pull that off?"

"Gifted," I said. "You're a Gifted One."

Jean-Luc tittered nervously. “Not so fast, my friend. That sort of thing is only a legend, and besides, I have not been able to reproduce the effect a single other time.”

“Somebody want to fill me in?” Squid asked. “What exactly is a Gifted One?”

Simone answered him. “An ancient vampire legend and a term for one of us who becomes powerful in leaps and far faster than usual. A Gifted One, as the legend goes, will lead the vampires to world domination.”

“You’ve always been more powerful than your age,” I said. “It makes perfect sense for you, all legends aside. And I’m sure there must be a physiological explanation.”

“In all your years, have you ever seen a Gifted One?” Jean-Luc asked sourly.

“No, I guess not,” I answered. “But maybe now I have.”

Jean-Luc scoffed. “As I said, nothing more than a fluke. It doesn’t matter.”

“It matters a great deal,” Simone said. “It’s the only reason Gaius contacted you. Now he sees you as a true threat.”

“Why *did* he contact you?” I asked.

“He wishes to start a movement to attain worldwide vampire dominance,” Jean-Luc answered, “and he wants me to join him.”

"Tom Carson already did join him," I replied. "He alluded to the same sort of plan. Right before I cut his head off."

“Like I said, anger problem," Squid quipped. "But one hell of a coincidence, huh? I mean, this Gifted One baloney, and Gaius wanting Jean-Luc to join up. You think he believes the legend?”

“Who knows, but I doubt it,” I answered. “If Gaius is going to make this kind of move, he needs to collect some powerful allies. And Jean-Luc is even more powerful than any of us thought.”

“It’s just like Saint Michel all over again,” Squid said.

“What do you mean?” Jean-Luc asked.

“Gaius was in cahoots with Chrissy’s aunts centuries ago and had pretty much taken over the Luberon Valley,” Squid answered. “It all fell apart somehow, but the worst part is that Chrissy had no idea it was going on.”

Jean-Luc and Simone both appeared shocked.

“Is this true?” Simone asked.

“Unfortunately, yes,” I mumbled. “And now it looks like Gaius is at it again."

"I'm sorry, Titus. I know how much your aunts meant to you, and to learn this must be quite unsettling," Jean-Luc said.

"Unsettling doesn't quite describe it," I replied. "Where do you stand with Gaius now?"

"We have a truce," Jean-Luc said, "while I decide to join his cause or not."

"Good," Squid said. "String him along. It'll buy us some time to come up with a game plan."

Jean-Luc looked abashed. "Stringing him along was, of course, part of my intent, but to be completely honest, I'm actually considering his offer."

Actually considering his offer?

I nearly fell out of my fucking chair.

CHAPTER 45

Once all the shouting died down, Jean-Luc's office was filled with an uncomfortable silence. Simone looked as if she might faint, while at the same time she seemed to want to punch through the nearest wall. The Squid fidgeted mightily and appeared as if he'd just caught a case of the "I want to get the fuck out of heres".

I don't know how I looked, but I felt as if I'd been poleaxed. The only one in the room who seemed calm was Jean-Luc.

Finally I found my voice, the calm one, thank the gods, not the shouty one that I generally used when I was feeling as confused and angry as I did right then. "Jean-Luc, you can't be serious. Gaius is a psychopath. You know that. He can't be trusted."

"I said I was only considering it. My mind is far from made up," Jean-Luc replied evenly. "As for Gaius's psychopathology, he plays the madman for you and you alone, just to annoy you, I suspect."

I couldn't believe he was taking this tack. I was totally flustered. "Playacting or not, Gaius is a sociopath at the very least."

Jean-Luc smiled. "Being a vampire immediately makes one a sociopath, at least by human standards."

"You know what I mean," I spewed out. "He tried to kill you and Simone, for God's sake. He killed Rodrigo and Miranda."

The Frenchman remained infuriatingly composed. "I know that, and his actions were in retaliation for my attacking him when I came to your aid. It is not the man I would flock to, it is the cause."

"The cause," I scoffed. "You haven't been into this kind of crap for the last seven hundred years, unless you've been bullshitting me, too. And for the record, I never asked for your help."

Jean-Luc paused, pensive for a moment, and then said, "You're quite right. You didn't ask, but nonetheless, I felt obligated. But no, I have not been bullshitting you. I've always had sentiments that leaned toward vampire dominance. You know it well. It is no secret. And I think Gaius might be quite correct. The time may be right. Besides, as he pointed out to me, he's not in it alone. He will have to have significant support from our community, and because of that, it could not possibly be his one-man show to run as he saw fit.

"He's honored the truce he made with me thus far. Furthermore, as long as you don't interfere with his plans or attack him, he's agreed to leave you all alone. I have that to consider."

Squid rolled his eyes. "How fucking sweet of him."

My blood was starting to boil again. "I don't need Gaius's protection, or yours, Jean-Luc. I can't believe you could be so naive, especially having firsthand experience with his track record. He's going to fuck you the first chance he gets. Count on it."

"He already has," Simone barked. "He broke your precious truce when he attacked Montreal, Adrienne's city."

Jean-Luc remained self-possessed. "He had the accord with me, not Adrienne."

"I think you're splitting hairs there, Frenchy," Squid said. "But even so, have you considered what happens if you fail?"

Jean-Luc shrugged. "Then we die."

"Yeah, I know, but I'm not sure it'll be in the way you mean *we*," Squid replied. "I realize that people of this era don't believe in much, especially when it comes to vampires and the like. And governments have a way of suppressing information that they don't think would sit well with the masses, but this is the era of instant communication. If you start something as big as a war and lose, no amount of suppression is gonna hide the fact that we exist. We'll be hunted down and exterminated as a race. One thing humans are still very good at is killing."

I hadn't even considered the angle Squid had taken. Thinking about it was chilling. But it didn't seem to affect Jean-Luc at all.

He said, "Then *we* will die."

Squid's eyes locked onto Jean-Luc's. Their old animosity seemed to be instantly rekindled to even greater levels than before. You could feel their anger bounding around the room, ready to boil over at a moment's notice.

With a deadly, quiet calm, Squid said, "I'd just as soon you didn't make that choice for me."

Their eyes remained locked, and the moment played out. I

thought for sure that at Jean-Luc's next comment, Squid would go at him. I got ready to intervene.

But Simone shouted and broke the spell. "Jean-Luc, you idiot! He's using you. He'll use you, and then he'll toss you away with the rest of the trash."

"He might not need Jean-Luc all that much," Adrienne said from the doorway. "You need to take a look at what Doc just sent me." She made her way to Jean-Luc's computer and punched it up as we gathered around. "It's the video from the security cameras on the night of the attack in Montreal." Adrienne forwarded through quite a bit of the film and froze it just after the first explosion. She zoomed in on two of the assailants and then magnified their faces even more. "Recognize anybody?"

I was pretty sure I did. "It's grainy, but I think it's Harrison and his daughter."

"You think correctly," Adrienne replied. "Doc confirmed it with facial recognition software."

"Ha, you see," Jean-Luc said. "It wasn't Gaius at all. It was the Harrisons."

"It might not be all that simple," Adrienne said and panned the view to another part of the film. She focused in on one of the other assailants firing a machine gun into the bar crowd. Wearing a tailored black suit, white shirt, and a thin black tie, the man looked quite formal. "Recognize the look?" Adrienne asked.

Jean-Luc turned his eyes from the screen and remained silent, but I didn't.

"Sure, the Reservoir Dogs look," I said. "I'd know it anywhere. That's one of Gaius's men."

Jean-Luc mumbled, "Doesn't prove anything."

Adrienne looked curiously at Jean-Luc. Evidently she'd missed quite a bit of the conversation and the yelling match we'd had before she entered the office. She went on. "Now here's the really interesting part. Watch the Harrisons in real time."

She cued the recording up to speed, and I watched, not knowing what I was watching for at first, but then it became very obvious.

As usual, when it came to talking, the Squid beat me to the punch. "Holy Jeez, look at them go. That old fuck was fast anyway, for a human, I mean, but he's like greased lightning now. And the daughter, my God, she's a one-woman slaughterhouse. They move like us, and they're not fledglings, either."

"Yes," Simone chimed in. "The girl looks like a five-hundred-year-old, and the father isn't too far behind."

"If they were turned, they couldn't be this far advanced," I said. "Unless…"

"Unless, that rumor about the enhancing drug is true," Jean-Luc added.

There was a stunned silence until Adrienne said, "It would be just like Gaius to take vampire hunters into his employ. Sometimes I think he invented *shock and awe*."

Squid nodded. "It's definitely his style, but I can't believe Harrison would ever agree to team up with him. That old man hates vampires. Exterminating us is his life's work."

"Desperate," I said. "He must be desperate."

"This is all hypothetical at best," Jean-Luc said. "But it gives us much to think about."

I turned to Jean-Luc and put my hand on his shoulder. "I hope so, my friend. I hope so."

He smiled at me, and I turned and headed for the stairs. The information that had just come to light was confusing, and I needed to think about it alone and without distraction. But there was something else I needed to do first.

"Where are you going," Squid called out after me.

"To see Jake."

CHAPTER 46

I called Jake's sister, Elise, on the short drive over to the house where Jake was being held in the Garden District. She didn't pick up, so I left as unalarming a message as I could, only lying a bit—well, maybe more than a bit. I told her everything was fine—the lie part, but I asked her to get in touch with me as soon as she could, as it was kind of important—the not so lie part.

Before I entered Jake's bedroom, I noticed one of the two vampires on duty at the house was Nick Boudreau, the bartender from the Absinthe House, and more importantly, Miranda's old boyfriend.

He said, "Hello Titus. Good to see you again."

I smiled. "Hey, Nick. How's he doing?"

Nick shook his head. "Terrible. He's hardly taking any blood now, and only when we force him. He's really starting to fall apart. It's accelerating. You better brace yourself."

I nodded grimly. I'd seen vampires kill themselves by blood starvation before. It was never pretty. I steadied myself and started into the room, but then I noticed that Nick didn't look so good himself. I stopped. "How are you doing, Nick? You okay?"

I didn't think he was going to answer for a moment. He lowered his head, but I could still see his lip quivering. When he looked up, his eyes were way too shiny.

"Not as bad as Jake, but not so hot," Nick replied. "After our breakup and things settled down, Miranda and I became friends again. Jake didn't like it at first, but then, he got used to it. Eventually, he came to think of me as a friend, too, you know?"

I nodded.

"I never hid it. I still really liked Miranda, maybe even loved her." He paused, choking up, and lowered his head again. When he looked up this time, tears were flowing down his face, but anger flared in his eyes as well. “You’ve got to promise me, if you do anything about this, if you’re going to try to take that bastard out, you’ve got to promise to take me with you.”

I hardly knew Nick, and I definitely didn’t know what tactical or combat skills he might or might not possess. All I had to go on was the look on his face, but it was a look I couldn’t say no to. “If I go, I promise you’ll be with me.”

He smiled at that.

“I need to see Jake now,” I said.

Nick took hold of my arm. “Are you sure you want to go in there? I don’t think there’s much you can do now. And it’s going to stick with you.”

Nick was right, but it didn’t matter.

“I have to,” I replied.

He let go of my arm, and I opened the bedroom door. The stench hit me right in the face with all the subtlety of a sledgehammer. As I closed the door behind me, I saw Nick’s partner trying to stifle his gags.

Jake’s flesh, without the benefit of blood, was rotting from his bones. In human terms, the smell would be the same as the stench of a rotting corpse, but vampires don’t die that easily, and Jake, unfortunately, was very much alive. But Nick’s assessment was spot on: he didn’t have much time left. Jake was too far gone.

He lay on his bed with his eyes closed, his chest barely rising and falling with infrequent and labored shallow breaths. I sat as quietly as I could on a chair next to his bed, studying him, looking for some sign of the Jake that I knew, and failing miserably. He was a wreck.

The ravages of blood starvation would even hit a vampire of my advanced age quickly, and very hard. For Jake, being little more than a fledgling, the process was all the worse, and much faster.

Thankfully, the covers were pulled up high, nearly to his neck, so I didn’t have to see much of his body. But his face—his formerly boyish face—was a horror. There were open, weeping sores scattered randomly all over it. Yellow, putrid fluid seeped from them, and from his eyes. It was as if the flesh on his face was melting away, and it hung limply from his bones. His lips were a drawn, hard line. His formerly thick brown hair had become wispy, thin, and snow-white. It did little to hide the scabrous, inflamed mess his scalp had become.

Seeing him like this made we want to fucking cry. I loved the kid.

He stirred, as if sensing me. His eyes fluttered, and then opened slowly. For a moment he looked up at the ceiling, as if getting his bearings. Then he turned his head slowly toward me. I swear I could hear the tendons in his neck creaking with the effort.

His eyes were glazed, rheumy, and draining that God-awful fluid. But when he recognized me, they sharpened up some. He worked up a small smile that came out looking more like a grimace. The effect was hideous. I could see, and smell, his rotting teeth.

He wheezed out a chuckle and whispered, "I wasn't expecting any visitors. I would've spruced up some."

"You know me, Jake. I never stand on ceremony."

His momentary attempt at graveside humor faded fast. "I knew you'd come, Titus. I'm glad. I hoped to see you before..." He stopped short of spelling out his meaning. "But it won't do any good. My mind's made up. I don't want to live without her."

"Miranda wouldn't want that," I replied. "She'd want you to go on, to live, to be happy."

His breathing took a hitch, and the flow of that gross yellow fluid coming from his eyes increased. Jake was crying, or as close as he could come to it in his ultra-debilitated state. His harsh whisper of a voice grew coarser. "I knew you'd say that, but it doesn't matter what Miranda would want. She's dead. Burned alive by that fucking madman."

"Then live, Jake," I implored. "Live to pay him back."

He shook his head wearily. "I'm not strong enough for someone like him. I've got to leave that to you, or Jean-Luc."

If I had told Jake that Jean-Luc was thinking about joining up with Gaius, it would've probably killed him on the spot. Considering the slow, horrible death the kid was facing, telling him might have been doing him a favor.

"She was your woman, Jake. Not very manly of you to leave it to others."

He wheezed out another putrid-smelling laugh. "I knew you'd try to goad me, Titus. You're really pretty predictable."

Jake was right, and I so hated being predictable.

"Well, how about this, then? I don't want to lose you," I told him honestly. "I don't have many friends, and you're one of them. How about that?"

He smiled, and I could almost see the eternally young twenty-year-old Jake powering through his rotting death mask. Almost.

"Look, Titus. I've had enough second chances," he said. "The first one was when I got lucky and lived through a vampire attack. Then with you fixing my pathetic life, and finally, with Miranda. But I'm all out of second chances now. I'm through."

I couldn't give up, at least not yet. "What about Elise? How do you think she's going to take losing you again, and for keeps this time?"

His eyes sharpened up another degree, and if Jake had had enough facial muscles in working order, he probably would've been shooting me an extremely dirty look right then. "I hoped you wouldn't bring her into this, but I knew you'd do that, too. She'll be okay. She's strong, a lot stronger than me. And I know you'll take care of her."

Back in my day in the Roman legion, there was no such thing as psychology. And even if there had been, I would've sucked at it. I'd lived through the Renaissance and many other "enlightened" eras, and to tell the truth, I still never got a single touchy-feely psychological concept. In the end, what I am and what I'll always be, way deep down in my bones, is a Roman centurion. Under duress, that's the well I always go to.

I rose, feeling my anger rising right along with me. "I have you pegged for a lot of things, Jake, but a coward's not one of them. And that's what you are, a fucking coward!"

His eyes blazed, and he tried to struggle up to a sitting position but couldn't manage it.

I laughed. "Oh, that's rich. Oh no! The rotting corpse boy is going to teach me a lesson. What are you going to do, ooze on me?"

He hissed. "Get out! Get the fuck out!"

"Don't worry, I'm going. But look at yourself, lying here, giving up like this. You should be ashamed. Miranda fought to the very end and burned for her trouble. You're not half the vampire she was, and you're dishonoring her memory. You're a fucking disgrace. Why don't you have some balls and torch yourself. It'll save us all some time."

Jake tried to scream at me, but all that came out was a muted, inarticulate rasp. He fell back on the bed, spent. I turned on my heel and left, slamming the bedroom door behind me.

I leaned back against the wall in the hallway and closed my eyes, taking a few deep breaths. I felt like shit after what I had just pulled, but it was the only thing I knew.

"You okay, Titus?" I heard Nick ask.

I opened my eyes and shook my head. "No, not really." I started for the door.

Nick escorted me. "Is there anything you want me to do?" he asked.

"What is there to do?" I answered, but then reconsidered. "Yeah, actually there is. Make sure there're no matches or lighters in Jake's room, okay?"

Nick nodded, and as I left, the sound of Jake's hoarse sobs followed me out into the street. It nearly killed me.

CHAPTER 47

Once again the Harrisons, this time with Steve Conti along for the ride, found themselves being escorted by Richard the footman through the maze of Gaius Acilius's mansion. They finally arrived in the great room and took the long walk up to the edge of the dais. Bill noted that an additional "throne" had been added for Lisa Brownell, who was seated next to Acilius. She wore her usual nonchalant smirk, but Bill thought there was an uncharacteristic nervousness playing across her eyes.

Davy Stein stood off to the side, far better dressed than when Bill had first met him. He looked twitchy and fidgety. Next to Stein was a handsome, dark-haired young man that Bill didn't recognize.

Richard announced them formally. "The Harrisons and Dr. Conti."

The footman moved toward a side door, but didn't leave. He stood waiting there at parade rest as Gaius Acilius rose and spread his arms in welcome, smiling his phony shark's smile. The smile never touched his hard, blue eyes.

"Better late than never, eh, Bill?" Acilius began. "And Dr. Conti, what a pleasure."

Conti replied stiffly, "Steve will do."

Acilius let out a high-pitched laugh and clapped his hands together. "Informality it is, then. I think I'm really going to like you, Steve-O."

Acilius's behavior was always affected and erratic, but this was different, and it put Bill on high alert. The young, dark-haired man looked completely relaxed, but Lisa, Stein, and even Richard, appeared coiled and ready. Ready for what, Bill didn't know exactly, but he knew he didn't like it. One glance told him Molly and Steve had noticed the tension in the room as well.

Bill said, "I'm sure you've gotten a report by now, but we had some problems in Montreal, suffered some losses."

Acilius interrupted with a wave of his hand. "Oh, tsk-tsk, you and your group performed admirably. I couldn't be more pleased. Your entire cell is a great asset to me, far greater than you know. But there have been some new and very interesting developments." The vampire turned to sit back down, and his eyes rested on the young man next to Stein. "Oh my goodness, how rude of me. Allow me to introduce a new associate of mine, Giorgio Zanazzi. Don't you just love the sound of that name? *Zanazzi*. I don't think I'll ever grow tired of saying it."

Bill ignored the introduction. "What developments?"

He was so focused on the group near the dais that he didn't notice the blur of movement coming toward them from the shadows along the side of the room.

But evidently Conti did. "Molly, look out!" he shouted. He shoved her aside.

A long silver blade slashed through the air, just missing Molly Harrison, but it didn't miss Conti. He'd put himself in harm's way, and harm was not a forgiving mistress. His head, neck, and a good chunk of his left shoulder thumped to the floor in a fountain of blood. The rest of his torso startlingly remained standing for a few beats. Then, as if it finally realized it was dead, it fell to the floor with the rest of him.

Although they were shocked and taken off guard, Bill's and Molly's reflexes kicked in, and they immediately drew their weapons: she her sword and he his shotgun. Molly's draw was just in time to deflect a second deadly sword thrust directed at her. Bill rounded on Molly's assailant, as Acilius's shout cut through the air. "Don't do it, Bill."

Harrison quickly scanned the room. Everyone, save Acilius, had pulled a weapon. Even Richard had somehow produced a huge double-barreled shotgun, but Bill noticed it was not pointed at him, but at Molly.

"That's right, Bill," Acilius said. "If you do anything, they're not going to shoot you. They'll shoot Molly."

Bill froze. He lowered his weapon and slowly turned toward the harsh clang of the sword song.

Molly had locked swords with her assailant and finally had a moment to take a good look at her. Molly's face appeared as stunned as Bill felt. "Amy," she whispered.

Amy snarled at her. "That's right, bitch. Surprise!"

They broke, and Amy went on the attack, lightning fast. Molly was backed up on the defensive, but more out of shock than from Amy's skill. Amy was formidable for sure, clearly a vampire, but Bill thought she was still no match for his daughter.

As if she were reading his thoughts, Molly's face hardened, and her movements became more swift, more precise. She quickly turned the tide and backed Amy all the way across the room. Their swords crashed together faster and faster.

Although it was perfectly clear that Amy was going to lose this fight, and her life, she didn't appear afraid, but more determined, and more and more enraged that she would fail.

Stein suddenly dashed across the room and tackled Molly. Although Molly had handled him easily before, Stein seemed every bit her match now. After a short struggle, he managed to tear her sword away from her.

When Bill moved to defend his daughter, he felt Richard's shotgun planted firmly in the small of his back. Bill hadn't even heard him move. He looked over his shoulder at Richard.

The elderly footman took his gun away.

By the time Bill looked back, Acilius had Amy in a bear hug from behind. She kicked and fought like a madwoman, but he was implacable. He whispered soothingly into her ear, and finally she seemed to calm down. Acilius took her sword, kissed her cheek, and set her down next to Zanazzi. The young man hugged her warmly, and Amy seemed to melt into his arms.

Acilius was flushed and looked genuinely happy. He said gleefully, "Now that was a helluva thing, wasn't it?"

Bill snarled out, "You double-crossing fuck. We lived up to our end of the bargain. What's this all about?"

Amy shouted, "That no-good cunt of a daughter of yours killed me and turned me into a vampire. How's that for starters? But you already knew that, didn't you, Bloody Fucking Bill?"

"Now, now, Amy dear, no need for name-calling," Acilius chided. "That might be counterproductive, and we have oh so much to get through."

Molly, who remained next to Stein, said, "We're listening."

Acilius sat back down in his chair next to Lisa. "First," he began, "I'd like to apologize for Dr. Conti. That was not supposed to happen. It was a pure-D accident, and that's all. You see, Molly, I'd made certain promises to Amy regarding the opportunity to face you when you arrived. Luckily, concerning your *most* fascinating enhancing agent, things seem to be mainly about production rather than research. So I'm hoping the late Dr. Conti's services won't be too sorely missed. As to services he provided to you, Miss Molly, I'm too much the gentleman to even hypothesize about those."

Lisa laughed uproariously, and Molly replied, "Oh, you're just too fucking funny, Acilius."

Bill noticed that Molly didn't look at all bothered that Steve had died, and gruesomely, defending her to the last. He thought, *They had their falling out, but even so. Maybe she just takes after me, or maybe it's that fucking drug.* "Can we just cut the shit and get to it?" he said. "So Amy turned, big deal. You told us last time that we were on our way to becoming vampires. I don't see that as earth-shattering, and it's certainly no reason to turn on us like this."

"Fuck you," Amy blurted out. "It's pretty fucking earth-shattering to me."

"Amy," Gaius said, all of his false cheer gone. "Keep your fucking yap shut."

She lowered her head and mumbled, "Yes, Dominus."

Acilius went on. "It's not that she turned, Bill. It's about the specifics of her turning, and what our research has shown thus far. First, I need to ask you, did you leave any of your *donors* alive?"

"Why should we tell you anything?" Molly asked.

Acilius rounded on her, uncharacteristically serious and more than a bit scared. "Because, Molly, it could change everything—the entire world, if you will—yours and mine, and not for the better. I assure you it has nothing to do with your current predicament, but it's vitally important that you tell me. And if any were left alive, I need to know where they are, and immediately. If you make me resort to torture, I will, and believe me, it will be far worse than anything even your dear old dad could think up."

He doesn't look scared, Bill thought. *He looks completely panicked.*

Bill didn't really care about Acilius's threats for himself, but he had Molly to consider. He couldn't stand the thought of her being tortured, and he knew for certain that was exactly what Acilius would do. Bill couldn't see why the information might be vital or of any use as a bargaining chip, so he made the snap decision to tell him. "No, none were left alive, and with no chance of turning, either."

"Are you sure?" Acilius asked.

Bill drawled out, "Sure, I'm sure."

Acilius let out a sigh of relief, and again took on his false cheer. "Really excellent, Bill, really. Now as for you and your girl, here's how things are."

Lisa spoke up for the first time. "Remember, darling, leave the good part for me. You promised."

Acilius patted her on the hand. "Of course, my dear. Now where was I? Oh yes. First, I'm excited to tell you that despite the safeguards put into the formula by Dr. Conti, we've reproduced your little drug and fairly effectively. Oh, it's not quite as good as his, but rest assured, we'll get there. You know, you two could help us speed things along."

The comment was met by the Harrisons' stony silence.

Acilius sighed again and went on. "No, I suppose not. Well, in any case, even our less potent drug works fairly well on humans. As you may have noticed, Richard is well on his way to becoming as you are. And for established vampires, PEDA17 is quite the wonder drug as well. I'll bet you didn't know that. After all, why would you? You were far too busy killing vampires to even think of using them as test subjects. But I digress, don't I?

"The drug, it seems, affects the younger vampires proportionally greater than it affects older vampires such as myself. The effects are temporary, unfortunately, but even one dose can give enhancements lasting several days. You see how, for instance, it has upgraded Davy, and my dear Lisa can already go out into the sun again.

"And most remarkably, it seems to diminish our need for blood. It has even caused slight improvements in me at my very old age. But even as slight as they are, they should be more than enough to greatly surprise a certain old friend of mine."

Bill interrupted him. "All good things for you as far as I can see. Again, why the double cross?"

"Always to the point for you, Bloody Bill, hmmm?" Acilius smiled. "Very well, as you wish. Let's discuss Amy here, turned by our very own Miss Molly. She is clearly a *standard* vampire like me, but now, because of that darn drug of yours, has certain enhancements, which seem to be permanent. No light sensitivity, and she's far stronger and more developed than a new vampire should be. I'd put her at about the century mark and with less blood requirement. She's passed a lot of these goodies along to Giorgio, albeit in a somewhat attenuated fashion."

"Again, where's the problem?" Molly asked.

"My, my, I do go on, don't I?" Acilius grinned. "Well, when Amy and Giorgio found me, they graciously agreed to undergo some testing. We discovered that Amy is far more infectious than your run-of-the-mill vampire, and Giorgio is, too, but again, less so. We think in another generation or two, the infectivity rate will be down to standard fare. As it is now, Amy would have a conversion rate of one hundred percent, and Giorgio, at least in the high eighties. But as for you—"

Lisa put her hand in Acilius's arm. "You promised," Lisa said, pouting.

"Of course, my dear," he answered. "Go ahead."

Lisa's eyes sparkled with malevolent glee. "You, Molly, and you, Bloody Fucking Bill, are absolutely teeming with HVSV. Your subtype is extremely infectious and very human friendly, since Conti did such a bang-up job of hiding it from your immune system. You're both one hundred percent infectious."

"So what, you little bitch," Bill growled. "Your boyfriend just told us Amy is, too."

Lisa laughed out loud. "Yeah, for dead people. You know, the good old-fashioned way. It seems, though, that you and your little bitch are a hundred percent infectious for the living, too. You're some kind of a hybrid human vampire, thanks to that drug of yours. You can actually turn living humans with a single bite, make them just like you, and then they'll go on doing the same, being just as infectious as you are."

The color drained from Bill's face and from Molly's as well. The room seemed to have gone as still as a vacuum, and Bill's ears felt as if they'd suddenly become congested and blocked. *That can't be right. I didn't hear that right,* he thought. He could feel the pulse starting to hammer away in his temples, and he barely managed to stammer out, "You're...you're full of shit."

Acilius responded in an uncharacteristically quiet, and maybe even sympathetic, tone. Even so, in the stony silence of the great room, his voice echoed to the very top of the fifty-foot-high ceiling. "I'm afraid not, Bill. Our scientists are fairly certain of it. We *will* need some additional testing to confirm things, and that's where you come in. But the truth is, you and your daughter are a plague, a scourge, if you will. It's ironic isn't it, but you're far, far worse than any of the vampires you've hunted and killed over all these years. You and your lovely girl are little more than a pestilence. You're like one of those comic book vampires—you know, the end of the world sort of thing—apocalypse. One bite, one vampire, and exponential growth until all that's left are vampires and vampires and vampires, with fewer and fewer humans to quench our blood thirst. Except it isn't comic book fiction anymore, Bill. It's fact. You and Molly *are* the fact. You and Molly could end the world as we know it.

"I'm certainly crazy, but even I'm not crazy enough to allow you two to roam free. Your drug is a powerful weapon—maybe the most powerful weapon the world has ever seen. But it needs to be strictly controlled, and I will be the one to control it."

Bill's throat had gone desert dry, constricted, almost to the point of complete closure. He managed to croak out, "You may have us, but you don't have Ted and Tracy. What are you going to do about them? When we don't contact them, they're gonna scatter."

Acilius's eyes locked onto Bill's. There wasn't one speck of his usual false humor in them. "They're dead, Bill. Aunt Fanny's Family Motel. They put up a good fight, but we only needed a few test subjects. More could prove dangerous."

Tears welled up in Molly's eyes. "He's lying, Dad. Don't listen to him."

Acilius answered Molly, but his eyes never left Bloody Bill's. "I assure you, Molly, I'm not lying. But if you insist, I could have their heads brought in."

Bill assessed Acilius's look, and he knew with absolute surety, one killer to another, that he was telling the truth. "No, you don't need to do that. So what do you want? Why didn't you kill us, too?"

"We need to do more tests," Acilius replied, "and it would be best to use live subjects. But if you force me to study you postmortem, along with Ted and Tracy, I will."

Bill smirked. "What's in it for us—being your guinea pigs, that is?"

Acilius smiled. "I grant you, not much. You and your daughter will live a bit longer. And on the outside chance we find something, something that could control or alter your current state, then perhaps I'd let you live."

Bill scoffed. "Chances of that are slimmer than a snake turd."

Acilius laughed out loud. "You know, I do like you, Bill, and you, too, Molly. If there *is* a way for you to survive this, I would be genuinely happy to find it. But I won't bullshit a bullshitter, as the saying goes. *Way* slimmer than a snake turd, but better than no chance at all, eh?"

Molly spat out through clenched teeth, "No, Dad. Not like that. Let's go at them now."

Acilius's pasted-on, patently phony smile widened. "Now why did I know it would come to that with you two?"

Heavy footsteps echoed through the hallway. Bill thought it sounded like a battalion, and he wasn't that far off. Upward of forty heavily armed men trotted into the room from the various entrances. They surrounded Bill and Molly and leveled their guns at them.

Bill took a slow look around the room, and then his eyes rested on Molly. She was totally revved and ready to go at them, despite their numbers and her being weaponless. More than just being ready, she was going to go.

"Molly," he said softly. Her rate of breathing was increasing, and she didn't respond. "Molly," he repeated, louder.

Slowly, as if her neck was fighting her brain, she turned toward him. Her eyes were wide and lifeless, the eyes of the half-vampire killer she'd become.

For a moment Bill considered letting her do it. It would be over quick for both of them, and maybe that would be for the best. It would be over here and now, and for good. But he was still a father, and if there was even the slightest chance of Molly living through this, he had to take it. He said firmly, "Molly, you are *not* going to do this. I'm still in charge here. Stand down now, girl. I mean it."

Molly's breathing accelerated into a pant, and for a moment, Bill didn't think she'd obey him, but then her breathing slowed. Her eyes took on a more human look: a bit softer and less the monster's, but still plenty dangerous.

"Okay, Dad, we'll play it your way," she said emotionlessly.

Acilius clapped his hands together. "Excellent. Now give us the rest of your weapons, please."

Molly turned to Stein, who still had her sword, and asked incongruously, "Davy, can I have my sword back?"

Taken aback by the request, Stein appeared flummoxed. He turned to his master, Acilius, to help him make sense of the ludicrous request.

He evidently did exactly what Molly had expected him to do. Just as he turned, she hit him with a blinding combination of three vicious shots to his face. The last shattered his nose. Stein staggered, but unfortunately for him, did not go down, so Molly followed up by breaking the arm that held her sword.

As it clattered to the floor, she casually kicked Stein across the room. He crashed into a wall and fell to the floor, unconscious. It was over in less than three seconds, before anyone could even fire a shot.

Molly very deliberately did not reach for her sword and raised her hands above her head. "Sorry," she said with a smile. "Don't know what came over me."

Acilius roared with laughter. "Oh, I am *really* going to miss you two."

CHAPTER 48

The minute they were locked into the "guest-suite" cell, Molly rounded on her father. "What the fuck were you thinking, Dad?"

"I was thinking of keeping you alive for a bit, that's what," Bill replied. "And watch your language. Last time I checked, I'm still your father."

"Sorry," Molly said, rolling her eyes and sounding about as genuine as a three-dollar bill. "And why didn't you take that shotgun away from the butler—"

Bill moved forward quickly and clamped a hand over his daughter's mouth. Her eyes flew open wide, and she made to struggle, but Bill held firm. He pointed to his ear several times before Molly got it. She nodded, and he released his grip on her mouth.

"Hey, I don't know about you, but I'm thirsty," Bill said affably, as he ambled over to the refrigerator in the kitchenette. "Why don't you see if there's anything on the tube."

Molly made her way to the living area, turned on the TV, and jacked the volume to deafening levels. She plopped down on the couch. A moment later, Bill joined her. He handed her a Bud Light.

Molly whispered, almost inaudibly and for Bill's ears only, "Shit, I'm sorry, Dad. I was pissed, and I wasn't thinking."

Bill whispered back. "No worries. We caught it in time. I didn't see any cameras in this room, at least not any obvious ones, but I'm sure old Gaius has got this place bugged up the yin-yang."

Molly nodded. "So why'd you let the butler keep that gun on you?"

"He's a footman, actually," Bill answered. "Didn't want to tip anymore to them than I had to. They'd already gotten a good eyeful of how good you've become when you fought Amy."

"Oh shit. What a dope I am," Molly answered, sounding

completely embarrassed.

Bill waved the comment away. “Don’t worry about it. No choice. You had to defend yourself. Amy’s pretty advanced, though, isn’t she?”

Molly nodded. “I’ll say. At first, I was so shocked that the little bitch nearly did me in. If I had known we were infectious, I would have taken her head, after we…”

“Can’t cry over spilled milk, or blood, in this case,” Bill said. “She’s really got it in for us now. Just what we need—another enemy.”

Molly scoffed. “Not that it’s going to make any difference. I doubt we’re getting out of Chez Gaius alive, unless you’ve got something up your sleeve.”

Bill shook his head. “Not much. These are nice digs he put us in, but I’m sure we’re bottled up pretty good. But we should go through this place to make sure.”

“And after that?”

“We wait. There’ll be a lot of contact with his people, interactions to do their testing on us. One of them is bound to slip up, and when they do, we’ll have to be ready.”

“And what if they don’t slip up?” Molly asked.

Bill took his daughter by both shoulders. “When we think it’s getting close to the end, we go right at them like you wanted to do a few minutes ago. But it’s my call. Agreed?”

Molly nodded. “Agreed.”

Bill took Molly into his arms and hugged her. “Moll, I’m so sorry I got you into all this. Things would have been a lot easier for you if I’d really been a farmer.”

She looked up at her father and smiled. “A lot more boring, too. And it was Mom who got us both into all this, not you.”

“But I could’ve, should’ve put a stop to it, especially after she died. I was just too damned used to being a hunter. And you, too, I guess.”

Molly sighed. “Me, too.”

Her sigh struck a direct hit on Bill’s heart. It was the lament of a person who’d missed a vital chance, and now it was too late. All was lost. If Bill were a different sort of man, he might have cried at that moment. But Bloody Bill wasn’t that sort of man.

Instead he smiled a bit. “Spilled blood again, I guess.”

Molly smiled back wanly. "Spilled blood."

"Hey, by the way, I'm real sorry about Steve," Bill said. "In the end, he did right by you."

Bill expected some type of reaction from his daughter, but got none. As a matter of fact, her eyes took on a hint of her vampire, stone-cold killer look.

"I'm not sorry," she said. "I grant you, he did save me from Amy, but that doesn't make up for exposing me to HVSV without me knowing it and turning me into a vampire. I've heard of betrayals before, but that one takes the cake. Jeez, couldn't he just have had an affair, like a normal guy?"

Bill laughed out loud at that, and Molly joined in. When their laughter died out, Bill murmured, "How many vials of PEDA do we have left?"

Molly answered, "Four. It's funny, but whenever guys frisk me, they make damn sure my crotch and boobs aren't harboring any concealed weapons. They almost never even touch my head."

Bill laughed again, but a bit more subdued this time, thinking about what he would like to do to the guards who'd searched Molly. He had to admit, though, Molly never seemed to let that sort of thing trouble her. *Different era, I guess*, Bill thought.

She smiled at her dad, as if she could read his thoughts and see his mental images of the devastation he'd like to subject those guards to. "You know, I always hated my hair growing up," she said. "Dull brown, and so thick I could hardly get a brush through it. But now it sure does come in handy. I could probably weave a dozen vials into it, and nobody would notice."

Bill had always thought Molly's hair beautiful and envied her for its thickness, which came directly from her mother. Bill's hair, in fact, had begun to thin, but that had been before the PEDA had re-thickened it. *Shit's way better than Rogaine*, he thought. "We better be careful doling it out," he whispered. "No telling how long we'll need to make it last."

Molly was about to answer when Bill saw her eyes flick over his shoulder. Her mouth dropped open. Bill turned quickly, expecting trouble, and instead found himself looking at a cute little redhead.

Bill and Molly were stunned mute.

The uncomfortable silence played out, until the young woman finally said, "Sorry, but the TV woke me up. I'm Elise Little."

CHAPTER 49

Gaius Acilius sat in the cozy, well-appointed study that adjoined his master suite. He pored intensely over the numerous reports, printouts, and spreadsheets that were strewn about his desk. It was as if he were trying to absorb all the multiple sources of print data simultaneously.

He slowly looked up at the man sitting across from him. Desmond Ashcroft was painfully thin, with thick glasses and hair that would make Einstein's coiffure look neat. Under Acilius's scrutiny, he immediately upped his level of fidgeting, and that level had been quite high to start with. He shifted in his chair, crossing and uncrossing his legs and nearly spilling his laptop—which, oddly enough, was in his lap—onto the floor. He caught it, barely, and then began loudly tapping his fingers on its hard surface at an alarming rate.

For the last thirty minutes, that noise had accompanied Acilius's studying of the various reports that he was trying to digest. The sound was so annoying that despite Acilius's laser-like concentration, he couldn't help but fantasize about ripping each of the good doctor's fingers off one at a time. And that was before the recent increase in speed and volume. Acilius placed his hands flat on his desk. If he didn't, he feared they would go on a finger-plucking expedition all by themselves. His voice was surprisingly calm when he said, "Dr. Ashcroft, could you please desist from that dreadful tapping?"

Ashcroft tried to gulp down his huge Adam's apple and failed. He cleared his throat, but only managed to squeak out a high-pitched, inarticulate voice crack. After one more huge gulp and a second throat-clearing that seemed to last nearly twenty seconds, Ashcroft managed to respond in his usual reedy, British-accented half whisper. "Of course, Gaius. Sorry."

Acilius studied the man for a moment longer. He may have been the oddest vampire that the old Roman had ever known, and Acilius had known quite a few of the real screwballs.

Ashcroft had been a brilliant scientific and medical researcher when he was accidently turned in the late 1700s. After a period of depression, he managed to carry on by continuing his research, at first in the human world. He soon discovered the futility of that and turned his formidable mind to researching his world, the world of vampires. Much of what vampires knew about themselves and their own physiology was due to Ashcroft.

Acilius shook his head at that thought, as by the look of him, Ashcroft would appear to have difficulty tying his own shoes. Bald when he was turned, he never seemed to get used to the idea that he'd regrown a full head of hair. He let it sprout randomly, in any manner it saw fit. He wore thick spectacles, but Acilius knew that they were made of clear glass and were an affectation. Ashcroft didn't need them; no vampire needed corrective lenses.

The one time Acilius had asked Ashcroft about his eyewear, the scientist managed to stammer out, "I've had glasses all my life, Gaius. My nose doesn't feel right without them."

The good doctor's clothing style had managed to keep up through about 1940, but stopped there. And although retro could certainly be chic, this did not apply at all to Ashcroft, whose ill-fitting, mismatched, wrinkled clothing would even make Davy Stein wince.

Correction, Gaius thought. *It would even make the old Davy wince. My new and improved Davy is quite the clotheshorse these days.*

Although he was painfully thin, somehow Ashcroft's tweed jacket was far too tight for him. His black pants were pleated and big enough for two Ashcrofts. His neckwear fit him like a garrote rather than a tie. His shoes were a nondescript mud brown.

Or are they just covered in mud? Acilius wondered.

Under this intense scrutiny, Ashcroft once again went through his leg-crossing ritual. When his hand moved into tapping position, Acilius barked out, "Stop!"

Ashcroft started back in his chair at the sound of Acilius's voice. Acilius, for his part, felt somewhat bad about shouting at his scientist. As quirky and annoying as the man could be, he was absolutely brilliant, and invaluable. So much so in fact that Acilius had essentially isolated him and his research from the rest of the world at large. For the past thirty years, Ashcroft had worked for Gaius, and Gaius alone.

Acilius sighed. "My apologies for raising my voice, Doctor. But I wonder, were you always such a fidgety nerd, even back when you were a human?"

"Well, I was always fidgety, but the term *nerd* didn't exist in the eighteenth century and..." Ashcroft's words trailed off, and his eyes glazed over and angled upward and to the left, the way they always did when he was deep in thought. After a moment, he went on. "Applying today's parameters to my behavior and correcting for the cultural differences of my time, I would say yes, I was always a nerd."

Acilius favored Ashcroft with a sour smile. "Wonderful analysis, Doctor. Now to the matter at hand. I think I've made sense of most of your endless reports, but I'd like you to give me a summary of your findings to make sure that I have completely grasped the situation."

Ashcroft opened his laptop. "I suspected you would want a summary, so I prepared a PowerPoint presentation. It should only take—"

Acilius's voice was low and dangerous. "I don't need a PowerPoint presentation, Dr. Ashcroft. Do I look like a PowerPoint kind of guy? Gods, you are so fucking annoying. Just tell me."

Ashcroft humphed and cleared his throat, while taking on that indignant look that the British seemed to have somehow mastered. "Really, Gaius, how rude. Very well, then. I know you like your reports complete, but at their briefest. And in my defense, this is quite a difficult dichotomy to master. So to be very brief, nearly all of my initial surmises were correct. I have now scientifically proven the majority of them. I'm quite certain that I'll prove the few that are left to be correct as well. After all, my hypotheses were all tied together, and logically so." The doctor paused, seemingly for effect.

Acilius sighed again and rolled his hand forward, beckoning Ashcroft to go on.

The scientist looked perplexed at the simple hand motion, and so Acilius finally had to say, "And..."

After a pause, the imaginary light bulb evidently lit over Ashcroft's head. Understanding showed on his face, and he finally must have realized that this time Acilius wanted a bit more than the briefest of the brief.

"*And* the hybrids are totally infectious, even to the living," Ashcroft said. "This has been confirmed. Any humans converted in this way will be just as infective as well. We injected some of the Harrison saliva into human test subjects, and they showed cellular signs of turning within two days. All subjects were put down and incinerated."

Acilius nodded. "What about those turned after death by the hybrids, like Amy?"

"My surmise was once again confirmed by testing," Ashcroft replied. "Such beings will be jump-started, if you will, and enhanced in terms of physical attributes, including a complete lack of sun sensitivity. These effects appear to be permanent.

"They are also more infectious than standard vampires, but not so much as to turn the living, as the hybrids are capable of. All of these traits will wash out generationally, as shown by young Mr. Zanazzi. I initially thought that would happen over a few generations, but now with study, I see that the washout effect will take at least five to six generations to return to the norm."

Acilius smiled. "So Amy, and even Zanazzi, could in effect breed super vampires?"

Ashcroft grimaced and shook his head in response. "Not super vampires, but if you mean, say, precociously advanced vampires, then yes. That would be a far more descriptive term."

Acilius smirked. "And far more stupid. What about the drug?"

Ashcroft humphed again. "It clearly suppressed the urge and need for blood in vampires, and even in the hybrids. The Harrisons' initial blood lust came at the time when they first completely turned. Any such subsequent urges, I would venture to say, are more psychological than anything else. Right now, the girl's blood needs, and her talents, are somewhere around those of a standard six-hundred-year-old, and the father isn't too far behind. Given more of the drug, I have no idea where this advancement would stop, or if it would at all."

Acilius's eyes opened wide. "Really? Those two are even more dangerous than I first presumed. And the drug's effects on vampires?"

"Enhancement of all vampire traits," Ashcroft replied immediately. "And although I thought more so in the younger than the older, this may be purely dose-related. Older vampires may simply need a larger dose for proportionate results."

"I see," Acilius said. "Long-term effects?"

Ashcroft shook his head. "That would be pure conjecture, Gaius. As you know, HVSV will only naturally reproduce and survive in a human host. Animal models are extremely limited at best. It might take years of study to properly assess the long term."

"And our long term is so long, eh, Doc? What about the formula and production?"

"Production isn't difficult, but the formula was ingeniously sabotaged by Dr. Conti. My PEDA is still quite deficient by his standards. He must have been quite an intelligent young man. I would like to have met him."

That was the fucking idea, Acilius thought. *Until that stupid bitch Amy hacked him in two.*

"Unfortunately that's not possible any longer," Acilius said. "Do you think you will be able to get by Conti's sabotage and produce PEDA 17 in its purer form?"

Ashcroft smiled proudly. "Most assuredly, Gaius. It's only a matter of time."

Gaius smiled to himself and stood. When Ashcroft rose in response, Gaius came around the desk and shook his hand. "Excellent work, Dr. Ashcroft, really excellent. If you check your offshore account tomorrow, you'll find triple the amount that we agreed upon."

Ashcroft stammered out, "No, Gaius. I couldn't accept that. We had an accord."

Gaius took him by the arm and began walking him to the door. "Nonsense, Desmond. You have been of great value to me in this task. I reward those I value. One more thing—when you isolate the formula to your satisfaction, I want you to destroy all your research about it, except for one record of your work. You will hide this record to the very best of your ability. Given your phenomenally high IQ, I know the formula will be hidden so well that even your hero, Sherlock Holmes, would never be able to find it. When you do this, you will tell me and me alone where you've hidden it so that only the two of us will know. Understood?"

Ashcroft smiled again, likely at the idea of besting his one hero in life: Holmes. "I'm sorry to say that no matter how well I hid it,

Sherlock Holmes *would* be able to find it. But fortunately for us, Mr. Holmes is a fictional character. I will do exactly as you say, Gaius."

Acilius bowed slightly. "Thank you, Doctor. Will you please send Davy in on your way out?"

Acilius sat back down at his desk to wait for Stein. He contemplated the fact that once the formula was isolated, he would likely have to kill Dr. Ashcroft. It would be a loss, and a huge one no doubt, but he had trouble conceiving of any discovery that he might make in the future to be more important than PEDA 17. That agent was far too dangerous to have anyone else, even Ashcroft, know too much about it. Acilius trusted Ashcroft as far as a person of his ilk could trust anyone, but that wouldn't even come close to keeping the good doctor alive, if his death served Acilius's purposes. *I'll cross that bridge when I come to it,* Acilius thought.

Stein poked his head in the office. "What's up, Boss?"

Acilius looked at Stein and smiled. "Davy, it's time."

"Time for what, Boss?" Stein asked.

Acilius opened his arms wide. "Time to make a phone call, of course. No, check that. What do you say we truly embrace this modern era? Let's Skype."

CHAPTER 50

Needless to say, the events of the past few days left me not in the best of moods and totally distracted. So much so that I'd forgotten to hunt. Now on my fourth day without blood, I physically felt like shit, and this beautifully blended with how I felt psychologically: yep, shit again, due to my piles of trouble with Gaius, Jake, and Jean-Luc. Sure, I needed blood, but more importantly I really needed to make a nice clean kill to get my head on straight, and then maybe take a five-year vacation to Tahiti. Yeah, that might be just the ticket.

All vacations aside, I hoped that a nice hunt might put me in better humor and clear my thought processes a bit so I could perhaps come up with a solution to my sudden logjam of nearly insurmountable problems. On the other hand, whether it helped really didn't matter. I'm a vampire, and even though at my age I really don't have to kill anymore, or very much, for the amount of blood I require, I find I need to kill more for the psychological reasons.

If I don't kill at least a few times a month, I quickly become a depressed basket case. I know this kind of sucks for all the humans out there, but my decades of pretending to be human and drastically limiting my natural urge toward homicide taught me that cold, hard fact the cold, hard way. It nearly drove me nuts.

I stalked my prey on Frenchman Street as he left one of the music clubs there around two a.m. He was alone and headed east, away from the Quarter and toward more residential areas. The streets were dark and deserted as I closed in on him. This was going to be perfect.

I pegged him at about forty, wearing dark, Goth-type clothes and sporting a lot of ink. He was bald on top, with greasy black side hair pulled back and tied in a loose baldy-tail.

I came up on him from behind, took him by the shoulders, and spun him toward me. Totally taken off guard, he opened his eyes wide. I locked my eyes onto his and pushed out my vampire telepathy, suggesting, "Relax."

No soap there. He was resistant. I remedied that small glitch by giving him no time to react. I dove directly into his neck and bit him, and his warm, red life began spurting into my mouth. I began gulping it down, and it was absolutely delicious. Blood always was.

Oddly, he didn't scream, or even struggle, but after he got over the initial shock of my attack, he began mumbling softly. He didn't beg for his life, or uselessly talk out loud to the loved ones he'd never see again, but said rather dreamily, "I knew it, I knew it. All these years, I knew it was true."

He kept going on like that, which was annoying enough, but throw in the fact that he had a ludicrously high, scratchy voice, and it's probably no surprise that his blood started to lose some of its flavor. Well, I tried to concentrate on the blood and the blood alone, but he'd already pretty much wrecked my "nice, clean kill" idea, and the pain-in-the-ass, squeaky-voice bastard wouldn't shut the fuck up. I mean, would it kill him to die quietly, with a little dignity at least?

To make matters even worse, he changed his tune to the flip side and started repeating, "I'm going to be a vampire. I can't believe it. Me, a vampire." He droned out more of that same sort of shit, over and over again, with the litany getting louder and louder.

Finally, I couldn't take it anymore. I stopped drinking, let him go, and shouted, "Will you please shut the fuck up?"

He staggered a step back from me, holding his neck.

I went on. "Jesus, you've got a big fucking yap. And just for the record, you're not going to be a vampire; you're going to be dead."

Now that seemed to get his attention. He took another step back and managed to squeak out, "But, but…"

"You think I'd turn a dope like you into one of us?" I said. But then I noticed how much his neck was pumping red. If I didn't act soon, I might end up turning him, dope or not.

He had totally ruined my urge to kill, and of course, greatly worsened my already beat-down mood. I grabbed him, bit one of my own fingers, and roughly rubbed my blood on his neck. His bleeding immediately stopped, and his wound was well on its way to healing completely in seconds. I let him go and growled, "Beat it."

He stood there, looking at me like the dope that he was, and once again started up with the "but, but, buts."

"But, but, but," I mimicked. "Isn't it bad enough you ruined my entire fucking night? Now you're going to stand there saying, 'But, but, but'?"

I took him by the shoulders, spun him around, and booted him a not-too-gentle kick in the ass to start him on his way. He broke into a fairly brisk, rather feminine walk, with one hand holding his neck and the other holding his ass. It was probably the weirdest gait I'd ever seen.

He took a quick glance at me over his shoulder, and I said, "By the way, you're a little old for that Goth shit, aren't you? Maybe it's time to clean up and get a job."

Well, of course this little episode did absolutely *zilcho* to clear my muddled head. I figured to cut my losses and head back to my hotel and call it even for the night. The little blood that I got from the Goth idiot would have to hold me over until tomorrow.

About halfway back to my hotel, my phone buzzed. I was beginning to think my gutter-low attitude couldn't get any worse, when Jean-Luc spoke up at the other end of the line. The tone of his voice told the story and made my multiply-traumatized mood want to shout out, "See you later, gutter! Storm drain, here I come!"

"Titus, could you come over to the Absinthe House?" he asked. "I need to speak to you."

My stomach did a flip-flop. Jean-Luc was throwing in with Gaius. I still couldn't believe it. "Why don't you just say what you need to say now? I already know how this is going, Jean-Luc."

There was a long pause, and then he said, "Please come. I don't want to do this over the phone, my friend."

I told him I would be there and hung up. I stopped and rested against a lamppost and proceeded to get a first-class case of the shakes. It didn't make any sense. Jean-Luc, one of my best friends in the world, was going to join up with my worst enemy. It was insanity. I felt horrible, jittery, and began to start my typical angry, slow burn toward uncontrollable rage. I couldn't meet Jean-Luc feeling the way I was feeling right then. Our meeting might degenerate into physical violence, or worse. I knew what I had to do.

I broke into the next house I came across and slaughtered a family of four. I wasn't proud of it, but I wasn't ashamed of it, either. Afterward though, I felt a whole lot better, calmer even. You see, I'm a vampire, and every now and again, I need to kill.

~~~

Just after 3:00 a.m., I strolled through a jam-packed Absinthe House. The place was rocking with a great band. It was, in fact, the same band that had been playing the night I danced with Becca, Jen, and Maddie. I barely heard the rocking beat as I thought back.

It was about three years ago, right after my separation, when I was first learning to be a vampire again. The three of them danced with me all at once and wildly so. Later, after my party, they *all* stayed with me at my suite at the Monteleone, and I don't think I've ever had a better sexual encounter in my life. But as fantastic as it was, somehow it's the dance that's really stayed with me. As silly as it seems, I've always thought it was that dance that set me on the right path more than anything else, the right path to truly accepting what I was—a vampire—once and for all. But they're dead now—Maddie, Becca and Jen—blown up by a Harrison bomb.

As I headed down the stairs to the dungeon, Simone passed me on her way up. Her beautiful face was streaked with tears. I knew what was wrong, but I stupidly asked anyway. She didn't speak. She couldn't. She just viciously shook her head back and forth. I reached out for her, but she pushed me away—and almost through the nearest wall—as she raced by me, taking three stairs at a time.

I entered the office and found Jean-Luc at his desk, his fingers steepled in front of him and his eyes a million miles away. There were two glasses of red wine poured and waiting on the desk, and I noticed a third smashed on the floor.

I strolled up to the desk, picked up the wine bottle, and read the label. "A 2000 Lafite Rothschild. You really are trying to soften the blow."

"It is a celebration of sorts, no?" Jean-Luc said. "The beginning of a journey."

"I don't think Simone saw it that way."

Jean-Luc shrugged. "Women, eh?"

I lifted my glass. "To the women, then."

We drank. The wine was ridiculously good. I'm not sure if it was quite worth the $1,600 per bottle that it was priced at, but it was pretty damn close.

We sat in silence, savoring the wine.

"You know, Titus, this is something I must do," Jean-Luc began. "I believe in this cause, and I also believe the time is right."
~~~

"I understand," I replied, even though I didn't. "As to the timing, I'm not sure I agree with you. But I have to be honest. I despise the fact that you're joining Gaius. And it's not about feeling betrayed by you. Well, it is. But it's also the fact that he's going to screw you. You know it. It's only a matter of time. I'm worried about you, Jean-Luc."

"Gaius has kept his word to me on all matters so far. He has provided me a partial list of some of the vampires who have joined with him. I have confirmed this information. And most of the elders who have chosen to move forward with this are levelheaded, respected vampires. He has assured me that he will not harm you or any of our friends as long as they don't interfere with him."

"You mean *my* friends," I replied.

Jean-Luc rolled his eyes. "As you wish, *your* friends. In any case, my mind is made up. You shouldn't try to dissuade me. Considering our long history together, I wanted to tell you in person, of course. I know things will not be the same between us, but I hope we can continue with some semblance of friendship."

"I hope so, too," I replied, but I sincerely doubted it. "Let's leave Gaius out of the equation for a moment, Jean-Luc. Did you give any thought to what Squid said? You know he's right. We're not in the Dark Ages anymore; this is the age of information. If you do this and fail, we'll be outed permanently. It won't be a simple lay low for a few hundred years until things blow over and the humans forget about us. They'll never forget this time. Their damn computers and Internet and social media won't let them forget."

He waved his patented limp-wristed backhand at me disdainfully. "You give them far too much credit, Titus. Those things you mentioned are simply toys, tools perhaps, but the humans are still running them. And you know as well as I that they have a gigantic talent for explaining away things that do not neatly fit into their little universe. I do not think that we'll fail this time. But if we do, rest assured, they will forget about us again, given enough time."

I raised my glass and took another sip. Outstanding. This time when the flavor hit me, I couldn't help thinking that the wine might be way *underpriced* at $1,600. "I hope you're right, but you and Gaius and the rest are making the decision for a whole lot of vampires without their consent. There'll be plenty more besides the Squid who don't like it."

"There's nothing that can be done about that," Jean-Luc replied.

I nodded. "When do you leave?"

"In a few days. Godfrey and Archambaud will be meeting me in California as well."

I was saddened that Jean-Luc had involved those two, but not surprised in the least that they were going. They'd follow Jean-Luc to the gates of hell. He must have seen the expression on my face, because he said, "Before you say it, I did not encourage them to come. Quite the opposite, in fact, but I had to tell them. And once I did, they could not be stopped."

"I understand," I replied, this time really meaning it. "One more crusade for the three old friends, is it?"

Jean-Luc smiled. "Something like that."

"Actually, as I think on it, I'm glad they're going. I'll feel better about you being around nutcase Gaius knowing that Godfrey and Archambaud have your back. By the way, have they tried to convince you yet that God had a hand in all this?"

The Frenchman tittered. "Several times."

I glanced over at Jean-Luc's family cross. It was pure gold, nearly three feet high, and intricately inscribed with Latin and various holy depictions. I observed it was more prominently displayed than it had been in the past.

"I notice that your cross is more out in the open these days. So of course, it makes me wonder if those two old fruitcakes finally got to you. You know, lured you back to the one *true* faith?"

Jean-Luc scoffed. "Godfrey and Archambaud can be quite persuasive, but there is absolutely no chance of that. But to be perfectly honest, I find as of late that kneeling before the old relic as I did when I was human somehow centers me. It is not to do with God or religion, but more to do with remembering when I was human, and having faith in myself and in my friends. As for the Almighty…"

Jean-Luc punctuated *the Almighty* with an extra-disdainful wrist wave, and we shared a laugh.

When the laughter died down, we were left with nothing more to say. It seemed a ridiculously banal dénouement for a friendship that had lasted over two hundred years.

Having nothing more to say had never stopped me in the past, so I said lamely, "So your mind is made up, then."

He nodded gravely and stood. He raised his glass. "A toast. To none of us getting hurt."

I stood. "To none of us getting hurt."

We drained our glasses. It was the most full-of-shit toast I'd ever drunk to.

CHAPTER 51

The buzzing noise kept drilling its way into my dream. I know it was vivid. All my dreams were, but it was one of my rarer varieties that I couldn't quite remember the details of. One thing I could remember—that incessant buzzing didn't fit into it. No matter how much I tried, that damn noise kept swinging through my dreamscape like a cacophonous wrecking ball. It refused to play nice and take on a supporting dream role. Oh no, it just had to be the star, unceremoniously refusing to blend in and be explained away.

Finally, my overworked and underpaid subconscious mind threw up its hands in frustration and said, "Damn it, Titus. I'm sorry, but there are limits to what even I can do. Time to wake up."

I opened my eyes. It was my cell. I'd forgotten to silence it in my haste to try to get to sleep. I glanced over at the bedside clock as it clicked over to 8:02 a.m. I groaned. After talking with Jean-Luc, I'd gone back to the Monteleone Hotel and immediately hit the sack. Considering our discussion and the level of tension it had caused, all that trying to get to sleep accomplished was me tossing and turning away the next few hours. I finally nodded off just after six, and now this: an early buzzing, wrecking ball of a dream-destroying wake-up call.

Finally the phone quit, going to message, I presumed. I let out a sigh of relief. But about two seconds later it started up again.

"Shit," I said, as I placed a pillow over my head to try to muffle the sound.

When buzz-buzz cycle three started, I ripped the pillow off my face and snatched up the phone, meaning to silence it, or perhaps to throw it out the window. Now I really don't have a great explanation as to why I didn't silence it when it rang in the first place instead of going for the self-suffocation, pillow-over-the-face technique. But that's what less than two hours of sleep will do for you.

I was in mid-silence, or mid-throw, when I noticed the caller ID was flashing Jean-Luc's name. I keyed the phone on and grumbled, "Jesus, haven't you fucked me up enough for one day?"

"It's Gaius. He wants to speak to us."

The mention of my nemesis' name shocked me awake way too fast for my taste. The cobwebs fairly exploded off of me, but enough remnants were sticking around to gum up the gears of my half-asleep brain.

"Us? Who's us?" I asked.

Jean-Luc replied. "All of us, Titus. Please be in my office before ten o'clock."

Cold dread crept over me. Realizing the danger we all were in, my sleep-fogged head rapidly finished clearing. "He's here? Gaius is here in New Orleans?"

"No, not at all. He will call at ten. Please be here. I have to contact the others."

Before I could ask another question, the line went dead.

~~~

Everyone was in Jean-Luc's office by quarter past nine. A light breakfast had been prepared, but nobody had much of an appetite, except the Squid. Adrienne and I pretty much stuck to the coffee, while Simone didn't even do that. She paced the room like a caged animal, with Jean-Luc attentively watching her walk back and forth.

Squid was finishing off his fourth breakfast when he noticed me staring at him. "What?" he asked.

I shook my head. "I don't know how you can manage to eat at all at a time like this, let alone so much."

He let out a belch so loud that it actually echoed.

Simone absently slapped him on the back of the head as she paced by.

He flinched. "Hey, watch it, beautiful. I might get the idea that's some kind of rough foreplay."

She gave him a very wan and very un-Simone-like smile and continued her walk to nowhere.

The Squid lit up a Camel and puffed out a cloud of smoke. "What, I'm supposed to lose my appetite over an asshole like Gaius? Not in this lifetime."

"Not in any lifetime, for that matter, my love," Adrienne chimed
~~~

in.

"You're right about that, hon." Squid laughed. Looking around the room, he added, "You know, Jean-Luc, it might help everyone's appetite if you'd just lose the dungeon theme down here. You know, maybe some soft pastels, track lighting?"

Jean-Luc didn't reply and appeared deep in thought, with his head resting on his fingertips. His eyes were straight ahead, looking right through the thick stonewalls of his office.

When he didn't respond, Squid went on. "Hello? Earth to Frenchy. Are you there, Jean-Luc?"

Jean-Luc blinked, startled. "I'm sorry, my friend, I was lost in thought. Did you say something?"

Squid waved the comment away. "Nah, just a bad joke."

It was five of ten, and I could see and feel the tension in Jean-Luc's office. Adrienne appeared calm and cool as usual. The Squid wore his customary rakish half smile, as he always did no matter what the circumstances. But he was more fidgety than usual. He was really well beyond fidgety: he was scared. Shit, we all were.

Jean-Luc looked pale and drawn, and I figured I didn't look that much better. But Simone—Simone looked like she wanted to crawl right out of her own skin. Gaius had that effect on people.

Nick Boudreau, out of breath, stuck his head in the office. "Am I too late?"

"No, not at all," Jean-Luc replied, waving him to a chair.

"No offense, Nick," I said, "but what are you doing here?"

Before he could answer, Jean-Luc did. "Gaius specifically requested Jake to be here. Jake, for his part, was far too weak to come, so he sent Nick in his stead. I saw no reason to disallow it."

I shrugged, and Jean-Luc looked over at a huge flat screen that had recently been added to his office wall. "It's nearly ten. I'd best turn this on."

He remote-controlled the screen to life, and just as he did, the landline phone on his desk began ringing. That benign little ringtone somehow seemed to suck all the air out of the room. Noting everyone else's expression, I knew I wasn't the only one who was feeling a distinct lack of oxygen.

Jean-Luc stared down at his phone as it lay ringing away on his desk. It was as if he didn't know what to do with it. But as I watched him further, I saw that he wasn't looking at his phone in confusion:

he was looking at it as if it were a poisonous viper. I don't think he was so far off the mark. As the phone rang on, it seemed as if even the dungeon itself was holding its breath.

"Jean-Luc," I said softly.

Even though my tone was quiet, the little Frenchman jumped as if he'd been buzzed by a cattle prod. He let out a startled, "Huh?"

"Answer the phone," I said.

Jean-Luc nodded and keyed his phone. The blank flat screen crackled to life with the signal from the cell phone, and in the next instant, Gaius's oversized face was eyeballing us all the way from California. His phony, shark-toothed grin was already in place, firmly cemented to his sharp, angled features. The smile never touched his eyes, however. It never did, and those ice-blue killer's eyes slowly took a turn around Jean-Luc's office.

"Well, well, well. It looks like the gang is all here—except where is young Jake Lyons?" Gaius's voice boomed out way too loud.

Looking at Gaius this way—all head, no body—made me feel as if I were in an audience with the Great and Powerful Oz. If Jean-Luc had adjusted the color to turn his face green, it would've nicely completed the image. The thought took a firm hold on me, and I had to cover my mouth to stifle a potentially horrible case of the giggles. Of course, Squid noticed it right away and mouthed, "What?"

I shook my head and looked away from him quickly. If I let him in on the joke, both of us would be rolling on the floor, laughing, in no time. We'd done it before in serious situations, and it never went over too well.

Nick spoke up, answering Gaius's question. "Jake is indisposed. I'm Nick Boudreau. I'm here to represent him."

Gaius's cold eyes fixed on Nick, who tried his best not to shrink away from that malevolent gaze. "A piece of advice, Mr. Boudreau. In the future, you might want to be more careful about whom you choose to represent."

Nick swallowed and stammered a bit, trying and failing to come up with a retort, so I jumped in. "All right, Gaius, enough of your shit. We all stupidly agreed to take this conference call, or Skype, or whatever the fuck it is, so let's not waste any more time than we have to. And would you mind zooming out a bit? Your ugly face looks like that gigantic green head in *The Wizard of Oz*."

Squid pointed at me. "That's what you were cracking up about.

Not bad, Chrissy. That's pretty funny."

Gaius's eyes whipped over toward the Squid. "You've always had a singular sense of humor, *Neal*. I wonder just how long you're going to manage to keep it."

Squid looked at the screen, all good humor gone in an instant. "Fuck you, you murdering cunt. When you're worm food, I'll be pissing on your grave and laughing the whole time."

The Squid always had a way with words. It was a way that Gaius decidedly did not appreciate. His eyes narrowed to a murderous squint. And with this much zoom, and in high def, it was pretty fucking murderous. He said in a calmly dangerous tone, "Oh, there'll be a fucking all right. But rest assured, you oversized lout, you will be on the receiving end."

I actually cringed for Gaius. I knew from experience that it never did well to give the Squid such an easy setup line.

The Squid smiled. "That'll be okay. From what I hear about your tiny cock, I won't even know you're there. And if by some miracle I do feel that miniscule needle dick of yours, I'm sure I'll be able to fart it out."

Everyone, with the exception of Jean-Luc, roared with laughter, as Gaius's still overly blown-up face did not turn green like the Great and Powerful Oz, but an alarming shade of red.

Before anyone could speak again, Jean-Luc stepped in front of the screen. "Please, let's not do this. I'm quite sure this is a serious matter for serious discussion. We need to all calm down and stop the insults, please. I, for one, wish to know what is on Gaius's mind."

With an obviously heroic effort of will, Gaius again adopted his false good cheer, and his face regained its usual color. "You are the voice of reason, Jean-Luc, and quite correct. This childishness needs to stop, on both sides."

"Agreed," Jean-Luc replied, walking back to the desk. "I am lowering the volume of the feed on my end. And Gaius, would you mind zooming out? Your current appearance on-screen is somewhat distracting."

This time I caught the Squid stifling a laugh, as Gaius replied, "Of course, Jean-Luc."

Gaius panned back his camera, revealing that he was likely in one of his numerous offices scattered throughout his mansion, and that he was not alone. There were four others seated around his desk, but for me there was only one other—Lisa.

A tiny black miniskirt barely covered her crossed upper thighs, and if she'd sneezed, her cleavage would've spilled out of her ultra-low-cut top. Blood-red lipstick adorned her smirking, full lips, and her hair fell around her shoulders, lustrous and loose. I had to admit she looked great—a bit on the slutty side, but great nonetheless. But, it was great in that same way that the Greek Sirens looked to all those sailors, right before they smashed their boat on the rocks.

"How are you, Lisa?" I asked.

"Just fine, Titus." She smiled. "Gaius is taking very good care of me."

I was about to respond when I heard Squid murmur, "Davy? Is that you? What the hell are you doing there?"

My eyes flicked to the right of the screen, and I noticed Davy Stein for the first time. I didn't recognize him initially because he was so well dressed, not wearing his usual clownish garb. Stein appeared extremely nervous under Squid's scrutiny.

"Yeah, it's me, Squid," he replied. "I'm working for Gaius now."

Clunk. A piece of the puzzle fell through the fog of my dense mind and right into place. The near deathtrap at Gaius's, Dom getting whacked, and Gaius seeming to know every move I made. Stein. Of course it was Stein. He was an expert purveyor of illicit information.

I scoffed. "Working for him *now*, my ass. You've been working for him all along, you little weasel."

Stein shifted in his chair, but before he could respond, Gaius jumped in. "Now, Dad, we've just agreed to be nice. What difference does it make when Davy came to work for me? It's all water under that proverbial bridge, isn't it?"

I decided to let it go for now, but I promised myself before this was over, I'd make Stein pay. There was a young blond woman and an even younger dark-haired boy sitting behind Lisa to Gaius's left. I had no idea who they were or what part they were meant to play in Gaius's little game.

"I suppose it is," I replied. I gestured toward the two people in his office I didn't know. "By the way, just for the sake of introduction, who are your two new playmates?"

"Oh, please forgive. How rude," Gaius said. He gestured over his shoulder. "They're brand new turnees and my new associates, Amy Polanski and Giorgio Zanazzi. Don't you just love that name,

Zanazzi? I can hardly stop saying it."

Adrienne chimed in. "Yeah, it's a fucking peach. Can we get on with this?"

Anger flared in Gaius's eyes, but his voice remained calm. "Of course, Adrienne, my dear. It's a pleasure to know you're just as uncouth as I remember you. But my, oh my, what has happened to your taste in men?"

She was about to snap off a comment, but I spoke before she could. "All right, enough of this. Let's. . ." My eyes were drawn to the painting hanging on the wall behind Gaius. I recognized it, but it couldn't be. I looked back at Gaius.

His eyes danced with a malevolent glee. "Cat got your tongue, Dad?" he asked.

I turned to Jean-Luc. "Give me that fucking remote."

Simone asked, "Titus, what is it?"

I shook my head, as I fruitlessly fiddled with the goddamn device. Finally, on my third try, I was able to zoom in on the painting. Gaius smiled away the seconds with an ominous patience. The zoom confirmed what I already knew.

The painting was the Vermeer that Dom has stolen from the Gardner Museum for my aunts. I didn't have the beginning of a clue as to how the fuck Gaius got his hands on it, but I was sure as hell going to find out.

Being a near expert at the remote now, I was able to zoom out more efficiently than I'd zoomed in. Gaius's smile had grown so fucking large I thought the ends of his mouth might meet somewhere on the back of his skull and the top of his fucking head would fall off. Wishful thinking.

"You want to tell me why you stole that painting, you slimy fuck?"

Gaius's expression went from uncontrolled glee to an over-the-top, silent-movie style, mock surprise. Both hands flew to his chest, directly over his nonexistent heart.

"Whatever do you mean? I can't believe you would accuse me of such a heinous crime. I own dozens of paintings." Glancing over his shoulder, he added mock realization to his growing list of mock expressions. "Oh, you mean the Vermeer? I assure you I did not steal it."

I scoffed. "I suppose Mary and Katie just gave it to you."

"If you mean Enanatuma and Ninbanda, then yes, they gave it to me. In their will, the poor things."

I was shocked that Gaius knew my aunts' real names. Mary had finally told me their actual names just after Katie was killed by Bill Harrison, and only minutes before she took her own life.

I slumped back in my chair, shocked, all the energy drained out of me. It was bad enough learning what I learned about my aunts and Gaius in Saint Michel, but this—this was worse. I wanted to think Gaius was lying, but I could tell he wasn't. Unfortunately, I knew him well, and I could hear the truth in his voice. He once again patiently waited for me to recover as he smiled on and on and on.

Both ends of the conference call sat in silence, while I sat looking blankly at the screen and the Vermeer. When Gaius realized I wasn't likely to respond anytime soon, he picked up where he had left off. If the malicious joy in his voice increased one iota, he'd have to sing instead of talk.

"Didn't you know that we'd had an ongoing relationship, Dad?"

He thought I didn't know, and I didn't, not until Saint Michel. "I knew," I fired back. "I figured it out in Saint Michel. Big deal. You had some dealings hundreds of years ago. From what I can figure, it didn't take *you* very long to sour them."

Gaius laughed. "Finally, you were able to figure something out. That first centurion of yours was quite correct, Titus. You are slow-witted. Do you really think that was the end of my dealing with our aunts, or the beginning, for that matter? We've always kept in touch, and one of my greatest joys was knowing that they never told you. I guess they thought you far too sensitive to deal with it."

I shouted, "You're a fucking liar! You hated them. You told me you were happy they were dead."

"I only did that to irritate you," Gaius replied in the calmest of tones, neatly counterpointing my near hysteria. "The truth is I may not have loved them or been totally enamored with them as you always were, but I came to appreciate them, respect them even. And do you know why? Because they never gave up on me the way you did, *Dad.* They were smart enough, and not anywhere as bullheaded as you, to realize that they couldn't mold me into their own image. They accepted me for who I was, and perhaps even respected *me* for it. Again, something you could never do.

"I could really rub your upturned little nose in it and detail all the times over the years they helped me, but we don't have the time for that, do we? I think it's good enough that you know how it really was. Truth is, I miss the two old hags. I wish they'd never pulled your fat out of the fire at the Harrisons' farm. I wish you had died there, and they were still alive. They might have been powerful allies in my new endeavor, or powerful enemies, but either way, they would've been a hell of a lot more interesting than you, and more fun for sure.

"And since I'm in such a truthful mood, I'm going to tell you that I don't know why they kept all this from you. I suspect they had their reasons, though. They always did. Or perhaps they thought I'd eventually spill the beans at some point. But with those two, you never could be sure what they were thinking."

My head was reeling. But what he just said, that was key, maybe a slight glimmer of hope for me in this total debacle.

I scoffed a Gaius-worthy, phony scoff. "Well, Junior, looks like you've royally fucked up yet again," I began. "You should have told me way back when. And you say I'm the slow-witted one? All you ended up doing was depriving yourself of years of argument and stress between Mary and Katie and me. You might have even driven a permanent wedge between us. Think of all the centuries of gloating you've left on the table. You really blew this one, sonny boy."

Squid shifted in his chair. I could tell he realized something I didn't. In my current state, though, after this shocking turn of events, I was lucky to be able to realize my own name.

Gaius's smile phonied up again. "I considered that, I really did, and my youthful zeal nearly caused me to come out with it when they first reconnected with me. Did you know, by the way, that that was only a scant forty years after I first left you in Rome? No, I don't suppose you did, did you? But I digress.

"Even though this little secret was as juicy a piece of intelligence as I'd likely ever have concerning you, I made a deal with myself about it, and in fact about any information to do with you. I would never act in haste. I would file each and every tidbit away for the exact right moment to cause you the greatest harm."

Dim realization began to seep into my muddled head. I opened my mouth to speak, and then it hit me. But the words wouldn't come.

Assessing my expression, Gaius clapped his hands together, startling me. "Ah, the ten-watt bulb has finally come to life," he said. "That's right, Titus. I saved it for the correct moment, the perfect moment, the moment it would do maximum damage, didn't I? Oh, it was a risk, and a great one, considering the potential value lost. Such a secret would become totally worthless if discovered, or if one of us died first, but if *our* aunts passed away first, well then…"

"You really are a no-good little prick," Squid growled.

"That is the first correct deduction you've made in a long time, I would wager," Gaius responded. He turned his attention back to me. "Then Dad, after they died, I'd get to tell you of our secret dealings, as I just did. And that, in and of itself, would bedevil you.

"But even worse for the bullshit Renaissance vampire that you believe yourself to be is that you'll never get to ask them why they kept the secret from you, or how they could've ever accepted a horror such as me back into their lives. You'll never understand the relationship I had with them, and you'll never get to have those soul-searching, handwringing, overthought discussions about it with them that you so love. You'll never know their reasons why, because they took those reasons to their graves, and you'll have to take your questions to yours, never knowing why.

"In the end it will eat you alive, and do *you* know why, Titus? Because in the end you'll have to accept that maybe, just maybe, they didn't trust you as much as you foolishly thought they did. But that's merely assumption on my part, isn't it? I think, though, the part that will end up galling you the most is that they were every bit *my* aunts as they were yours."

A grave silence gripped the room. All I could do was stare at the screen, looking from Gaius's smug face to the Vermeer and then back again. I felt as if every drop of blood had been drained from me. I was totally defeated.

Gaius was right. I'd never know the whys in this mystery, and this mystery related to two of the most important people in my life. It would vex me as long as I lived.

Jean-Luc stood and looked at me. Even through my bewilderment, I could clearly see that every nuance of his expression shouted out concern and barely avoided spilling over into pity. Jean-Luc was a good friend, but that pitying made me angry. It made me want to wipe it off his face.

"Gaius, I'm sure this is not why you set up this conference," Jean-Luc said. "I fear at this point it would be wise to finish this another time."

I growled. "Fuck all that, Jean-Luc. Let's get this over with."

Gaius replied, "Good old Dad. What he lacks in brains, he sure makes up in backbone."

"Please, Gaius," Jean-Luc said, still trying to be the peacemaker. "What is it that you want?"

"Actually," Gaius replied. "I mainly wanted to speak to you. Oh, the others are—might be—involved, but it's mainly you. You see, I'm going to have to renege on part of the deal I initially proposed to you."

"You see!" Simone barked, stopping in mid-pace. "What did I tell you, Jean-Luc? You can't trust him, and you know it."

"Come, my dear," Gaius soothed. "I think your judgment is being clouded from that unfortunate misunderstanding when I last visited you in New Orleans. In retropsect, I'm forced to admit, I made a bit of a mistake, but it was all in good fun."

"Good fun?" Simone replied incredulously. "You killed two of my close friends and nearly killed me!"

"Hmmm, I see your point," Gaius said thoughtfully, rubbing his chin. He broke into a huge grin. "Well, it was fun for me, anyway. Can't we let bygones be bygones?"

"Jean-Luc?" Simone fumed.

"Wait, Simone," Jean-Luc said. "I want to hear what he has to say."

Simone stomped to the nearest chair and plopped down, clearly seething. Burning with red-hot anger, she stared at a wall, avoiding both the screen and Jean-Luc.

"As you can plainly see, I am not going behind your back to double-cross you," Gaius explained. "But as I thought about it more, it came to me that part of the deal, the part concerning Titus and his close circle of friends, would never hold. I knew it would eventually cause a rift between us, and therefore cause great trouble in this extremely important endeavor we are about to embark upon."

"I'm listening," Jean-Luc said.

Gaius smiled and went on. "I'd said that I wouldn't harm Titus or any of the others, as long as they didn't interfere. But the truth is this: he will interfere. Most everyone in this little conference knows it."

"Now hold on a damn minute," I objected.

"Why don't you let me finish, *Dad*," Gaius replied. "Then you can have the floor."

With a great effort, I remained silent.

He went on. "Look at the history we've had. No matter what I might have been undertaking through the centuries, if Titus *judged* it to be beneath his very high standards, he's always found a way to enmesh himself in my doings, whether directly, or by his influence, or by using others as pawns. He's done this repeatedly, and to be perfectly honest, quite effectively. Frankly, I'm touched that he's so interested in his wayward son and more than overjoyed to annoy him to the point where he felt he had to become involved.

"But most of those little projects were mere dalliances for me. This, this is far too important and requires every bit of my concentration and effort. I can't be constantly looking over my shoulder and watching and waiting for dear old Dad to stick his big Roman nose into things whenever he sees fit. We all know that he will. No matter what he says, he'll find a reason and likely take you all along for the ride. When it comes to me, *Dad* can never leave well enough alone."

I had thwarted Gaius in many of his schemes through the years. But I would have done the same if any vampire had done what he had done, wouldn't I? It was about the horrible actions he'd taken, not about Gaius, the individual. At least I thought it was. Was I as obsessed with him as he was obsessed with me? No, no way. And God damn it, my nose was not that big.

"What do you propose?" Jean-Luc asked.

Gaius opened his arms wide and smiled wider. "Just this: that Titus and his inner circle of vampires come and face me and mine. It's very simple, really. If they win, my movement is effectively stopped, and if I win, it will go forward. In any case it will end this animosity between us once and for all."

I scoffed. "Oh, what an offer. We're just supposed to march into your compound with your legion of human bodyguards armed to the teeth. Yeah, right. I think I'll take a pass."

"I think you won't," he replied smugly. "But you have my word of honor, my guards will be dismissed when you arrive."

"Word of honor, my ass," I said. Then the video feed from Montreal flashed into my head. I paused for a moment, thinking about it. "By the way," I asked, "do the Harrisons count as human these days? With that enhancing drug onboard, I'm not sure how you'd classify them."

Gaius's smile faltered, and his eyes narrowed. "The Harrisons will not be joining this party. They have unfortunately outlived their usefulness to me. No, it will be just you and your little handful of intimates against me and mine."

"So me and my little group here against yours?" I waved my hand at his confederates on the screen.

Gaius refound his smile. "Oh, I'm sure you'll bring a few other vampires along for the ride, and perhaps I'll have a few more as well. Wouldn't want to take all the fun out of it, now would we?"

I eyeballed his group: basically fledglings with Stein at just over eighty. Now Gaius might have some heavy hitters hiding in the bull pen. In fact, I was sure he did, but he'd expect the same from me. No, this didn't add up. His group wouldn't stand a chance against mine. We clearly had the weight of years and experience in our favor. Once again, the Montreal video feed ran through my head, along with something the Squid said about the Harrisons in that video. "Jeez, they move like us."

Could it be the enhancing drug worked on vampires, too? Could that be the reason Gaius would risk his entire plan by fielding a team of rookies against me?

"You know, looking at your crew there, Gaius, it seems to me you don't have a lot of age or experience on your side," I began. "It's not like you to give away an advantage. It's started me wondering why you'd have so much confidence in this little ragtag group you've put together. Could it be that enhancing drug works on vampires as well."

For the second time in our conversation, Gaius's smile faltered, giving away that my inference was correct.

A smile formed on my face, replacing his.

"Look at the brains on Dad," Gaius said quietly. He brightened. "Perhaps your centurion was wrong, after all. But as to your hypothesis, I wouldn't say yes, but I couldn't say no. You'll just have to come and find out."

I shook my head. "No way, Gaius. You think I'm going to walk into that death-trap mansion of yours, just because you want me to? No, I think I'll bide my time and hit you when you least expect it. Or maybe I won't hit you at all. Maybe I'll spend my time talking to every influential vampire I can and doing my best to turn them against you. I wonder how your movement will fare if I go ahead and do that."

"I knew you'd say that, Titus, or something like it, so as usual, I'm quite prepared to respond." Gaius nodded toward an area off-screen.

Two extremely large guards, wearing Team Gaius's standard black suits dragged a petite old lady on-screen. Her head was lowered, and her scraggly gray hair hung in her face. When I noticed a few streaks of red mixed with the gray, the icy finger of dread touched my heart, causing it to skip a beat. Gaius roughly grabbed the "old lady" by the chin and lifted her face for the camera.

It wasn't an old lady at all, of course, but a vampire in the middle stages of blood starvation. Even though there was a fair amount of tissue breakdown, there was no mistaking who she was. It was Elise Little.

Gaius roared with laughter, and all of his cohorts joined in. When he finally settled down, he said, "Oh my, Titus, if you could only see the expression on your face. It's absolutely priceless. I see you've recognized young Miss Elise, your dear Jake's baby sis, no less. That's why I really wish that pain-in-the-ass computer geek had shown up today. But in any case, I turned her. And you, Titus, you led me, or should I say Davy, right to her."

I burned with rage, and my eyes flicked to Stein.

He squirmed under my gaze.

I said with a deadly calm, "Before this is over, Davy, I'm going to rip your fucking head right off your shoulders, and I'm going to take my time about it."

Stein gulped, and Gaius said, "So I take it you're coming then, Dad?"

"Oh, I'm coming all right, you no-good prick."

"My, my, the temper on you," Gaius replied. "But wonderful, I'm already looking forward to it." He turned toward Jean-Luc and said, "Jean-Luc, please stay out of this. If you come, even if you declare for me, I will kill you. I couldn't trust that you wouldn't be executing a stratagem for dear old Dad. I know you're conflicted in this, so stay in New Orleans and let it play out. If it goes the way I think it will, you and I will have a long and glorious history together."

I held my breath, waiting for Jean-Luc's response, but it never came. All eyes were on him, but he simply sat, mum, staring at the screen.

Gaius was still holding Elise by the chin, but then he theatrically whipped her head around, putting her nose to nose with him. He studied her face for a moment and said, “At the rate she’s breaking down, three more days without blood, and I’d say she’s dead meat.” With that, he clouted her a harsh backhand, driving her across the room into a wall. She crumpled to the floor, but never made a sound, tough little bitch that she was.

I flew to my feet and took a step toward the screen. I stopped, realizing the futility of it, but not before Gaius and his crew had another long laugh at my expense.

“What are you going to do, Dad, charge me through the screen?” he scoffed. His tone quickly turned deadly serious. “One more thing, Titus. Whether Elise blood starves or not, if you’re not here within three days, I’ll kill her.”

With that, the screen went black.

CHAPTER 52

The second the screen turned off, Stein twitched to his feet and started in. "Jeez, Gaius, why the hell did you tip him that I was the one who fingered Elise Little? Titus is gonna kill me for sure."

"Oh, tut-tut, Davy, he'll do no such thing," Gaius said soothingly. "I had to make sure he would take the bait, didn't I? The comment about you was merely icing on the cake. You're far too important to me to let anything happen to you."

Stein managed to look sullen and happy at the same time at Gaius's comments.

The old Roman turned to the room. "Bravura performance by the rest of you. Your well-timed laughter at Dad's expense will rile him to no end."

"Who was performing?" Lisa replied. "I *was* laughing at him. He's pathetic."

Gaius smiled and gestured toward Elise, who was still crumpled on the floor. "Take her back to her cell."

The two guards hustled forward and yanked Elise to her feet. Before they could drag her out of the room, she said, "You're making a big mistake, fuck-wad. You're calling in an airstrike right on your own head. I've only known Titus for a little while. How come I know not to piss him off, and you don't?"

Gaius put a finger under Elise's chin and smiled coldly. Suddenly he struck her with a head-rocking slap. She sagged in the guards' arms, and blood gushed from her smashed nose and ran freely onto the floor. Gaius roughly pulled her head up by the hair. Elise's stunned eyes swam around the room before they were able to focus on Gaius.

He waited patiently for her to regain her wits, then hissed, "We'll see if I've made a mistake or not, you little bitch! But you won't. I'm going to kill you right in front of your big brother and the rest of them just before the party really gets started. What do you think of that?"

Elise smiled and spat a huge wad of blood directly into Gaius's face. The color drained from his face, and an uncontrollable rage came over him. He released Elise's hair, took her by the throat, and began squeezing.

Elise gurgled and choked on her own blood. She fought as hard as she could, but it did no good. Gaius slowly tightened his grip, cutting off her air and blood supply. As her face turned purple, Gaius smiled serenely. He looked and felt so relaxed that he might have been holding a martini glass at a swank evening party instead of throttling the neck of a struggling, bleeding woman.

Stein and Lisa moved to intervene. They tried to force Gaius's hand off Elise's neck, but it was like trying to move granite. Elise lapsed into unconsciousness.

"Gaius, stop!" Lisa shouted. "We need her alive! They'll demand to see her or talk to her before they come. We need her."

Gaius barely heard her words. It was as if his ears were plugged with cotton wadding. When he worked himself into a killing rage, almost nothing could penetrate his sensorium. Gaius was much like his "father" in this.

Lisa began beating on his back, and Stein shouted at him. Finally, some of their efforts made it through the wall of his fury, and he let up on his grip. Elise sagged forward and took in several hitching, choked-off breaths.

Gaius shouted at the guards, "Get her the fuck out of here!"

The guards quickly dragged her out the door, with her head lolling back and forth between them.

Gaius turned his back to the room and took some slow, deep breaths. The little bitch had almost goaded him into killing her. If not for the others, he would have. That would've been giving away a huge advantage, and that was something he could not afford to do. It was the stress—the huge stress of what he was about to take on.

This wasn't like his previous schemes, which were small-time compared to what he was now going to attempt: a gigantic coming-out party for vampires as a world-dominant class. All but for Titus; fucking Titus once again. He steadied himself, willing himself not to stumble now, not to stumble when he was so close.

Gaius had to say something to his associates. He knew the longer he waited, the more nervous and fidgety everyone would become—everyone except Lisa, that is. In a very short time, she'd somehow learned to deal with nearly all of his moods, even his most volatile. This brought a small, wry smile to his lips. *Lisa knows how to handle me,* Gaius thought. Though he despised the thought of being "handled", somehow when it came to Lisa doing the handling, he didn't seem to mind so much.

He turned to face the room. Stein was yanking at his neck collar as if he were Rodney Dangerfield lamenting his lack of respect. Amy quickly averted her eyes rather than meet Gaius's gaze. The boy, to his credit, steadily met his scrutiny, but it didn't take much observation to see that although Giorgio was doing his best to hide it, he was terrified.

And then there was Lisa, who wore her patented small, pouty smile. Acilius wished he could end this meeting and kiss her full lips, but there was too much to do. Lisa's eyes sparkled with a secret knowledge of the inner workings of Acilius's mind, and there was something else. They sparkled with a complete acceptance and absolute love for him, no matter all his shortcomings, of which there were many. The thought of that sort of feeling for him forced him to suppress a shudder.

He spoke in his most mild tone. "I apologize for my outburst. That was amateurish at best, and a potentially huge mistake. Thank you, Lisa, and you, Davy, for helping me see the error of my ways."

"*De nada*," Stein responded, and Lisa favored Gaius with a slight nod. Her smile increased, showing a bit of her sparkling white teeth, her very full lips pouting themselves fuller somehow.

Gods, she is so damn sexy, Acilius thought. *If I don't fuck her soon, I'm going to burst.*

Lisa had totally distracted him, and Acilius could tell by her smug look that she knew it. "Now, where were we?" he managed to mumble.

Amy spoke up. "Before the call, we'd been talking about the Harrisons and when to kill them. I don't see the point in keeping them around any longer. You've done all your testing, haven't you? I don't care about the old man, but I'd be happy to kill him if you want me to. Molly, she's the one I want. Why do we need to wait anymore? They're dangerous. Let me kill them before Titus and his friends get here."

"I understand your desire to kill them," Gaius replied, "and I agree they need to be eliminated before Titus gets here. But Dr. Ashcroft is in an absolute frenzy, cramming in as many last-minute tests as possible. He has impressed upon me the need to keep them alive until the last possible moment. But I promise you, I will save the pleasure of killing the Harrisons for you, Amy."

"I agree with Amy," Stein chimed in. "They're dangerous. Why risk keeping them around?"

Acilius smiled. "Aside from the testing, I can't help thinking that they may yet be useful to us somehow, although I'll be damned if I know how. Maybe I have a soft spot for that nasty old coot, Bloody Bill. He reminds me of...well, of me. What's the worry, Davy? You've assured me they're completely under lock and key, with no chance of escape. Has that somehow changed?"

Stein fidgeted. "You know it hasn't."

"Good," Acilius replied. "You know, I even toyed with the idea of letting them loose on Titus. I'm sure Bloody Bill would love to take down the vampire who organized the attack on his farm, wrecked his life, and killed his wife and two younger daughters. But the Harrisons are far too infectious and resourceful and dangerous for that. Given the chance, I'm sure they'd use the opportunity to elude us."

Stein said, "Or kill us, but—"

Amy cut him off. "Before we move on, Gaius, I'd like to ask one more thing. When the fighting starts, I'd like you to keep Giorgio out of it. He's too young, too untried."

Giorgio flushed and bristled.

Acilius replied, "He's not very much younger than you, Amy."

"True enough," Amy said, "but he has no experience. I was with the Harrisons for years. That sort of thing ages you fast."

Acilius laughed. "No doubt. But why not ask Giorgio himself?"

The young man spoke up immediately. "I love Amy, Dominus, but she spoke from passion and from her urge to protect me. I feel I am on a great adventure, and it would be an honor to stand with someone such as you."

Acilius stepped toward the boy and embraced him with a warm hug. He looked into his face with a kindly, very un-Gaius-like smile and kissed him on both cheeks. The boy was surprised at the gesture and smiled in return.

Acilius patted him on the cheek and said, "Such eloquence and loyalty from someone so young. Ah, if I only had another hundred like you, Giorgio. You see, Amy, he wants to stand with us, and who am I to deny him? Besides, you worry too much. With us using the enhancing agent, Titus and his little group don't stand a chance. Even young Giorgio here will be more than a match for most of them."

Amy did not appear convinced, but she said, "Yes, Dominus."

Lisa asked, "Do you think Jean-Luc will come?"

"I don't know," Gaius replied, shaking his head, "but I truly hope he doesn't. He could prove invaluable to our endeavor. If he does come, however, he'll be in for quite the surprise."

"Along with the rest of them," Stein chimed in.

"Indeed, along with the rest of them," Acilius echoed.

Stein asked, "So what's the game plan?"

"First, we make sure all is ready to spring the trap," Acilius replied. "Then we saturate ourselves with PEDA 17."

CHAPTER 53

The greatest silence breaker in the history of the world broke the silence of Jean-Luc's graveyard-still office.

The Squid turned to me and said, "I'm in. So when do we leave, Chrissy?"

I couldn't help but smile.

Adrienne spoke up. "Let's hold on a minute here and think. There's no question that this is a trap, and one full of surprises. Caution and patience is what we need."

"And let that little girl die?" Squid replied, shaking his head. "No way, no way, Addie. We all know it's a trap. Big deal. And we'll work out a few surprises of our own. Speed is the key here, getting there well before the deadline."

Adrienne took on an expression that said she knew she was wasting her breath, but she tried anyway. "Would it do any good to remind you we'd be walking into his home turf, his castle, if you will, and he knows how to defend it?"

Squid waved a contemptuous hand at her. "Oh come on. Then he's in a siege mentality, and that crap went out with the invention of gunpowder. Speed and mobility are the key, and with me in the equation, we'll have plenty of both."

I laughed. "You, my friend, are the slowest vampire that I have ever known. As I recall, you weren't that quick as a human, either."

He scoffed. "Quick enough to save your ass a couple of times, as *I* recall."

The lightness of my mood quickly sobered. I realized that I could get Squid and everyone else in the room killed right along with me if they went to Gaius's. I stood and walked over to where the Squid sat. I put my hand on his shoulder.

He looked up at me inquisitively.

"Adrienne's right," I said. "You all need to proceed with caution. I have no choice. I have to go. It's really me he wants, anyway, and it's my fault Elise is there with him. I owe it to her."

Squid rose to his massive height, towering over me. I'd really enjoyed looking down on him as he sat. It was one of the rare occasions that I'd seen him from that perspective since we'd met. At this close range, I had to crane my neck so much to meet him eye to eye that if I were human, I'd be loading up on Motrin come morning.

As if reading my thoughts, he smirked and shuffled back a bit. "Owe, schmoe. Save your breath, Chrissy. All these years and we've always had each other's back. I don't see how that's changed here, so I'm going. It's as simple as that."

If after two thousand years I had a bit more human emotion left in me, I might have shed a tear, but on second thought, probably not. Truth was, dangerous or not, deep down, I wanted the Squid to stand with me. In situations like this I always would. I clapped him on the shoulder. "Okay," I said, "but coming along with me proves your lack of speed is only matched by your lack of brains."

"Nice," he said. "If you're done insulting me, what's the plan?"

"Yes, what is the plan?" Simone asked. She walked toward me, looking long, tall, and on-fire hot, as usual. "I hope you can come up with something better than you did at the Harrisons' farm."

I laughed.

She gave me a long hug and kissed me on the cheek.

"Yeah," I agreed. "I'll have to do better than that."

Nick approached our little threesome. "I'm coming, too."

I turned to face him. He looked scared to death. "I know what you said back at the house, Nick," I began, "but I'm not holding you to that. You had no idea you'd be signing onto a suicide mission when you said it. You don't owe me anything."

"No, I don't," he replied. "But I owe Miranda. I'm coming."

Adrienne had just hung up her cell. I'm pretty sure it was the third call she'd made since the Squid indicated he was coming with me.

"Oh great," she chimed in. "Another blockhead. Just what we need. Well kid, you got any skills? Security, weapons, explosives, anything that might be useful?"

Nick looked abashed. "Kind of mediocre with all that stuff. Truth is, I'm pretty much average with most things, except mixing drinks, that is."

Adrienne rolled her eyes. "Oh Great. Maybe you can get Gaius and his crew really drunk before the fighting starts. That ought to be a big help."

Squid stepped forward and slapped Nick on the back, nearly knocking him over. "Oh, don't be so hard on the kid, Addie. He's got big balls. That ought to count for something."

"And he's cute. That definitely counts for something," Simone added with a smile as Nick blushed through about thirty-two shades of red.

"Maybe, but he's really not my type," Squid replied.

Adrienne favored Squid with a rather unsavory look and began dialing her phone again.

"May I ask who you're calling?" I asked.

"Really," Adrienne sighed and eye-rolled me as well. "Do you think I'm going to leave this assault entirely up to you? The best you're going to come up with is to draw your sword and storm the front gate."

I was going to retort, but there was really nothing I could say. Adrienne had pretty much summed up the depths of my military strategy. She shot me a quick "yeah, you know I'm right" expression and started in on a fresh phone conversation.

"I hate repeating myself, but here I go again," Squid said. "So what's the plan?"

I threw a quick glance at Adrienne, who was jabbering away on her phone. Then I threw a quicker one at Jean-Luc, who remained at his desk, still as a statue, staring straight ahead.

"I think Adrienne is working up something already," I answered. "But for now, Squid and Simone, why don't you hit up the locals for as many weapons and as much tech support as you can scare up."

"Maybe we can get a few more bodies to join the cause, too," Squid said.

Simone shook her head. "I doubt it. The general feeling in New Orleans is that it's best to stay out of this feud."

"Understandable," I replied.

"Fuck 'em. We've got more than we need anyway," Squid added. He turned to Simone. "Let's go, beautiful. We've got a lot of work to do."

"Nick, you any good with computers?" I asked.

He opened his mouth to answer, but after a moment, it fell shut.

So I answered for him. "Let me guess. Mediocre."

He shrugged.

"Okay," I said. "You're with me, then."

"And where exactly are you two going while Simone and I do all the work?" Squid asked sarcastically.

I gave him a one-word answer that shut him up. "Jake."

Squid nodded, and he and Simone started up the stairs with Adrienne close behind, still yammering away on her cell. Nick and I fell in line and started the long ascent.

I looked back at Jean-Luc. He was still staring out into the room without really seeing it. I almost asked directly, asked him what he was going to do. But in the end I chickened out. I was too afraid of the answer.

CHAPTER 54

A rather pale-looking guard let us into the safe house. The smell of putrefying flesh was still there, but it had lessened quite a bit. There probably wasn't that much of Jake left to rot anymore.

"Is he still alive?" I asked.

The guard shrugged. "He was ten minutes ago."

On second look, the dude wasn't only pale; he was bleached and clearly disgusted by the horrible duty he'd had the misfortune to pull. I can't say that I blamed him. Deathwatch on a blood-starving vampire was the absolute worst.

"You can go," I said.

Hope glimmered in his eyes, and his color magically got a little better, but then he sighed himself back to his pasty whiteness. "I can't. Jean-Luc's orders."

"Really, it's okay," I replied, putting a hand on his shoulder. "Nick and I've got this. You have my word."

My standing in the community, and the fact that I had made a promise steamrolled over what was left of the guard's disintegrating facade of resistance. As it crumbled to dust, he machine-gunned out, "Thanks so much Mr. Beauparlant."

And let me tell you, the front door didn't stand a chance of hitting him in the ass as he raced through it.

I glanced at Nick and opened the bedroom door. The odor that didn't seem so bad with the door closed now had its way with my unfortunate sense of smell. I felt as if my nostrils wanted to implode and burst into flames. Evidently there *was* still a lot of rot left in my poor boy, Jake. The stink was different from before, still horrible, but now in a completely novel, nauseating way.

It was an overpowering, almost cinnamony odor, dry and sweet, the way a mummy might smell after five hundred years, but nowhere near that sterile. Oh no, we weren't that lucky. Mummies are dead. There was still life in this room—not a lot, mind you, but enough to wreak havoc with my nose and my gut.

My stomach did a triple backflip with one and a half twists and then decided to settle down and behave itself, at least tenuously so. I steadied myself and walked into the room. Nick followed and closed the door behind him, sealing us both into Jake's crypt of a bedroom.

Even though it was my friend Jake lying there, his stench made my skin crawl. Suddenly I had an overpowering fear that if I didn't get out of this room, I would somehow catch what Jake had and start rotting right along with him. It was totally irrational, of course. Vampires can't catch anything, and especially Jake's particular malady of the heart, so I shook the thought out of my head and steeled myself for what I had to do next. I eased up to his bedside and forced myself to sit down next to him when every fiber of my being screamed, "Get the fuck out of there!"

His covers were moist, with what, I didn't want to think about. Mercifully, Jake's head was turned away from me, but the back of his head was bad enough to deal with. It was skull-like, with what was left of Jake's thin, parchment-like skin tightly stretched over it. In some spots I could see through to bone, but the few dozen clumps of wispy, snow-white, scraggly hairs protruding randomly from his ruined scalp were somehow the worst. I found myself transfixed by them. I couldn't take my eyes from them, for some reason. That did it. My gorge started to rise. I whipped my head away barely in time to fight off the urge to vomit.

I thought, *Wouldn't that have added nicely to whatever the moisture is on Jake's sheets?*

Not my brightest thought, given the circumstances. Once again, a fresh geyser of vomit tried to spew its way up my gullet. I managed to beat it back down where it belonged with a hiccupping, nasty-tasting swallow-belch.

I took a few deep breaths, centered myself, and turned back to Jake. I reached down and gently took his head in both of my hands and turned it toward me. Touching him made my fingers want to run away and hide. His skin felt like wax paper with no wax on it, all cheap and flimsy. There was hardly any tissue left beneath it. His skull felt like ancient porcelain, as if a puff of a breeze could pulverize it to dust.

Seeing my friend's face didn't make me sick again, only dreadfully sad. Even though he was a total ruin, in my mind's eye I could still see Jake clearly, still see him as the handsome young man he'd once been, and not the rotting monster that he was now. My stomach didn't lurch this time, only my heart.

"Jake," I tried to say, but it came out in a barely audible whisper. I cleared my throat and said it louder.

The eye that hadn't rotted out and drained down on his cheek tried and failed to swim itself open. I spoke his name louder, but with no luck. As gently as I could, I shook him by the shoulders, but he didn't wake up. I shook a bit harder, and still it was no good. He didn't respond at all. He was too far gone.

I guess I should've felt bad for him being in this state, but somehow seeing him there, not responding to me, seemed to bring out the one consistent emotion I could really count on—anger. I started a slow burn, and my hard, Roman sensibilities jumped into play. Vampires never lose the basics of what they were as humans, no matter how old they get.

Jake was taking the coward's way out when his sister was in mortal danger. Now he couldn't possibly know this, and to be honest, I'd probably been most responsible for putting Elise in danger, but that did nothing to stop me from redlining. Here I was trying to tell him what was going on, and this fancy little fuck couldn't even give me the courtesy of coming out of his fucking coma for a minute to acknowledge me? To hear about the sister he supposedly loved more than anything? No fucking way would I let this stand.

Hefting him by his shoulders, I sat him up, and my gods, he was nearly weightless. I tried one more time to shout and shake him awake, and when that didn't work, I began methodically slapping what was left of his face. Forehand, backhand, forehand, and then all over again. I was working up quite a rhythm and started to feel like a tennis player in a long baseline rally. "Yoo-hoo, Jake, anybody home?"

"Stop! You'll kill him!" Nick shouted.

I found that remarkably funny, considering the situation Jake had already put himself into. I roared with laughter and kept the rally going. No drop shots from me, only good, solid ground strokes: forehand, backhand, and forehand again. Nick tried to stop me, but I easily brushed him aside and sent him crashing across the room.

When I looked back at Jake, I saw his one good eye opened and locked onto mine. I think it looked seriously pissed, but with all the gooey green drainage coming out of it, and the way his cornea was clouded over, it was kind of hard to be sure.

"Oh, finally. There you are," I chirped. "Just thought you should know, Gaius kidnapped your sister and turned her. He's going to kill her in three days."

Jake's paper-thin, lashless eyelid opened wide. This time I was sure of what I was seeing there. His eye glowered with rage. In a whisper he hissed something that I couldn't make out.

I shook my head. "Didn't get that."

He took a very dry swallow, and then slowly, his chin ratcheted down to his chest. I thought he'd gone unconscious again, but his right arm suddenly heaved itself up from the shoulder, and his claw of a hand took hold of my shirt collar. With what must have been a last-ditch effort, he mustered whatever small reserve of strength he had left and pulled me toward him. A small child could have easily resisted, but I could not.

His face was intimate, close to mine, the distance that lovers' faces might be as they whispered their secrets and promises to each other while lying in their beds, blanketed by the still embrace of the night.

His eye lost focus, just for a moment, and then relocked onto my face. I think he might have smiled, but with no lips left, that was kind of hard to tell. His last three teeth were black with rot, and to call his breath rancid would've been an insult to good old Mister Rancid.

He swallowed again. It looked so painful that I winced.

He took a deep breath and croaked out, "Blood. Get me blood."

CHAPTER 55

Elise Little was unceremoniously heaved back into her room. The door slammed and locked behind her as she bonelessly rolled across the floor.

Bill Harrison jumped to his feet to help her.

Before he got there, she lithely got up on her own. "You know, being a blood-sucking ghoul does have some advantages," she said with a smile. "Gaius beat the shit out of me, and I already feel a lot better."

Bill smiled and began to respond, but Elise cut him off with a stop-sign hand signal and then pointed to the bathroom. She led the way, and Bill and Molly filed in after her, squeezing into the small space. Elise turned the shower on full blast, and Molly did the same with the faucet in the sink. Bill settled himself down on the toilet, with his bony knees nearly coming up to his chin.

Two days ago the TV service had been cut off. Although unable to find them, Bill was still convinced there were listening devices in the room. He'd decided that any important discussions should be whispered in the bathroom with the water on. It wasn't ideal, but it was the best he could come up with. *If they shut the damn water down, we'll be in a hell of a pickle,* he thought.

Elise began speaking in a low tone. "I finally know why they're keeping me around. You two always made sense to me, you know, to experiment on, but me? Now I get it. I'm bait for my brother."

"For your brother? Who's your brother?" Molly asked.

"My brother's name is Jake Lyons. From what I'm able to pick up out there, he hurt Gaius somehow with his computer skills. Gaius Skyped a conference call to a bunch of other vampires, but Jake wasn't there. That's got me worried.

"Anyway, Gaius is using me as bait to get Jake and the rest of them to come. They've got three days before Gaius kills me. But I don't think Gaius is really after Jake, at least, not all that much. He's really got it in for Jake's vampire friends, and one in particular, Titus Acilius."

"What?" Bill blurted out.

Molly's face went pale, and she whispered, "Julian Brownell."

"Who?" Elise asked.

Bill replied, "Just another alias for him, for that same vampire. Brownell was the name we first came to know him by way back when."

The steam was starting to rise from the bath and shower, turning the small bathroom into a Turkish bath.

"He's the one who organized the attack on our farm, the attack where my mom and two sisters got killed," Molly said. "We've been looking for him for three years. What's Brownell to you? Why would he come to save you?"

Elise shrugged. "He reintroduced me to my brother after I thought he'd been dead for the last twenty years. He's kind of bristly, crazy even, but I sort of like him."

"Too bad," Molly replied curtly. She turned to her father. "You think Gaius will let us out to help him fight Brownell when he comes? I'd sure like a piece of that bastard and the rest of his crew."

"Say, bitch," Elise said with a calm, deadly glare. "My brother will be in that crew."

Molly returned Elise's glare in kind.

Bill was struck by the thought that Elise's Jake had to be the very same Jake who was at the family farm on the night of the attack. *Oh shit!* Aloud, he said, "The two of you cut it out. We ain't getting let out. We're way too dangerous for that. I'd say it's likely we're dead meat long before they let us out of here."

The two young ladies continued their deadly stare down, but after a moment the intensity slipped a notch or two. With the wall of steam getting thicker and thicker, it was getting too hard to maintain any eye contact, let alone a stare down.

"There's more," Elise said. "From what I heard, Gaius is moving ahead on some kind of "Dr. Evil" plot, where vampires will take over the world or something like that. He seems to think he's got a good chance at pulling it off."

"Who's Dr. Evil?" Bill asked.

"Never mind, Dad," Molly answered. "Where does Brownell fit in?"

"Gaius thinks Titus—Brownell—will try to stop him," Elise answered.

"Damn," Bill said, rubbing his chin. He shifted uncomfortably on the toilet seat. "Puts us in quite a situation, don't it? If we do pull off a jailbreak, that is."

"Yeah, like which group of no-good bloodsuckers should we kill first?" Molly replied.

Elise smirked. "For the record, we're all no-good bloodsuckers now."

Molly smiled dryly. "Thanks for the reminder."

Elise shrugged. "No problem. But if we do get out—and that's a pretty big if—we could of course just make a break for it."

"I ain't running," Bill replied immediately. Bloody Bill Harrison had never run away from a fight in his life, and he wasn't going to start now.

"Me either," Molly said. "There's too much payback potential all grouped up in one place."

"I'm not running either," Elise said. "Just thought I'd throw it out there. I owe that fuck Gaius big-time, and I have my brother to think about."

Molly turned to Bill. "So what do we do, Dad?"

Bill thought for a moment before he answered. He rubbed his chin once again while looking up at the moisture-covered ceiling. He wasn't a deep thinker, but a logical one, and it didn't take him long to make sense of the almost unfathomable conundrum of who might be their allies and who might be their enemies. "The way I see it," he said, "back on the farm, and before that, we were at war. We would have won that night except for those two little old ladies. It still flummoxes me as to who they were and where the hell they came from. No matter, Brownell and his group ended up on top. But in the end, they were true to their word, letting me and you go."

Molly spat out. "After killing Mom and Shannon and Cathy!"

"You don't think I know that!" Bloody Bill shouted.

Elise and Molly jumped.

He took a few deep breaths to get himself back under control and went on in a secretive whisper. "I apologize for shouting. They nearly killed you, too, Molly, but once again were true to their word, healing you. Believe me, I know what they did. I'll never forget it. But like I said, it was war, and we lost.

"Gaius, he's cut from a different cloth. He's a two-timing cheat who's double-crossed us, and a passel of others, I'd reckon. If he had the chance, he'd stab us in the back again, anytime it suited him. Throw in the fact that he's cooking up some kind of crazy world-domination plan, and it seems to me the answer is obvious."

Molly mumbled, "Throw in with Brownell—if we get out of here."

"If we get out of here," Bill echoed.

"You're right, Dad," Molly said. "But if I got a chance to take a shot at the other ones, I'm not sure I could stop myself."

"If you hurt my brother, I'll kill you," Elise said calmly.

Bloody Bill was quite confident about his daughter's self-defense skills. Elise was a mere fledgling, someone he hardly knew from a hole in the wall, but he got the sense that she wasn't to be taken lightly. As a matter of fact, he liked the kid, and he knew that Molly did, too. Elise Little had a boatload of guts, and that made her dangerous.

Damn, Bill thought. *Just how I want to spend the last few hours of my life. Sitting on the shitter in a steamy bathroom, refereeing two wildcat crazy women.* The image got Bill chuckling.

"What's so funny?" both girls asked at the same time.

Their simultaneous question got him laughing for real.

Elise and Molly looked at each other, then back at Bill, clearly peeved.

Oh great, Bill thought. *Now they're pissed at me instead of at each other. I guess that's something.* He got himself under control. "Nothing's so funny, but you two need to stand down. The likelihood we get out of this cell is about zero, so you're fighting over nothing."

Molly looked over at Elise and shrugged.

Elise smiled.

"So what do we do?" Molly asked.

"Load up on the last of our PEDA and be ready," Bill answered. "This party's gonna start, and soon."

CHAPTER 56

I hadn't slept a wink in the last twenty-four hours. I was too jacked up, and there'd been too much to do. Adrienne continued making her undoubtedly complex plans to help us in our assault on Gaius's mansion, but for now, she was keeping most of those plans close to the vest.

Oddly, her joking reference to what I'd propose for our initial incursion *was* right out of my playbook: draw our weapons and walk in the front door. When I kidded her about it, she buried me in a spate of four-letter expletives that would've made a sailor blush. The flurry of magnificently foul language coming out of this petite beauty created such an odd dichotomy that it set me off with a case of the uncontrollable giggles. This did little to brighten Adrienne's foul mood, and I'd had to flee the room to save myself significant physical harm. I hoped that I would have the chance to kid her about it again when this was all over with.

For about the hundredth time, I pored over the surveyor's map for Gaius's grounds and the blueprints for his mansion, looking for something, anything that might give us a slight advantage. There were two hours to go before we left.

~~~

With the aid of Nick and other local vampires, Jake Lyons drank down gallons of blood. Needless to say, the missing persons report for New Orleans that week was going to be extra-long. He'd regained some semblance of a normal human appearance, but he was far from being all the way back to his usual self. By the end of his blood-immersion therapy, he ended up looking like a gray-haired, nasty old man with a bad case of psoriasis.

When he felt strong enough, Jake got on his laptop and began the arduous task of trying to hack into Gaius's extremely secure
~~~

computer systems. He wasn't sure he'd be able to break in before he had to leave. But he wouldn't give up until the last possible second because Elise's life might very well depend on it, and he was determined not to lose her for a second time. If all else failed, he vowed to himself to do his best to wring Gaius Acilius's neck, or die trying. He was not going to let his Little Red down.

Nick stuck by Jake's side the entire time, helping him with his work as best he could.

~~~

Adrienne made dozens of phone calls, hatching plans and doing her best to give her group some advantage—an advantage they'd sorely need, considering the meat grinder they were most assuredly walking into. She did this for her own self-preservation and the preservation of Titus and the rest of them, but she did it mostly for the Squid. She would do anything to protect him.

~~~

Simone spent those last few hours with Jean-Luc. They did not exchange a single word. He knelt in front of his family's cross with his eyes closed and his forehead propped on the hilt of his broadsword. Simone stood behind him with her hand lightly resting on his shoulder. He was completely motionless, except for his lips. They moved silently. Jean-Luc appeared to be praying.

~~~

The Squid felt the way he always felt before trouble began: relaxed. He lay flopped on his hotel bed with his hands behind his head, watching Canadian football on the flat screen. He managed to swill down three six-packs of Bud before the half.
~~~

CHAPTER 57

The Squid leased a private jet and uneventfully flew us into San Francisco. If we'd tried to fly commercially, it would have been pretty damn eventful considering the tons of weapons we were carrying. All the metal detectors within a mile radius of us would've rung off louder than those super-cheap slot machines in Reno.

Squid arranged for a huge old-style van to be waiting for us at the airport. It was a nondescript dark blue and looked like the sort of thing Scooby-Doo and his homies would be tooling around in. But in point of fact, it was way too dull for that talking mutt. Scooby's van, the Mystery Machine, may have been old-school, but it was styling, at least for an old cartoon.

On second thought, our van was more like something a serial killer, or maybe a rapist, would use. Even with three generous bench seats in the tub, there was plenty of room in the back, behind them, to do whatever nasty shit any self-respecting serial killer or rapist might come up with.

We got loaded up fast and piled in, with Squid taking the wheel. I started in on him right off the bat. When it came to busting Squid's balls, no matter how serious the circumstances, I just couldn't help myself. And I could always count on him to return the favor.

"Nice choice for a rental," I began. "Exactly what is Hertz charging these days for a rape van?"

"I knew it. I just knew it," he shot back. "You can't keep your fucking mouth shut, can you? Unless you didn't notice, there are seven of us. What am I supposed to do, rent one of those teacup ragtops that you like so much? And by the way, at over two thousand years old, aren't you over your middle-age crisis yet? Do you really need to be driving a convertible at this stage of the game?"

"Touchy, touchy," I said. "You should try a ragtop. That way that oversized melon you call a head wouldn't have to scrape the roof of that shit-box that you drive."

"Hey, hey. Insulting me is one thing, but insulting the Squidmobile is going too far. It's a classic."

"Yeah," I answered. "A classic shit-box."

"Considering our lack of time and the task before us, I would think you two might want to interact in a more fruitful manner," Jean-Luc said.

I looked behind me to take in Jean-Luc's small, pursed-lip smile. I couldn't even describe how thankful I was to hear his voice as we drove to meet our fate at Gaius's. I was so relieved that he had chosen to stand with us—with me.

"We're only kidding around, Frenchy," Squid said. "This *is* fruitful interaction for us. It's been going on for almost three hundred years, and I doubt it's going to stop anytime soon."

"Let's hope not," I said. "But Jean-Luc's got a point. If anyone would like to say anything, anything at all, before we get there, now would be the time."

"What exactly do you mean, say anything?" Adrienne asked.

I felt kind of silly having made such a statement. It was fatalistic, for one thing, and kind of touchy-feely, for another. I usually didn't tend toward either direction. "You know what? I don't know exactly what I meant myself. Let's drop it. Dumb idea."

"Maybe not," Simone said. She paused, looked all around the van, and then went on. "On that night you dueled Jean-Luc, when you first got to New Orleans, I found you attractive even then, Titus."

Jean-Luc shot her a "what the fuck" look, but someone as refined as he would never say what the fuck out loud.

"He very nearly killed me, Simone," Jean-Luc said incredulously. "How could you have been attracted to him?"

Simone shrugged. "Chemistry."

I was flabbergasted. "Chemistry? Your dirty look alone could've killed me that night. And you didn't speak to me for like, three years after the duel."

She smiled. "I didn't want to tip my hand too early. A girl must have her secrets, and besides, you were a bit pompous back then. It took a while to get used to you."

Jean-Luc tittered.

"Oh great," I said. "Why do I feel like I just opened Pandora 's box?"

"I slept with Adrienne," Squid blurted out.

In the seat next to me, Adrienne jumped as if she'd been goosed.

"Duh, numb-nuts," I replied. "I know you've been sleeping with Adrienne. We all do."

"I didn't," Nick said.

Squid went on. "Not sleeping. Slept. Way back in Montreal, when I was still human."

What the fuck, I thought. And I was nowhere near refined enough to not say it. I was totally flabbergasted. "What the fuck? *You* slept with Adrienne when you were still human, and I was living with her?" I blabbed out. "She hated your fucking guts. She nearly killed you after I turned you. And do you realize what I might have done to you, you know, me being a vampire and you being a human, if I'd found out?"

"I didn't know you were a vampire back then, numb-nuts," Squid replied. "Besides, it wasn't my fault; it was hers."

I turned to Adrienne. "You want to tell me what he means by that?"

Even though the van was dark, I could tell she was blushing. And it was no easy trick to make Adrienne blush.

"Well," she began. "You were so enamored with the big oaf—"

"Hey!" Squid interrupted.

Adrienne reached forward and touched Squid's shoulder. "Sorry, my love. Anyway, you were so enamored with him and your friendship and this whole Squid thing, I just wanted to see what it was all about. I'd had a bit too much absinthe, and one thing led to another. I probably intended to hold it over your head at some time or another, but the right time never came up."

"Three hundred years, and the right time never came up," I said disbelievingly. "Oh, I see."

"No worries, Chrissy," Squid interjected. "Adrienne told me I was horrible. The worst sex she'd ever had in her life."

"I lied," Adrienne said. "Actually, it was among the best, if not the best, sexual experience I've ever had in my life."

Squid whipped his head around to face her, his eyes and mouth shocked open. With him looking in exactly the wrong direction, the car veered suddenly, scraping and bouncing off a guardrail. Sparks flew up from the collision.

"Watch out!" I yelled.

Squid turned back to face the road, working furiously at the wheel. The van zigzagged and skidded back and forth for a few hairy moments before he was able to right it and steady out our ride.

"Jesus, will you keep your eyes on the road?" I said.

The Squid mock-wiped sweat from his forehead with the back of his hand. But considering how the big fucker could sweat, there might have been nothing mock about it.

"Whew," he whistled. "Yes sir, eyes on the road. No argument there. But no wonder I nearly drove us into a ditch. Do you believe this shit? Women."

I had to agree. "Women."

Jean-Luc spoke up from behind me. "I'm actually Italian."

I nearly choked. "What?"

Squid started laughing. "Jesus, Chrissy. This is turning out to be a damn interesting ride. You really did open Pandora's box."

"You mean all of this French accent and culture and the rest of it is bullshit?" I asked. "I mean, I always had my suspicions about the phony accent, but what the fuck?"

Jean-Luc managed to look uncomfortable and insulted at the same time. He shifted in his seat. "I assure you, there is no bullshit, and my accent is quite authentic. I happened to be born in Campania, Italy—in Nocera de' Pagani, to be specific. My family moved to France when I was a small child."

I shook my head. "So when we strip it all down, you're a greaseball, just like me."

"I'm afraid so," Jean-Luc said. He let out a brief, high-pitched titter, which he quickly sealed off by placing his hand over his mouth.

"Will wonders never cease?" I laughed and reached back to Jean-Luc and shook his hand. "My paisan."

Jean-Luc tittered again. It seemed that most everyone in the van thought Jean-Luc's revelation was quite fascinating, but Jake, who was sitting next to Jean-Luc, apparently did not. He kept his head bent to his laptop, his scraggly, white, old-man hair hanging into his eyes as he feverishly tapped away at the keyboard.

"What about you, Jake?" I asked. "I suppose you're about to tell me you're really my father or something like that."

Not bothering to look up from what he was doing, Jake grumbled, "I don't have time for this shit."

I really wished he had looked up, just for a moment, because at that point I'd even have welcomed the permanent scowl he'd plastered on his face the past twenty-four hours. I was worried about him. Since Miranda had died, he'd become a different person. But I couldn't really blame him.

If we made it through this night and he was going to last as a vampire, he'd have to even out his emotions. I didn't think Jake wanted to make the effort, though. It seemed his only purpose now was saving Elise, and I suspected he didn't care one bit if he lived or died in the process, although I'd wager Elise would. Once we got to Gaius's, I'd have to watch Jake closely—as if I didn't have enough to think about.

I turned to face Nick in the front passenger seat. "How about you, Nick? Anything you want to share?"

He looked around the van nervously. "Hell, I barely know most of you. How about after? I'll come up with something afterward."

"That's really hedging your bet, Nicky-boy," Squid said. In the past few days, Squid had taken a liking to the kid.

Nick smiled, and Simone said, "I guess that leaves you, Titus."

Shit. Now I'd have to come up with something, and I really hated this sort of thing: revealing myself, even to my dearest friends. I guess I'd always had trouble letting anyone get close, even when I was human. The one person I'd let in back then was my daughter, and then she died and look where that got me. Why did I have to bring this whole thing up? If I could have kicked myself in the ass while sitting in this damn rape van, I would have.

Adrienne chimed in from next to me. "Yes, come on, Chris. Your turn."

"Okay, okay," I said. "Give me a minute."

I folded my hands in front of me, racking my brains for what seemed like an eternity and coming up with exactly zilch. Was I that closed off? Was I anal? Or maybe it was that I'd always been blandly forthcoming with impersonal matters that really didn't matter, while subconsciously burying my true feelings. Or worst of all, maybe I was a colossal bore.

That last thought got my brain working at full speed, and still, I drew a blank. I fervently hoped my brain was actually only functioning at half speed, and then a thought began to form. "Ah, ah," I stammered.

"Oh come on, you tight-ass," Squid scoffed. "Stop thinking so much and just come out with something."

"Aha. Remember I told you I was with Cortes?" I started hopefully. "Well, all that stuff he got credit for doing, I really did most of it."

Adrienne stifled a pretend yawn. "Boring."

I actually broke into a light sweat. Why was this shit bothering me so much? But more frightening, I wondered if I'd caught Squid's hyper-perspiratory tendencies. The idea of going through life sweating like a mule sent a shiver down my spine. And damn it, I was still baffled by the show-and-tell bullshit that I'd brought up. Talk about shooting yourself in the foot.

I came up with something else. It was still historical, but *I* thought it was a doozy. "I was Belisarius."

From the backseat Simone asked, "And who exactly was Belisarius?"

I was crestfallen. "Eastern Roman general. After the fall of the West, he—I won back nearly all of the Western Empire from the Vandals."

The van was utterly silent.

I went on. "The Ostrogoths? The mid-sixth century? No?"

Squid spouted out sarcastically, "Oh, sure the Ostrogoths. They're my favorite."

"And they say I'm a stiff," Jean-Luc added.

"I'll say one thing for you, Chrissy," Squid said. "You sure like to fuck around with history. But you're missing the whole point. It's got to be something personal, you know, like how an utterly charming human fucked your girlfriend behind your back in Montreal."

Everyone in the van, even Adrienne—no check that, especially Adrienne—cracked up at the Squid's joke. Over the centuries I'd become quite used to being on the shit-end of his wit.

When the laughter petered out, a thought hit me, and it was definitely personal. "Okay, how about this? I've never really gotten over my daughter dying, even after two millennia. I think about her every day. And I just realized something: Elise reminds me of her. My girl had blond hair, and Elise's is reddish, but she reminds me of her anyway. There's something in the face, in the eyes. Elise looks like my daughter would've if she'd had the chance to grow up. At least it's how I imagine she would've turned out."

What little was left of the laughter stopped abruptly, and the van grew uncomfortably quiet. I saw out of the corner of my eye that even Jake took some notice, bringing his wrinkled face up from its locked-down, computer-staring position.

I immediately regretted my mood-sobering comments and wished I could've taken them back. We'd been having such fun, and considering what we were about to face, I would have preferred letting the good times roll right up to Gaius's front gate.

"That was in the right line, Chris," Simone said, "but a bit of a buzzkill."

"That's my buddy," Squid added with a laugh. "Buzzkiller of the century."

Well, you can never go back, and you can never take words back. Life doesn't work that way. So I tried again. "How about this then?" I said. "I love you all."

Nick piped up. "Even me?"

Shit, I thought. *I forgot about him.*

"Well, maybe not you. But I do like you, and I respect you for sure."

"Jeez, it sounds like you're trying to get into his pants, Chrissy," Squid said. "I always thought you were gay."

The laughter restarted. The Squid had once again rekindled it from the dead, as he'd done millions of times before.

"You wish, big guy," I replied.

The good mood and the laughter burned a bit more brightly as we drove on toward Gaius's mansion and whatever was waiting for us there.

CHAPTER 58

Bloody Bill and Molly Harrison sat mutely on the couch of their cell staring at the blank flat screen on the wall. Elise Little had been easily extracted from the room and taken away, and there wasn't a damn thing either one of them could've done about it.

Molly broke the silence. "We should've tried something, anything, when they took her."

Bill shook his head. "There wasn't anything we could've done. When they put that flamethrower nozzle through the slidey hatch in the door, it was all over. If Elise didn't go out, they would have baked us all, simple as that. That wasn't a baby one, either, like the one we cooked up for the vampires. It was Army issue. It would've fried the whole suite. There would've been nowhere to hide."

Molly grunted. "Then we're screwed, Dad. We were kidding ourselves the whole time. We don't have a chance. At least Elise is out. I guess that's something, but the next time they come down, they'll either cook us or machine-gun us through the door. I don't want to go like that, without a fight."

Bill took his daughter's hand. "I'm not gonna bullshit you, Molly. I never did before, and I ain't about to start now. You're right. We're probably screwed, but we'll have our chance. I know for a fact that they're not just gonna kill us through the door."

"How, Dad? How do you know?"

Bill smiled a deadly smile. "I'll tell you how I know: Amy. That girl's got a bee in her bonnet about you, hon. And Gaius probably threw me into the deal for good measure. She'll open the door, all right. She's gonna want to take you out, up close and personal. Count on it. That'll give us our chance."

"With them armed and us not?" Molly replied. "Not a very good chance."

Bill laughed. "I didn't say it was a good chance, girl, just a chance. Besides, we've made pretty crummy chances payoff in spades before, haven't we?"

Molly smiled back. "We sure have, Daddy. I only wish whatever was going to happen would happen soon. I'm jittery as hell with all this waiting around."

"Me, too. But it's probably because of all the PEDA we've taken," Bill answered, mouthing the last words silently.

Although he doubted they were being listened to any longer, Bill was being careful just in case. Their execution order was no doubt already signed, sealed, and delivered, making them yesterday's news. And Gaius, no doubt had plenty of fish to fry with those other vampires on the way. But that didn't mean Bill would throw caution to the wind. That sort of thing wasn't in his makeup.

"You look as jittery as a fart in a skillet," Molly said, and immediately started giggling.

"Hey, that's my line," Bill said. He chuckled along with his daughter.

When the laughter died down, Molly said, "No kidding, though. I'm so ramped I feel like I could rip the door off the wall with my bare hands."

"Already tried it," Bill replied. "Creaked a little, but no way. It's reinforced steel."

"Doesn't matter," Molly said. "We're going to give them a hell of a go, aren't we, Dad?"

"Damn tootin', girl." Bill answered. "I only wish I hadn't gotten you into this."

"I could've walked anytime. I almost did more than once."

Bill's hard, flinty eyes locked onto his only surviving daughter. He could feel them want to fill with tears, but he wouldn't allow it. "No, not now—way back when you were a kid. It was your mother's idea to let all you girls in on what we did, and at an early age. She said she didn't want to have to be deceitful with her own kids in her own house, and I knew that was part of it, but I always thought she had other reasons. Anyway, I didn't want to at first. I didn't think it was right, but your mother…"

Bill trailed off, and Molly finished for him. "Mom was hard to say no to."

"That's the understatement of the century." Bill smiled.

"I wonder what she would've thought of this mess we've gotten ourselves into," Molly said.

Bloody Bill nearly jumped out of his seat at the thought. "Holy Jumping Jesus! Why'd you have to come up with that one?"

"Shit. Sorry, bad idea," Molly replied.

Bloody Bill felt seriously nervy over the idea of Helen judging their current circumstances, even though she was over three years dead. "Your mother would probably have put the both of us down."

Bill and Molly stared at each other for a moment, and then burst out laughing, even though they knew it was true. The laughter once again felt good for a bit, but the idea that Bill had gotten his daughter caught in a death trap wouldn't shake free from his mind. He again grew somber, and the tears started to come once more. This time he couldn't stop them.

Molly appeared shocked. Bill was not the crying type, and she probably could've counted the times she'd seen him cry on one finger. "Dad, what is it?"

"God damn it," Bill said, viciously wiping the tears from his face with the back of his hand. "I don't want you to be here, that's all. I should be facing this by myself, God damn it. I shouldn't have drug you along for the ride." He put his head down.

Molly reached out and took his hand. "Water under the bridge, Dad. It doesn't matter, anyway, because we're gonna show them, aren't we? We're gonna show them and good."

Bill looked up. His eyes were once again hard and dry, just the way they should've been. The cold smile that he wore would've scared the living daylights out of anyone—anyone but Molly, that is.

Bloody Bill Harrison said, "Oh, we're gonna show 'em. We're gonna show 'em, all right, girl."

CHAPTER 59

It was just after dusk when we arrived at the main gate of Gaius's property. The driveway, dimly lit by tasteful late-1880s-style streetlamps, wound aimlessly up a hill and then vanished into the trees. The gate was open wide, beckoning us to come in and stay for a while, like maybe forever. It looked like the maw of some giant of a hideous animal monster, like Fenrir, the huge, gruesome wolf of Norse mythology that had swallowed Odin, horse and all.

I couldn't get that damn vision out of my mind: that if we drove through that awful gate, it would somehow chomp down on us, metal on metal, chewing through the rape van, and then chewing us to pieces. It would finally swallow us, leaving no trace behind. I looked around the van. Nobody else could've been thinking the same crazy thought that I was, but they sure as hell looked like they were.

Adrienne broke the spell. She reached up, absently touched her earpiece, and said, "Acknowledged. We're at the gate."

"I'm guessing you're not chatting with a telemarketer," I said. "Mind telling us who's on the other end of the line?"

She looked distracted for a moment, still intently listening. Then she said, "I've got Doc and Cat-Juice already on the inside."

"That's good," Squid said.

I was pissed at her. "Thanks so much for letting us in on it."

Adrienne shrugged. "Would it have made a difference?"

I wanted to come back with a snappy, Squid-like response, but she was right. I hated when she was right.

She went on. "There's more. Gaius lied, of course. He has a good number of his human guards on hand."

Squid said, "That's bad."

"The boys don't have an exact number, but they think it's probably fewer than usual," Adrienne added.

"Well, that's good," Squid said.

"Okay, okay wise-ass," I said to Squid. "You're very funny. You want to cut the crap?"

"I'm just trying to have some fun," he replied.

"Unfortunately, they think the rest of the force may be somewhere off the property, ready to attack when signaled," Adrienne said. "Or hidden somewhere, perhaps underground."

Squid said, "That's—"

"Enough already!" I yelled.

"Jeez, touchy, touchy," Squid said.

"Anything else you want to let us in on, Adrienne?" I asked.

She looked at me soberly for a moment. "Yes, the boys have rigged explosives in the subterranean levels. We can use them as a last-ditch tactic, or at the very least, a serious distraction. Problem is he's not sure if they'll bring the entire house down or not."

Squid looked over at me, but thankfully didn't speak.

Jean-Luc did. "This time I'll say it. That *is* bad."

"You see?" Squid added.

"One more thing," Adrienne said. "We have human help of our own coming. I'm hoping they'll arrive shortly."

"Who did you get?" But then I realized exactly who it must have been.

Adrienne said it before I could. "The people from Saint Michel, of course."

Oh, damn it.

I didn't want this for them, to put them in harm's way again after what they'd just been through. But as much as I hated the idea and was pissed at Adrienne for doing it, it was the logical choice and something that had to be done. I'd never have done it, even if I'd had the brains to think it up, because in a lot of ways I'm still a bit of a softy—when I'm not in my cold, vampire-killing place, that is.

But Adrienne had a mean streak a mile wide. At times like this, I envied her.

"Now what?" Squid asked.

I looked to the road in front of us, and thankfully, the open gate miraculously looked like a gate again, with no wolf fangs or anything. "Home, Jeeves," I said, pointing my index finger up the drive.

Squid laughed and started us up the road.

"Everybody, gear up," I said. "Jake, are you in?"
Old man Jake looked up and nodded grimly. "I'm in."
I smiled. "Great. Shut him down. Let's let these cocksuckers know we're here."

CHAPTER 60

Elise half walked and was half dragged up to the great room. She feigned weakness, forcing the guards to carry her at times, but she didn't want to overdo her act. *Gaius is too fucking observant, too fucking smart,* she thought. *I won't tip my hand too early no matter what.*

The fact was, because of the overdose of PEDA she'd taken, she felt stronger and better in many ways than she ever had. But on the other hand, she felt like and looked like shit from the lack of blood. That was okay in her book because what she thought of as her "old-lady look" would go a long way toward keeping Gaius thinking that she wasn't a threat. She would need blood, and sooner rather than later, but considering what Gaius had in store for her, the lack of blood would only be a problem for later if there was a later.

The guards shoved her into the great room, and she fell face down on the floor. When they pulled her to her feet, she noted the smug, mirthful expression on Gaius's face. His man-bitch, Stein, and the others mimicked their master's look. *Just give me the chance,* Elise thought, *and I'll wipe the smug look right off your fucking face.*

Near the dais, she was once again pushed forward. This time she didn't fall. Instead, Gaius caught her by the wrist and twisted viciously. Elise shrieked in pain, and it was no act. He'd nearly broken her arm.

Gaius smiled and looked at her benevolently, maybe even paternally, for a moment. That caused Elise to flash back to the treatment she'd received at the hands of her own father, and because of it, she found herself hating Gaius even more.

Gaius must have picked up on it, maybe from the look in her eyes, because he looked at her contemplatively. "My, my, could there be some fight left in you after all, little Elise?" he asked. He paused for a moment and then waved his free hand as if waving a stray thought away. He beamed at her. "No matter now. In any case, I'm so happy that you could make it to my little party. In many ways you *are* the guest of honor, after all"

"I'm flattered," Elise replied.

Still firmly grasping her wrist, Gaius took her chin in his other hand. All pretense had vanished. His smile was gone. His eyes were stone cold and deadly. But even so, Elise thought she might have seen something else in those killer's eyes: fear.

He said softly, "It will all be over for you very soon now, dear."

"Maybe for you, too," Elise fired back, just as softly.

Gaius twisted her wrist harder, and she shrieked again as both bones in her arm snapped like twigs. The pain was ridiculous, white hot and shooting all the way to her shoulder and into her neck. Almost worse was hearing the sickeningly wet, snapping cracks of her arm breaking. She vomited and started to gray out, but a hard slap rocked her head back. When the stars cleared from her vision, she found herself nose to nose with Gaius.

"No, no, no, not so easy for you!" Gaius snarled, spittle flying from his lips. "No sleeping on the job here. You're going to be wide awake for every *last* second. Do you actually believe your pathetic Jake and his imbecile friends stand a chance against me? I don't think so, you silly little bitch. Today is my day."

As if on cue, all the lights in the great room winked out. After a moment, the backup generators hummed slowly to life, revving the emergency lighting up to its subpar level.

The force on Elise's wrist relaxed some as Gaius slowly panned around the room before settling his gaze onto Stein, who twitched and fidgeted in response. When he finally looked back at Elise, she beamed a thousand-watt smile at him. "Well, Gaius old chum, it looks like my big brother is here."

Gaius flung Elise headfirst into a wall, knocking her unconscious.

~~~

Gaius turned back to Stein. It took every bit of his willpower to stop himself from killing him on the spot. "Davy, you told me that our systems were secure," he began, oddly sounding quite calm. "That no one would be able to get into them ever again."

"Yes, Boss. That's what our computer guys told me."

"Then why the fuck are the lights out?" Gaius screamed.
~~~

Stein flinched, but held his composure. “I don’t know, Gaius. They’re the experts. I gotta go with what they tell me. It’s that fucking Lyons kid. He’s a goddamn genius.”

Gaius felt as if he were on the verge of a complete rage-fuel meltdown, but he knew he couldn’t afford it. He had to remain calm and act. Even with the power gone, his security systems and monitoring gone, he still had the advantage, and he wasn’t about to give it away by throwing a hissy fit.

“And you’re a moron, Davy,” Gaius replied conversationally. “Get the fucking power back on.”

Stein took out his cell and started dialing. Gaius took a deep breath and went on. “Amy, take Giorgio and get to the holding cell and take care of the Harrisons immediately. There’s no time for indulgence; kill them quickly and be done with it and get back up here.”

Amy smiled. “Consider them dead already.”

Gaius smiled sourly. “It would be wise for you not to be so cocky, Amy. Even locked down and weaponless, the Harrisons are very dangerous. Take two guards with you.”

“But there are already two down there,” Amy replied. “That’s more than—”

“Humor me,” Gaius interrupted coldly.

She gulped, nodded, and pointed at two guards as she left the room. They fell in behind her, with Giorgio bringing up the rear. The boy carried a huge shotgun that looked bigger than he did.

“And what should we do, my dear?” Lisa asked.

“Gather your weapons and be ready,” Gaius answered. “And spread out. I don’t want to give them an easy target.”

Lisa laughed. “Oh come now, Gaius. With all the PEDA we’ve taken, and all of the little surprises you’ve put together, Titus doesn’t stand a chance.”

Gaius turned and walked over to Lisa until they were face-to-face. Although he loved her, or at least supposed he did, all he felt for her now was an ice-blue rage. At that moment, instead of speaking to her, he wanted to smash her face to serve as a lesson for her stupidity.

His tone was low and menacing. “Don’t tell me you’re getting as foolish as that silly bitch Amy, are you, my love? Or perhaps as reliant on our technology advantage as Davy?”

Lisa stammered out, “But—”

"Lisa, shut the fuck up and listen for a change," Gaius interrupted, his cheeks taking on a dangerous ruddy tone. "Even with all of our preparation, all of our supposed advantage, are you actually dumb enough to believe this is going to be easy? Are you actually that fucking stupid? When Titus, *your ex*, locks down all of his emotional baggage, he is the deadliest and most brutally efficient killer that I have even known. Now I realize you've never seen this part of him, but trust me, I have. It would be wise of you not to underestimate him."

Given the look on Gaius's face, Lisa kept her mouth shut. She was not fucking stupid.

CHAPTER 61

Bill and Molly jumped off the couch when the lights went out.

"It's time," Bill said.

They took their positions as the emergency lighting started to wink on. Molly stood to the side, with a desk lamp in hand. Bill squatted behind the couch right in front of the door. He'd try to get them to commit to him and then heave the couch at them. Hopefully it would distract them enough so that Molly could make her move from the side. It wasn't much, but it was the best he could come up with given the circumstances.

Bill peeked up over the couch at Molly. She smiled and gave him a thumbs-up. Bill smiled and shot back his own thumbs-up, although nothing about this situation made him feel at all thumbs-uppy. The thought that this was the last time he was probably ever going to see Molly began trying to creep into the back of his mind.

No fucking way, Bloody Bill thought. *That's just the kind of shit that'll get the both of us killed. You'll see her again, all right, old man.*

His self-admonishment calmed him and he was ready; ready to fight to save his little girl.

A soft thump came from outside the door, then another. The room was soundproofed, and no human would have heard the noises, but Bill and Molly's new and improved vampire hearing picked them up easily. He peeked at Molly once again.

She mouthed, "What should I do?"

Bill put out his hand in a stop sign and mouthed back, "Wait."

The door silently swung open. Bill's fingers tensed under the bottom of the couch, ready to heave it into the air. Every nerve in his body sang with anticipation, and his already slow and steady heartbeat slowed even more, as if calmly waiting for him to act before speeding off in an adrenaline-fueled frenzy.

A mirror, stuck on the tip of a bayonet, edged around the door, checking both blindsides. On the second pass it steadied down on Molly.

Shit, Bill thought. *We're screwed.*

A very large man in Army fatigues and with camouflage paint on his face glided around the corner. He had some kind of heavy-duty sniper rifle trained right on Molly. Never taking his eyes off her, he spoke to someone outside the room. "Confirmed. It's Molly Harrison. She matches the photos in the intel report."

Molly tensed to attack as the Army man spoke again. "Mr. Harrison, please show yourself."

Bill didn't respond.

"I know you're both vampires, but I'm loaded with .700 Nitro Express ammo. I know you know what that means. Even if I miss your daughter's head, and at this range let me assure you I won't, I'll still blow a hole in her as big as a basketball. Don't make me do that. Show yourself."

Bill had no choice. He stood, a little quickly, hoping to draw the man's aim off, even a fraction. That would've been enough for Molly to make a move. But the man's aim never wavered, and the red dot from the soldier's laser scope remained steadily seated right in the middle of his daughter's forehead.

A second soldier glided around the corner with a similar rifle trained on Bill. Soldier number two said, "Confirmed, Juice. Bill Harrison. Let's do this and move on. We're running out of time."

The first soldier, the one with the odd name, said, "Hold your horses, Doc. I'm thinking."

"Thinking about what?" Doc asked. "They're the enemy."

"Maybe, but haven't you heard the saying about the enemy of my enemy?"

"Sure I have. But do you think that's enough? Leaving two as dangerous as them alive, given our mission parameters?"

"That's exactly why I'd be doing it, Doc, for the mission," Juice replied. "We don't stand a snowball's chance in hell, and you know it. We're totally outclassed and outgunned, even if the backup gets here on time."

Doc said, "So what? Then the mission fails. It happens."

"Yeah, and Addie and the major and all the rest die. Isn't part of our mission keeping them safe?"

Doc looked disturbed by this statement, but his eyes never wavered for a moment from Bloody Bill.

Bill waited, somewhat shocked, thinking that he and his daughter might still have a chance. The next exchange would spell it out. He readied himself to make a suicide rush if it went the wrong way. He glanced over at Molly and could see that she was ready, too.

Doc said, "You've got rank. Your call."

Keeping his eyes dead steady on Molly, Juice said, "Mr. Harrison, it seems you've fallen afoul of Gaius Acilius, with you and your daughter being under lock and key here."

"You're damn right about that," Bill drawled.

Juice went on. "At the present time there's an assault in progress against him. From what I've read, you may bear a grudge against my team, but as you're well aware, in time of war, alliances frequently change. If I were to release you, again given what I've read about you, I believe you would join the fight rather than retreat."

Molly answered for him. "You're damn right about that, too."

"That would serve my purposes," Juice replied. "But I must have your word of honor, Mr. Harrison, that you will not harm any member of my team."

"You have it," Bill replied immediately.

"And your daughter's as well," Juice added.

Silence ticked out in the room. Bill looked over at Molly. With her arms defiantly folded over her chest and the red laser dot still on her forehead, she glared at the soldier called Juice.

Bill said, "Molly, for God's sake!"

She turned her glare to Bill. "How could you, Dad? Those are the ones who killed Mom and Shannon and Cathy. How could you promise not to harm them?"

Bloody Bill spoke to Molly as if he were chastising a child, not as if both of them were about to have their heads blown off. "Darn it, Molly. We've been through this. You promise this man right now."

Molly wasn't usually much of a pouter, but this time she came close. Exasperated, she finally said, "All right. I promise."

A flicker of a smile touched Juice's lips. "Thank you. Now my associate and I are going to leave. If we see a head look out that door before say, ten Mississippi, we'll be forced to blow it off. Understood?"

Bill nodded.

Doc said, "Just for the record, I think this is a very bad idea."

"Duly noted," Juice replied. He turned to the Harrisons. "Good luck, Mr. Harrison. Good luck, Ms. Harrison."

With that, Juice tipped an imaginary hat to Molly, and both soldiers were gone like smoke.

Molly rounded on Bill. "How could you?"

"Oh sure, we could've taken your tack and had our heads blown off," Bill scoffed. "What the hell were you thinking, girl?"

"I'll tell you what I was thinking—"

Bill interrupted her. "You can tell me later. I think we've got plenty else to worry about. Ten Mississippi. Let's go."

Bill looked each way down the hallway, and then very carefully, they stepped out of the room and to their freedom for the first time in many days. The two guards that Gaius had stationed outside their cell were dead on the floor, their throats neatly slit. Bill took their weapons while Molly checked out a metal locker down the hall.

"Convenient," she said with a smile.

Bill looked up. "What?"

Molly tossed Bill his Mossberg shotgun. "All our stuff is right here, Dad."

Bill smiled. "Let's gear up and go hunting."

The two of them cocked and holstered so many weapons that the resulting clicks and clacks sounded like an old freight train lugging up a steep rise.

Their hunt didn't last very long. They rounded the first corner and almost walked into two of Gaius's guards. Molly nearly cut the first one in half, and Bill quickly drew his bowie knife and buried it in the forehead of the second one. They fell to the floor, dead. And there, about thirty feet beyond them, looking as shocked as all get out, were Amy Polanski and Giorgio Zanazzi. Amy had a sword, and the boy carried a huge shotgun.

Bloody Bill smiled his deadliest smile. "Well, well, well. What do we have here?"

The boy squeezed off a shot in response, filling the hallway with a deafening roar. Molly and her dad were peppered with some very widespread and essentially harmless buckshot.

She laughed. "I think your boy-toy needs more training, Amy. He's got the choke on that shotgun all screwed up."

Bill added, "Yep, it's pretty useless firing at that distance when you're dealing with vampires, unless you're a good shot like me."

Bill smoothly raised his Mossberg and fired, taking the legs out from under Zanazzi, who went crashing to the floor. Molly charged at Amy, and their two swords clashed and caught together as the two girls strained at each other. They released, and the swords met again and again, singing their deadly metallic song.

Bill advanced on the boy as he regained his feet. This time, he put a charge directly into his chest. Blood flew, and Zanazzi was blown back flat on his back. Bill cocked his weapon and moved forward for the headshot.

~~~

Giorgio Zanazzi lay on the floor, his chest ruined and in horrible pain, but somehow he'd managed to hold on to his weapon. He could already feel his body healing as the overdose of PEDA was doing its work. He knew Amy was good with her sword, but that horrible Harrison woman was far better. If he were going to help Amy, Giorgio would have to dispose of this nasty old man.

I am destined for great things, he thought, as he sprang to his feet and fired his big gun from the hip.

~~~

Bill felt his head pushed back gently but firmly, as if by a strong wind. There was absolutely no pain, but even so, he couldn't help falling to his knees. He thought he heard screaming, but he couldn't be sure with all the ringing in his ears.

He fought to remember what he'd just been doing, but he was having trouble thinking. It was as if his thoughts were wrapped in thick cotton wadding. His vision darkened and blurred and came in and out of focus. At least the left side of the hallway did, anyway. He couldn't see to the right.

That boy, he couldn't bring back his name now, was coming toward him, his big shotgun in hand. He seemed to be moving in slow motion as he cocked his gun while advancing forward. Bill couldn't hear the click, but he sure as hell saw him do it. He made to cock his own weapon, but his left arm wouldn't seem to move. Firing a shotgun with one arm was pretty damn stupid, and he wasn't even sure if his Mossberg was cocked.

Bill thought, *What the hell.* He swung his shotgun up and fired.

The boy's head exploded from his body in a bloody pulp.

The gun's kick drove Bloody Bill backward to the floor. His vision swam again and then came back, affording him a fine view of the hallway ceiling. *I'm dying,* he thought calmly. His mind was muddled, his thoughts were getting slower and slower, harder to corral, but one of them kept pounding its way through the confusion: *Molly. Shit,* he thought. *Just let me live long enough to get her out of here. That's all I ask.*

Bill had never been a religious man, and that was about as close to a prayer as he'd ever come in his adult life. But even in the state he was in, the second he thought it, he knew it was bullshit. He was too badly hurt. His vision swam again and threatened to darken for good this time, but by sheer force of will, he didn't let it. He had to see Molly again.

This time, maybe his prayer was answered. Her face appeared above his.

~~~

Tears ran in torrents down Molly's face as she looked at her father. His right forehead, from the eyeball up, was blown away. His left eye swam aimlessly around as if trying to follow a pesky housefly that he just couldn't hold sight on. Blood ran from his nose in torrents, soaking his moustache. The "good" side of his face seemed to want to droop and melt down into his chest. His breathing rattled erratically from his chest.

Molly sobbed out, "Oh, Daddy."

The sound of her voice seemed to focus him. The one eye he still had locked onto Molly. A small smile touched the right corner of his lips. He swallowed. "Get out of here. You get out of here, girl."

His voice was so thick and garbled that Molly could barely understand him. A fresh gush of tears sprang from her eyes. She shook her head. "No, Daddy. I'm staying with you. It's going to be all right. You'll heal. You'll see."

"Liar," Bill managed to croak out. More blood pumped from his nose, choking him.

Molly tried her best to wipe it away, but it wouldn't quit gushing.

Bill coughed weakly. His breathing slowed to a halt, and his eye rolled away from her.

"Daddy, Daddy?" Molly cried out.

Bloody Bill took a congested, hitching breath, and he found his daughter's face for the very last time. His good arm floated up
~~~

slowly, and he lightly touched her cheek. "Live, Molly," he whispered. "You live."

Bloody Bill Harrison took a last shallow breath and closed his eye. His hand fell lifelessly to the cold stone floor.

Molly screamed at the top of her lungs. Tears exploded from her eyes, and she screeched, "No!" over and over again.

After a time, her screaming petered out, and her tears slowed to a stop. She was done—done for now, anyway. She knew there'd be gallons more tears later, but they would have to wait. If she stayed like this any longer, she'd be a sitting duck. If anything, Molly was a practical girl. After all, she was Bloody Bill's daughter.

She stood, finally looking away from her dad. But then she looked back at him, and the tears wanted to start all over. "No," she said out loud, and viciously fought them back.

She bent back down and picked up her father's Mossberg. She kissed him goodbye on what was left of his ruined forehead. She stood once again, and when she looked back at him this time, she had a cold, hard expression on her face. If a mirror had been available, she would have recognized it in an instant. It was the look Bloody Bill Harrison wore when he had killing to do.

"I'll live, Daddy. I promise," Molly said. "And while I'm doing it, I'm gonna kill every last motherfucker in this place!"

CHAPTER 62

Amy ran through one of the many side entrances of Gaius's great room. When Gaius saw her, cold dread touched his heart. Her left arm was missing just below the elbow, but the bleeding had already slowed to a trickle. Amy stopped before him, panting like a bull.

Amy's butchered state indicated a serious turn of events. Even so, Gaius could never resist the opportunity to display his sarcastic wit. He looked to where her arm should have been and smiled. "You forget something, Amy?"

"What?" Amy replied, appearing dumbfounded. Then she looked at the stump of her arm. "Oh, my arm. That bitch, Molly, cut it off. I barely got away."

Gaius's phony humor evaporated quickly. "Got away, did you?" The volume of his voice rose dangerously. "Just how the fuck did you let *them* get away when they were locked up tighter than a fucking drum? Would you mind explaining that one to me, Amy?"

The color drained from Amy's face, and she backed away, taking first one tentative step and then another. "I swear, Gaius, they were already out when we got there. I don't know how. They killed our guards, and then Giorgio. Poor Giorgio." She began crying.

"Giorgio is dead?"

"Yes," Amy sobbed. "But he killed that fucking old man first."

"Giorgio killed Bloody Bill!" Gaius blurted out.

Amy nodded as tears ran down her face.

"Too bad he's dead. I liked the boy." Gaius ruminated over the situation. "Killing Bloody Bill Harrison was no easy trick. No telling what poor Giorgio may have accomplished, but no matter. I presume Miss Molly is on the prowl?"

Amy looked as if she'd prefer to have her other arm cut off rather than to answer the question. She managed to squeak out, "Yes, but—

”

Gaius cut her off. “Davy, what’s the status of our power?”

Stein closed his cell phone with a snap. “Zilch, Boss. That Lyons kid fucked up our shit but good.”

“Eloquently put, Davy,” Gaius replied with a smirk. “We’ll have to make do without our security systems. No matter. We’re still more than a match for them. Rally all of our human troops.” He turned back to Amy. “And you, take some men, a lot of them, and go find your fucking arm and Molly Harrison. Do not fail me this time, Amy. Am I understood?”

All Amy could manage was a slight spastic nod. Before she could start on her way, the door at the far end of the room opened, and through it walked Titus Acilius.

As the rest of his group filed in, Gaius said in a low tone, “Too late for that now, my dear. Davy, give old one-arm one of your machine pistols. Maybe she can be of some use before one of our guests takes her head.”

~~~

I opened the main door of Gaius’s great room. The emergency light was dim, but not so much so that I couldn’t see Gaius, Lisa, Stein, and Amy Polanski at the far end of the room and armed to the teeth. Elise lay crumpled on the floor against a wall. I thought she was still breathing, but I couldn’t be sure from this distance. Jake took a quick step forward.

I put a hand on him. “Stop,” I said in a low tone. “That’s just the kind of thing he wants us to do.”

Jake glared at me for a moment, and I didn’t think he was going to listen, but then reason slowly found its way back to his face. He nodded, and I released him. The seven of us spread out into a loose skirmish line at the far end of the room.

“Daddy!” Gaius said with mock cheer. “I’m so glad you could come.”

“Wouldn’t have missed it for the world, Junior,” I replied. “By the way, we killed several of your guards on our trek through your oversized barn here. So much for keeping humans out of this. But you always were a fucking liar, weren’t you, Gaius?”

“Oh Dad, come now,” he answered. “Liar is such an ugly word. How about exaggerator, or better yet, jokester? Yes, a jolly jokester, that’s me. I think I like that one. Besides, it’s all in the name of good,
~~~

clean fun."

I scoffed. "Looks like the joke's on you. Only four of you? Your legion's a bit light, don't you think?"

"You know, I was just thinking the very same thing," Gaius replied. He looked over to his left.

From out of the shadows walked John Dodd. He wore a beautifully tailored dark blue suit, and as per usual, looked the epitome of the perfect gentleman. He said in his clipped British accent, "Hello, Titus. So sorry that we're meeting like this."

I was shocked. Dodd was an old friend that I'd known for over a hundred years. "John, what the hell are you doing here? I *know* the mayor of London is dead set against the sort of thing that Gaius is cooking up."

He replied matter-of-factly, "As was the deputy mayor. They both held onto that view right up until the very moment that I killed them."

Squid leaned in and whispered, "So you know this guy. Big deal. It doesn't change anything. And if you ask me, he looks like a bit of a pansy."

"He was Jack the Ripper, you idiot," I replied.

Squid shot Dodd another assessing look and then replied meekly, "Oh."

I turned back to my nemesis. "I still only count five, Gaius."

"More than enough for your sorry group," he answered with a smile. "But I do see your point."

He looked to the other side of the room, and to my utter shock, Godfrey and Archambaud walked to the center and joined Gaius's group.

Jean-Luc sucked in a loud breath.

Shit! Not those two, I thought.

"Do you stand against me?" Jean-Luc asked disbelievingly. "After all our years as brothers?"

It was Archambaud who answered. "Not against you, Hugues, but *for* this glorious cause. God has spoken to us."

"I think you guys need to pick a new god, then," Squid said. "Gaius is a bit of an asshole, isn't he?"

"It is these godless heathens that you associate with who have led you down this path, Hugues!" Godfrey shouted angrily. He collected himself and continued speaking calmly. "We have been brother knights for centuries. We have crusaded together. We suffered the terrible ordeal of turning together, and many others, both before and after. We are blood, my cousin. I beg you, in the name of God, please walk away from this now."

Jean-Luc did not hesitate in his response. "You know I cannot do that, cousin." He turned to me and drew his broadsword. "Those two are mine. It is my fault that they are here at all."

I nodded and said to Gaius, the only "son" I would ever have, "If you're done with little surprises, I'm getting a bit anxious to kill you."

I started forward at a slow walk, and my group followed suit, but Gaius dashed over and snatched Elise off the floor. He held her in front of him and twisted her arm viciously, making her moan in pain. She was a wreck. Gaius, the bastard, had blood-starved her, and she was breaking down. Somehow, she still had managed to keep one defiant streak of red in her unkempt gray-white mop of hair.

"Not so fast, *Dad,*" Gaius said. "You see, I've got a few more things to say to you, things you really need to hear about your aunties and a lot more. And since you're going to be as dead as dog shit in a few minutes, this is my very last opportunity to bring you up to speed. I wouldn't want you to go to your grave without first being totally fucked up by what I'm about to tell you. So unless you want little Elise here dead right now, you all better stop."

Our skirmish line, including Jake, to my great relief, stopped in its tracks.

Gaius smiled benevolently. "That's better. Now—"

That fake smile, and whatever Gaius was about to say, was wiped away in an instant. With her free hand, Elise grabbed the arm that Gaius was using to hold her and whipped it backward at a horrible angle. The snapping sound of bones breaking even made me wince.

Gaius howled in pain. But somehow, even with his arm shattered, he managed to hang onto Elise for a moment. For a moment, until she sank her fangs into his arm. This time he didn't howl; he screamed. Elise shook free of him and bolted for the side of the room, spitting out chunks of Gaius's arm as she ran.

And then all hell broke loose.

CHAPTER 63

Oddly enough, it was Stein who reacted the quickest. He whirled, whipped out a machine pistol, and peppered Elise's back with bullets, driving her face-first into the floor. Squid opened up on him with his machine gun, forcing him to duck for cover. Jake made a beeline for his sister, with Nick close on his heels, but Lisa body-blocked him, knocking him flat and sending him sliding across the floor. Nick fired his shotgun at her, and shockingly, hit her, blowing her back before she could get to Jake.

Adrienne and Dodd were tangled together as they hacked at each other with long knives that were already dripping with blood. Simone was busy with Amy, who despite being down an arm, seemed more than a match for her.

I took all of this in at a glance as I drew my gladius and ran straight for Gaius. Amazingly, his arm seemed to have already repaired itself. He rushed directly at me with the purest look of abject hatred that I've ever seen in my life. But I suppose at that moment, my expression was pretty similar.

As we closed, I noted he hadn't even bothered to arm himself. Fine by me. This wasn't a contest in chivalry, and I'd be ecstatic to hack him to pieces, weaponless or not. I timed my blow perfectly, aiming to cut his head in two. And I hit exactly nothing. Somehow, he'd eluded me and then rammed into me with the momentum of a freight train. The wind whooshed from my lungs, and I sailed across the room and crashed into a wall. The back of my head hit against solid stone with a dull *thwack*.

Bright stars flashed across my eyes, but I didn't have time for stars. I rolled out of the way of Gaius's kick just in time. Its force knocked a huge chunk out of the wall and would have broken my head had it landed. I righted myself just as Jean-Luc, Godfrey, and

Archambaud danced across my field of vision, thrusting and hacking and parrying with their long swords. The speed at which Jean-Luc wielded his weapon, fending off his two attackers, amazed me. But I didn't have the time to be amazed. Gaius was already on me.

I feinted and came in low, hitting him two satisfying, rib-crunching body shots. An uppercut caught him square on the jaw, and I followed up with a head-butt directly to his ugly face.

He staggered back a step or two, his hand reaching up to his nose as bright red blood flowed through his fingers for a moment, but then suddenly stopped. When he lowered his hand, he was smiling. His face looked perfectly normal, as if it hadn't even been hit. "Not bad, Dad, but nowhere near enough today."

He flashed forward and struck me with a backhand that felt more like a sledgehammer. Once again, I went sailing across the room and crashed down in a heap. This smashing into walls shit was getting old.

It's that drug, that fucking drug, I thought. *We're all as good as dead.* I staggered to my feet and brought up my hands in a semblance of self-defense.

Gaius put his hands on his hips and roared jolly laughter. "Why don't you take a moment and look around the room, Titus?" he asked. "No, really, go ahead, I won't attack you. Scout's honor. I want you to take it all in before I kill you. You and your little friends are way overmatched. You are all going to die here tonight."

A head came skittering across the floor. For a moment, I thought it was Jean-Luc's, but to my great relief, it was Archambaud's.

"Oh, well," Gaius said offhandedly. "Most of you are overmatched. This enhancing agent that good old Bloody Bill and his crew came up with is quite the ticket. I told those two religious nut jobs to use it, but they refused, and now look at Archambaud, headless and everything. But no matter. Go on. Take your look. I want you to appreciate what you've gotten your friends into before I rip your head off."

I took my look. Nick, Elise, and Jake were nowhere to be seen. Lisa had gone missing as well. Dodd was backing Adrienne out a side door, beating on her the entire way. She was covered in blood and pretty much defenseless. Squid was down on the floor with Stein on top of him and choking him for all he was worth. The Squid's face had turned an alarming shade of blue. Simone looked as if she was ready to pass out on her feet. She was bleeding from what looked to be a thousand wounds. Amy, one arm and all, circled her nonchalantly, and every now and again darted in and cut another piece out of her with a saber.

Gaius chuckled. "You see, Titus, it's over for you. Oh, maybe a few have gotten away, and if they have, rest assured they will be hunted down like the dogs that they are. Now you old fuck, it's time to pay the piper." He took a step toward me.

A barrage of ear-shattering explosions ripped through the room. I was blown high up into the air, and everything went dark.

CHAPTER 64

Elise, Jake, and Nick raced through the corridors of Gaius's subbasement, with Lisa and a squad of guards right behind them. Once they'd managed to get out of the great room, they'd tried to make it outdoors, but all the exits were blocked. They ended up being chased into the lower levels of the mansion, and finally the subbasement. Elise knew it wasn't the best idea, but they'd had no choice. It was retreat down there or die.

Jake led her by the hand, with Nick bringing up the rear. As they sprinted along, Jake kept telling her repeatedly that everything was going to be all right and that he'd get her out of here. Elise very much doubted both assertions.

At one point they ran right by the body of Bill Harrison. The sight of him lying there like that saddened Elise. In the short time she'd known Bill, she'd come to like the old man. She wondered if Molly was still alive.

Their pursuers closed in once again, and a fresh spate of machine-gun fire drove those thoughts from her head. Pain ripped through her back when some of the bullets found their mark. The three took a quick turn, then another, and then one more, and ended up dumbly looking at the blank wall of the dead end they'd run into.

More gunfire shook them from their "now what the fuck are we going to do" stupor, and they took cover as best they could on the floor against the walls, returning fire at Lisa and her guards.

Jake tried to call for help using the communications earpiece but got no reply. He shouted over the roar of gunfire, "It's either jammed, or there's no one left to respond!"

More gunfire pelted down the hallway, noisily ripping stone fragments from the walls. The stench of cordite was suffocating.

Nick peeked around the corner and ducked back quickly, barely eluding the barrage of bullets that could have taken off his head. "We have to make it back to that last intersection," he said. "It's our only chance."

"Not much of a chance," Elise replied, tossing a few shots around the corner. "For all we know, it's another dead end."

"In a little bit we're going to be out of ammo," Nick answered. "Then they can stroll down the hall and blow our brains out. If you've got a better idea, I'm all ears."

Elise didn't. All she could do was shake her head. Her ears rang from the continuing roar of the guns.

Nick got up and crouched at the corner. He looked like a sprinter waiting for the starting gun to go off, and in this death-trap corridor, there were plenty of guns to choose from.

Jake put a hand on his shoulder as Elise continued to return fire. "Where do you think you're going?" he asked.

Nick looked back at him. "It's the only way. I'll go straight at them, and you two try to get around the corner."

Jake nodded grimly.

Elise stopped firing. "What are you talking about?" she shouted. "We'll all go together and take our chances."

Jake shook his head. "No, sis. He's right. If we all go out, we'll just get cut to pieces. It's the only way. Except Nick's not going, I am."

"No, Jake, you can't," Elise pleaded. "I just got you back. I can't lose you again. I can't. We'll all go together."

Nick spoke up. "No, Jake. I'm going, not you."

Jake's head snapped toward Nick. "We don't have time for this. Before we left New Orleans, you promised me you'd do everything you could to save my sister, promised you'd do what I said. Are you a liar, Nick?"

Jake's question was punctuated by a grenade exploding just around the corner. They all ducked their heads, and luckily, none of the shrapnel reached them.

"Oh, man," Nick replied sadly. "No, I'm no liar."

Jake turned to Elise and touched her cheek with his hand. She burst into tears. "No, Jake. Please."

Elise knew she looked like an old crone, and so did Jake, but her brother looked at her the way he had when she was a little girl all those years ago. He looked at her with pure love. "I got you into this, and I'm going to get you out," he said. "I love you, Little Red." He pulled her toward him and kissed her on the forehead.

She wrapped her arms around him and hugged him tightly.

Jake looked over Elise's head and said to Nick, "Count of three and then go." He forcibly removed Elise's hands and held them in front of him for a moment, smiling. He winked at her, and then he dashed around the corner.

The barrage of weapons fire somehow managed to increase in intensity. Elise screamed, "Nooooooooooo!"

Nick counted slowly.

At three, he grabbed Elise by her hand, yanked her to her feet, and sprinted around the corner, making for the intersection.

They took some fire, but Jake, already a bloody mess and barely recognizable, took most of it. Even though he was being pulped with round after round, somehow he managed to keep moving forward.

Seeing him like that, Elise tried to slow down, but Nick yanked her around the corner after him, never breaking stride. Elise looked back at Jake as she ran, and she thought he looked at her, too, but with all the blood, she would never be sure. She thought he might have smiled at her just before a flamethrower burst lit him on fire.

Elise passed out.

CHAPTER 65

Molly Harrison made her way to the ground level of the mansion, leaving quite a number of Gaius's guards, along with two fledgling vampires, dead in her wake. She followed the sound of gunfire to the main door of the great room, and there almost came face-to-face with one of the soldiers who'd released her, the one called Juice. They trained their guns on each other for a tense moment, and then he smiled and lowered his. Molly followed his lead.

They peeked through the door and were greeted by an astounding sight. It was a vampire battle, the likes of which Molly had never seen. They used swords, knives, and guns, or fought hand-to-hand as they fairly flew around the large room. The leaps and oversized strides and speed at which they fought made them look like something out of an overdone special-effects-laden martial-arts movie. But this was no movie; this was real. One thing was quite certain even after only a quick glance. Titus Acilius and his group were losing and losing badly.

Molly stepped back from the door as Juice was unslinging a sleek, compact rocket launcher from his back. It was an RPG that had several small charges arranged on a circular feeder belt. As far as she knew, automatic, multi-shot RPGs didn't exist except in video games.

Juice smiled at her admiring glance and motioned her to the door. Molly put her hand on the doorknob and silently counted down on her fingers. *Three, two, one!*

She threw the door open, and Juice stepped over the threshold. He methodically fired seven well-spaced RPG rounds into the room. The explosions were ear shattering. Juice dropped the launcher, hefted his machinegun, and advanced into the great room.

Molly followed right behind and was shocked at the devastation. The place had been reduced to rubble and was nearly unrecognizable from the room she had peeked into seconds ago. She scanned the debris carefully as she moved forward, her dad's Mossberg at the ready. She saw no movement at all. Everyone was down.

From the far right side, some of Gaius's men entered the great room. Juice greeted them with withering machine-gun fire, and they retreated through the door they'd just come through.

Molly caught a blur of motion out of the corner of her eye on the left. She turned and saw Gaius speeding toward Juice. "Look out," she shouted. But it was way too late.

With the side of his hand, Gaius struck Juice a nonchalant blow to the head. He never saw it coming. Juice took two more steps and fell to the floor, dead, his skull crushed.

"Bastard!" Molly screamed and began pumping shotgun blasts into Gaius.

Gaius was rocked and staggered by the impacts but managed to heave himself out of the room.

Molly followed close behind.

CHAPTER 66

My head really hurt. I couldn't remember why, but I figured I must have had too much absinthe. Hangovers don't last too long for vampires, like maybe an hour, tops, but even so, an absinthe hangover can be pretty nasty.

Someone was shaking me. I tried to ignore it. Better to sleep it off. Another twenty minutes, and I'd be fine.

Then I heard a familiar voice. "Chrissy. Come on, Chrissy, wake up."

It was Squid. Yep, it was absinthe, and I was in McKibbin's Pub, tanked to the gills.

"Leave me alone," I grumbled.

"Jesus, will you wake up? We need to get out of here!"

Then it hit me. It wasn't McKibbin's at all. I was in Gaius's mansion. My eyes flew open, and then my head swam, and my vision doubled. I felt like I was going to puke. After a moment, my stomach and my eyes decided to cooperate. Squid's oversized head sharpened into focus, and luckily, I didn't throw up on him. Blood and soot were smeared across his face.

He sighed with relief. "Oh, thank God. I thought you were a goner. One of those rounds landed right at your feet. You were blown all the way up to the ceiling. Christ, Chrissy, you look like a Swiss cheese. You must have a dozen holes blown through you."

He reached for my face and head, and exquisite bolts of pain erupted at his slightest touch.

I winced. "Cut it out! Oh shit, that hurts like a bastard."

"Stop being such a baby," he admonished. "The right side of your face is meat. You're not going to win any beauty contests today."

"Was I ever?"

He chuckled. "Good point. Your skull is crushed on the right, too.

Doesn't look like any penetration into the brain. The way you heal, you ought to be okay soon enough."

"Thank you, Dr. Squid. Who the hell was doing all the shooting, anyway?"

"No idea." He started to lift me to my feet. "Come on. We're getting out of here."

A loud voice stopped us. "Titus Acilius, you will pay for your sins!"

It was Godfrey. I turned to see him stagger into the room. He was gore-soaked from head to toe. In one hand he held his broadsword. In the other, like some horrible bloody trophy, was the head of my friend, Jean-Luc Leclerc.

The Squid took in a deep, whistling breath, and I rasped weakly, "Oh, no."

Godfrey held the disembodied head of my friend by its long dark hair, and it swayed back and forth like some sort of grisly wind chime in a light summer breeze. Jean-Luc's beard was matted with blood, and his mouth was frozen shut in a final rictus of pain, but his eyes were by far the worst. They were unseeing and shocked open wide by the ultimate surprise, the last horrible surprise that Jean-Luc would ever experience.

Hideously mesmerized, I couldn't seem to tear my eyes away from the horrible sight, and my shrapnel-peppered stomach decided it had had enough for the day. I leaned over and vomited. It felt as if I were heaving up hot lead.

Godfrey went on with an uncontained rage. "You see what you have made me do? You and your cohort of godless heathens, you are to blame for this. You led my brother astray. You forced me to be the terrible hand of God's retribution. And now you and all of your kind will pay."

Squid looked at the gladius I held in my hand. "Can I borrow this?" he asked conversationally.

Somehow, through everything, I'd managed to hold onto it. An old soldier's instinct, I guess.

I didn't have a chance to answer before Squid took the sword, stood, and threw it in a perfect end-over-end spiral. It buried itself right in the center of Godfrey's forehead.

His head rocked back on his neck from the impact. He dropped his sword and Jean-Luc's head and began staggering around the room.

Squid unhurriedly strolled up to Godfrey, picked up his broadsword, and with one smooth stroke, lopped off his head. When Godfrey's teeth stopped chattering, Squid picked up his head, spat in its face, and flung it across the room. Then the Squid picked up Jean-Luc's head, smoothed out the hair, and closed the eyes. "That was for you, Frenchy," he said as he reverently set it back down on the rubble-strewn floor. The big oaf sauntered back to me, whistling one of his patented out-of-tune melodies. "Those religious whackos really piss me off."

"Me, too," I agreed. "Hell of a lucky shot with my gladius, by the way."

"Nah. Did a stint in a knife-throwing act in the circus eighty years ago," Squid replied. He tried to muster up a small smile, but didn't come close. Jean-Luc was dead. "I'm sure I told you about it."

"No, you didn't tell me," I said.

"You sure?" he asked. "I have a distinct recollection of mentioning it to you."

I was about to respond when Squid went flying across the room, crash-landing in a pile of rubble. In his place, very unfortunately for me, stood Gaius Acilius. He smiled down upon me.

Stein, Amy, and Richard stood about twenty feet behind.

"I'll take care of that idiot sidekick of yours shortly," Gaius began. "Rest assured of that. But you, dear old Dad, are always first in line with me."

I began struggling to my feet, but a vicious kick sent me sprawling.

"Don't stand on my account, *Dad*," Gaius went on. "You know, you've really caused me far too much trouble this day, maybe even a bit more than I expected you would. But then again, you've always been quite the troublemaker when it comes to me, haven't you? And as much as I want to prolong my enjoyment of your abject failure, time seems to be of the essence at this juncture." Gaius's face grew stone-cold. His eyes looked as if they could barely contain the psychotic rage pent up in them, a rage that if it were to escape him, would be powerful enough to kill me in and of itself. "Goodbye, Titus."

"Fuck you, Gaius," I replied.

A hint of his phony smile reappeared. "Eloquent to the last." He took a step forward, but the noise of a shotgun cocking stopped him. He looked over his shoulder at Richard and smiled. "Richard, my dear man. I appreciate the sentiment, but I hardly need your assistance."

The shotgun roared. I cringed and closed my eyes, but I felt no pain. Was I already dead? I didn't feel dead.

I opened my eyes to see that a huge hole had appeared directly in the center of Gaius's chest. Gaius staggered and turned to face Richard. The old footman's face was flushed. He looked scared to death but exhilarated at the same time. Stein's and Amy's mouths opened wide. They were pale and stunned into inaction. Hell, so was I.

Ashen-faced, Gaius swayed on his feet, but even so, he managed to smile at Richard. His voice was surprisingly even, full of its usual mocking good cheer as he said, "Why, Richard, I didn't think you had it in you."

Richard chambered another round.

Gaius glanced over at me, still smiling, and I think I saw an expression on him that I'd never seen before. Relief.

The shotgun blasted again, and Gaius's head exploded. His blood and brains splattered all over me. My mind flashed back all the centuries, back to when Gaius had been human, a loyal soldier and a good guy. I should have let him die back then. I'd acted impetuously when I turned him, and I didn't have the right to do it. Look at all that had happened today, all the death and destruction. And for what? I should've left well enough alone. My heart seemed to gain weight and sink into my already nauseated gut.

As Gaius's headless body hit the floor, Stein wheezed out, "Jeez."

Richard seated his shotgun under his chin. He looked right at me. "I never wanted this. I never wanted any of it." With one more squeeze of the trigger, Richard joined his master.

Stein, now over his shock, looked at me with hardened eyes. There was murder written on his fleshy, liver-lipped face, and I didn't care one damn bit. I wondered if when the cheap, dime-store hoodlum killed me, I'd be wearing the same expression as my son, Gaius: relief.

I was going to simply lie there and take it, but something deep inside me clicked. I couldn't just sit back like that. It just wasn't in me. I was a Roman soldier, for God's sake, and that's what I'd always be. I had my soldiers, my friends to think about—if any of them were still alive, that is. Even though I wanted to give up on myself and lie down and die, I couldn't because if I did, I'd be giving up on them as well. And that was one damn thing I couldn't do.

Badly hurt or not, feeling like shit over Gaius and Jean-Luc and all the rest of the mayhem I'd caused today or not, I was going to do my very best to make good on my promise and rip Stein's ugly fucking head off of his ugly fucking shoulders. No boohooing for this old centurion, no fucking way.

I heaved myself to my feet.

Stein started forward. It was Amy who stopped him. Maybe she saw the expression on my face or something in my eyes and figured it could go way wrong for Stein no matter how badly I was hurt. I don't know. But anyway, she grabbed him.

"No, Davy, don't," she said. "He'll kill you. He'll kill you! It's over. Let's get out of here."

I could see the chaos written all over Stein's ugly mug. He wanted to do me, to risk it all and stand against me right then and there, to finish the job for his dead master, the ultimate loyalty. But in the end he was too smart, too calculating for that, and he allowed himself to be pulled back toward a door by Amy.

He pointed a finger at me as he backed up. "This isn't over," he said. His voice couldn't have sounded more outraged. "I'll be seeing you, Titus. Count on it."

I smiled. "You better hope not."

I really did want to kill him, needed to even, and I was healing, albeit probably not fast enough to chase them down. But I had the Squid and the rest of them to worry about. The centurion that I once was fairly shouted out in my mind, *No time for attack now, Titus. Retreat. Form up what's left of your century and make a controlled retreat.*

He—I—was right. I made my way over to the Squid. He was lying on his back, his legs tucked under him at an odd angle. He was breathing, thank the gods. I squatted down next to him.

"Back's broke. Not too bad," he said conversationally. "I can already move my toes. Should be better soon."

The big dope always was a fast healer for his age. "Okay, we'll hunker down here for a bit and then try to collect the rest and beat it. I'd hate to have to lug your giant ass out of here. Probably give myself a hernia."

"Nice," he replied. "You okay? I mean with Gaius and everything. I know you hated him and all, but..."

"I'm not sure," I answered. "I'll have to mull it around. You know me, slow thinker and all. I'll let you know in a few weeks."

"Considering how this day's been going for us, a few weeks sounds great to me," he answered. "Can you fucking imagine? This is probably the first time in the history of the world that the butler actually did it."

"Sorry to burst your balloon, but Richard was actually a footman."

Squid rolled his eyes. "Just like you to try and wreck one of my best jokes. Footman, butler, what's the difference? Close enough in my book."

Quiet sobbing short-circuited our conversation. I turned to see Lisa kneeling and crying over Gaius's body.

Godfrey, Gaius, and now her? Jesus fucking Christ, I thought. *This room is like a who's who of people who want to kill me.*

"Who is it?" Squid asked. He couldn't see from where he was, and he still couldn't move enough to get a good look.

"You know, buddy, I'm beginning to think we're never getting out of this room alive," I answered. "It's Lisa."

"Oh shit," Squid whispered.

"How're you doing," I asked.

"No good. Legs are still too weak."

"Just stay put, then. Don't move."

"Like I have a choice?"

I looked back over at Lisa, and her eyes, unfortunately, were already laser-locked on me. Stein may have had murder on his ugly mug, and Gaius was full of psychotic rage, but Lisa—Lisa wore the expression of a rabid dog. I was still hurting bad, and she was hopped up on that fucking drug. I was in serious trouble.

I had just managed to stand when she screamed out an inarticulate war cry and rammed into me full tilt. For about the fiftieth time that day, I had the wind knocked out of me, and we went rolling and tumbling through the debris field that the great room had become. She rained blows down on me, striking me over and over again. What little blood I had left in me flew all over the room. Lisa was crazy-stoked to the max, fueled by her rage and that damn drug.

I really need to get my hands on some of that shit!

A perfectly delivered roundhouse kick landed squarely on my already crushed face, knocking that thought out of my head and making me feel like it had exploded. She would never have been able to kick me like that if I hadn't paid for her kung fu lessons way back when. Now that just didn't seem fair.

As I once again kissed the floor, the reality of my situation started to sink in. I was tremendously injured, weakened, and nearly bloodless, and this ramped-up fledgling, my ex-wife no less, was about to beat me to death. *After all I've been through today,* I thought. *No fucking way.*

Now I fully realize that divorce is a tremendously cruel and a remarkably stressful event. I've even heard tell that people have died when they were going through a divorce. But there was no way I was going to let that sort of thing kill me. I straightened up and hit Lisa a hard left-right combo directly to her pretty little nose.

She screamed and staggered back, bleeding. I waded in, hoping the tide was turning. But when she took her hand away from her mangled nose, I saw that the loony look in her eyes had climbed several notches on the "fucking nutso" scale.

Shit, I thought, *She's not just a rabid dog. She's Cujo!*

She plowed right into me again, nailing me over and over with knockout kicks and punches.

The whole time she was laying into me, she screamed, "You were a shitty husband, a fucking liar, a bigger bore! You turned me when I said no! You were lousy in bed, and your dick is tiny!"

She punctuated the last comment with a kick perfectly delivered to my balls. I don't know what hurt worse, the kick or the tiny dick comment. But, really, it was the kick. It was excruciating. I fell back against a wall and hunched over, feigning I was hurt worse than I was, albeit, I was hurt pretty damn badly. After two thousand years of being a vampire, pain still sucks, but with a lot of practice you can learn to ignore it.

Lisa moved in, and I reared up suddenly and grabbed her by the head. With a quick twist, I snapped her neck. She fell to the floor, paralyzed, but to my amazement, her neck almost immediately straightened out. Her legs began twitching and moving a second later. I stood there spellbound, watching that enhancing drug of theirs do its work once again.

Within five seconds, her arms were functioning, and she made to get up off the floor. "You're going to have to do a lot better than that, asshole!" she screeched. "I'm going to rip off your nuts and stuff them down your throat!"

It was the thought of dining on my own testicles that prompted me to action. I reached down for her, but her hand flew out and clamped, viselike, on my already aching nuts. She twisted them hard, and white-hot pain shot from my groin all the way up into my throat, nearly making me vomit. I staggered back, and didn't the bitch use my own momentum to pull herself up? She pulled herself to her feet, using my nut sack like a helping hand!

I crashed into a wall, and there was Lisa's smiling face, nose to nose with mine. She clamped her free hand on my neck, choking me out, while somehow she managed to increase the pressure on what was left of my hapless genitals. The pain was beyond description. I was losing oxygen fast, and the room was starting to swim. Lisa was saying something—something real witty, I'm sure, but I couldn't hear her. It was as if my ears were clogged with wax on account of all the blood that was backed up in my skull from Lisa's more-than-effective stranglehold. If my balls had somehow miraculously developed a sense of hearing, I'm sure they would've been stone deaf by now as well.

Lisa droned on and on, and I couldn't hear a goddamn thing. It was like watching an extremely unpleasant silent movie. Unbelievably, the pain in my groin ratcheted up another notch, and mercifully, things began to go gray.

This is it, I thought. *This is where she makes good on her threat.*

I looked at her, thinking it would be for the last time, and I really didn't mind that much. Because the truth was, when you got by her outer facade, she really was an ugly bitch.

As the room got darker for me, I noticed that Lisa was wearing her patented smug little smile, one that I'd come to know all too well during our years of marriage. It was the kind of smile that said, "Oh, of course, dear, and isn't it so cute that you stupidly think that when we all know that my way is correct? After all, I'm always right, aren't I? And really, the only reason I let you speak to me at all is so I can correct you and show you the error of your ways, the error of your completely faulty and idiotic thought processes."

It was the kind of smile that even though you were in "love", whatever the fuck that meant, bothered you a little, though you really couldn't quite figure out why. But the minute you split up, you knew you hated the fucking thing, and you knew exactly why. It condescended you; it put you down; it made you feel like a lowly piece of crap and for no real reason—no real reason, that is, except to undeservedly elevate the wearer of such a butt-ugly smirk, to make her feel superior, and at your expense. And guess what? When you were married, you let it go. You had to pick your fights, didn't you? You couldn't get into it for something as minor as a patronizing smile.

In the end, it wasn't the fact that I was a rough and tumble Roman soldier or a two-thousand-year-old killer vampire that got me going. It wasn't the fact that my nuts were about to be ripped out of their warm and cozy sack and then rammed unceremoniously down my throat. It wasn't even the fact that I was about to die, as unbelievable as that sounds.

It was that smile. It was Lisa's smug, know-it-all, I-told-you-so, no-good-bitch of a smirking smile that got me going. I was sick to fucking death of it.

My nearly lifeless hands floated up and clamped themselves on the sides of Lisa's head, crushing that fucking smile off her ugly face. Now it was my turn to smile.

My thumbs made their way toward her eyes. I meant to pop them like grapes. She released my neck to defend herself, and I heard, more than felt, my deep, whooshing breath as it entered my lungs. One hand wasn't helping her much as I crushed on and on, so finally she released my balls so her second hand could get into the fray.

My body had somehow gotten used to the intense pain coming from my groin, and when it suddenly let up, the effect was staggering. My knees nearly unhinged, and Lisa almost shook loose. But I knew if I let her go now, that would be it. She'd kill me. It was now or never for me. I didn't have anything left.

I grimly increased the pressure on her head, and she went wild, tearing rents in my face with her fingernails, pummeling my torso with blow after blow as we staggered across the room in what must have looked like the oddest ballroom-dance hold in history: the old hands-to-head two-step.

She struck me in the left side of my gut, and I felt my spleen burst, filling my abdomen with what little blood I had left. The pain was ridiculous. It shot through all points of the compass of my battered belly. That was it. I couldn't hold on anymore, so I did the only thing I could think of: I snapped her neck again. But this time I held her and didn't let her fall to the floor. I could feel her neck healing itself, the bones moving like they were alive, writhing under her skin.

Now I realize that I'm an ancient vampire, a killing machine if you will and have seen and done some really freaky shit in my time, and that I heal pretty damn fast myself, for that matter. But even for me, her healing *this* fast and all that moving bone and tissue was totally gross. It was like something out of *Alien.* I blew chow all over the floor.

Lisa's arms were already starting to twitch and move, and far more quickly than before. In my current sorry state, I really couldn't have any of that. Besides, we Romans weren't big on letting our enemies off the mat once we had them down.

I twisted Lisa's head again and felt a very satisfying snap. Then I gave another nasty twist, and another, and another after that.

"Noooooo!" Lisa screamed as I ripped her head from her body.

As a matter of fact, I think she screamed it for a full ten seconds after her head was detached. The fountains of blood from her neck soaked me and then pumped themselves to a stop as her eyes twittered shut.

I looked into her face, and to be honest, even after everything that had happened with Lisa during our sham marriage, even after everything that had happened over the past three years when she'd become a rogue vampire, even after everything that had just happened in this horrible battle with her, I still wasn't quite sure how I felt about what I had just done to her.

Then I was sure.

I took one oversized step forward and punted her head high into the air across the room. It was a beautiful end-over-end kick that had a damn good hang time. It finally landed out of sight with a dull, splatty *thwack.*

The Squid had just managed to stand. "Jesus, Chrissy. I guess the divorce is final."

I shrugged. "I guess so."

"Nice punt, by the way. You ever play football?"

"Nah. Just got lucky."

"So tell me," Squid asked, "which did you like better, killing her the first time, or the second time?"

I smiled. "No contest. The second time."

He laughed. "Come on. Let's get the fuck out of here."

We turned to see Molly Harrison slowly dream-walk into the room. Her eyes look dazed and blank.

"For Christ's sake," I said. "What is this place? Grand Central Station?"

"It's big enough," Squid said. "What's left of it, that is."

"Molly, are you, okay?" I asked.

She looked over at me and tittered out a shrill, breathy, out-of-control laugh. It sounded like broken glass, and it sent a chill up my spine.

"I didn't kill them all, Daddy," Molly said. "I killed a lot of them, though. And Gaius, Gaius got away from me. I'm so sorry."

She dropped the shotgun she was carrying and plunked down on the floor, crying and still clutching her bloody sword.

Squid spun his finger at his temple. "Crazy cakes."

"Shhhhh," I hushed him. "It's okay, Molly. He's dead. Gaius is dead."

She didn't respond. Squid put his huge paw on my shoulder. "Come on, we have to go."

"I completely agree," a lovely, high-pitched voice piped out from the far end of the room.

Squid and I turned to see Adrienne standing at the main entrance. She was bloodied and soot-covered, but her eyes sparkled and that beautiful smile of hers beamed. Man, she was gorgeous.

Squid lit up like a Christmas tree. "Addie!"

He took a step forward and nearly keeled over from his back injury.

I managed to catch him before he fell. "Whoa. Hold on, big fella."

Adrienne's smile faltered. "Squid, are you all right?"

"I'm good," Squid replied. "Be as right as rain in a few."

Adrienne warily advanced a few steps into the room, looking back and forth. "Gaius?"

"Dead," I answered. "So are Lisa and Godfrey and Archambaud. What happened to Dodd?"

Her smiled widened. "Quite dead, and it was truly a pleasure. And the Saint Michelers have landed. They're trying to fight their way in past the guards. Now come on, you two. We have to go."

A glow appeared around Adrienne for a moment, making her look even more beautiful, like a bloodied angel, perhaps an angel from *Paradise Lost*. The ones who had helped the Almighty beat back the forces of Satan.

But I knew it wasn't that. It wasn't a glow; it was fire. Adrienne's face took on a look of surprise, and her eyes quickly darted toward Squid.

"No," Squid whispered weakly.

The flamethrower blast completely engulfed Adrienne in its scorching, yellow embrace.

Squid tried to stagger toward her, but in his injured state, it didn't take much for me to hold him back.

Adrienne took two uncertain steps into the room and fell to the floor, already burned to char.

"Let me go!" Squid bellowed. "I can save her. I can put the fire out. I did it before."

"Squid," I said softly, "she's already dead."

He looked as if he were going to hit me for a moment. But then he sagged against me, crying.

Someone tossed grenades into the already ruined room. Squid and I cringed and hit the deck when they went off. I noticed Molly still sitting serenely, semi-catatonic, in the middle of the floor. She hadn't even flinched when the grenades exploded, and luckily for her, none of the shrapnel hit her.

"Come on, Squid. They're gonna rush us," I said. "We gotta make a run for it."

He didn't respond, but I felt him nodding against my shoulder. I heaved him up, and we started lumbering for a side door. It was like Paris all over again, except this time Dom wasn't going to be coming to save us.

As I ran, I shouted, "Molly, come on! Follow us!"

Molly placidly sat on. There was nothing I could do about that. I had the Squid to worry about. The gunfire started up, but none of it found us—yet.

As we rumbled along toward an exit, a deep voice called out. "Major, Titus, please stop. It's Doc. Please stop."

I wanted to keep running anyway. It didn't matter if it was friend or foe behind us now. I had an incredible urge, no, a need to get the fuck out of that no-good fucking great room. I was certain that if I didn't leave and now, I'd die there. Even though everyone else who'd tried to kill me there had failed, this no-good son-of-a-bitch of a room in and of itself would somehow do me in.

Squid slowed me, saying, "Hold up, Chrissy. It's Doc. Hold up."

Even though every self-preservation reflex I possessed screamed, "Keep going," we stopped.

Despite everything, Squid managed to straighten up and take on the semblance of military bearing. He took his arm off my shoulder and limped toward Doc. "Report, Sergeant."

Doc snapped off a crisp salute. "I scattered the flamethrower unit that was about to attack you, but they'll be back soon. We need to get out of here fast."

"Tell me something I don't know," I scoffed.

"Anything else?" Squid asked.

"The Saint Michelers have secured the perimeter," Doc replied. "There's still some minor skirmishes going on, but things are under control."

"Casualties?" I asked.

"Heavy," Doc answered. He shot me a quick glance and went on. "The woman Brigitte and Yves are dead. Many others."

All of a sudden my legs felt like Jell-O. I sat down hard on some rubble that was conveniently placed directly behind my butt. "Oh shit," I said.

It was hard to imagine that beautiful, vital young woman was dead, but at that moment, Yves somehow bothered me more. I knew of course, that this would change in time. But the thing was, I had no relationship with the guy, barely knew him, and really didn't like him. Nonetheless, he was dead on account of me. He got dragged into this because he worked for Adrienne, and she got dragged into this because she knew me, and now they both were dead, and it was my fault. I put my head in my hands.

"What about the rest of our group," Squid asked. "Any word?"

Doc answered, "Elise and Nick made it out. Jake didn't. He's dead, sir."

Jake was dead. Jesus Christ, would this ever end? I couldn't believe it. Jake was dead. Hot tears spilled from my eyes.

"Oh, oh my," Squid stammered. "Simone? Did Simone get out?"

"Yes, sir," Doc replied. "She's hurt bad, but she'll be okay."

"Well, at least there's that," Squid said.

My head snapped up. Tears ran down my cheeks. "Oh, at least there's that, is there? Are you going to tell her about Jean-Luc? Or maybe we should flip a coin to decide who gets the honor."

The Squid winced at the tone of my voice and the nastiness of my comment.

I immediately felt like shit about it. "I'm sorry, Squid. That was uncalled for."

A wan smile crossed his lips. He looked over to where the head of Jean-Luc lay and then to the charred ashes that up until a few minutes ago had been the love of his life. "No apology necessary, Chrissy. This has been one hell of a fucking day." He turned back to Doc. "Anything else, Sergeant?"

"Yes, sir," the soldier shot back. "Juice rigged a boatload of explosives to go off down in the basement. Last resort sort of thing. He's got the detonator, but if they're not keyed, they're on a simple timer as a backup. They're going to go in sequence any minute now."

Molly Harrison's dead, flat voice drifted over to us. "Your friend, the other soldier, the one you called Juice—he's dead. Gaius killed him." Her arm floated up slowly with her index finger pointing out. "He's over there."

Doc stayed rigid at attention. "May I, sir?"

Squid nodded. "Of course, Doc. You want to get his tags?"

"No, sir. I'm going to take him out of this hellhole. I can't leave him here."

Squid nodded, and Doc walked over to where Molly's gesture directed him. His head bobbed down for a moment as if in prayer. Then he straightened up, saluted his comrade, and hefted him over his shoulder in a fireman's carry.

A low rumble ripped through a distant corner of the house. The floor vibrated ominously. Doc, carrying the body of his friend, hustled over to us. Tears streaked his face, wrecking the effect of his camouflage paint. "We need to get out of here now. That's the first charge. This whole place could go."

Doc headed for the door, with Squid limping along behind. Squid stopped for a moment and stood over Adrienne's charred remains. He put his head down and spoke softly to her—so softly that I couldn't hear. A single tear fell from his eye and mixed with what was left of her. Then he knelt down on one knee. I was shocked. In all my years of friendship with the Squid, I'd never known him to be a praying man. But he didn't pray; he scooped up a handful of Adrienne's ashes and stuffed them into his pocket. He stood and turned to me. "Come on, Chrissy, let's go."

Hesitating, I looked over at Molly Harrison.

Squid eyeballed her for a moment. "Leave her, Chrissy. She wants to die; it's obvious. Besides, she hasn't exactly been a great friend of ours through the years, now has she?"

He was right, of course, but it didn't matter. For some reason, I didn't want to leave her there. I think it was because I'd had enough killing and dying for one day, and leaving one more person, no matter who that person was, to perish in Gaius's Great Fucking Room of Death didn't sit well with me.

"You go ahead," I said. "I'll be right along."

Another rumbling explosion ripped through the mansion. This time it was closer.

Squid shook his head reproachfully. "I hope you know what you're doing. And whatever it is, hurry the fuck up about it." He headed toward the door.

I eased over to Molly. "Molly, come on. We have to go."

No response. She sat there, staring straight ahead. I tried again, and zilch. Another explosion went off. This time the floor didn't vibrate—it shook.

I really didn't have time for this shit, so I did what I did best. I reared back and hit her a solid slap in the face.

Her head rocked back, and despite her near catatonia, that damn sword of hers flashed out at me.

She was fast, but I was ready. I caught her arm, and after a brief struggle, took her sword from her.

She remained seated the entire time, like some demented yogi, and didn't fight back very hard. She glared up at me.

I could see her old man in her expression.

"You should listen to your friend," she said. "Go!"

"Come on," I replied. "You don't really want to die in this house of horrors do you? Let's go."

She scoffed. "With you?"

My mouth took off. "Sure, why not? If you change your mind later, there's always suicide."

Her glare turned into a "what an asshole" look. It was a look that unfortunately I was well acquainted with. Even in the most trying circumstances, I had to contend with my mouth, my goddamn big fucking mouth. Molly turned away from me and stared at the wall.

Another explosion went off. This time the floor rocked. I swayed on my feet and looked up, nervously waiting for the roof to cave in on us.

When it didn't, I turned back to Molly. "Look, I'm sorry I said that. It was stupid of me, but we're running out of time."

"Why would you possibly care about me?" Molly asked, still facing the wall.

I shook my head slowly. "I really don't know. I just don't want you to die in here. So please, live."

With that last comment, her head snapped back to me. Her eyes intently searched mine. For what, I had no idea. But I did know that for some reason, the last thing I'd said affected her.

I extended my hand to her and repeated it. "Live."

Her eyes went from my eyes to my hand and then back again. After a moment, she put her hand in mine, and I helped her to her feet. She extended her free hand toward me. I didn't know what she wanted at first, but then I got it. She wanted her sword. I gave it back to her.

"Take the shotgun," she said.

As I bent to pick it up, for a disquieting split second I was certain that she was going to take my head. She didn't, but when I straightened up, she had a very odd look in her eyes. Maybe I was being paranoid, but after the day I'd had, who could blame me?

Another blast, sounding as if it were right under our feet, ripped through the mansion. The room started to shower down huge pieces of its stone ceiling. I grabbed Molly by the hand again, and we sprinted for the door. As we cleared the mansion, we were greeted by a cool, fresh breeze. The air had never smelled so good to me as it did this night, and I doubted it would ever smell as good again.

We kept running from the house as four more explosions in rapid succession tore through the night.

Molly and I stopped and looked back. It was as if the entire mansion was on the receiving end of a gigantic goose. It appeared to jump five feet into the air. And then, with a crescendoing rumble, and what seemed to be at a physics-defying, way-too-slow of a rate, that fucking godforsaken place imploded on itself and crumbled to the ground.

EPILOGUE

I spent the next several weeks keeping as busy as I could, trying to distract myself as much as possible to keep my mind off what had gone on at Gaius's mansion. I was doing a fairly good job of it, at least during daylight hours. But my subconscious mind refused to play ball, and I was plagued by recurring nightmares that forced me to relive the horrors of what had happened there.

The doozy of them all, to my great consternation, had premiered about a week ago—and to excellent reviews, I might add. It was currently enjoying a sellout run at Titus's Nightmare Cineplex and was wreaking havoc with my REM sleep. It featured the snippet where Gaius confronted me, just after Squid had killed Godfrey. Except in my dream, Richard didn't kill Gaius; he just stood smiling, along with Amy and Stein.

I was at the part where I said, "Fuck you, Gaius."

"Eloquent to the last," he responded and walked toward me.

I looked at Richard, but he held the shotgun at port arms, never aiming it at Gaius, never shooting him. He smiled on and on.

After seven nights' worth of replays, I knew without a doubt that it was a dream, but that didn't stop the abject terror from gripping me as Gaius's hands tightened around my neck and I was lifted into the air.

But knowing it was a dream didn't help one damn bit, because what was coming next just totally sucked. I'd feel the tendons ripping in my neck and my spine cracking, and then, just before my head was torn off, I'd wake up in a cold sweat, shouting out loud, panting, and gasping for breath.

As I dream-waited for the inevitable, head-ripping, nasty climax of this shitty nightmare, I felt a gentle tugging on my arm. This was a new twist. I looked down and saw Sarge once again using my arm for an oversized chew stick. His deep brown eyes sparkled as they smiled up at me, and the speed of his wagging tail could've matched the RPMs of any decent outboard motor.

I was really liking where this could be going.

Sarge turned and pulled me along with him. I easily slid from Gaius's death grip. My good old boy began to lead me away with not only his tail, but his entire rear end wagging, just as it always did when he was taking part in the ridiculous activity of the dog leading the master.

I looked back over my shoulder and saw that my dream enemies now seemed nearly transparent and frozen in time. They continued to look to where I should have been but was no longer, their unmoving, murderous smiles frozen on their faces. Gaius, frozen as well, still held his hands up, choking away at thin air instead of yours truly.

Sarge led me through the main door of the great room, and instead of ending up in a corridor, where we should have, we exited directly to Cutler Park.

Now this is all right, I thought.

Cutler was one of my favorite places for taking Sarge on a walk. It had a biggish pond that he loved to swim in. Being a Lab, he and water had fallen in love at first sight. Very early on I gave up on trying to break him of the habit of jumping into each and every body of water he came across. It was like asking the wind not to blow.

He went crashing ahead of me and dove in headlong, while I strolled along the path next to the pond, looking at the trees and listening to the birds sing their springtime songs. We'd taken this trip so many times we had a "prearranged" meeting site where Sarge would come to shore. Then, we'd take the rest of our walk together on dry land.

I sauntered up as he was getting out of the water. As usual, he waited until I was good and close before he started up his water-shedding shake. To me, that definitely proved Sarge had a sense of humor. He never seemed to shake off water until he had a good audience and well within soaking distance.

After he'd succeeded in exposing me to a fair amount of pond water, Sarge looked back at me with a huge doggy grin on his face. A few tail wags later and he was bounding off down the path. He bounced from tree to tree, finding anything and everything irresistibly fascinating and peeing on most of it. Where the hell he stored all that urine, I'd never know. The dumb mutt always pissed so much, he had to have had at least three bladders.

It was that funny, late time of day, when the sun was slanty and the trees of the forest surrounding the pond threw dark shadows, but in between, the sunlight was startlingly bright. I loved walking with him in the woods at that time of day because he pulled off that trick that only the blackest of black dogs could do. And Sarge was as black as they came.

As he flitted about through those end-of-the-day shadows and back into the sunlight again, it was as if he would disappear and then reappear again like magic. Smiling, I walked along behind and admired his Houdini routine as I always did.

We got to the part of the walk where we always cut left to circle the pond and head back to the car. But Sarge surprised me. He kept trotting on straight, toward the deep woods. When he was fifty feet in, he stopped and looked back at me. His ever-wagging tail wagged a slow, steady beat, back and forth, back and forth.

I nodded to the left. "Come on, boy, this way. We always go this way."

He half huffed, half barked, and his deep brown eyes said to me as just clear as day, "Come on, Titus, how about going somewhere different for a change? You're not going to let me go on by myself, are you?"

I thought again of all of my superstitious friends who'd warned me about dream-following my long-dead Sarge. They said he was trying to lead me to the *other side* to be with him. What exactly the other side was, I didn't know, but the thought of it made me laugh out loud. The laugh felt so genuine that I was quite sure I was laughing in my sleep as well, neatly tucked into my bed.

Even in their dreams, I imagine that people cut from more careful stock than I was might have hesitated, considering what they should do next. But for me, there was nothing to consider.

I took my first step to follow Sarge, and his tail-wagging immediately increased to motorboat speed. He bounded off into the deep woods, barking happily, with me right behind.

What the hell, I figured. Where my good old boy wanted me to go couldn't be any worse than where I'd just been.

Besides, Sarge would never lead me astray.